Ransom!

The Story Of A Lost Child; Intimate Chapters Of A Film Star's Life

By
Grace Allen Hardy

VOLUME 2; NUMBERS 14 - 26

Published by
GIANT SQUID AUDIO LAB COMPANY
2021

No. 14

Price 10 Cents

Ransom!
the Story of a Lost Child

Intimate Chapters of a Film Star's Life

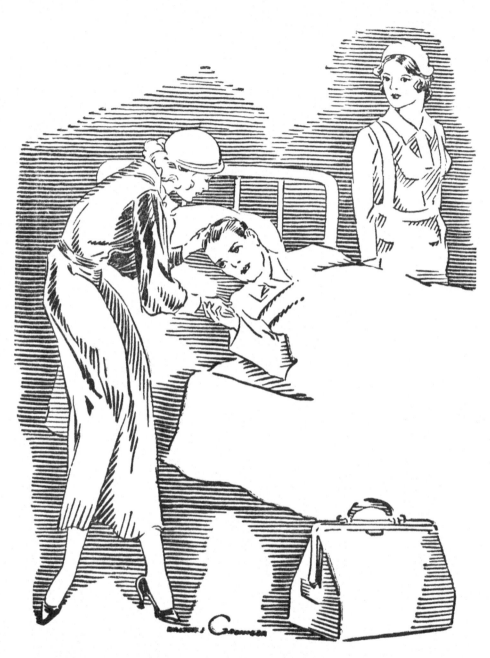

Half-laughing, half-crying, Janelle bent low above the man she loved and kissed him. "Please — take care of him for me, Nurse!" she begged unsteadily. "Of course I will—you run along now and don't worry! I'll see that he's all right — anything that wants him will have to get me first!" said Nurse Judkins firmly. (See Page 440)

Chapter 45

"CAN A MOTHER'S HEART BE WRONG?"

IN THE DIM lit room Sherman stared at Janelle, quite sure that for the moment she had lost her head. She was sitting forward, tense, pallid, her hands gripped tightly together, her eyes on that screen across which the shadow of a handsome little boy was toddling gaily, as much at home as he had ever been in Amelia Stuart's pent-house apartment.

Another close-up showed him, curly-haired, laughing, his tiny teeth gleaming—an adorable baby, as the little involuntary exclamations about the room told Janelle the others in the audience found him.

"My—little lost baby!" she gasped, trembling, the tears slipping down her white face. "My—baby!"

"My darling, are you sure?" asked Sherman quickly, yet gently. "It's been a long time, you know—almost a year!"

"And he is almost a year older than when they took him from me? Is that what you mean?" asked Janelle swiftly. "Ah, but Sherman—I'd know him if it had been years! He's mine—a part of me—can a mother's heart be wrong about a thing like that?"

The picture had been nearly over before the child made his appearance. When the last foot of film flickered out and the lights went on once more, Janelle was on her feet and hurrying towards the little improvised booth where the projecting machine had been concealed.

To the operator she made swift question.

"How can I find out something about the child who played in the last reel?"

"Cute kid, isn't he? My wife has a fit about him every time she sees this picture—bet she's seen it a dozen times just because of him. She'd like to adopt him I guess!" said the operator, smiling.

"He is my baby—he was kidnapped a year ago —we thought that he was—dead! I've—got to find out how long the picture has been made, and by what company!" said Janelle swiftly and passionately.

The man stared at her as though he thought she had lost her mind. He even edged a little away from her as though he thought she might become violent.

"The picture was made by an independent company—a 'quickie' company. The exchange could give you all the dope on it!" he suggested.

Janelle made a note of the name and street address of the film exchange that had handled the distribution of the picture. She thanked the man and hurried back to Sherman, who was watching her eagerly, anxiously. More than at any other time since he had been ill he resented his helplessness — his forced inactivity, at a time when he ached to help her.

"I've got the name of the exchange that handled the release of the picture—I'll have to get the other information I need from them!" she explained to him swiftly.

He caught her trembling hands and held them close.

"Darling—are you very sure? Sure that it was not just a marked resemblance?" he asked quietly. "Try not to get your hopes aroused too high—it makes the disappointment so much more bitter! You see—I know!"

Janelle bent swiftly and kissed him, her eyes tender.

"Of course you do, dear—and I'll try! But—it's my baby, Sherman, I know it is! He's grown a little—and they've cut his hair—and I think he's got another tooth—am I being silly, Sherman? I'm his mother and I've missed him—so terribly!" she choked a little.

"Of course you're not being silly—you couldn't be silly, being you, darling!" Sherman assured her gravely.

They talked until Nurse Judkins came into Sherman's room, scandalized that an invalid should keep such late hours, and she shooed Janelle off to her own room.

Janelle lay awake throughout the night. Why try to sleep when her whole brain was teeming with excitement with a hope that her trembling heart scarcely dared to accept. This was her child—of that she was certain. A mother's heart could not be wrong about such a thing. The only question now was—had the picture been made before that pathetic little skeleton had been found near Greenwich? If not—then her baby might still be alive. She must find out WHERE the picture was made, and WHEN and go on from there.

The woman, Annie Green, who had written her. Could she be in league with the kidnappers, and taking this circuitous route to return the child, collect the reward, and go scot-free? If she could only reach Annie

Green—only convince her and any one who might be working with her that she had no interest whatever in the matter save that of finding her baby if he still lived. That she had no desire to punish the kidnappers —that she was willing to leave to the Divine Justice that saith, "Vengeance is mine." She wanted only her little lost baby brought back to her empty arms and her hungry heart. If only she could get that word to the woman Annie Green, whoever she might be, and to the people with whom she was connected.

Her brain was fretted with puzzles. Who was Annie Green? What was her connection with the case? Was she a go-between to connect the kidnappers with the payer of the ransom, whoever and whatever it might be? Or had Annie Green a more powerful hand in the dangerous game? Or perhaps she was what she claimed to be—merely a woman with knowledge of a crime in which she had had no part, but from which she hoped to profit—fairly or unfairly.

If Annie Green really lived where she said she did, why was it that old residents of the community did not know of her? And if she did not live there, what arrangements had she made to receive the answer to the first letter she had sent to Janelle?

Again—why had Annie Green waited more than a year before approaching Janelle with her guilty knowledge? Was she, after all, only a crank who, reading the story of Janelle and Sherman, had thought to "chisel" her way into some easy money by pretending a knowledge she did not have?

Had Annie Green any connection with the person or persons who were instrumental in putting Billy-boy into this picture she had seen tonight? She had a fleeting memory of the movie director who had dropped in occasionally at Amelia Stuart's tea-parties. He had been interested in the baby. She tried to remember his name—perhaps he could help her.

The element of time was so precious. If the picture, "The Guilty Woman," that she had seen tonight had been made prior to the finding of that little body off a lonely Connecticut farm road, then it would not prove so much — only that Billy-boy had lived long enough after being torn from his mother's arms to take the first step on a path that might have led to fame and fortune for him. If the picture had been produced AFTER that date—then—she trembled at the thought —then it would mean that the tiny grave beside Bill's, back there in the little City of the Dead did not contain Bill's son!

It was that thought that kept her awake throughout the long night. That thought that made her oblivious of the tropical beauty of the night, velvet dark, with a star-strewn sky in which the Southern Cross seemed to bend so low that one might almost stand on tip-toe and touch it.

And in his own room where he had slept peacefully night after night joying in the knowledge that Janelle was near him, and that she was his as utterly as he was hers, Sherman lay awake, too, staring into the fragrant, soft darkness.

Had he made a terrible mistake in identifying that pitiful little body? In taking it home to Fair Oaks, in laying it beside the man he felt so sure was the baby's father? Had he, in trying to help Janelle over a great heart-break in her life, inadverdently done her a great wrong? This woman Annie Green, whom his detectives could not locate—this baby who had laughed so deliciously from the screen that women in the audience had felt a little tug at their heart-strings—who were these two? Was there a connection between them?

The child that he had so sadly so pityingly, brought back to that quiet country churchyard, to lay beside the boy who had gone down to death in the very flower of his young manhood—was there no connection between those two? The baby—and the young man?

He lay wide-eyed, staring into the darkness tortured by his bewilderment. He feared that in trying to help the girl he loved so dearly, he had done her a very great wrong.

In thought he went back to that bleak, gray day in November when he had stood beside a tiny open grave there in the little cemetery and the old minister, with tears in his eyes, had read above that small white casket the beautiful, solemn words of the burial service. He went once more over the agonizing details of the identification—the gruesome, but necessary measurements, comparisons—the many little, unpleasant but essential things that had had to be attended to in order to prove that the child they were laying here beside the young man was that young man's son.

The dark room grew gray with morning light while sleep was still far away from him. The lack of rest, the worry, the bewilderment had caused a slight fever that Nurse Judkins greeted with a little disappointed frown when she came in to bring him his breakfast and to make him comfortable for the day.

For the first time in weeks he did not react to her pleasant, friendly greeting and, perplexed, Nurse Judkins wondered if it could be possible that he had quarrelled with Janelle. She couldn't believe that—they were too deeply devoted to each other. Their love was a clear, shining, steady flame that was too fine and beautiful for the casual wind of a quarrel to blur it.

Chapter 46.

THE OLD HEARTACHE.

HEN JANELLE came in, she was already dressed for her trip into town. A thin, smart w h i t e crepe frock, a loose-fitting three-quarter length white coat, a broad-brimmed shady hat, w h i t e slippers, her white gloves and bag in her h a n d, she l o o k e d young and lovely, and somehow, pathetic.

Sherman, looking at her with his heart in his eyes, raged helplessly that this girl, so young and sweet and lovely, should have been dragged through so much horror and shame and sorrow. This girl who should have been sheltered in the home of an adoring husband, her baby protected, her life made sweet and happy.

"I'm going in town to the exchange, Sherman, to find out more about the picture!" she explained as she kissed him, and for a moment his arms held her close.

She straightened and looked down at him.

"What was the date—the day—you brought him home to—his Daddy?" she asked levelly.

"The ninth of November!" said Sherman so promptly that she knew he, too, had held the same thought.

She drew a long hard breath and squared her shoulders.

"Then if I find that the picture was produced BEFORE November 9th, I haven't proved a thing! I —can still believe that—my little lost baby is there with Bill, his father!" she said quietly. "But—if the picture was made after November the 9th—then—I know that he is still alive! And somehow—I'll find him!"

"Somehow, darling, WE'LL find him!" Sherman corrected her, and put her hand against his lips.

She bent swiftly and kissed him.

"I'll hurry back, dear!" she promised, and hurried out of the room.

Sherman lay for a long time staring after her, his eyes wide, his jaw set. If the picture had been produced AFTER November 9th—he started a little when Nurse Judkins spoke to him.

"Don't take it so hard — she'll be back!" said Nurse Judkins teasingly.

Sherman looked at her as though startled to find her in the room with him.

"Yes—of course she will—why not?" he agreed politely.

But he did not rally to her teasing, and Nurse Judkins looked down at him, troubled. She was fond of him—she was a middle-aged woman, childless, who had taken up nursing because of a heart that ached to mother a suffering world of pain-wracked people. She could not regard her patients impersonally—they were friends, people she liked and admired. Sherman's bravery against the almost unsurmountable obstacles of the jungle—his love for Janelle—the loveliness of the

romance between them all touched the kindly, senti-
mental heart of the nurse, and now that for some reason
her patient seemed to go backward instead of forward,
worried her.

Meanwhile Janelle had reached the city, and her
taxi had taken her straight to the film exchange in a
side-street. A slightly bored girl greeted her, and when
Janelle asked for the manager the girl doubted whether
he could be seen. Janelle said firmly:

"I must see him—it is most important—I wish
to buy a print of the picture shown last night at the
American Hospital! He may set his own price!"

"What is it, Miss Johnson?" asked a man's voice,
as a middle-aged, sunbronzed man clad in immaculate
white stepped through the door of an office at the back
of the room.

"I want to find out something about the picture,
'The Guilty Woman', which was screened at the American Hospital last night—and I would like to purchase,
at whatever price you care to ask, a print of the last
reel!" explained Janelle swiftly.

Instantly the man's manner altered.

"Won't you come in?" he motioned Janelle into
his office, and sat down opposite her.

His eyes took in the beautiful cut of her garments, their obvious expensive simplicity, and he smiled.

"Let's see, that was a picture in which James
Marvin, the new screen sensation, played the lead?" he
suggested with a little wise smile. "A great many of
our feminine fans are raving about him—but few of
them, I'm sorry to say, go to the length of wanting to
buy a print of his picture!"

Unsmiling Janelle faced him quietly.

"I don't know who is in the picture—save the
child who is seen at the very end!" she explained. "I

—have reason to believe, by every instinct of my heart —that he is my child!"

The man's smile vanished and he looked startled.

"I'm afraid I don't quite get you!" he stammered frankly.

Janelle leaned towards him, her gloved hands folded tightly in her lap.

"I'm Janelle Elliott—almost a year ago, my baby was kidnapped by Alexis Forgio!" she said levelly. "I —was sent to prison for Forgio's murder the following day—I was kept in prison, convicted of his death, and sentenced to execution—until on the morning set for the execution the woman who really killed Forgio, confessed!"

"Of course—I remember the case!" said the man swiftly. "It was revived a short time ago by your rescue of Sherman Lawrence, American business man, who crashed in the jungle. Mrs. Elliott, I am honored —delighted to meet you! Anything that I can do—you have only to ask!"

"I had believed that my baby was—found dead! In the last week something has happened to make me think that—that it might not be true!" said Janelle swiftly. "Last night when I saw 'The Guilty Woman' I recognized my baby instantly—what mother wouldn't? What I have to find out now—is when that picture was produced and by whom?"

"I can tell you when it was released and by whom it was produced!" the manager offered, and turned swiftly to his files while Janelle waited tensely.

While Miss Johnson was looking up the required information, the man dug out a set of the still-photographs—enlarged scenes from the actual production of the picture—and a press-book made up of interesting items about the picture, the stars, etc, such as is supplied to the manager of a theatre running that particular picture.

Janlle ran through the stills, throwing aside those showing the lovely star, Gladda Romaine and the "new screen sensation," James Marvin, with no interest at all. Suddenly, as she shuffled the nine-by-twelve inch photographs, her hands grew still and tense—her eyes widened, and she caught her breath. For there in her two hands was the picture of Billy-boy! Her little lost baby!

Tears dimmed her eyes as she studied him. Standing between the two screen stars, laughing up at them, his adorable baby-grimace that narrowed his laughing eyes and wrinkled his small button of a nose, and showed his small, pearly teeth. Her baby — clinging with one chubby, small fist to Gladda Romaine's hand, with the other to James Marvin's trouser-leg, as though trying with all his baby-might to bring together these two people whom the finished picture would have you believe were his estranged mother and father.

Allen, manager of the exchange, was watching the girl and he saw her white face, the distended eyes —the trembling of her body.

"It is your baby?" he asked unnecessarily.

She lifted her eyes, wide and filled with tears.

"There isn't the faintest doubt!" she told him unsteadily.

"Would you like to see the movie again—the part in which the child appears?" he asked gently. "I'll be glad to run it off for you!"

"Thank you—you are more than kind! I WOULD like it—very much!" she stammered.

Allen led the way into a small cell of a room with white-washed walls and an excellent screen at one end. There were wicker chairs, and he seated Janelle before he went back and spoke to the operator in the booth.

"Just the last reel, Joe—the kid isn't on until then!" he murmured swiftly.

A moment later the lights were switched out, and a round white beam of light fell upon the silver screen. A moment later—and the interior of a house was shown —a nursery, with painted rows of Peter Rabbits, and Mickey Mouses and other beloved toys of childhood days around the wall. There were dainty pieces of furniture in the right size for a child's use, and there was a trundle bed down front.

The scene shifted to a close-up—a baby asleep in the trundle bed, and Janelle put a shaking hand over her mouth as she saw the beloved little blond curly head against its pillow, one little curled fist flung back against the pillow—the way Billy-boy had slept! The hundreds of times she had bent over him as he lay just like this! Her heart was beating so thickly that it shook her body as she leaned forward, tense, her eyes fastened on the screen.

The child stirred, awoke and sat up. He laughed, joyously clapped his little hands together, and hurled his teddy-bear out of the bed. Apparently he heard a noise that caught his attention. He listened, then he laughed again, and climbed out of the bed. When he landed solidly, he merely grunted, and heaved himself to his small, unsteady feet. Janelle all but cried out as she saw that he was clad in a one-piece sleeping garment of the type he had worn the last time she had put him to bed.

He pattered across the floor and out of the scene. The next scene showed the two stars, the lovely Miss Romaine, and the stalwart and handsome Mr. Marvin in the role of the child's parents. Apparently they had just come in from the theatre, and they were quar-

"I'm terribly sorry, Mrs. Elliott, that we haven't been able to find out what became of the baby after the picture was finished!" Maxie went on smoothly. "Right now I got scouts out all over town, at every studio, and at Central Casting—everywhere there's any possible chance he could be and lots of places he COULDN'T be — trying to find him!"

(See Page 451 in No. 15)

reling. Miss Romaine, in an elaborate evening gown, drew her magnificent fur-coat about her shoulders haughtily and turned her back upon the equally angry· Mr. Marvin.

Here came another close-up of the baby on the stairs. Clinging to the banisters with one hand, his teddy-bear clutched beneath the other arm, he came down the steps one step at a time, his eyes dancing as he saw the two at the foot of the stairs. Reaching them, he shrieked "Boo!" and flung himself upon them.

Throughout the rest of the reel the baby's antics drew the estranged couple closer together until at the very finish, there was a close-up of the two stars holding the baby between them, a chubby arm about each of them, drawing their heads closer together.

When the last scene flickered out and the lights went back on in the room, Janelle sat back in her chair, for a moment, her shaking hands over her white face, tear-stained, ravished.

Allen looked at her, sympathetic, troubled.

"You are quite sure now, Mrs. Elliott, that this is your child?" he asked unnecessarily, for her manner had already told him how certain she was of that.

"Here are the dates on that picture, Mr. Allen!" said Miss Johnson from the doorway.

"Ah, yes — thanks, Miss Johnson!" he accepted the notes, and looked them over swiftly.

"Mrs. Elliott, the picture was produced at the studios of XL Art Productions on Vine Street in Hollywood, and released January 4th, of this year!" he told Janelle.

She caught her breath and stared at him, wide-eyed.

"Then—then that means—that my baby was alive after November 9th?" she cried unsteadily.

"Well, I don't know about that. Mrs. Elliott. You can't always tell anything about when a picture was made by the date of its release. Usually the picture is released shortly after it is made—sometimes, they are held over for months!" explained Allen gently. "However, XL Arts is a small independent company—one of the kind that turns out its stuff so quickly that it is called a 'quickie' company. I imagine that they would release their stuff as rapidly as they could get it ready!"

He was looking over the notes the girl had brought to him.

"Strange the name of the baby doesn't appear in the cast—his part is rather a good one!" he puzzled.

Janelle, trembling, asked swiftly:

"Could that be because whoever put him in the picture knew that he had been—stolen? That I might be able to trace him?"

Allen smiled a little as he shook his head.

"I hardly think that would be it!" he answered. "I think it is possibly because Miss Romaine and Mr. Marvin were fighting so hard for honors in the picture, that they kept the cast-list down as low as they could!"

"Mr. Allen—if you were in my place—what would you do? How would you go about finding him?" asked Janelle swiftly.

Mr. Allen flung his notes on the desk.

"I'd take the first boat for the States — I'd go straight to Hollywood—I'd make the rounds of the casting directors, and of the main casting office, Central Casting Bureau, with photographs of the child. If he is on call at any of the studios, they will be able to help you find him!" he told her concisely.

She stood up.

"Thank you, Mr. Allen—that's exactly what I shall do!" she told him quickly.

"Good! I'll give you the name and address of my company out there—the owners of this exchange, and I'll write them today, asking them to look out for you, and to offer you any assistance possible!" he said as he shook hands with her and walked with her to the door, where he watched her hail a taxi and get into it.

He turned back to the office, his eyes snapping.

"Miss Johnson—take a letter to the home office —publicity department — greatest story we've had in years—'The Guilty Woman' with this front-page tie-up ought to gross a million!" he cried enthusiastically. "Know who that woman was? Janelle Elliott who was sentenced to death for the murder of her lover, a Russian named Forgio whom she accused of kidnapping her child! And she rescued this bird Lawrence from the jungle—think they are going to get married—and she thinks the kid in 'The Guilty Woman' is her stolen child. Boy, will the press-crowd in the home office yell their heads off when this gets to them? They ought to crash the front page of every newspaper in the country!"

Chapter 47.

"GOOD-BYE, MY LOVE—FOR A LITTLE WHILE!"

HEN Janelle reached the hospital, she went straight to Sherman's room. Nurse Judkins and the doctor were just coming out of the room, and as she saw Janelle, the nurse pulled the door shut behind her, and she and the doctor faced Janelle.

At the look in their faces, Janelle's heart sank. She had been so engrossed with thoughts of the baby—she had all but forgotten that Sherman was still far from well. Out of danger, yes —unless there should be a recurrence of the dread jungle fever! And they had fought so hard to avoid that. Yet now the doctor and the nurse looked grave-eyed, troubled.

"What—what's—wrong?" she stammered, one hand up to cup above her breast where her heart thudded so wearily.

"I'm afraid we'll have to ask you to tell us that!" said the doctor gravely. "Yesterday Mr. Lawrence was getting along splendidly! Taking his nourishment, sleeping soundly, making great strides towards recovery.

Yet today we find him—slipping back. He has a touch
of fever—he won't eat—and he didn't sleep last night.
That's mighty dangerous business for a man who has
gone through what he has gone through! Nurse and
I thought you might be able to help us find out what's
troubling him!"

The two were studying her gravely, waiting.
Janelle put up her hand to shade her eyes. Was it
always to be like this? Was she one of those tragically
unfortunate people who brought only sorrow and tragedy to other people? First Bill—then Forgio—then her
father—perhaps her baby—and now, because of her affairs Sherman was dangerously ill again. But for her,
Sherman would not be here. But for her he would be
back in Atlanta, carrying on his enormous business,
living a sane, normal, rational life. Instead, because
he had loved her, and she had failed him at a moment
when he had needed her terribly—he had started off
on this flight that had ended in disaster. And now here
he was, wasted in health and strength, poorer in money
as well as in other ways. And all because he had loved
her!

"He's—worrying about me, doctor—not so much
about me as about—my baby that we thought was dead
—but that I've seen in the movies—the uncertainty—"
she stumbled and then stopped.

"I'm very sorry for you, my dear—but if you
want him to get well, you must relieve his mind. Make
him stop worrying!" said the doctor as though it was
as simple as that and turned and walked away.

Nurse Judkins looked after him smiling a little,
wryly, shaking her head.

"Aren't men the limit? Telling you to relieve
Mr. Lawrence's mind as casually as though all you had
to do was press a button and, presto! his mind is at

peace! Go in and tell him the truth—and try to make him feel it's going to be all right—maybe it is!" said Nurse Judkins almost grimly.

When Janelle opened the door of Sherman's room, he was lying still and white against his pillows, relaxed. Her heart turned over in her breast at the sight of his pallor, his wasted body that had been big and strong and vital. He lay so still that at first she thought he scarcely breathed, but as she crept closer to the bed he heard her in his heart, if her foot-steps were too faint to reach his ears, and his eyes opened, and he looked at her, that little glad, joyous laugh that always shone in his eyes when he looked at her, flashing into being.

He put out his hand and closed it over hers, drawing her close to him.

"You're so lovely!" he told her, and to Janelle's ears, even his voice sounded weaker, more faint than it had sounded yesterday. "I love you so!"

"And I love you, dearest—my dear!" she said unsteadily as she bent above him, kissing him tenderly.

They rested so for a long moment, as though each of them joyed in the little contact—as though he drew strength from her own vitality. And then, after the little pause, he looked up at her.

"Tell me what you found out, darling—I've worried and wondered—I loathe myself for being helpless and an invalid when I want so much to help you!"

"You help me, darling, by—loving me and believing in me! That helps more than anything else in the world!" she told him unsteadily, kissing him again and holding him very close before she drew a chair up beside the bed and related to him the happenings of the morning.

He listened intently and when she had finished

he said promptly,

"You must go to Hollywood at once, and see what you can find out!"

"You—you don't think I should send a detective? I hate to leave you when you are so ill——" she stammered, and Sherman smiled at her ruefully.

"Yet it breaks your heart to think of turning over to a detective a search that you're aching to make yourself—sweetheart—I understand! You're sailing on the first boat—and I'll be quite all right here with Nurse Judkins and old Doctor Fuss-Budget — he's a good scout at that! And the minute you find the boy —God grant that you do find him. dear—and this busted flipper of mine let's me travel, I'll be after you!" he told her humorously.

And in the end it was settled that way. There was a boat sailing at midnight that night. By rare good luck Janelle was able to get passage on it. It wrenched her heart to say good-bye at the last to Sherman. The doctor very keenly and frankly disapproved of her going—but Sherman was firm in his insistence that she go ahead, and Nurse Judkins insisted that she would take care of Sherman.

In the event of any further letters from the mysterious "Annie Green," Sherman was to wire Janelle and keep his detectives advised. A little after ten o'clock she was ready. Her baggage stowed in a taxi down-stairs.

Dressed for travelling she stood beside Sherman's bed looking down at him, as he smiled valiantly up at her. She knew that his own heart was torn at the parting as hers was. She was strangely reluctant to go. It was as though some ominous dread of the future— some portent of evil—made her cling to him, unwilling to be separated from him even for the few weeks of this very important trip. Was it a whispered foreboding of evil—some instinct that told her long, cruel months of anxiety and heartache might stretch between them before ever they met again? Was it a fear of the future that made her drop suddenly to her knees, her face hidden against Sherman's shoulder, her arms clinging to him almost frantically?

"Oh, Sherman darling—I can't go away and leave you like this—ill—and needing me. Oh, dearest, I can't —I can't—I'll send a detective——" she wailed suddenly.

Sherman's arms closed sharply about her, almost convulsively, as though the effort of parting was too much for him. As he held her close, his face looked white and sick. his eyes dark and lonely as untended hearth-fires. They had come through such trials and tribulations — so much of sorrow and heartache and tragedy had held them apart for so long—and now, when they were together—when the day of their marriage was set—when all life stretched ahead of them, a rose-strewn, flowery path of peace and happiness— they must be torn apart again! It was almost more than human heart could stand.

And yet he knew that every minute that she clung to him—every day that she lingered at his side, waiting and fretting for news from Hollywood, she would be miserable. Far better, far more wise, for her to make the journey herself—to see at first hand just what was to be done—than for her to linger here, feeling herself chained to Sherman by his helplessness. Loving her as he did, he could not but see the whole thing sanely and clearly—and, seeing it so, he found somewhere in the innermost recesses of his heart the strength to send her from him, knowing that in the activity the busyness of searching for her child she might find a peace of mind that she could never know, chained to his side, tortured by uncertainty.

"Sweetheart—my dearest—listen to me!" he told her gravely, and she could never know the courage that it took for him to say it. "I'm quite all right here—and you can keep in close touch with me by cable. You must go out there and find out for yourself—if this is Billy-boy—think of the great happiness we three will know together! And if it isn't—then your mind will be at rest! You MUST go, beloved—for my sake, for yours—most of all—for the baby's!"

"Here, here, here—I can't have my patient upset at this hour of the night!" Nurse Judkins, her eyes suspiciously moist, interrupted suddenly. "Here, young woman—don't you know taxis charge money for just standing still? Be off with you now—yes, you may kiss him once more, and then you scoot—do you hear me?"

Half-laughing, half-crying, Janelle bent low above the man she loved and kissed him.

"Please—take care of him, for me, Nurse!" she begged unsteadily.

"Of course I will—you run along now and don't worry! I'll see that he's all right—anything that wants him will have to get me first!" said Nurse Judkins firmly.

(A homely, not too funny little joke, meant merely to brace the girl's spirits. But afterwards they were both to remember those words and to shiver at the thought of their real meaning!)

Janelle tore herself away at last—and, from the window, Nurse Judkins saw her get into the taxi and the door slam behind her. She turned back to Sherman with some light remark, but he was lying very still with both hands over his face—and the nurse, a little shaken by the pathos of that still, silent figure, turned and tiptoed out of the room in search of a sleeping potion that would guarantee him the sleep he so badly needed.

At midnight Janelle stood at the rail of the ship, a small, lonely figure, her white face turned towards the hospital, that lay in its beautifully landscaped grounds, only a few lights glowing here and there to mark a room where a patient fought his lonely, tragic battle with the Gray Shadow that her love had routed from Sherman's room. Tears slipped down her cheeks and she held out her hands in a little, pleading gesture.

"Good-bye, my love—my dear—for a little while —but only for a little while!" she whispered as though the fresh, springing breeze that caressed her white face might take her message to him. But only the sound of the night wind answered her.

Chapter 48.

IN HOLLYWOOD.

IN THE luxuriously appointed office of the President, a group of men employed in producing, selling and exploiting the productions of the XL Art-Productions, Inc., a studio not quite as large as its name, the President himself was addressing his employees.

"A picture we've got that can be tied up with one of the biggest newspaper stories of the year—and you don't even know how to find the child! A child who comes in to our studio, who works for two, maybe three weeks, who draws twenty-five dollars a day for his work—and nobody in the studio knows his name or his address! I ask you—what kind of an organization is this?" he demanded savagely.

"The dame that brought the kid to the studio gave us a fake name—we found that out later!" the casting director tried to explain. "She said she was Mrs. Green, and she called the kid Junior. Central Casting sent her over—but the address she gave them was a cheap little hotel on a side-street—and when we telephoned there, they said she had moved and left no address!"

"Excuses—excuses—that's all I'm getting is excuses!" blazed the President furiously. "With that child in the studio now, and this newspaper story breaks — the kidnapped baby — the mother that was almost sent to the chair—the guy that crashed in the jungle —the woman that rescued him—and she sees her kidnapped baby in one of our pictures—she's on her way here now to find the kid—and we don't even know the name of the people that rented us the kid!"

The little group of men about him stirred unhappily, but nobody dared to ask him a question, or to offer another excuse. The stout little President's thick black cigar spouted creamy, thick smoke for a few moments. He was almost in tears.

"A story that puts the name of my company on the front pages of the world's newspapers! Another production with that child in it, and I could retire and live like a gentleman! But no—we can't find the child!" he wailed.

Suddenly he pounded his fist so vigorously on his solid rosewood desk that the solid gold pen and pencil set bounced indignantly.

"Well, why are you standing around here like numbskulls? Go out and find the child! He's gotta be somewhere—ain't it? Well, find out where that is!" he ordered, and the little group melted thankfully away.

As they left the room a woman entered. A woman who was smaller than her screen fans would have thought, and not quite so beautiful. But so smartly, so expensively gowned that, for a moment, one did not notice her lack of beauty.

"What's the matter, Maxie? Goodness, you're running a temperature—and over what, I ask you? Tell little Gladda!" she cooed sweetly, perching herself on the corner of the rosewood desk, and lighting a cigarette between her own lips from the President's cigar.

He looked at her with sudden eagerness.

"Look, Glad—you remember the picture, 'The Guilty Woman?' Sure you do—you played in it!"

She frowned in annoyance.

"Sure I remember it — that's the picture that Wayne let Jim Marvin hog from me!" she snapped.

"Never mind that now, Glad—it's this I'm asking you. You remember the child — the little feller that played in it?" Maxie begged her to remember.

"You mean the one the publicity department cooked that wild story about — claimed I wanted to adopt the brat? Is that the one you mean?" asked Gladda puzzled.

"Sure—sure—that's the one! Maybe you remember his mama—who brought him to the studio? Where he lived, maybe?" he begged eagerly.

Gladda stared at him, puzzled.

"What's it all about, Maxie? Sure I remember the brat — but I don't remember anything about the woman who brought him, except that the youngster was scared to death of her! Wayne had to get her off the set before he could get a giggle out of the child!" answered Gladda carelessly.

"You remember, maybe, what she called him?" Maxie hated to give up.

Gladda slid down from the desk, and pressed the light from her cigarette in the ash-tray on the corner of the desk.

"Sure—that's an easy one! The only thing I ever heard her call him was 'Hey, you'! And in a tone that said she meant it, too!" she laughed. "I'll drop in again, Maxie, when you aren't so hot and bothered. I've got a little bone to pick with you about that part Wayne is trying to give me in his next picture—how about tipping that bird off to the fact that I'm a star—and NOT a supporting player for his discovery, Martin?"

And she walked out of the room, closing the door behind her, giving no further thought to her employer's troubles.

*　　*　　*　　*　　*　　*　　*　　*　　*

Janelle, as she reached Los Angeles and a hotel realized that the one vitally important point that she must keep in mind was that of the time of the actual production of this picture. If "The Guilty Woman" had been shot prior to November 9th, it would not prove that her child was alive. If, however, the production date had been AFTER November 9th, she would know that her child had been alive and here in California, when that pitiful little skeleton had been consigned to its last resting place there at Fair Oaks beside Bill.

When she had unpacked and straightened her things and had a bath and was freshly dressed, she came out into the bright, warm sunshine, and hailed a taxi.

The driver smothered a grin as she gave the address of the XL Art Studio on Vine Street. Another movie-struck dame, he thought. Evidently one not very wise to the racket or she wouldn't be heading for a studio on Poverty Row, where the chief out-put was "shot 'em up Westerns" and melodramas of the poorer sort, where salaries were small and work was scarce. The drive from the hotel to the studio was a long one, however, and the driver was duly grateful for his fee.

Arrived at the studio, Janelle walked into the office, and to the bored, haughty young girl behind the window marked "Information," she addressed herself.

"I'd like to see——" she began, but the girl waved her hand negligently.

"Nothing today. Leave your pictures—we'll call you!" she said wearily.

"I'm not applying for work!" stated Janelle almost sharply. "I want to see someone who can tell me something about the players in a picture your company made called 'The Guilty Woman.'"

The girl looked up, startled.

"Are you Mrs. Elliott?" she demanded.

Startled, Janelle stared at her, wide-eyed.

"Yes—but how in the world did you know?" she gasped.

The girl waved her hand airily.

"Oh, we've been expecting you since early this morning!" said the girl casually. "I'll see if Mr. Cason can see you now!"

Janelle stared at her, bewildered. How in the world—and then she remembered. Mr. Allen, of the exchange, in Havana—he had written them. They were receiving her as a friend—she felt a little rush of relief. She was no longer among strangers.

The information clerk, no longer haughty and bored, showed her into the inner office where a stout, immaculately groomed man of middle age, with a thick black cigar in his hand was awaiting her.

"Mrs. Elliott, this is a great pleasure!" he assured her shaking hands with her, and putting her into a comfortable chair at his desk. "We are anxious to help you in any way possible!"

Janelle looked up at him gravely.

"Then—you know what I've come for? News of

my lost baby." she added eagerly.

Mr. Cason waved his pudgy hand on which glittered a rather awe-inspiring diamond.

"Sure, sure—Allen wrote us—a great story, Mrs. Elliott—a great story!" he assured her eagerly.

"A great story? I don't think you understand, Mr. Cason—the child who played in one of your pictures——" she began, but Mr. Cason waved her to silence.

"Sure, sure — but the newspapers ate it up—that story! By the end of the week every newspaper in the world will carry a story of it—the search for the kidnaped baby, seen in a production by the XL Art Company!" he cried.

"You've given the story to the newspapers?" cried Janelle aghast.

Mr. Cason shrugged.

"Sure—why not? It's good publicity—swell publicity! If only we had another picture with that baby in it—we'd make a fortune!" he assured her.

She leaned towards him tensely.

"Mr. Cason—does that mean—you know where he is—my baby?" she stammered.

Sadly he shook his head.

"I only wish I did—but we haven't been able to find a trace of him, though we've searched the town!" he admitted.

A little wave of desolation swept over Janelle. After a long moment, she spoke tensely:

"It's—terribly important for me to know—when that picture was produced—the actual time that—my baby was here in your studio! Have you a record?" she asked.

Cason took up a slip of paper.

"The picture started shooting—November 1st!"

he told her, and added without realizing the importance to her of what he was saying: "The scenes of the baby were the last made—he started working on November 28th!"

Janelle caught her breath, and it seemed to her that Mr. Cason and his voice were miles away. The only thing that seemed real and vivid to her was—that her baby had been alive and in Hollywood on November 28th—and that tiny baby had been buried back at Fair Oaks on November 9th.

Her heart sang with one mad, exultant thought —her baby still lived!

Continued in Next Number.

"Maybe—these Japs all look so much alike I never try to tell one from another!" Maxie agreed carelessly. "Have you had this one long?" asked Janelle idly. Now she was sure that the Jap was listening. (See Page 470)

Chapter 49.

A STARTLING OFFER!

ELL, NOW — if the child in 'The Guilty Woman' WAS your baby, Mrs. Elliott — was working in this studio on November 18th, and for four days after that!" said Maxie Cason, president of XL Art Productions.

Janelle caught her breath and swayed back in her chair, her hands over her eyes. Then — the identification of that tiny body back there at Fair Oaks was a mistake. It was not her baby that slept in the tiny grave beside Bill. Her baby—her little, adored Billy-boy—still lived! Her mother's-heart had not been mistaken!

When she had finally managed to regain a measure of her self-control, she looked up to find Maxie's eyes on her, studying her shrewdly, taking her in from the top of her smart, expensive hat to the tips of her small, polished slippers.

"I'm terribly sorry, Mrs. Elliott, that we haven't been able to find out what became of the baby after the picture was finished!" Maxie went on smoothly. "Right now I got scouts out all over town, at every studio, and at Central Casting — everywhere there's any possible chance he could be and lots of places he COULDN'T be —trying to find him!"

Through her tears, Janelle smiled at the man gratefully.

"That's awfully kind of you, Mr. Cason!" she stammered.

Maxie made a little gesture, disclaiming her gratitude.

"It's not kind at all, Mrs. Elliott—frankly, we'd like mighty well to find him, for our own sake—to put him in a picture. If we could release a picture with that baby in it right now, while the story is 'hot' in the newspapers—well, I could gross a million on it! So you see, I'm a business man—maybe it's good business I should help hunt your baby—a prospective star!" he assured her quite frankly.

He was studying Janelle sharply, shrewdly, and any one who had ever worked with Maxie Cason would have known that in that fertile, shrewd, canny brain of his, he was revolving a smart idea. Suddenly he leaned towards her, and asked baldly,

"Ever work in pictures, Mrs. Elliott?"

Janelle laughed a little and shook her head.

"No, of course not—I was never in Hollywood before in my life!" she returned, smiling.

"Ever on the stage?"

"No!"

"But you've posed for artists — you and the baby?"

"A little!"

Maxie leaned towards her persuasively.

"Mrs. Elliott, I got a little idea—how I can make a lot of money and you can, maybe, find your baby!"

he told her solemnly.

"How?" Janelle begged to know, leaning towards him tensely.

"By working in a picture for me!" said Maxie.

Janelle stared at him, puzzled.

"You mean—act—me? Oh, but Mr. Cason, I've just told you that I've never had any movie experience, or stage experience, either!" she protested.

"And I'm telling you that makes no difference! I got a director that can show you everything you need to know about acting—you stand in front of the camera, say the things you are told to say, in the way you are told to say them, and do the things you are told to do, the way you are told to do 'em—and you'll be a hit!" he assured her eagerly. "Mind you, first we have a test —to see how you photograph—but I got a camera eye —I can tell now that you screen great!"

Janelle flung up a little protesting hand.

"But, Mr. Cason—I don't want to be a picture actress—I want to find my baby and go back to Cuba to the man I love, and be married and settle down!" she protested. "Of course, I'm grateful to you and all that—but I can't see that this would help——"

"All right—you can't see that it would help— then I'll show you!" Maxie cut in swiftly. "First of all, we have a story turned out here in the studio about you and your search for your baby and the man you love—a story based a little on your own life, you see? We'll use pictures of your baby—maybe some film from 'The Guilty Woman'—and as a feature of the advertising about the baby, we'll offer a swell reward to anybody who can help up locate the baby! Is that an idea, or isn't it? I'm asking you!"

He was so proud of the idea that Janelle hesitated to veto it. She did not particularly like the idea

—yet—it had its possibilities. Through the picture the baby's features would become so well known that there would scarcely be a spot in the world where he could be hidden. Through the offer of the reward, the kidnappers, whoever now held him might be tempted to return him, by pretending that they themselves, had taken him from some one else and were innocent of his original capture. There was, too, the fear that this broadcasting of an appeal for the child, the difficulty of hiding him any longer, might lead to his death—still, that was a chance that must be taken, and the hope of his return for a heavy money reward was much greater than the fear of his destruction.

"You see, Mrs. Elliott, the power of the motion picture, the power of the press and public opinion will all be on your side, and I'd be almost willing to guarantee you that the baby will be returned to you within a month of the release of the picture! I'll pay you a good salary—and if you screen as well as I believe you will—who knows but what you may become a great star? A movie sensation. What do you say?" coaxed Maxie, more and more thrilled over his idea which in his own mind he described as "terrific."

"The only thing about it that interests me is the thought that it might lead me to my baby—I'd like a little time to think it over!" she said at last.

"Of course, of course—but now that you are at the studio, why not have the tests made now? Then we can develop them while you are thinking the proposition over, and if you decide to accept—we'll be that much ahead. We'll have to work fast, you know, while the story is 'hot' on the newspaper front-pages!" he coaxed, and Janelle consented.

Maxie turned back to his desk a minute, scribbled rapidly on a note-pad, and when he walked with Janelle through the office, he gave the note to the telephone operator. As the door of the outer office closed behind Janelle and Maxie the telephone operator rang the scenario editor's telephone.

"Hello, Joe? Mr. Cason wants you to dig up the files on the Janelle Elliott story—yeah, that one. She's going to do a picture here, and Maxie wants it written about her life—sure, go to it. He'll probably want to start shootin' before six o'clock tonight! Yeah, she's a good-looking dame—what did you think? Maxie's not 'THAT goofy!"

Chapter 50.

A NEW CHAPTER BEGINS!

ANELLE walked with Maxie down the little street between the dressing - rooms and administration offices of the XL Productions, to one of the sound-stages.

A huge sign hung on the door. "Shooting. Do not enter!"

Apparently the sign meant nothing to Maxie, for he opened the door and drew Janelle with him into a place that seemed to Janelle a perfect bedlam of chaos and confusion. Piles of scenery, heaps of furniture, tall canvas screen, wires, cables, boxes of lights—a bewildering confusion through which she threaded a cautious, uneasy way behind Maxie, who strode pompously ahead of her, thoroughly at home in all this chaos.

Before them was a elegantly furnished room. With only three walls. The fourth wall had given way to a barrage of cameras, sound apparatus, borders of lights. A flood of brilliant, bluish light poured over the two people who were in the room, while outside a white chalk mark, in front of the missing fourth wall, stood a group composed of camera-men, technicians the director and his assistant, the attentive script-clerk.

The atmosphere was tense and bitter.

"For the last time, Wayne, I'm telling you that I will NOT play the script the way its written. I am a star—not a supporting player!" a woman's voice was saying acidly.

Janelle saw her—a woman whose beauty was almost hidden by the thick smear of cream-colored grease-paint, the mascara that fringed her eyes, the purplish hue of her lips.

"And for the last time, Miss Romaine, I am the director of this picture, and the script has been okayed by the front office and New York—and it's going to be shot the way its written—or not at all!" said a man's voice, thick with suppressed fury.

Maxie thrust himself forward with the gesture of one who spreads oil on troubled waters.

"Now, now, now—what's all this? Quarrelling and wasting the company's money? Tchk, tchk, tchk, Gladda — I'm surprised at you!" he said soothingly. "Wayne, what's the matter?"

"Miss Romaine objects to the script, to the leading man, to the director, to the assistant director, to the script-clerk, property boys—to the color of the draperies in the set—in fact, if there's anything about the production that Miss Romaine doesn't object to, I've yet to find out what it is!" said the director wearily as he dropped into a canvas chair labelled simply, "Wayne."

"It seems impossible, Maxie, for him to get it through his head that I'm a star——and until he does, the picture can go to blazes for all I care!" snapped Gladda, and, lifting the trailing skirts of her velvet gown, she stalked out of the scene.

Maxie looked after her, unperturbed.

"She'll get over it—she wants to play this picture

—it's a great part for her!" he said grinning.

"I'm sorry, Maxie—but if she plays it, then I won't direct it!" said the director. "I'm fed up on her whims and tantrums—it's all I can do to keep from strangling her!"

"And who said you had to direct her?" demanded Maxie happily. "Wayne, my boy, I got the biggest sensation of the year—for you to direct!"

Wayne looked up at him suspiciously.

"Maxie, if you've brought me another beauty contest winner, so help me, Hannah, I'm through!" he threatened ominously.

Maxie laughed, and drew Janelle forward.

"Mrs. Elliott, this is Mr. Wayne, the best director in Hollywood, or anywhere else! Wayne, will you give Mrs. Elliott a test for this new part I'm having written? Let her do a scene with Marvin here and see how she screens!" said Maxie happily.

"But, Mr. Cason, I'm not at all sure——" began Janelle, protesting.

Maxie waved his pudgy, beautifully manicured hand.

"I know, I know.—but I'M not at all sure, either —until I see how you screen! That's all—it's a test!" he assured her.

Wayne looked down at Janelle, and as he took in the planes and angles of her face, the slim, graceful carriage of her body, and heard the tones of her voice, a look of faint interest dawned in his eyes. After all, she would not be the first "over-night miracle" of the screen, and, mollified, with the interest of a discoverer, he turned her over to the make-up man.

In a dressing-room at the side of the stage—one of the small, portable sort, of which she had read in the movie magazines—Janelle sat down and took off her hat. With a towel fastened carefully over her hair, her head tilted back so a merciless light beat directly upon her face, the make-up man studied her carefully from every angle. before he began applying cold cream to her face, wiping it off, and then applying a pale yellow grease-paint, mascara and so on.

When he had finished, and she surveyed herself in the mirror, she looked into the wide eyes of an utter stranger. Surely nothing so grotesque, she told herself, dazedly, could possibly photograph as anything but a freak!

But when the make-up man led her back to the little group that stood about Maxie and the director, she heard expressions of approval, and appreciation to the make-up man.

Evidently Maxie had told the director something about Janelle, for his apparent interest had deepened, and he was very pleasant and helpful in his suggestions.

"Now, Mrs. Elliott, you come into the set through this door! You are wearing your out-door things, so it's evident you've been out for a walk, or shopping or something. While you were gone, this letter has been delivered by special messenger! It tells you some news of your baby—he has been found! You start up the stairs, and you meet Mr. Marvin on his way down. And he tells you that the letter has been proven a fake, and that there is no truth in it. Your baby is dead!" Wayne described the little scene with gestures, and when he had finished, he added, "You understand? Behave exactly as you would if all this were quite true. Try to make yourself feel that it IS true!"

Janelle nodded. She had time to wonder if there was a girl her own age in America who wouldn't have thrilled to the tips of her toes over such an opportunity as this to enter the movies. She felt, desolately, the unfairness of such a chance coming to her, who did not want it, when there were probably girls here in Hollywood, starving, homeless, yet talented enough to take advantage of such a chance.

"I understand!" she answered Wayne's instructions, and took up the position he indicated outside the set-door.

She was trembling a little, but she was conscious of no nervousness. She was going through that door to find news of her baby—that thought was uppermost in her mind, as, at Wayne's signal, she stepped through the door, closed it behind her and crossed to the table where she stood pulling off her gloves.

Then her eyes fell on the letter, and, startled, she picked it up. It was addressed to her, in a scrawling writing, and she ripped the envelope open, swiftly, drawing out a single sheet of torn paper across which was written the words,

"Your baby has been found alive and well—bring the ransom money!"

For a moment she forgot that it was all a made-up scene. So long she had waited, hoped, prayed, for such a message. She had all but despaired of ever getting it—and now, here it was in her hands. She caught her breath, the letter crumpled between her trembling hands. Her hand went up as she struggled for composure, and from beneath her eyelids two crystal tears slipped.

A sound on the stairs caught her attention, and she whirled to see a man coming down the stairs towards her. Dimly she remembered instructions. She was to go towards this man — she stumbled towards him, with outflung hands that held the crumpled note, and she clung to him with both shaking hands as he caught her.

"Why, darling, what is it?" his voice was well modulated, pleasing.

"They've—they've—found my baby!" she stammered, still held in the grip of the image her thoughts had created.

The man took the note and read it. He looked down at her pitying, reluctant to hurt her, yet knowing that it must be done.

"My darling, you must be brave—you MUST be!" he told her gently.

Dumbly, she stared up at him, the light fading from her face was the light as snuffed from a candle by a winter wind. For a long moment she stared at him, wide-eyed—and then she whispered barely above her breath.

"You—you mean—it isn't—true?"

"I mean, darling, that—it can't be true—for—your baby is—DEAD!" said the man with an almost cruel emphasis.

Not even the bonds of make-believe could hold her through that. Her shrinking heart could not face even the belief of that — and she cried out sharply against it.

"No, no, no!" she cried sharply, her voice breaking beneath the weight of its grief and anguish. "That isn't true—it isn't true! I won't believe it—I WON'T believe it!"

She was sobbing now, and scarcely heard the director's cry of "Cut!" that told of the finish of the scene. Marvin, the leading man who had good-naturedly helped with the test, was a little aghast at her behavior and he patted her shoulder ineffectually.

"Here, here, Mrs. Elliott—please! Brace yourself—it's only a test—of course it isn't true! Ye gods, Wayne, why didn't you tell me she'd really lost her kid?" he demanded of the director.

By now Janelle had managed to pull herself together, and she tried to stammer an apology to the men who looked a little embarassed and very sympathetic.

The make-up man took her back to the portable dressing-room, where the make-up was removed, and where he gave her a small glass containing aromatic spirits of ammonia, which helped to strengthen her composure. When she came back to the place where Wayne, Maxie and the others were waiting for her, she found Wayne and Maxie in close conversation.

". . . . a natural!" she heard Wayne say enthusiastically. "In a story written especially for her —and a tie-up with the newspapers——" he broke off as he discovered her approach.

"Mrs. Elliott, suppose you have dinner with Wayne and me tonight!" suggested Maxie. "By that time we will have seen the test and you will have had time to think over the proposition, and maybe we can come to terms!"

Janelle agreed, thanked them all pleasantly, and was sent back to her hotel in Maxie Cason's Rolls-Royce behind an immobile Japanese chauffeur, who, to Janelle, looked somewhat like the servant who had on a long ago night, let her into Alexis Forgio's apartment! That night that her baby had been stolen! She shivered at the thought and was heartily glad when she reached the hotel, and the chauffeur, with an odd glance at her had driven away.

Chapter 51.

LETTERS.

HEN SHE came into the hotel the clerk handed her a letter, and when she saw, in an upper corner, the return address of the American Hospital in Havana, she hurried to her room to read it.

The first thing she noted, as she drew the letter from its envelope, was that the handwriting was strange. Her heart sank a little at this. She had felt so sure the letter was from Sherman. She turned swiftly to the signature and saw that the writer was Nurse Judkins.

"Dearest:" the letter began, simply.

"Nurse Judkins is being the good scout I've always known she was, by acting as my secretary for this letter. I'd write it myself but this darned fever has my hands shaking so that if I did write, you'd probably think the letter was in Chinese or ancient Arabic and be running around Los Angeles, trying to find an interpreter.

"Your letter mailed at Colon, and at other

points along your route, were grand. darling, and I was so happy to know that you had a pleasant journey. It was selfish of me, but I was glad, too, to know that you missed me and were lonely! Because, sweetheart, I miss you like the very dickens. and am as lonely as sin!

"I hope by now you have found out something about our baby—you don't mind if I call him OUR baby. do you, darling? Because when we find him—notice I say we, for even if I am not with you in person. I'm there in spirit! And when we find him, we'll settle down somewhere, the three of us, and you and I will make for our baby the happiest home any baby ever had, to make up to him for all that he's missed these three years of his life! Maybe we'll send him to college. eh. Janelle. darling? We'll start studying catalogues, and be sure we pick him out a grand place!

"Seriously. my sweetheart, my thoughts are with you always. Wherever you go, whatever you do, I'm with you in my heart, even if this crooked old body of mine is chained here to a bed that I loathe more with every hour that goes over my head!

"I'm getting along fine though and will join you soon in Los Angeles, and then we'll follow the trail no matter where it leads, firm in the knowledge that eventually it will lead us to 'a harbor of delight in a sea of happiness.'

"Goodnight. my dearest — all my love and my thoughts for you, always.

"Yours, alone,

"Sherman."

When she had read the last words of the letter and pressed her lips to them, Janelle saw through her tears that a smaller slip of paper had fallen out of the letter into her lap. She took it up and opened it. It was a postscript from Nurse Judkins, herself.

"Dear Mrs. Elliott:
"This is just a private little note to tell you that I am taking the best of care of Mr. Lawrence. I have to confess that he is not reacting as I had hoped he would.

"I am afraid that he is fretting about you, and I know that he misses you so badly that it is retarding his recovery. I don't like to tell you this, for I know it will worry you. Still, I know that you will want the truth, and as nearly as I can, I mean to give it to you!

"He is in no present danger — but should his condition take a turn for the worse, I will cable you, and you can get a plane that will bring you here very quickly. I am sure that is the way you would want it!

"With best wishes, I am
"Sincerely,
"Georgia Judkins."

Janelle sat for a long time with the two letters in her hands, looking out of the window over the lovely landscape, starred with flowers, shaded with beautiful pepper and eucalyptus trees, with a towering palm tree here and there.

She was seeing, instead, the hospital room in which Sherman lay on a high, narrow bed, his brown face no longer brown, but pale with the pallor of a long illness. His eyes tired and bleak and lonely. With the eyes of her heart, she could see him as plainly as though he were before her—and her heart cried out to him in loneliness.

She was so lonely—she missed him so. And she knew that he was even more lonely than she, that he needed her much more than she needed him.

Wasn't it, after all, a cruel thing for her to do —to leave the man who loved her devotely and who had gone through a living hell, who needed her—just to make a wild-goose hunt for a child that every possible clue had failed to find?

She wavered piteously, tragically, between the need to stay here and search for her child, and the urge to go back to the man she loved—the man who needed her.

Once she came so near a decision that she stood up abruptly and turned to her baggage to pack for the return. But even as she did, her eyes fell upon the picture of her child—the picture that went with her wherever she went. The picture of Billy-boy, with his collie pup—Billy-boy, laughing, ecstatic, happy.

She stood for a long moment, studying that picture. He was so little, so helpless. He had suffered so much before she had found him. She thought of him as she had seen him there in that grimy little shack in Florida—in the power of those two brutes who had beaten and starved and neglected him.

She saw him as he had been when she had brought him to New York- -a little, frightened. starved. abused animal so accustomed to blows and anger and cruel neglect, that her kindness, her love, her gentleness had been utterly strange to him.

She saw him as he had been the night she put him to bed—the last time she had ever seen him. He

Janelle put both her trembling hands on his arm, her face uplifted to his.
"Oh, Mr. Marvin—tell me—what was it?" "The only time I ever remember the little fellow calling her anything at all except 'yes,
ma'am and 'no, ma'am,' was one day when he called her—
Annie!" said Jim quietly. Janelle caught her breath.

(See Page 480)

had been so happy, so confident—all the fear of the past had vanished—swallowed up in his happiness and his confiding love for his "Muzzie."

And that had been the child wrested from her arms, by a man's wicked lust for her beauty! A man who had wanted her so much despite her hatred and loathing, that he had cruelly thrown her innocent little child to his brutal gang, as callously and as without compunction as though it had been some small animal.

She stood there before the picture of her baby, her eyes lingering on that lovely, laughing, baby-face —and even the claims of the man she loved with all her heart melted before her baby's need of her. She had no way of knowing where he was—how he was—who had him.

But—if he were in the hands of crooks—murderers—thugs—people who would mistreat and abuse him—if he were cold—hungry—frightened—oh, dear God, while even the faintest hope that her baby yet lived, existed in her heart, she could not turn back from the search to which she had dedicated herself. Not even to answer Sherman's need for her.

She sat down at her desk, and drew paper and pen towards her. She wrote swiftly, outlining to him the plan that Maxie Cason had offered her that morning, and asking Sherman's advice on it. She told him of her discovery that the baby had worked at the studio on November 18th———nine days after that pitiful little funeral at Fair Oaks, when Sherman and her father had stood bareheaded in the drizzling rain and had watched a tiny white casket lowered into the kindly earth.

"I want to come back to you. my darling— I miss you so! We've lost so much time, my dearest—so many days and weeks and months when we might have been so happy together, that I'm jealous of every minute that we spend apart now!" she wrote, swiftly. "But—I can't leave now, while there's even the faintest chance that I may find him. I know you will understand and that you will want me to stay—but—oh, my dearest, I miss you so! Hurry and get well, and come to me here!"

She thought of him forlornly. But he would want her to stay she knew, and to do anything that she could to find the baby. Tears fell from her eyes as she read the little paragraph, "our baby!" That had been the only thing needed to make her feel at peace about the baby. To know that Sherman would welcome him, that he would be the third and completing link in their chain of happiness—that had been the final touch to complete her happiness.

She was a little puzzled when it came to dressing for dinner. She had seen enough of the handsome, elaborate costumes at luncheon and at tea in the hotel patio to warn her, however.

So she wisely chose a dinner gown of corn-flower blue crepe, that had a row of tiny brilliants outlining the decolletage, and the wide arm-holes of its sleeveless bodice. The skirt was quite long and full, depending on the beauty of the material and the suavity of the cut for its decoration.

When she came down to the lobby to meet Wayne and Maxie, her costume completed by a brief little jacket of blue and silver squares, that had wide puffed sleeves lined with silver, she knew by the expression in the eyes of the two men that she was looking her loveliest, and that they were more than pleased with her.

"Well, where shall it be, Maxie?" asked Wayne when they had greeted Janelle.

"Where? You're asking me where? When it's Wednesday night, and we've got a new star to lunch? Where would it be but the Cocoanut Grove at the Ambassador?" demanded Maxie as though amazed at the ignorance of his friend.

The Rolls-Royce was waiting, and the same impassive yellow-faced Jap chauffeur was behind the wheel. Janelle felt his eyes on her with a queer look for a brief moment as she paused with one silver-shod foot on the running board of the beautiful car. The chauffeur turned swiftly away, and Janelle got into the car, settling herself between Maxie and Wayne, staring at the chauffeur's head.

"Your chauffeur looks rather familiar to me, Mr. Cason—I can't help feeling I've seen him somewhere before!" she said suddenly.

She thought the chauffeur's head turned a fraction of an inch towards the speaking tube beside him, and realized that he must have heard what she had said.

"Maybe — these Japs all look so much alike I never try to tell one from another!" Maxie agreed carelessly.

"Have you had this one long?" asked Janelle idly.

Now she was sure that the Jap was listening.

"He's practically an old family retainer as servants go, nowadays!" said Maxie, lighting one of the thick, fat, black cigars that he adored. "He's been with me more than a year!"

Janelle relaxed a little, a tiny frown between her brows. This chauffeur had worked for Maxie Cason more than a year.

It had been "more than a year" since Alexis Forgio had been shot to death. It had been "more than a year" since her baby had been lifted, sleeping soundly, from his little crib, and carried away in the darkness, a sinister green and purple orchid left in his bed; it had been "more than a year" since an impassive, yellow-faced Japanese butler had opened the door of Forgio's studio to her.

Could the presence of this man here mean that he had had anything to do with the presence of her baby in this motion picture city? Had this man had anything to do with the theft of her child?

She was trembling a little as she watched him, and wondered. But she spoke of him no more to Maxie, for she knew that the chauffeur was listening intently and that she must be very careful.

Chapter 51.

DAY-TIME STARS AT NIGHT!

N COMMON with almost every normal girl of today, Janelle had gone to the movies, had read movie magazines with avidity, had been interested in the stars and their doings. She had heard of the Cocoanut Grove at the Ambassador, and she knew that on certain nights of the week it was a favorite resort for those of the stars rich enough to afford it.

So, forcing herself to put the puzzling question of the Japanese chauffeur out of her mind for the time being, she went up the walk to the hotel and through to the Grove, walking between Maxie and Wayne, and pleasantly conscious that they were proud of her because she was beautiful and exquisitely dressed.

A waiter-captain showed them to a choice table near the dance-floor. Maxie and Wayne were kept busy acknowledging greetings, gay salutations from surrounding tables and from the dancers.

Maxie was beaming as he gestured about the room, pointing out to Janelle this and that star.

"There's Bebe Daniels—there, in white, with that goodlooking young man. Sure, that's her husband, Ben Lyons—everybody's crazy about those two kids—they grew up with Hollywood, and are still two of the most popular stars—way out in front of lots of newer people that think they own the earth just because they've had stage experience!"

A slender girl, with blond hair, dressed in ivory satin of a regal cut, danced past in the arms of a broad-shouldered, darkly good-looking young man with humorous dark eyes and a well-cropped, dark mustache.

"That's Connie Bennett, and her husband, the Marquis—he's such a 'regular' that everybody forgets he belongs to one of the oldest families of France, with a title and what-not. He likes to be called just plain Hank!" Maxie went on when the waiter had been dispatched with their order.

Wayne leaned towards Janelle, smiling, his strong, sensitive hands folded on the white cloth before him.

"Don't let Maxie bore you pointing out all the celebrities, Mrs. Elliott—you're going to be one yourself in another six weeks or so—by the time 'Legacy of Love' is finished!" he told her pleasantly.

Janelle looked her bewilderment.

"That's the name of the script you're to begin work on Monday!" he told her quite frankly. "Your test this afternoon was a tremendous success — you screen like a million dollars, cash money, and by the time this picture is turned loose throughout the country, you're going to have one hundred and ninety million people, at a low estimate, helping you to find your kidnapped child!"

Janelle caught her breath, and her color faded a little. Her eyes widened and suddenly she leaned towards Wayne, one hand on his arm, Sherman's marquise-cut diamond ring glimmering with a thousand different lights from her finger.

"Mr. Wayne—do you honestly, in your heart, believe that my allowing this picture to be made—my working in it—is going to help me find my baby?" she asked him earnestly.

Wayne hesitated a fraction of a moment. Across her head Maxie signalled him swiftly, and there was a threat in his eyes that made Wayne say with perhaps a little more conviction than he really felt,

"Of course I do, Mrs. Elliott—how can it fail? Your story will be presented to movie fans all over the world in a way that no amount of newspaper space could ever manage. People all over the world are going to weep with you in your sorrow, and burn with indignation, to help you—why, it can't fail!"

Janelle drew a long breath and lifted her lovely head.

"I—hope you are right. And I've no reason for thinking you may not be. So—I'll try it! After all, the picture will cover the world—I couldn't hope to cover a tenth, a hundredth of that much territory in a personal appeal in just six weeks!" she agreed finally.

"Then — you'll make the picture?" demanded Maxie so eagerly that she realized how little hope he had had that she would listen to reason. "Good! Then I'll have a contract ready in the morning!"

"I was wondering if I might break in on this little party long enough to ask Mrs. Elliott to dance?" said a pleasant voice, and Maxie and Wayne rose to greet Jim Marvin, the new screen sensation, who was standing beside the table. "After all, Mrs. Elliott, if we are going to work in a picture together, we might as well begin by being friends!"

"Why not?" agreed Janelle, and with a little apology to Maxie and Wayne she rose and let Jim Marvin take her into his arms.

The music of Abe Lyman's band was ingratiating, the floor smooth as lemon-yellow ice. There was plenty of room as yet, for it was too early for the supper-crowd that would come in after the theatre.

"I'm delighted that you and I are to do a picture together, Mrs. Elliott—Gladda Romaine has impressed it upon me so forcefully that I am an amateur and a newcomer, that I'll be glad to have another newcomer to play around with!" said Jim smiling.

"I'm afraid you won't be delighted long!" Janelle apologized. "You see, I've had neither stage nor picture experience—and I'll probably be an awful dud!"

Jim laughed.

"Somehow, I can't seem to get terribly worked up over that possibility—I'll confess a secret: I've had no stage experience, and very little movie experience! I was driving a truck when Wayne 'discovered' me— his car broke down one morning on his way to the studio, and I picked him up and gave him a lift downtown—and we got to talking, and he suggested I drop in for a test—and the next thing I knew I was playing the supporting lead to Gladda Romaine in 'The Guilty Woman'! And that's how it all happened you see!" he told her gaily

Janelle missed a step and looked up at him sharply.

"You worked in 'The Guilty Woman'—then you must have worked with my baby—he was in that picture. He was supposed to be your child, and Miss Romaine—don't you remember him?" she asked swiftly.

Jim looked down at her keenly—and suddenly, he asked a question.

"Look here, Mrs. Elliott—is this kidnapped baby gag on the level?" he demanded frankly.

Janelle looked her bewilderment.

" 'On the level?' I don't quite understand!" she confessed her puzzlement.

"I mean—all this stuff in the newspapers—about your baby being kidnapped—about your being charged with the murder of the man who had him kidnapped— about the jungle business—and you seeing your child in this picture—is that all true? Or is it just a gag for newspaper space?" he was quite frank in admitting his doubt of the truth of the newspaper headlines.

The look in Janelle's face was conviction enough.

"I—only wish it were a newspaper 'gag' as you call it! Unfortunately—it's all—quite true—horribly true! I'm here for one purpose, and one only—that of finding my baby!"

"Gee—I'm sorry!" Jim apologized swiftly with a little winning, boyish smile. "But I guess I've been around Hollywood so long that I'm beginning to doubt anything that I see on the front page of the newspaper, if it concerns somebody in the movies! I thought the whole thing was a swell 'set-up' for the advent of one of Maxie's 'discoveries' into pictures!"

"But now that you know it is true—can't you remember anything about Billy-boy that night—give me a clue as to who had him—or where they may have gone?" she pleaded.

Jim frowned in concentrated thought.

"I remember the little fellow, of course—cute little tyke—he took quite a fancy to me, and that burnt Gladda up—she didn't care for him herself, but it annoys Glad to find anything alive prefers anybody in the world to herself!" he said at last. "The woman who used to bring him to the studio was a hard looking customer—she had henna'd hair, and the face and eyes of a woman who had gone 'through the mill' if you know what I mean!"

He saw the look in Janelle's eyes, and he added swiftly,

"But I don't think that she was ever unkind to him! I mean to say he didn't seem actually afraid of her! Although she was pretty strict with him!"

Janelle controlled the quivering of her lips, the tears in her eyes.

"Did he call her—'mother'? Or do you remember?" she asked after a moment.

Jim was silent for a moment, thinking. He hadn't paid a great deal of attention to the little fellow—yet because Janelle was so lovely and so troubled and so intent on his answer, he tried hard to think of something that would be consoling.

"N-n-no, I'm quite sure I never heard him call her mother—I can't quite remember just what it was that he DID call her—the only thing I ever heard her call him was 'hey, you'!" he returned.

The music ended on a long drawn out "hot" note, and Janelle stood still beside Jim, looking up at him, her great darkly blue eyes steady and grateful.

"Thank you!" she said evenly. "And — if you CAN remember anything that you heard—my baby call that woman—won't you please—tell me right away? It MIGHT help, you know!"

"Of course I will—and I'll rack what I laughingly call my brain until I remember what it was!" he assured her as he led her back to Maxie and Wayne who were waiting for her, and then excused himself.

Dinner was on the table and waiting. Janelle tried hard to eat, to enjoy the food—Maxie and Wayne were so anxious that she should be happy, that she should enjoy herself.

She felt the interested eyes of people about the room upon her. By that mysterious wireless telegraphy that exists in such places, the news had winged its way about the room that the blond beauty with Maxie and Wayne was XL Arts new star—and everybody craned for a peek at the girl.

People came up to be introduced. Leading men, hopeful of jobs, and anxious to be "pleasant" to the new star; people who had been stars yesterday, but today would be glad of the smallest part that would give them food and lodging and the clothes so vitally necessary in their business; newspaper people; columnists; representatives of the movie fan and trade magazines; present-day stars securely enough established to be able to look with interest and friendliness at this newcomer, rather than with jealousy and suspicion.

Janelle, thrilling a little despite the darkness in her heart, saw Marion Davies looking lovely and gay and vivacious in a black velvet frock; Lilyan Tashman, gowned in a strange, bizarre gown that no doubt would heighten her much-advertised reputation as "the best dressed woman in Hollywood," dancing with her good-looking husband, Edmund Lowe, who seemed in his usual excellent spirits.

They pointed out to her the exotic Marlene Dietrich with her good-looking, blond husband, and the dark gentleman who was Joseph von Sternberg, credited with the lovely Marlene's discovery; she saw Renee Adoree, of whose plucky fight against illness in the loneliness of a desert sanitarium, had been rewarded with complete recovery, and who was surrounded by a group of welcoming friends; impish Polly Moran, her eyes twinkling with fun, her kind face making up for its lack of loveliness in the beaming smile that she was distributing among her friends, while William Haines, as usual her devoted escort, put on his usual side-splitting comedy act. They were all there, it seemed to the slightly dazzed Janelle—stars of the day-time, here at night in this lovely place. Ronald Coleman, making an infrequent appearance with a beautiful blond, creating considerable excitement since he was so seldom seem at such a place.

Robert Montgomery, Douglas Fairbanks, Jr., and Laurence Olivier, "The Three Musketeers of Holly-wood," as they called themselves, all very busily explaining that their wives were out of town or working, which gave the reason or excuse for their own presence in a "Stag-party."

In short, Janelle saw a cross-section of Holly-wood such as the average movie fan would give a year of his life to see, and in addition, she had the added thrill of being introduced to a great many of the stars, because she was with a producer and a great director—and so, accordingly, well inside the inner section. When Douglas Fairbanks, Sr., and Mary Pickford arrived with a party of house-guests from Pickfair, Janelle felt that the evening had been an entirely full and complete one.

Finally, when the time came to go, she and Maxie and Wayne walked down the aisle, between tables that were crowded now with gay, laughing, chattering people.

The music was gayer than ever—the floor was crowded—but as she stood for a moment, waiting for Maxie and Wayne to get their coats, some one called her name, and she turned to find Jim Marvin coming towards her, his face alight with an eager smile.

"Excelsior — I just remembered!" he told her eagerly. "You wanted to know what the little fellow called the woman who brought him to the studio and I've been racking what passes for my brain, in an effort to recall—and just a minute ago, when the orchestra over there began to play a new tune, it suddenly popped into my head!"

Janelle put both her trembling hands on his arm, her face uplifted to his.

"Oh, Mr. Marvin—tell me—what was it?"

"The only time I ever remember hearing the little fellow call her anything at all except 'yes, ma'am' and 'no, ma'am,' was one day when he called her—Annie!" said Jim quietly.

Janelle caught her breath—and grew white as death, her eyes widening as though not quite sure that she had heard him right. The name struck her like a blow between the eyes.

"Annie!" she whispered. "Annie—Green!"

Continued in Next Number.

Janelle followed him into the office, and with a little smile declined
the cigarette that he offered her. "You don't smoke? Good! I'll
tell the publicity department — maybe they can put over
a story about it, 'Old-Fashioned Girl Clings to
Old-Fashioned Virtues'." (See Page 505)

Chapter 52.

A SINISTER SHADOW!

J IM MARVIN looked down at Janelle in surprise and concern. She was so white and distressed, as though the memory of the name of the woman who had brought her child to the studio had been some dreadful blow to her.

"You — you are— quite sure?" she stammered after a moment, when she had regained a measure of her shattered self-control.

"Sure about the name?" asked Jim, puzzled. "Why of course I am—I remembered it because in the music Abe Lyman and his band are playing they interpolated a few strains of 'Little Annie Rooney,' and all of a sudden it popped into my mind that that was what the little fellow called the woman—Annie!"

She was trembling violently, and Jim touched her arm in an attempt to steady her as he bent over her, concerned.

"Are you ill, Mrs. Elliott?" he asked anxiously.

"No, no—it's only that—your remembering that —gave me a sort of a clue! It may help me to find my baby and—I am so grateful to you!" she stammered her thanks as Wayne and Maxie came up, and Jim, with a little bow, went away.

Wayne saw Janelle's pallor, her trembling, and he asked quickly,

"Why, Mrs. Elliott—what's wrong? You're ill?"

"Maybe something she ate!" suggested Maxie comfortably.

"No, no—it was something that Mr. Marvin told me—it may be a clue to — my baby! It startled me, that's all!" she exclaimed, and let them draw her out of the hotel into the exquisitely cool fragrance of the California night.

The Rolls-Royce was waiting, the impassive yellow chauffeur at the wheel. Janelle felt his narrow brown eyes upon her as she walked between Maxie and Wayne to the car. But there was nothing in the servant's manner to make her feel that he was being rude, or even that he was aware of her as anything save a guest of his master.

As they settled themselves in the car, Maxie said with a little frown,

"So Jim remembered something that might help you find your baby, eh?"

With her hands tightly clenched together in her lap, Janelle looked at the dark head of the chauffeur outlined against the glass in front of her. Did he have anything to do with this whole miserable business? Was he innocent?

Did he merely bear a facial resemblance to Forgio's servant — or WAS he the man who had been Forgio's servant? She couldn't be sure—but she had learned to be suspicious, and knowing that the speaking tube was beside the chauffeur's ear, she said with an attempt at lightness,

"Oh—he merely remembered the child playing with him in the picture—and that—he and—Billy-boy became friends. It was—something of a shock to find that someone here at the studio actually remembered my baby!"

Wayne shot her a swift look, his eyes narrowed. He knew that Janelle was not telling the truth. Something far more dramatic had happened there in the few minutes while he and Maxie had gone for their coats.

But for some reason that he could not now guess, Janelle had lied to him and to Maxie. What was the discovery she had made? It puzzled him—made him curious.

When Maxie and Wayne had left Janelle at her hotel with a promise that she lunch at the studio the following day, to discuss the story which the script department was whipping together tonight, the two men got back into the Rolls-Royce which drove away towards Wayne's apartment.

Maxie was silent, sitting hunched forward in his seat, leaning on his cane, his hat on the back of his head, deep in thought. Suddenly, he spoke.

"Wayne, we've got to keep her from finding the youngster until after the picture is released!" he said firmly.

Wayne looked at him, startled.

"What the dickens do you mean, Maxie?" he demanded.

Neither of the two men noticed that the chauffeur was sitting rigidly, his ear almost against the mouth of the speaking tube, his hands clenched about the wheel.

"I mean, Wayne, that the minute she finds the youngster, she'll walk out on us!" said Maxie. "And I mean, also, that the minute the baby is found, our plans go 'phooey'! For without the hunt for the kidnapped baby, we got no story—we got no tie-up with the news-papers—we got nothing except a woman on our hands that knows nothing about acting and that the public has no interest in!"

Wayne was listening, interested. He could fol-low Maxie's lines of reasoning perfectly, of course.

"You see, the way things are now—we make a picture in which a heart-broken mother proclaims to the world the loss of her baby, and tries to enlist the aid of the whole world in finding that kidnapped baby! Right away the newspapers are interested again. They rehash the story of Forgio, the jungle flight—all of that —and then wherever the picture plays, its 'hot news'— and we make maybe a million dollars. You follow me, Wayne?" demanded Maxie.

Wayne grinned cynically.

"I'm way ahead of you, Maxie!" he agreed.

"Suppose she finds the baby tomorrow — she walks out on us without even making a picture! We lose a big chance to put over some swell publicity and make the 'big money boys' give us a tumble, for, maybe a new studio and a heavy spending account!

"But suppose she's half-way through the picture, and she finds the baby — we're stuck with a lot of useless film — even if she should stay on and finish the picture, it would be no use. The whole thing would be finished! Am I right, Wayne?" demanded Maxie.

"For once, Maxie, I can do the 'yes-man' act, in all honesty. You're quite right, Maxie!" agreed Wayne.

Maxie spread his hands with a little gesture that made the impresive diamond on his finger glitter like a vindictive eye.

"So what? So we must see to it that she doesn't find the baby—no?" said Maxie simply.

Wayne stared at him as though he had never set eyes on the man before in his life.

"Maxie, you're a fiend!" he said simply.

Maxie shrugged carelessly, as though he found the term rather flattering.

"No, Wayne, I'm a business man—protecting my investment!" he said quite simply and honestly.

Wayne stared at him, grinned cynically and shook his head as though he gave up any thought of understanding the man for whom he worked, and asked curiously,

"Have you any idea where the child is? Who has him?"

Maxie shrugged, and once more made that little gesture that caused the diamond on his finger to wink wickedly.

"Maybe yes—maybe no!" he answered cryptically and Wayne realized that they had reached the apartment in which he lived.

"Well, good-night, you old marble-heart!" he grinned as he got out of the car.

Unoffended, Maxie laughed and waved his hand carelessly after Wayne as that young man strode up the walk and entered the apartment building.

If Maxie could have seen the face of Satsu, his chauffeur, as the car turned about and headed for Maxie's beautiful home in Beverly Hills, he might have been a little puzzled at the expression on a face that had always been impassive, expressionless, when turned to him.

He would have known by that expression that Satsu was elated by something he had heard and that he was very busily evolving a plan in his agile brain.

But Maxie, in the back of the car, was too deeply engrossed in his own thoughts to notice the slightly odd behaviour of his servant, and so missed a chance to check up on something that might have saved a lot of trouble later on.

That night before she went to bed, Janelle wrote Sherman a long letter, telling him all that had happened during the day, and especially, of the evening's occurrences.

The stars she had seen — those she had met— plans for the new picture that she was to make in the hope of enlisting the aid of interested movie-fans the whole world over, in the search for her baby. And at the very end, she told him of Jim Marvin's remembering what he had heard the baby call the woman who was his guardian.

"He doesn't want me to think that she was actually unkind to him, but he let slip the news that the woman called my baby 'Hey, you' and that the child seemed afraid of her—that she was 'very strict'." she wrote, and there were tears in her eyes and on her cheeks as she wrote. After a moment, she went on:

"He says that he heard the baby call her 'Annie' — Oh, Sherman, do you suppose that woman 'Annie Green' really knew something? Do you suppose she is the woman who had him here at the studio? The name is not an unusual one — she listed herself at Central Casting Offices as 'Mrs. George Smith, and child, George, Junior' and they sent her to XL Art Productions. The address she gave was a shady little hotel—and she checked out of that the day the picture was finished.

— 489 —

"Several other companies have tried to find
the baby, for use in their pictures — but the
woman has hidden herself so completely that
there isn't a trace of her. If it is true that
she is really the 'Annie Green' who wrote to
me in Havana — oh, Sherman, I don't know
what to think! I'm so distressed and I miss
you so — hurry and get well, darling, and join
me here!"

A tear splashed on the page as she signed her
name, and she blotted it carefully. She didn't want
Sherman to know that she was weeping — that she
needed him so desperately.

She was restless—the thought of sleep was far
away. She switched out the lights and drawing her
thin negligee about her, she rose and walked through
the darkness to the window, where she stood for a long
moment looking out into the soft, semi-tropic darkness.

It was quite late, and the moon was waning. The
air was cool and dewily fresh, laden with the fragrance
of orange-blossoms and roses and the thousand and
one blossoming flowers and shrubs that make Southern
California a delight to the senses.

Suddenly as she leaned there, she saw a slight
movement on the lawn before the hotel.

The shadow of a man who stood leaning against
a palm tree, and who had not been visible until he
stirred suddenly, and stepped from the shadow. In
the waning moonlight she saw his face upturned directly towards her window, and she caught her breath
and drew back a little, before she realized that he could
not see her, in the darkened room.

She was convinced that his eyes were upon

her window—that he was watching her, even though at the moment he could not see her.

And then as suddenly as he had appeared, he was gone.

So silently, so swiftly had he moved, that she blinked a little for a moment with an absurd idea that he had been, not a man at all, but a sinister shadow that had lain for a moment across her path and then had vanished like a puff of smoke.

But the discovery that she was being watched, shadowed, made her knees suddenly weak, and she sat down on the edge of her bed shivering as though suddenly cold.

Chapter 53.

THE MAKING OF A STAR!

HE FOLLOWING day at noon, Janelle arrived at the studio. Half a dozen hopeful aspirants for film fame waited in the outer office, patiently spending hours in the hope of gaining the casting director's attention for a bare five precious moments in which to impress one's worthiness of a chance at the screen.

As Janelle came in, looking very smart and trim and pretty in a white sports costume, the office-boy sprang to his feet, and swung open the door for her to the intense envy and curiosity of the others less fortunate in the office.

"Who is she? I never saw her before!" one girl murmured acidly to another.

"That's the dame who almost got electrocuted for murdering the man she claims kidnapped her baby!" said the other girl. "I read about it in the papers!"

"And for that they make her a movie star! Wonder who I could bump off?" suggested the first girl.

"My landlord!" suggested the other one so

promptly that the half dozen people in the office laughed.

Meanwhile Janelle was in Maxie's office, being introduced to the scenario editor and a couple of staff writers. There was also the head-designer, whose job it would be to design gowns and costumes that would effectively heighten Janelle's natural beauty and charm.

To these people Janelle was merely a sort of clothes-horse, on whom the scenario editor and the staff writers hoped to hang an appealing story; the dress-designer, to hang some effective clothes that would make people talk about his genius.

Maxie hoped to build from her tragedy and heart-break and her poignant search for her child, a small fortune in money; the press-department looked her over carefully, took up another notch in its collective belt, and plunged into the task of making the whole wide world "Janelle Elliott conscious."

To all of these people who surrounded her, who studied her as impersonally as though she had been a bit of plastic clay which they hoped to twist to shapes of their own conceiving, Janelle was an inanimate bit of material with which to fashion the things of their own dreams.

She was not a human being with likes and dislikes, with heart-aches and happiness and human emotions similar to their own. She was the stuff out of which these entirely serious and very much in earnest people meant to make a motion picture star!

And so the scenario people asked her questions that involved her deepest tragedy and most private thoughts; the press department insisted on the most intimate details of her life, and her adventures; the dress-designer studied her from every possible angle; Maxie looked on and beamed and figured his probable profits on his investment.

Only Wayne who was to direct the picture, sat a little apart and looked at her as a human being, a very beautiful woman through whom he would make people laugh and cry and suffer and sympathize.

Janelle was to find that the next few days were the most frantic, in point of work, that she had ever gone through.

For one whole day in the studio of the staff-photographer she posed for "advertising pictures" — in every imaginable costume and pose and attitude.

When at nine o'clock at night, after having been at the studio since eight, the photographer announced himself as satisfied and let her go, she was so exhausted that she had barely strength to get home and into bed.

Then next day she stood for ten long weary hours while the wardrobe department fitted to her an amazing number of gowns and wraps and hats and slippers and negligees.

Her head was spinning when at last they let her go, and that night she had to don a gown, wrap and accessories that the studio had sent over, and attend, with Maxie and Wayne, the premiere of a rival company's most ambitious production of the season.

In a white satin gown, with a band of sapphires for shoulder straps, and a white ermine evening wrap, with white orchids in an amazing cascade from her shoulder, she walked between Maxie and Wayne across the side-walk with gaping crowds of people held back by police on either side, and into the lobby of the theatre, where dozens of established stars and featured players were making brief, gay little speeches over the radio, or autographing books held out by eager fans.

Had she been less tired, less bewildered, less bedazzled by it all, she might have enjoyed it more. As it was, the battery of lights, the battery of eyes, the barrage of voices from the "fans' who had stood in line for hours to see the stars enter and leave the theatre, the crowds, the noise, and her weariness deadened her to everything except her own misery.

But Maxie was hugely delighted with the whole affair. With the attention that the youth and beauty of his prospective star had created, and with the generous amount of newspaper space given to her.

When Janelle returned to the hotel, Maxie and Wayne went with her into the lobby and saw the clerk hand her her key, together with a letter. Maxie saw her eagerness when she recognized the postmark and the writing.

"You'll excuse me, I know—it's a letter from the hospital where my fiancee is a patient—I'm anxious to know how he is, and what he thinks of my going into the movies!" she explained, eager to escape to her own room where she could read her letter in peace. "Good night, and thank you for everything—it's been a lovely evening!"

She hurried away to the elevator, and Maxie and Wayne walked out to the car where Satsu stood, holding the door open for them.

"She's too anxious about news from that fellow, Wayne!" said Maxie, when they were in the car. "Maybe he gets pretty sick, and she throws everything over, and goes back to him before the picture is finished? Then what?"

Wayne grinned a little.

"You think of everything, Maxie!" he applauded. "But how are you going to keep her from getting letters from him? Remember, if she DOESN'T get letters from him, she will be a lot more likely to kick over the

But—Alexis Forgio was dead! Yet—here was his message again! It was, of course, her stunned reason told her, a message from the kidnappers of her son.

(See Page 515 in No. 17)

traces and go back to find out what's wrong!"

Maxie nodded, his face still downcast.

"That's right, of course—but—well, I'd like it if I could, maybe, keep an eye on her mail until the picture is finished!" he confessed frankly.

Wayne looked startled.

"Heavens, Maxie—you don't mean you'd hold up her mail?" he demanded, actually shocked.

Maxie looked at him solemnly.

"Already I've got lots of money tied up in this girl—and in this story. It's the biggest thing we've ever done—it's the biggest thing, in point of publicity that any producer has had a chance to do—I got a right to protect my investment!" he said stubbornly.

"Maybe—but, Maxie, have a little sense, can't you? Nobody has the right to hold up Uncle Sam's mail—they put people in jail who do things like that!" cried Wayne, startled and protesting.

Maxie shrugged and spread his hands with that little, deprecating gesture that displayed his fine diamond to perfection.

"Who's talking about holding up anybody's mail?" he demanded. "But — letters get lost, sometimes, don't they? Well, can I help it if letters addressed to a star of my company gets, maybe lost, delayed—or even—destroyed?"

Wayne stared at him for a moment, angry, shocked, a little disgusted. And then, suddenly, unwillingly, he grinned.

"Maxie, you're a devil! Complete in everything except horns and hoofs—and I'm not TOO sure that the hoofs aren't there, and I'm beginning to suspect the horns of sprouting!" he commented as he got out of the car in front of his own door.

Maxie, entirely undisturbed by the quite frank

disapproval of his friend and director, leaned back in his seat, thinking deeply as the car turned in the direction of his own impressive home.

Meanwhile, Janelle had read her letter. Written once more by Nurse Judkins, but dictated by Sherman. It was gay and blithe—almost determinedly so, it seemed to Janelle. It expressed complete approval of her plan of producing a picture in which she could broadcast to the world an appeal for the return of her lost son. It assured her that Sherman was feeling great, and would soon be taking ship for California, and a re-union with Janelle, and it closed with a declaration of his love and his belief in her.

Janelle's relief at the tone of the letter suffered a sharp set-back when she unfolded the little note that Nurse Judkins had enclosed, as her own expression, unknown to Sherman.

"Dear Mrs. Elliott," the letter read. "I wish sincerely that I could echo Mr. Lawrence's assurance that he is feeling splendid. But—the truth is that he is not gaining at all. In fact, the doctor feels that he is losing ground, steadily if slowly. He is fretting so about your being there alone—he is mad with impatience to join you— and his sleeplessness, the necessity of giving him something to make him sleep, is causing him to lose all that he had gained before you left.

"His leg, I am happy to say, has healed and he is able to walk on it, though he is so weakened by fever and by his inability to take nourishment to regain his strength, keeps him in bed, despite the mended leg.

"I don't want to alarm you unduly—nor do

I want to deceive you. For the present you need not return—but if I think it necessary or urgent that you return, I will wire you, as I know you would want me to do, and a plane can bring you here in a few hours. Meanwhile, I will take the best of care of him as I promised before.

"May I offer my congratulations on your new business deal? I should look with keen interest, for your new picture.

Sincerely,
"Georgia Judkins."

Janelle was trembling when she put down the letter. Her heart ached to be with the man she loved—yet she had bound herself to stay here — to help put through this ambitious plan to recover her baby. She knew that Maxie had already invested heavily in the plan to put her over in this picture—and if she walked out on him on the search for her child, how could she hope ever to find the baby again? If she gave up now, when she had just started, she must abandon all hope of ever finding him. And—she could not do that! Even though her heart cried out for Sherman, its mate. Her first duty was to her baby—that tiny life that she had brought into the world. That little life into which so much of sorrow and tragedy and pain had so cruelly fallen — into which the only happiness and love and peace had been that she herself had given him.

She was here in Hollywood, in the very studio where her baby had spent days. She had the opportunity in making this picture, "Legacy of Love," to put before the whole world, the true story of her loss—of her suffering—of her plea for the return of her baby. And—she would not, she dare not—give up the whole plan—unless Nurse Judkins wired her to come at once. That would mean that only she could save Sherman—and against that plea, nothing else could hold her.

When she had finished writing this to Nurse Judkins, she switched out her light and went to stand beside the window, hidden by the curtains, looking out into the darkness. Yes, there was that sinister shadow that had been there every night since she had first gone to the Cocoanut Grove for dinner. A sinister shadow that merely stood and watched her window—and then vanished.

She fell asleep at last, puzzled, wondering and a little afraid.

Chapter 54.

IN HAVANA.

URSE JUDKINS stood beside the bed, and looked down at her patient, a little frown drawing her thick dark brows together, her kind eyes worried.

Sherman lay quite still, a wasted form beneath the light coverlet. He had again made the attempt to walk across the floor, and had failed. He was ashamed—humiliated. He was seething with rebellion against the weakness that held him here a prisoner, when with all his soul he wanted to get out of this bed and take the very next boat for California.

He had stood up out of his wheel-chair, and with a struggle that had brought the sweat out on his forehead and set his knees trembling, he had tried to hold himself erect and to walk across the floor—a distance of a few feet. Half-way across the room, he had collapsed, and so frail and wasted had he become during this long illness, that Nurse Judkins had been able to catch him, to lift him in her strong arms and to put him back to bed.

That had humiliated him to the very soul. As weak as a kitten—as helpless as a baby. To be lifted and carried about and put to bed as though he were a child! Never in all his life had he yearned so for strength and free limbs unhampered by illness.

He turned his head at last, when he felt sure that his eyes were free of tears, and looked up at the nurse. The look in his eyes, the set of his pallid face, the jaw hard, made Nurse Judkins more sorry for him than she had ever been in her life.

"Run along, now, Nurse, like a dear! I'm—all right. I'll just lay quietly here—as befits a broken piece of crockery!" he told her between his teeth.

"Don't be absurd!" scolded the nurse, though her voice was none too steady. "Broken crockery, my eye! You're going to be fine as silk in another week or two!"

"Or three or four—or more!" Sherman finished for her, his face set grimly, though his thin lips tried to twist in a smile. "Let's not kid ourselves, Nurse— I'm finished—licked!"

More than she had ever wanted anything in her life, Nurse Judkins wanted to sympathize with him. There were tears in her eyes, and her lips trembled. But she knew that there was no more certain way of utterly wrecking his morale than by letting him see the intensity of her pity for him. She must arouse him —make him angry—make him fighting mad—so that he would throw off this feeling of being utterly useless, and put up a fight against helplessness.

"Licked?" she said, and there was a deliberate sneer in her voice. "Well—of course you're licked—if you want to be! I've always felt that when a man admitted he was finished—that he was licked—it was usually because — he had a streak of yellow a mile wide!"

She held her breath, aghast at her daring. She watched the man before her, breathless, for his reaction. She saw the startled look that swept over his face, and then the dull, angry surge of red as the meaning of her words penetrated his consciousness. She saw his thin hands clench into taut fists, until the knuckles went white with the strain.

"So—you think I'm yellow, do you, Nurse? You think I've—laid down—that I don't want to fight any more? That I'm—quitting?" he said, his voice so low that it barely reached her ears.

In a panic she saw now that she had gone too far. That she had said more than was necessary. Swiftly she tried to repair the damage that in all kind-heartedness she had done.

"I'm terribly sorry, Mr. Lawrence—of course I didn't think that—I think you're great! Splendid! We all do! It was only that—I thought you didn't want me to pity you—to feel sorry for you! That was why I said that—please forget it! Of course I didn't mean it!" she stammered swiftly.

But Sherman's mouth twisted with a little bitter smile.

"It's quite all right, Nurse—I understand perfectly. And—I'm really quite grateful! You'll see—I'll prove it! And now—if you'll bring me whatever vile concoction it is that I'm supposed to have at this hour, I'll swallow it without a whimper!" he dismissed her so unmistakably that the look in his eyes told her she must not linger.

Hating herself for obeying an impulse that she now knew to have been wrong, she left the room and hurried down to the diet kitchen in search of some strengthening food that she could take to him as a sort of peace-offering.

Meanwhile, back in his room, Sherman lay quite still, his hands clenched into hard fists, his teeth set in his lower lip to control the unmasculine trembling of his mouth.

So Nurse Judkins, the kindest soul he had ever known, thought that he was a quitter. That he "had a yellow streak a mile wide" did she? Well, if Nurse Judkins thought that, what did other people think? What—would Janelle think? Janelle, whom he loved, and who needed him now almost as desperately as she had needed him before. He had failed her that first time she had begged for his help—and, alone, defenseless, fighting for her baby, she had set out along a trail of shame and sorrow and tragedy that had brought her within the shadow of the electric chair. It had always been a source of secret shame that he had been unable to free her from that shadow—it had taken Mariusa's death-bed confession to do that. He had, according to his code, failed her again. For without Mariusa's confession he would have been helpless.

And now, when once more Janelle needed him, he was lying here, like a log, while she was there in Los Angeles, alone—and faced with terrific odds in her effort to find her baby.

It had been bad enough to be ill and helpless to go to her rescue—but to know that people thought him —shamming—that Nurse Judkins who was the kindest and most sympathetic soul imaginable, thought so badly of him hurt terribly. He had not dreamed that there was anything in Nurse Judkins' heart for him but sympathy—and even now, when she had delivered her blistering remark about quitters with yellow streaks.

Deliberately he tried to steady himself and to understand what Nurse Judkins had said—to understand the way in which she had meant it. And from his effort to understand, to see the situation as she saw it, he began to wonder if she was right. Was it possible that some sub-conscious part of his own brain held him helpless? Was it for lack of some effort on his own part, that he was unable to walk? He had heard of soldiers injured during the war—shell-shocked— who had been held by some strange hypnosis of their own sub-conscious minds, that had crippled them until some great shock or fright had served to loosen the bonds of that hypnosis. Was that true of his case?

Nurse Judkins had given him a shock—would it release him? He threw back the covers, slipped out of bed, and stood up, bracing himself by clinging to the frame of the bed. He took a deep breath, threw back his shoulders, and, to himself, as though it had been the clarion song of a bugle calling him to fight for his country, he murmured Janelle's name. And then—he stepped forward. One step. Breathing hard, his body bathed in cold perspiration. Two steps. His knees trembling with weakness, his teeth set hard, his fists clenched. Three steps. A wavering of his limbs—a swimming of his senses — he lifted his foot for the fourth step—and staggered. The black waters of oblivion swirled over him as he plunged downward, and Nurse Judkins, coming in with a tray on which was a bowl of steaming broth, found him lying face down, unconscious on the floor.

Chapter 55.

A MYSTERIOUS MESSAGE.

ON MONDAY, when Janelle reported at the studio, she found Maxie waiting for her, smiling, urbane, pleased with himself.

"It will be an hour or more before they are ready for you," he told her. "Come on in my office — I want to talk to you! I got a plan for you!"

Janelle followed him into the office, and with a little smile declined the cigarette that he offered her.

"You don't smoke? Good! I'll tell the publicity department—maybe they can put over a story about it. 'Old-Fashioned Girl Clings to Old-Fashioned Virtues' —by golly, that's good!" he applauded himself, and made a note on the pad on his desk. "Now, Mrs. Elliott, here's the plan. I don't like your living there in the hotel—first place, it's too far from the studio, and, second place, you should have a nice house where you can receive the press, and give dinners for the important people it will be good business for you to entertain and so on! Since it is part of the company's plan, the company will pay for the house. Matter of fact, it's a house that I own and its furnished, and its eating its head off in idleness—much better you live in it, and get some servants that will keep it looking nice! It's not far from here and there'll always be a studio car at your disposal!"

Janelle was a little dazed, but she had already learned in the few days she had spent at the studio, the importance of what the amazing city called "front." Occupying a beautiful, well furnished home would give her more prestige than to live alone at the hotel. And since she had placed herself in the hands of the company, it seemed foolish to object to this one detail.

"If you think it's best, Mr. Cason—I'm a little tired of the hotel, anyway!" she agreed willingly.

"Good! I'll have my own house-keeper get some servants and get the place ready for you by Wednesday. All you need do is have your bags packed and ready Wednesday and I'll have somebody bring them down to the house for you—you won't need to bother!" he assured her, pleased that she had acceded so readily to what he really considered a very good move.

She hesitated a moment, and then said,

"Mr. Cason—you've been so kind and friendly— and I'm so alone here, I'd like to tell you something that has been troubling me!"

Maxie looked a little startled, but interested.

"For several nights—ever since the night that you and Mr. Wayne took me to the Cocoanut Grove for dinner—there has been a man outside the hotel, watching my window!" she burst out swiftly. "I don't know who he is, or what he wants. I've no way of finding out but—I'm—just a little frightened!"

"Well, of course you are—why wouldn't you be? I'll have this looked into at once! You just leave it to me! It's a good thing you are getting out of that hotel.

You'll be safer in the house—I'll put on a couple of body-guards who will watch the place and see that you are not bothered!" he said swiftly, and then, veiling his eyes a little, he said as though it had been an after-thought, "Oh,—by the way, have you received any—er — threatening letters, anonymous notes, or anything like that?"

"Why, no—why should I?" she returned, puzzled.

Maxie waved his hand so that the diamond ring twinkled diabolically.

"Oh, I don't know—the story about you making a movie in the effort to locate your lost baby has broken pretty well over the country—I thought it might be pos-sible that whoever has the baby might try to get in touch with you—and about the easiest and simplest way is through the mail!" he answered carelessly. "Maybe you'd better have your mail come in care of the company here—our other people do—and then we can help you check up on anything that looks suspicious."

Janelle smiled her relief.

"Thank you—I will! That's very kind of you!" she answered in simple gratitude.

Maxie grinned pleasantly.

"Oh—that's all right—that's all right! We want you to be comfortable and happy here!" he assured her.

"I'm sure you do—and I'm very grateful!" said Janelle, and hurried away to dress and make up for her first scenes.

Maxie, looking after her, lit a fresh black cigar inhaled the smoke, blowing several very perfect little smoke rings before he shrugged and reassured himself.

"After all, it's my money—I got a right to pro-tect my investment!" he assured himself almost grimly, as though his conscience might be offering faint protest for something he was merely thinking of doing.

Nurse Judkins swore at herself in half a dozen different languages during the week that passed, but she was forced reluctantly to admit that her well-meant, if on the surface unkind taunt, had had a fair effect on her patient, for, grimly, he was eating everything that she brought to him without argument. Taking his medicine. Obeying her as docilely as a child; plainly, he had set himself grimly to the task of getting his strength back as quickly as possible, and he was working towards that goal with an almost frantic intensity.

Late in the afternoon towards the middle of the week, a letter came for Janelle.

"A letter for Mrs. Elliott!" Nurse Judkins said, smiling, holding it up. "I thought you might like to write a little note to go with it when I forward it to her!"

Sherman glanced at it carelessly—and then his eyes became riveted to the envelope. A cheap, small envelope, smudged and grimy, addressed in scrawling pencil that was almost illegible.

Somewhere, he had seen that writing before. Of that he was quite sure. He put out his hand, that trembled a little in spite of himself, and took the letter. He held it in his hands, examining it with an almost fierce intensity. It had been postmarked at City Hall Station, New York City, and while it bore no distinguishing mark whatever, Sherman was certain beyond a doubt that the writer of the letter was "Annie Green."

"We won't forward it until in the morning!" he told Nurse Judkins. "I'll write her then—if you will help me. And—I'd like to keep this letter until then!"

"Of course!" said Nurse Judkins, and went away.

Outside the door, she met the night nurse.

"It's an absolute shame for a woman to go away and leave a man who loves her that much—no matter why she goes away!" said Nurse Judkins grimly.

"Of course it is, Juddie dear—but strange! men always fall for girls like that, while women like us who could really take care of them get left. There ought to be a law against it!" laughed the night nurse.

But inside his small, clean, bare room, Sherman lay against his pillows, staring at the envelope in his hand. It was an answer, he knew in his heart to the advertisement that Janelle had put in the New York Gazette—that ad meant as a message to "Annie Green."

He turned the letter over and over in his hands—and suddenly, with a decisive gesture he slit the envelope with his thumb and drew the paper out, unfolding it, holding it before his eyes with shaking hands.

"I seen the ad in the paper," the letter began, without any preliminaries. "I'm gonna give you one more chanct. And if you don't come through this time, I ain't gonna bother with you no more. If you'll come to New York at once and register at the Farraday Hotel—the address is given below—I'll know about it, and I'll let you know then what to do next. I ain't givin you enuff information for you to try to frame me—I'm holdin' all the cards in this game, and your gonna pay plenty for sittin in with me. I give you til the twenty-eight to get her—after that it's gonna be TOO LATE—get me?"

The letter was without formal signature, as it had been without formal salutation.

Sherman lay staring at the letter for a long moment. The twenty-eighth! If he could get a boat to-night —he would just be able to make it in time. If he forwarded the letter on to Janelle, it would be too late. If he cabled her, and she flew to New York by plane—but that was dangerous. Janelle, alone in New York, faced by Heaven alone knew what——

No, it wouldn't do! And then the decision came. HE must go to New York and look into this thing for Janelle! He must face this mysterious "Annie Green" and find out what she knew. If through this "Annie Green," he could find Janelle's lost baby and take him back to his mother—he had a vision of walking into Janelle's presence, with Janelle's baby in his arms, and the vision was so wonderful that he caught his breath.

His brain was a roaring, singing thing now. The blood sang through his veins. He flung back the covers, slipped out of bed. He steadied himself against the frame of the bed, until his eyes had cleared and he could see what he was doing.

Across the room, in a closet, hung the clothes that he had worn on the occasions when he had been allowed to sit on the veranda with Janelle before he had grown too weak to sit up. He managed to reach the closet, and with some difficulty, to dress himself. He was sick and weak, shaking when he had finished, but there was not a moment to spare. If any of the nurses, or attendants saw him, he would be put back to bed and they would refuse to let him help Janelle.

He crept across to the door and locked it. Then he went back to the window and examined the fire escape. His room was on the third floor. The fire escape led straight down, and the last flight was down a ladder. Well, he would have dropped down the fire-escape without a second thought. Sick and dizzy with weakness, he trembled at the sight, and cold perspiration broke out over his body. But it was for Janelle—for her happiness—and, setting his teeth, he climbed out of the window and set his feet on the steps of the fire-escape. Clinging, almost frightened, he went down, step by step until he was at last on the ladder. Eventually he stood on the ground, clinging to the trunk of a tree, for support until his head cleared a little. Then he set out for town, swaying with weakness, yet plodding doggedly on.

It seemed to him that hours passed—it was silly, but his mind was growing a little hazy—where was it that he was going? And why was he going? He was awfully tired—why was it that he must not sit down and rest? Funny — how dizzy a fellow's brain gets. Why, of course he knew where he was going—and why he was going there—the darkness of the tropic night swallowed him up.

•   •   •   •   •   •   •   •   •

Janelle was glad to be moved into the pretty stucco bungalow, with its lovely little patio in which a fountain tinkled—it reminded her a little of the fountain in the patio in the Sevilla-Biltmore in Havana. There were flowers in glorious profusion, and a few fruit trees—oranges, lemons, avocado—the house was beautifully and tastefully furnished, and the three servants whom Maxie's house-keeper had sent down were excellent. She had nothing to do save enjoy the home that was prepared for her, and which seemed to run on excellently oiled and quite soundless wheels.

The first night that she was in her new home, she stepped out of the living-room into the patio—and a burly man loomed up before her.

To Janelle's little frightened gasp he said:

"Don't be frightened, ma'am — I'm the night watchman!"

"Oh," said Janelle, with a little unsteady laugh. "I remember now, Mr. Cason was sending you over— I'm sorry I was frightened!"

The man took himself off, and Janelle sat on for a long time in the quiet and peaceful beauty of the night. Her thoughts went, as they always did when she was alone, to Sherman. Tonight she was worried about him. There had been no letter today from Nurse Judkins, and she had so confidently expected one.

She supposed that was the reason she felt so strangely lonely, so uneasy. She seemed almost to hear Sherman's voice, calling her urgently. To see him, with empty arms stretched out towards her. Was he worse? Did he need her urgently? Nurse Judkins had said that she would wire, if his need grew—if his condition was serious—yet Janelle could not rid herself of this uneasy, strangely ominous feeling.

She rose at last, assuring herself that she was merely tired and unduly nervous. She went into the house, passing the house-man, who was waiting to lock up the attractive little place. She said a careless goodnight to him, and went on up to her own room.

She looked about it in delight. It was charmingly furnished in mellow maple furniture, quaint and old-fashioned, with crisply ruffled organdie curtains at the windows and a flowered chintz drapery over the bed.

And as her eyes fell upon the bed, with its covers turned back, she caught her breath and recoiled, while an icy hand of terror clutched her heart. For there, against the pillow where her head was to lay, was a flower. A strange, exotic, unwholesome looking green plant — a green orchid with narrow, fang-like purple blossoms—the "snake-plant" such as the one she had found on Billy-boy's pillow the night he was kidnapped! Then she saw the note beneath the orchid.

Continued in Next Number.

Maxie leaned towards her across his desk, dropping his voice, speaking slowly, impressively. "Hoppy, I'm telling you confidentially— that I'm positive the child will be discovered alive and well, within a week after the picture is released!" (See Page 524)

Chapter 56.

GREEN ORCHIDS!

OR A LONG moment Janelle stood there, like a woman carved of stone, staring with wide, sick eyes at that sinister, u n l o v e l y green orchid that lay outlined s o starkly against the snowy pillow of her bed. She made no m o v e to touch it, or the note that lay beneath it.

She was going back in memory to a night in a New York penthouse apartment when she had stood beside the bed of her baby, and in the little round hollow of the pillow that had been made by his beloved little head she had seen just such a flower as this.

Then it had been a silent message from Alexis Forgio. A silent declaration of his power to make or break her happiness. But—Alexis Forgio was dead! Yet—here was his message again! It was, of course, her stunned reason told her, a message from the kidnappers of her son. People who must have known Forgio's manner of "signature" when he had completed the odious crime of kidnapping! Somebody who knew Forgio—somebody who knew what that green orchid would mean to the woman who stared at it, with wide, frightened eyes.

How had it come here? Had she found it in her room while she had been still at the hotel, it would not have seemed so terrifying. There it would have been a relatively simple matter for an enemy to have forced or bribed his way into her room, and left this sinister message. But here, in the lovely house to which Maxie had invited her to move—this house, enclosed in a stucco wall with a gate that locked, and with a guard on duty day and night—it destroyed utterly her former feeling of safety!

She forced herself at last to move forward, to lift the strange, weird flower, shivering at the cold, clammy, unpleasant touch of it, and to pick up the note that lay beneath it.

The note was typed on perfectly plain white paper such as can be bought in any ten-cent store in the country. There was no distinguishing mark there. It was folded once through he middle, and then again, and it had neither beginning of formal salutation, or signature.

"We know the purpose for which you are here!" read the note.

"It depends upon what you do, and what you say, whether or not your purpose is to be successful!

"Remember, YOU ARE NEVER FOR ONE MOMENT OUT OF OUR SIGHT!

"You'll hear from us again!"

Wide-eyed, dismayed, a little frightened Janelle reread the letter. It was neatly typewritten—the paper was smooth and cheap and guiltless of anything that could identify it.

"WE KNOW THE PURPOSE FOR WHICH YOU ARE HERE!"

That meant, of course, that they knew she was here in an effort to find Billy-boy.

"IT DEPENDS UPON WHAT YOU DO, AND WHAT YOU SAY, WHETHER OR NOT YOUR PURPOSE IS TO BE SUCCESSFUL!"

That, of course, meant that if she turned this letter over to the police, or made any efforts to trace the writer, her search would be unsuccessful.

"You are never for one moment out of our sight!"

That thought was the most terrifying of the whole letter. The feeling that she was being watched — that some sinister shadow dogged her foot-steps wherever she went—that she was never QUITE alone was well-nigh unbearable.

She read again the last line of the note—"you will hear from us again!" She looked down at the green orchid that lay like a splotch of green and dark purple on the blue Chinese rug. She moved it with the toe of her slipper, and felt that she moved the heavy, gleaming coils of the snake that the plant so weirdly resembled.

Who had been able to creep into her room, and to place this note and the flower on her pillow? She had dressed here for dinner—she had not been down-stairs more than two hours. She had been in the living-room, and would have seen any one going up the stairs.

Of course, it might have been someone using the back-stairs — in which case one of the servants might have seen them. And then she remembered that she really knew nothing about the servants—they were all strangers to her. A stout, friendly, pleasant negro cook who made her think wistfully of a younger Martha: a pert little maid, and the house-man, who had been out of work for months, who had a wife and several small children, and who was almost pathetically grateful for this job.

Somehow it seemed absurb to suspect either of these three — and yet — somebody had brought this flower and this note to her room, and in the last two hours. Somebody who was an agent of her enemies. Somebody who would not hesitate to destroy her, and her child as well, if she offered them the slightest danger!

She shivered uncontrollably at the thought, and impulsively she turned the key in the lock of her door, and locked the bath-room door as well. She searched her clothes-closet thoroughly, looked under the bed, and assured herself that the ornamental wrought iron grills before her windows made it utterly impossible for any one to enter her room that way, before she could compose her nerves enough to go to bed, where she lay wide-eyed for hours, going over and over again every angle of the whole miserable, unhappy business, before she finally fell asleep from sheer exhaustion.

* * * * * * * * *

Through the warm darkness of the tropic night, Sherman plunged on, his brain long numb, his body driven mercilessly despite a creeping, desperate weakness and weariness.

When he came at last within sight of the ship, that was preparing to sail, his shoulders straightened, and he felt the weariness vanish. He was going to help Janelle — he was no longer a helpless, broken crock of a man. He was a "Knight Courageous" going to the rescue of his beloved "Fair Damsel."

As he sought to mount the gang-plank, a ship's officer barred the way.

"Where's your ticket?" he demanded.

Sherman looked at him with feverish eyes, blank of any expression save bewilderment.

"Ticket?" he repeated, his tongue a bit thickened. "Don't need a ticket—got to get to the States!"

The ship's officer laughed grimly.

"Not without a ticket you don't, buddy — run along now, like a nice boy! Too much cognac and bacardi aboard YOUR ship already!"

Sherman looked at him stupidly.

"Go on—get going, buddy! You're drunk! But you're not sailing on this ship without a ticket!" said the officer roughly, and pushed him away as a party of tourists came up, presenting their tickets.

There was room in Sherman's poor, dazed, fever-stricken mind for only one thought — and that thought was the urgent necessity of getting aboard this ship, and eventually to New York where he could find the woman, "Annie Green" and find out whether she really knew anything about Janelle's baby.

There was no good in disputing the ship's officer's authority, however and so he wandered down the wharf to where a crew of laboring men were finishing loading the big vessel.

Sherman saw them passing him in a steady stream, each man laden with a bundle. Instantly he caught the idea as it sped through his mind. A stream of men, empty of hand, passed him coming from the ship's hold.

He fell in with them — and when they reached the piles of freight yet to be loaded, and each man seized a bundle, and turned back towards the ship, Sherman was still in the group, struggling beneath a laden sack that was almost too much for him.

Only the thought of Janelle and her need of him made it possible for him to stagger up that narrow gang-plank, to deposit his burden and as the others turned once more to the wharf to slip out of sight among the shadows and lose himself. He dropped, exhausted, on a box behind a great bundle of freight —and with the last remnants of his exhausted consciousness, he hid himself from prying eyes. He was on board the boat — what came next he didn't know. He was too exhausted to care — he relaxed in unconsciousness.

Chapter 57.

"IF A LETTER IS LOST?"

HEN JANELLE reported at the studio the following morning, she found a little pile of mail on her dressing - table, b u t though she went through it swiftly, there was no message of any k i n d from Sherman. There were the usual crank letters of which she had received so many since her name became front p a g e n e w s. There were advertising circulars — letters from movie magazines requesting information about herself — the usual thing. But nothing personal.

Before she permitted the make-up man to come in. and the hair-dresser, for their task of making her look her loveliest for the screen, she sat for a moment staring into space. It was so terribly hard to go on— without a word from Sherman. She missed him so— worried about him—again, she wondered if she would ever be successful in her search for her baby. Last night's message with its sinister green orchid—did it mean that she might some day regain her child? Or — would it be merely another cruel hoax, leading nowhere except into terror and despair for herself?

If only she knew how Sherman was! If only she could hear! It was small consolation to remember that Nurse Judkins had promised to wire her if Sherman became worse or needed her badly. She tried to console herself with that thought — but it was cold comfort after all.

There was a knock at the door — the insistent make-up man, the hair-dresser, the maid whom the studio provided to help her dress—wearily, she allowed them to enter, and turned herself over to their hands.

* * * * * * * * *

Maxie, in his office, looked up as his secretary came into the office. She was a tall, plain girl of past thirty, who was Maxie's right hand, and who knew more secrets about him than any other living soul. She earned a salary that was in three figures, and she could have ruined Maxie if she had ever chosen to betray a few of his secrets. But Maxie had the comfortable knowledge that she was faithful and devoted—utterly loyal.

She walked over to his desk and laid down a yellow envelope.

"Another cable for Mrs. Elliott — and they're insisting on an answer. You'd better send 'em one — unless you want them to ask the police to locate the Elliott dame!" she told him firmly.

Maxie picked up the cable-gram, frowning a little, turning it about in his fingers. Miss Hopkins, watching him, smiled faintly, cynically.

"Why not? You opened the other two—and destroyed them! Why get squeamish now?" she asked sardonically.

Maxie, undisturbed, looked up at her and grinned.

"After all, I got a right to protect my investment —ain't I?" he demanded.

Miss Hopkins shrugged a thin shoulder.

"Sure—why not? But you'd better send some sort of answer to that cable if you don't want these people hopping on your neck!" she assured him.

Maxie picked up a paper-knife, and slit the filmy yellow envelope open. He drew out the folded sheet and read,

"Amazed no answer to my former wires. Mr. Lawrence very ill. Please come at once.
"Georgia Judkins."

Maxie scratched his chin with the blunt end of the paper-knife, and reflected a moment.

"What would you suggest I say to her, Hoppy?" he demanded.

"Well, you COULD say that Mrs. Elliott was on her way down there! That's what this Judkins dame wants you to say—and after all, Maxie, Mrs. Elliott is in love with this Lawrence man. If anything happened to him — she'd probably want to murder you!" Miss Hopkins pointed out dispassionately.

"You mean I should let Elliott go to Cuba, now —when the picture is already started? When I got thousands of dollars tied up in it?" demanded Maxie, outraged.

Miss Hopkins' eyes narrowed a little as she looked at him, almost with a shade of disgust in her eyes.

"After all, Maxie, the poor guy will either get better or die in a week or two—that sort of business doesn't take long, you know! What difference would a week or two, more or less, make in this super-super-

super production of yours, anyway?" she demanded
with more rancor than she had used in speaking to her
employer, for whom she had worked fifteen years.

"All the difference between a great success and
failure—a million dollars—and the loss of the thousands
I got in the picture!" said Maxie dramatically. "Look
—the minute the kid is found—flooie! The picture is all
washed up—ready for the ash-can! We've got to work
fast to get the picture out before the kid is found!"

Miss Hopkins looked slightly startled.

"You mean you actually think the child will be
discovered? That he is alive?" she demanded wide-
eyed.

Maxie leaned towards her across his desk,
dropping his voice, speaking slowly, impressively,

"Hoppy, I'm telling you confidentially—that I'm
positive the child will be discovered alive and well,
within a week after the picture is released!"

For a moment Miss Hopkins was silent, startled
to complete, if temporary wordlessness. But, after a
moment, when she had regained some measure of her
composure, she said firmly,

"Then that means you know something about
where he is — Maxie, you've got something up your
sleeve!"

Maxie shrugged and selected another fat black
cigar, clipping the end from it very carefully, and
lighting it before he answered her with a little shrug.

"Maybe so—maybe no! Maybe I've got a hunch
—but I've told Mrs. Elliott that I'm sure the picture will
restore her baby to her—and you know me! I'm a man
of my word!" he answered grandly.

Miss Hopkins chuckled dryly.

"Sure — a man of your word — and WHAT a
word!" she commented. "Well, what are we going to

do about an answer to this cable?"

"Oh, yes—sure, we got to say something! I have it — take a wire, Miss Hopkins. To nurse Georgia Judkins, American Hospital, Havana, Cuba. 'Mrs. Elliott on location in High Sierras. Impossible deliver your message until her return end of week. Will do so then.' You'd better sign that, yourself, Hoppy!" suggested Maxie happily.

"I will not!" said Miss Hopkins swiftly and vigorously. "I'll sign it XL Art Productions, and blame it on the studio cat when Elliott finds out and raises the deuce, as she is sure to do!"

Maxie grinned as she went out of the room, and closed the door behind her with a bang. He looked down at the cablegram. He frowned. He was honestly sorry that he had had to take the action on these telegrams. He had twisted the old, old stage axiom, "The show must go on" until he felt that it really excused the despicable thing that he was doing. He had managed to convince himself that to protect the thousands of dollars that he and the stock-holders of his company had invested in the Elliott picture, he was justified in taking whatever means were at his command to keep Janelle in the studio, and working until the picture was finished. The "rushes" of each day's work, developed and screened each evening were enough to convince him that the finished picture would be the sensation he had fondly predicted. With the added publicity value of the fact that the story was based on facts, and that the mother had worked in the picture in the hope of enlisting the aid of the whole wide world in finding her stolen baby, he was confident that the picture would bring the greatest of any production that had ever borne the XL trademark. Through it, he hoped to be able to interest "the big boys" in the movie game—men whose name on a production guaranteed it a Broadway show-ing at the finest houses. Men whose story-budgets alone planned for the buying of screen-stories, far exceeded the total amount of XL's entire expense account for everything during a year.

Maxie was ambitious for the success of XL Pro-ductions. He was eager for wealth — he was quite honest in that. His was a single-track mind, set in the accomplishment of a great fortune for himself through XL Productions. Of course it was too bad that Janelle should be separated from her sweetheart—he regretted the necessity of holding up the letters and the telegrams—still, he was justified, he honestly felt, by the right to protect his investment. And so that still small voice of his conscience ceased to annoy him, and he sat wrapped in creamy cigar smoke, while he visioned the future when "the Big Four" of moviedom would be "the Big Five" with XL Productions making the fifth. It's a dream that was bloomed often in the minds of "quickie" producers on Poverty Row—and the fact that "the Big Four" is STILL the "Big Four" does not seem to disturb the dream, or the frequency of its dreaming, at all!

Chapter 58.

IN NEW YORK.

T HE HOTEL Farraday — which of course is not its right name— is one of the hundreds of cheap, furtive little hotels that dot the side-streets off Broadway in what was once "the roaring Forties". It has a small lobby, usually occupied by tooth - pick chewing vaudevillians "resting" or more frankly "at liberty"! by race-track gamblers; "small fry" gangsters and racketeers, and their hard-eyed, flashily dressed women; and a few innocent tourists from out of town who are attracted to the hotel by its amazingly low rates and its nearness to the shopping district and the theatres.

To the Farraday, one bright morning came a tall, well-set-up, nice looking young man, bronzed from an ocean voyage, and carrying a well-worn travelling bag of excellent make, that was monogrammed "L. S., Atlanta." He registered as "Sherman Lawrence, Havana, Cuba," and asked for a two-roomed suite. The price of ten dollars a day that the clerk, in a burst of daring set on the suite, seemed not to disturb the new guests in the least, and a thoroughly impressed bell-hop carried the well-worn, yet still handsome bag up to a front suite on the fifth floor. A tip of a dollar bill further impressed the now goggle-eyed bell-hop.

"Wonder if it would be possible to get a quart of something fit to drink around here?" asked the new guest idly. "Cuba's a great place, but I'm a little tired of Bacardi and that stuff—guess prohibition must have spoiled my taste — unless it tastes like shellac I can't seem to enjoy it!"

"I can get you some swell stuff, Mr. Lawrence— right off the boat!" the bell-hop assured him eagerly.

"Scraped off, I suppose!" grinned the pleasant looking, sun burned young man. "O. K.—hop to it!"

He flung the boy a five dollar bill, and the boy almost fell over his feet getting out of the room.

The minute the door had closed behind the boy, the pleasant looking young man whirled like a cat, stepped swiftly, to the window and shielding himself behind the sleazy curtains, looked out into the street. Apparently, what he saw there satisfied him, for he came swiftly back into the room and lifted his suitcase from the floor.

The bell-hop knocked and sidled into the room, with a package wrapped in a newspaper. He grinned and handed it over, reluctantly proffering two dollars in limp bills as change for the five that he had received.

"Stick it in your pocket, kid, and forget it!" laughed the young man, and the boy was only too glad to obey him.

The door closed behind the boy, and the man swiftly turned the key in the lock. He uncorked the bottle the boy had left, sniffed it, and wrinkled his forehead in disgust. There were two glasses on the stand in the bath-room, and he brought them to the living-room. He poured them both half-full of the vicious stuff from the bottle, and then went back to the bath-room and emptied them into the basin, swilling the contents about in the glasses, so that the scent would remain. He went back into the living-room, poured the glasses half-full again, and let them stay that way. Throughout this action he had worn rubber gloves.

He took a coat and a vest out of the suitcase and hung them over the back of the chair. Then he stood back and surveyed the scene. He seemed satisfied, and a slow, ugly grin twisted his face as he drew out a handsome black and silver cigarette case, with a monogram in diamonds in its upper corner. He selected a cigarette, lit it, and thrust the case back into his pocket.

He went back into the bath-room, selected a clean small hand-towel, and folded it until it was a bandage about three inches wide. He held it lengthways and tested it, a slow, evil smile twisting his face as he did so.

Suddenly the telephone shrilled sharply behind him, and with a look of sharp excitement he sprang to the telephone, picked it up, and spoke into it. His voice, lazy, drawling, careless, was in sharp contrast to the obvious tenseness of his pose as he listened.

"A lady calling to see you, Mr. Lawrence—says her name is 'Annie Green'!" said the desk clerk with the oily deference due the occupant of a ten dollar a day suite.

"Ask her to come up, will you, old man? Thanks!" said the pleasant brown-faced young man.

He hung up the receiver, walked to the door, unlatched it, and, with the bandage made of a towel held in his strong, cruel-looking hand, he took up his position just back of the door, waiting, tense, alert.

He heard the slow creaking of the elevator coming up. The stop. The door that opened, and clanged shut. The worn carpet on the floor of the narrow, dingy hall caught the faint footsteps of somebody who came forward hesitantly, as though reading the numbers on doors they passed.

The footsteps paused at the door behind which stood the brown, pleasant young man—who looked not at all pleasant now, as he waited, poised like some great cat for a spring upon an unsuspecting prey.

There was a knock at the door, and then the door was pushed open, and a woman stepped into the room. She was a woman no longer young, though her make-up and her clothes tried determinedly to foster the semblance of youth. Her hair had been henna'd, but the henna had been inexpertly applied, and gave her hair a greenish tinge; her face was sallow and lined, and the cheap powder and paint thickly applied only emphasized the fact. Her sleazy silk dress was cheap and badly made. The heels of her coquettish strapped sandals were run-over and badly scuffed.

She stood just inside the room, looking towards the open door of the bed-room, quite sure that her unseen host was in there.

But as she took a step forward, the door behind her closed softly, and before she could whirl around or cry out, the towel-bandage had gone over her head, and fastened cruelly about her throat, choking unuttered the scream of terror that bubbled in her throat.

She looked up, wide-eyed, into the face of the brown, pleasant young man. But the face was no longer brown or pleasant. It was sharp and wolfish with hate, and a sheer animal cruelty that struck terror to the woman's shabby soul.

"YOU! Oh, my God!" she mouthed, and even without the bandage that tightened so cruelly about her throat she could not have spoken above a whisper, so

Startled, she took up the receiver, and heard Jimmy's voice, excited, say·
ing, swiftly, "Janelle, did you tell me that this Sherman Lawrence
you're going to marry is in Havana, Cuba?" A nameless
fear lay like a chill hand against Janelle's heart.

(See Page 543)

savage was the terror that closed about her like a wall of ice, paralyzing the coursing blood in her veins, paralyzing the poor, dazed brain of her.

"So you were going to double-cross us, were you?" said the man very softly, and the hotel-clerk, the bell-hop would never have recognized this voice, silky with menace, acid with hatred, that whispered in the woman's ears. "You thought you could sell us out, and go scot-free, did you? You poor little fool!" You signed your own death warrant when you wrote that letter to the Elliott woman!"

The woman's claw-like hands struggled against that cruel gag, and she managed to whisper, her voice rasping in her throat,

"What—what are you—gonna do with me?"

"That's a fool question—what do we usually do to a rat that gets in our way? I'm going to kill you, of course! What else did you expect?" said the man, and deliberately he tightened the bandage about her throat —holding her easily, careless of her struggles.

Later, he lifted the limp body and laid it upon the bed. He looked swiftly about the room, as though to assure himself that everything was as it should be. Carefully he stripped off the rubber gloves. He put them into his pocket, and at the basin in the bath-room he washed his hands fastidiously, and dried them carefully on a fresh towel.

He combed his hair, put on a fresh collar and tie, tucking the discarded one into the waste-basket, as though with a sort of grim humor, knowing that both collar and tie had been bought in Havana, and never worn until today.

Leaving the room as it was, without a glance towards that still form on the bed, he unlocked the door and stepped through it. He closed it behind him and locked it again at the elevator before he put the key in his pocket, he very carefully wiped it free of any finger-prints on his handkerchief. Holding a letter in his hand, he laid the key against the letter so that there would be no new finger-prints.

Downstairs at the hotel desk, he slid the key gaily across the desk dexterously, without touching it save with the back of the letter which he thrust into his pocket.

With a little nod to the desk-clerk he crossed the lobby, stepped out into the street, and was lost in the rapidly milling crowd of noon-day.

* * * * * * * * *

Meanwhile, at Bellevue Hospital, doctors were examining a patient who had just been brought in.

"Stowaway — discovered aboard a United Fruit Company vessel that docked from Cuba this morning. Clothes are new, and with no distinguishing mark on them. No papers in his pockets—and no money. Still unconscious!" was the succint explanation of his entrance into the hospital.

He was found to be suffering from fever, from lack of food and from confinement in the close quarters where he had hidden himself. Until he should regain consciousness, he was relegated to one of the wards, and treatment outlined for him.

Chapter 59.

A JEALOUS WOMAN!

NEWS OF the success of the "rushes" on "Legacy of L o v e" went about the studios of the XL Productions on wings. People from other sets began to gather about the lines b e h i n d Director Wayne, and to watch the shooting of his scenes.

J a n e l l e was immensely popular with the production staff of the Wayne unit. She was friendly and courteous and kind. She was frankly ignorant of the technique of this new business into which she had so unexpectedly tumbled, and she was disarmingly eager for advice and suggestions. Because she remembered the camera-man's name, and was friendly and pleasant to his wife, one day when she called, the camera-man saw to it that Janelle was always photographed from the best possible angle. Because she was eager to take direction, and had no opinions of her own that conflicted with his, Wayne was delighted with her. Because she wasn't fighting for the best "spot" in a scene, but was perfectly satisfied with whatever "spot" was given her by the director, she became extremely popular with the other players in the company, particularly with Jim Marvin.

The publicity department found her willing to cooperate—to pose for as many special photographs as they wanted, entirely willing to talk to magazine and newspaper writers at almost any time they asked it, and because she was always delighted with whatever the publicity department did for her, they adored her to a man.

And one day when Gladda Romaine's secretary went into the press department to register her employer's complaint against some trifling bit of advertising, the secretary discovered that all the photographs had been taken down in the press department with the exception of a large and beautiful picture of Janelle.

It was a small thing — yet it served to open Gladda Romaine's eyes to something that had been going on about her, but that she had been too preoccupied to notice. She had been given a new director, the story she liked so much, and a leading man had been brought out from New York to work opposite her. Consequently there would be no danger of his taking any of the glory away from her for this picture.

Surrounded by the things she had demanded—a story, a cast and a director that she had chosen herself, and with gowns that she had selected for herself—she had been purring like a cat fed on cream. But now, with the incident of the photographs that had been taken down from the wall of the press department to make way for a single photograph of this newcomer, she was jarred to wakefulness.

She made it her business that day to leave her own set, and dressed in a white and silver gown, ropes of jewels about her throat and her arms, made-up and ready for her own scenes, when it should suit her fancy to make them, she strolled, with elaborate carelessness, over to Sound Stage 6, where Janelle and the Wayne unit were working.

The extra people grouped about the camera-lines watching the scene between Marvin and Janelle, drew apart, wide-eyed, a little awed, at sight of the beautiful and celebrated Gladda Romaine.

The script clerk gave up her own chair to the visiting star, and Gladda, without a word of thanks, dropped into it.

"Oh—hello, Glad—you here? What brings you for a visit?" demanded Wayne while the lights were adjusted for the final shooting of the scene.

Gladda lifted an exquisitely creamy shoulder in a little light shrug and said, smiling,

"Oh, I was bored—all the people in my company are actors of experience—I thought it would be amusing to see a couple of AMATEURS at work!" there was deliberate insolence in her tone as she smiled at him.

Wayne looked down at her, a little derisive light in his own eyes.

"I think perhaps it MIGHT be amusing—but I KNOW it will be instructive!" he told her brutally.

The color rose sharply beneath Gladda's thick make-up and her eyes flashed fire.

"You mean—you actually mean that this little—up-start—can teach me something I don't know about acting?" she demanded, incredulous that he should really mean this.

"She could teach you a great deal about sincerity, my dear girl! Your technique is marvelous—but—its cold! It's MERELY technique — this girl has warmth—she has sincerity—it shows in her work! Sit down, Glad, and watch this scene!" said Wayne coolly.

Gladda's breath was coming hard, and she had

set her teeth. Her eyes flashed fire, and her jewelled hands were clenched hard together. But she sat down again because she was genuinely curious to see the work of this girl from nowhere.

She listened with a curling lip, as the scene was rehearsed. She watched, her eyes narrowed, her manner amused, disdainful, as the scene was shot, and she would have died rather than admit the truth—which was that she was impressed by the work of Janelle.

When the scene was over, Janelle and Jim came together towards Wayne, blinded by the lights so that they did not see Gladda sitting so disdainfully in the canvas-backed chair.

"Good work, kids—darned good! And you didn't know that you had a highly critical audience — Miss Romaine, have you met Mrs. Elliott?" said Wayne smoothly.

Janelle's eyes lit up, and she put out her hand.

"How do you do, Miss Romaine? I've been so anxious to meet you—you worked in the picture with my baby—I remember so well!" she said eagerly.

Gladda apparently did not see the extended hand. She merely looked Janelle over coolly, and smiled an icy little smile.

"You mean this child you claim supported me in my picture! I was the star of 'The Guilty Woman'—the child was merely a 'bit-player'!" she said coolly. "I must congratulate you, by the way!"

Chilled by the woman's manner, Janelle looked a little uncertain.

"Congratulate me? You mean—my work?" she asked, her smile fading a little.

Gladda trilled a little, tinkling laugh.

"My dear—no! Your work is crude and impossible—any high school girl could improve on it!" she said disdainfully. "I congratulate you on your nerve! Your—brass-bound gall in trying to put over on the movie fans of the world this absurd hoax about a stolen child! It's clever, yes—but if ever they find out it is a hoax—you're finished! They'll hate you!"

"Gladda, for Pat's sake, be decent for once in your life!" snapped Wayne savagely.

Jim stepped closer to Janelle, and stood ready to back her up if she needed his defense. But Janelle, her slender back straight, her eyes looking straight into Gladda's, needed no defense.

"You mean—you think that—it is all untrue? A fake!" she asked quietly.

"Of course I do—what else COULD I think?" demanded Gladda contemptuously.

Janelle looked down at her for a moment—and then she smiled faintly.

"You'll find it hard to believe, of course—but the truth of the matter, Miss Romaine, is that—what you think is of no importance whatever to me!" said Janelle levelly, and walked away to her dressing-room.

There was a little breathless silence. Gladda looked as if someone had thrown cold water in her face. But the group of extras and technical people who had often suffered at the hands of the imperious star, were delighted.

There was a little soft, smothered chuckle—and then somebody turned away to laugh—and a little ripple sped over the entire group. Wayne and Jim Marvin were frankly delighted that Janelle had "talked back" so sharply to the star who had been privately known as "the studio terror."

Gladda's vanity could not stand ridicule, and seething with rage, she stood up and hurried away, scarlet with mortification as she heard the laughter that swept the crowd the minute her back was turned.

She would get even with Janelle for this, she promised herself, raging with fury. She would never rest until she had repaid this public snub. The fact that she had brought it upon herself—that she had been the aggressor meant nothing at all.

Someone had dared to laugh publicly at her—someone had dared to talk back to her—why, not even Maxie Cason himself would have done that! And she would see that this little up-start, as she called Janelle, should be taught a lesson.

As Janelle was ready to leave her dressing-room, there was a knock at the door, and she opened it to find Jim Marvin, also dressed for the street, standing there, smiling and eager, and very good-looking.

"I was wondering if you had a date for the evening, and if you didn't, whether you'd come and have dinner with me somewhere!" he suggested eagerly.

Janelle sincerely liked him, and he had been very kind and friendly and helpful. And she was lonely—so—after all, why not?

"Of course, I'd love it! Only—somewhere where we don't have to dress in evening clothes—I'm tired!" she stipulated.

"Good—we'll make it the Brown Derby! Ever been there?" said Jim, walking beside her out of the studio, and through the gates where a good looking roadster, all shining with black and silver paint and chromium-tire covers, was parked.

"No!" said Janelle, and then as he swung open the door of the roadster, she asked, startled, "Why—is this yours?"

Jim grinned, a trifle sheepishly.

"After I pay fourteen more notes, it is!" he assured her boyishly. "Everybody kept telling me I had to 'put up a front' out here, if I ever expected to get anywhere—so this is the beginning. Bought it before the ink was dry on my contract with XL!"

He helped her into the car and they drove off through the twilight that was frail with beauty, and soft with the magic of a cool wind fragrant with countless gardens through which it had slipped before reaching them.

They had dinner at the Brown Derby, and were amused and entertained by the movie celebrities who were present, and the tourists who had come to watch the movie folks.

Afterwards they went for a drive in the hills, and there in a quiet, secluded spot along the road Jim parked the car, and they waited for the moonrise.

Janelle was absent-minded. Her thoughts were busy with Sherman—busy with the problem of why she hadn't heard from him—wonder and worry about his condition—and suddenly, with a little guilty start, she became aware that Jim was talking to her—had been for several minutes, his voice not quite steady.

"——loved you since the first day I saw you, I think—I'm crazy about you, Janie, and we get along well together—I didn't intend ever to get married—not until after I had become a star, that is! But as soon as I met you——!"

"Jim!" gasped Janelle, wide-eyed and appalled. "What on earth are you saying?"

In the golden glory of the moon that was just pushing a shoulder above the farther-most rim of the world, she saw the surprise and the amazement in his face as he looked down at her.

"I'm saying that I love you, Janelle, and I'm asking you to marry me. Is that so amazing—or—so repulsive? Don't you like me — just a little?" he demanded, and his tone was hurt like that of a small boy.

Janelle put out her hand swiftly, and laid it on his in a little fleeting, friendly gesture.

"Jim, you're a dear, and I'm awfully fond of you, as a friend—you've been sweet to me, and I do appreciate it—but I thought you knew that—there can never be anything but friendship between us! I thought you knew—everybody knew—that I am engaged to Sherman Lawrence! We are going to be married as soon as he is able to join me here! He's quite ill in Cuba!" she told him, frankly and honestly.

Jim looked down at her in white-faced misery.

"You should have told me!" he protested bitterly.

"But, Jim, I thought you knew!" she pointed out unhappily.

There was a little silence, and she saw that he was looking away from her, out over the glory of the hills, bathed in that golden flood of moonlight. At last he shrugged, and bent to the gears.

"So that's that! Gosh, I thought I had the inside track for once in my life—but I guess it's my bad luck to always be an 'also ran'!" he said bitterly.

"But, Jim—truly—you'll forget me—you'll find somebody else, a girl who will love you and be worthy of you——" she tried to comfort him.

He smiled bitterly.

"Oh, sure, sure — but I'm warning you now, Janelle, if you offer to be a sister to me—I'll all but wring your neck, here and now!" he threatened.

"Then I won't—I'll just promise to be a good friend, Jimmy, and try to help you find a nice girl that will love you as you deserve!" she offered, and won from him a faint smile.

"O. K.!" he told her, the bitterness fading a little

from his eyes as he put the roadster into motion. "But, mind you, the girl must look as much like you as possible, and be nearly as nice! I couldn't expect her to be entirely as nice!"

Janelle, relieved that he was taking it so well, laughed.

"You're a dear, Jimmy—but you're a bit of an idiot!" she told him frankly.

The drive back to her house was made pleasantly, and at the patio gate where the watchman loomed up, to let her in, Jimmy held her hand for a moment.

"It's been grand being in love with you, and running a swell set of chills and fever in the hope of persuading you to marry me!" he told her. "But now that it's all over, I guess I might just as well stop kidding myself—anyway, I wish you happiness—he's a darned lucky bird, this—what did you say his name was?"

"Sherman Lawrence!" said Janelle, and her voice sang the words like a tender melody of love. "He will be here soon, Jimmy—and you must like him a lot!"

"I'll challenge him to a duel! Swords for two, and coffee for one!" he growled, but he drove away with the shadows lifting a little on his face.

Janelle said good-night to the watchman, and went on into the dark, silent house, and up to her own room. She had never entered the room without a little feeling of dread since that night when she had found the green orchid, and that mysterious message. Always, when she switched the lights on in her room, her eyes went first to her bed to see if the pillow held another of those sinister green flowers, and perhaps another note. But tonight, as for the past week, the pillow was innocent of any such message, and with a little breath of relief she began to undress.

She was ready for bed when the telephone rang

shrilly. Startled, she took up the receiver, and heard Jimmy's voice, excited, saying, swiftly,

"Janelle, did you tell me that this Sherman Lawrence you're going to marry is in Havana, Cuba?"

A nameless fear lay like a chill hand against Janelle's heart, and she had to wet her lips before she could answer him.

"Yes—he's ill there in the hospital!" she managed at last.

"Have you seen the evening papers, Janelle?" demanded Jim, and the tense excitement in his voice frightened her still more.

"Why—no, I haven't had time!" she answered. "Why, Jim?"

A moment's pause, and then he said quietly,

"Well, you might as well find it out that way, Janelle—I'll be right over!" and he hung up the receiver before she could ask him a question.

She caught up a negligee, wrapped it about herself and hurried down to the living-room, recklessly switching lights on as she went. The evening paper was folded on the table in the living-room, and Janelle took it up and unfolded it. The headlines seemed fairly to strike her between the eyes.

"WELL-KNOWN FINANCIER SOUGHT IN SORDID MURDER."

"Sherman Lawrence, well-known business man of Atlanta, almost equally as well known in financial circles here, was being sought by police today in connection with the murder of a woman in a shady hotel on the west side of Broadway, in the Forties.

"Lawrence, who was rescued from death in the jungle of South America a few months ago by Mrs. Janelle Elliott, herself well-known as an occupant of front-page newspaper pages for the past year or more, arrived in New York yesterday morning, and registered at the Farraday Hotel. He tipped lavishly, seemed well supplied with money, and took a two-room and bath suite. A little later, a woman called at the hotel, and asked for him. She was sent straight to his room, and an hour later, Lawrence came down from his room, surrendered his key, and stepped out of the hotel. He did not return, and this morning, when the maid went in to clean his room, the dead woman was found lying across the bed, and the alarm was given. Death was the result, according to the examining physician, of garroting—a towel had been folded, and used to strangle the woman.

"There were no signs of a struggle in the room. Two half emptied glasses of whiskey on the table, beside a bottle one quarter full indicated that the man and woman had had at least a few drinks together.

"No motive for the deed has been discovered. The woman was about forty, flashily, but cheaply dressed, and bore the unmistakable signs of dissipation. The clerk stated that the name she gave, when she asked for Lawrence, was 'Annie Green'."

Continued in Next Number.

Suddenly ahead of her, in the road, a man stepped from the shrubbery
and flung up his hand to stop her. With a shrill of protesting brakes
as she brought the car to a too protesting stop, she saw the man,
enveloped in a long cape, a slouch-brimmed hat drawn low
over his eyes, come towards her. (See Pag 576)

Chapter 60.

THE MISSING MAN!

OR A LONG, stunned moment Janelle stared at the lines of print until they danced maddeningly before her eyes. Sherman wanted for the murder of the woman, "Annie Green." Sherman, back in the States, and wanted for murder!

She put both shaking hands to her bewildered forehead. It couldn't be true! Sherman was ill in a hospital in Havana! Had he been able to travel, he would have come straight to her! She knew that he would not have gone to New York. Yet —"Annie Green!" The murdered woman's name was "Annie Green!"

She ran to the telephone, called the telegraph office.

"I want to rush a cable to Havana, Cuba, at once —the fastest possible service!" she told the operator breathlessly. "To Nurse Georgia Judkins, American Hospital, Havana. New York papers speak of Sherman Lawrence in New York. Wire immediately if this is correct. Have not heard from you for days. Am worried and anxious. Please answer at once. Signed, Janelle Elliott!"

She set her teeth in her lower lip as the operator droned the words back at her, made sure of the address and the signature, and by the time Janelle had hung up the receiver, there was a ring of the door-bell, and she answered it to find Jim Marvin and Mr. Wayne there.

"I ran into Wayne at the Montmartre and brought him along—is it possible, Janelle, that this is YOUR Sherman Lawrence?" demanded Jim breathlessly.

"Don't be an idiot, Jim—of course it isn't!" said Wayne swiftly. "I grant you the name is not a particularly novel one, but nevertheless, it's possible that there could be two people by the same name!"

"Hardly possible that both could be financiers, that both could have been rescued from the jungle by Janelle in the last few months, and have come direct from Havana, Cuba!" protested Jim with some heat.

"No, no — of course not!" agreed Janelle wild with anxiety. "But — there is some sort of explanation. It isn't true—it isn't true! Sherman didn't do it —why, he couldn't have done it. It isn't possible for him—why, he's been so ill that he couldn't even walk across the floor, yet they say he—he—garroted this woman — that takes real strength — doesn't it?" she begged them to agree with her.

"Of course it does—I'm sure that there's some terrible mistake!" soothed Wayne. "Don't you want to run along to bed and get some sleep? I've sent some wires to friends in New York, and we'll have the lowdown on this by morning!"

Janelle shuddered at the bare idea of bed.

"No, no—I couldn't! I couldn't! I've sent a wire to the hospital in Cuba—I've go to wait for an answer!"

she stammered, and her hands, as Wayne took them and chafed them, were icy cold.

"Then Jim and I will stay with you! Here, here, child, stop trembling so! Sit down here—I'll go make us all a cup of coffee! Jim, you stay with her!" ordered Wayne, and hurried towards the kitchen.

Meanwhile, Maxie Cason came home from a highly successful conference with several of his cronies who had seen the "rushes" on "Legacy of Love," and who were frankly envious of his chances of making "the Big Four" become the "Big Five" by taking him and his XL Productions into it.

As he came into the house his valet met him, trying hard not to look as sleepy as he felt.

"Miss Hopkins has been calling you, sir—she's most anxious to get in touch with you!" said the valet.

Maxie was a little startled, for well he knew that "Hoppy" would not be calling him at this hour if the business were not very urgent indeed. He went straight to the telephone and called his secretary's apartment.

"Hello—Maxie? Listen, Big Boy, you'd better step straight over to the home of your little new star and start explaining!" said Miss Hopkins swiftly. "If you don't know why, take a look at the evening papers. Her boy-friend who was supposed to be at death's door in Havana, has been in New York instead, dragging somebody else through death's door on the wrong side. And if you don't step lively, it's my guess your little star will be twinkling on her merry way to New York on the very next plane!"

"I'm half way there already—thanks, Hoppy!" said Maxie breathlessly, and left the telephone receiver dangling as he dashed out of the house, and to the drive before his chauffeur could put the Rolls-Royce up.

"To Mrs. Elliott's, Satsu—and make it snappy!"

he ordered and sprang into the car without stopping to note the servant's odd expression. Satsu said nothing —merely touched the visor of his cap and got into the car. But as he drove his eyes were narrowed to mere slits, and there was a puzzled, almost an apprehensive expression on his face.

When Maxie reached the pretty stucco home where he had thought that Janelle would be entirely safe from any interference from either her friends or her enemies, he found both his director and one of his leading men there ahead of him.

Wayne, hearing the sound of the car in the drive, anticipated the ringing of the door-bell.

"Never mind—I'll go!" he said, as Janelle rose to answer the summons of the door.

"Oh — so you're here!" said Maxie as Wayne opened the door and Maxie stepped into the big, cool, artistic reception hall. "How is she?"

Wayne looked grimly at the man who was his employer.

"How do you suppose she is after a blow like this? Her nerves are shot to blazes, of course—but she's a game little kid—she's taking it on the chin!" he said grimly. "I am a little surprised that you are here—I rather thought you'd—take it on the lam when you knew that she was about to catch up with you about holding up her mail!"

Maxie looked startled.

"Does she know that?" he demanded swiftly.

"Not yet—but she will very soon. She has wired the hospital in Havana, and should have an answer any minute! Then—she is leaving for New York on the first plane available!" said Wayne promptly.

Maxie made a little sound of distress.

"She's going away now — when we've only a

couple more weeks, maybe, before the picture will be ready to cut? And you let her talk like that?" he demanded, outraged. "You would let her go away——"

"Now listen, you—you—money-minded thus and so!" snapped Wayne roughly. "You've butted into this girl's affairs and tangled things up badly enough for her—and now you're going to keep your fingers out of her business—you hear me?"

Maxie made a little distressed gesture.

"All right—all right! I hear you—I'm not deaf! Sure I hear you!" he protested.

Janelle came to the living-room door, her face as white as the frail house-gown she wore.

"What is it, Mr. Wayne? Oh — it's you, Mr. Cason. How nice of you to come over—you've heard the news?" she greeted her employer eagerly.

Maxie made a little comforting gesture as he patted her shoulder as though she had been a child of five.

"Sure, sure—I heard and I came right over. Too bad—too bad!" he tried to soothe her.

"Oh—but it isn't true, Mr. Cason—it isn't true! Sherman was utterly incapable of a thing like that— he was the kindest, the dearest, and most gentle fellow that ever lived!" she stammered swiftly. "And even if he were not—he has been ill so long—why, he lacked the physical strength for such a thing. There's some dreadful mistake—I don't know what it is, but I DO know that there IS a mistake! Why, if Sherman had been able to leave the hospital—to travel—he would have come straight here to me—at once! I know it!"

There was an almost startled gleam in Maxie's eyes, but Jim Marvin created a slight interruption by coming in from the kitchen with a tray on which there were cups and saucers, spoons, cream, sugar, and a slender silver pot that gave forth the fragrance of excellent coffee.

"Come and have a cup of coffee, folks, while we discuss what's to be done! Come on, Janie—you're all upset!" he coaxed her, and when he had put her in a chair and gave her a fragile cup filled with golden brown coffee, she smiled her thanks faintly and said quickly,

"Oh, but — there's no discussion about that! There is only one thing for me to do—I must go to New York at once and find Sherman—and help him prove his innocence of this—hideous crime!"

"Oh, but you can't do that——" began Maxie, but unexpectedly Wayne cut in grimly,

"Maxie, so help me, if you say one thing about the necessity of protecting your investment in this— dratted picture—I'll—give you a poke in the eye!"

Maxie looked at him, startled, and decided that he meant it. So, hastily, he altered what he had been about to say.

"I was just going to say that it would be very foolish for her to go to New York, to hunt for Mr. Lawrence — when the chances are ten to one — a thousand to one, maybe—that Mr. Lawrence is secretly on his way here!" he said smoothly.

Startled, the others stared at him.

It was Janelle who recovered sufficiently to speak first.

"Why—what do you mean, Mr. Cason?"

"It's simple—he is in love with you—you are here! Naturally, he will come straight to you—isn't that right, boys? Isn't that good logic—a sound argument? I'm asking you!" demanded Maxie, triumphantly.

Wayne looked at him suspiciously, but agreed reluctantly.

"So good Maxie, that it makes me suspicious! What the heck have you under your hat NOW, anyway?" he demanded truculently.

Maxie grinned at him, entirely undisturbed.

"I'm trying to help her—by proving that it would be a foolish thing for her to go to New York—when she'd probably pass him on his way out here! I'm trying to point out that the wisest and sanest thing she can do is to stay right where she is—and go on with her work—and when the way is clear, he will come to her!" explained Maxie innocently.

"By George, he's right. Wayne! It's the logical thing—he will come to Janelle, or get in touch with her——" began Jim, but Janelle cut in sharply, swiftly,

"Don't say that—don't talk like that! You sound as though you thought he had really done this terrible thing — and I tell you, he didn't—he didn't! He just couldn't have done it! Why, he's sick in the hospital in Cuba—a lingering and malignant tropical fever— why, the last letter I had from him he couldn't even walk! Let alone travel to New York, and — and — STRANGLE a woman to death!" she was weeping now stormily, convulsively before she had finished, and the three men looked at each other uneasily, made uncomfortable by the familiar phenomenon of a woman in tears.

The sharp clangor of the door-bell came again, and once more, Wayne sprang to answer it. A messenger boy in the familiar livery of the telegraph office stood there, and Wayne signed for the telegram and came back into the room, looking grave and a little apprehensive.

"For you, Janelle!" he said simply, and held it out to her.

She shrank from it almost as though it had physical power to hurt her—and then with a swift revulsion of feeling she snatched it, slit the envelope open, and drew out the folded sheet. She read swiftly, her eyes widening, incredulously, her face paling.

She looked up at Wayne and then she cried out —a little short, stricken cry, and covered her face with her hands, the telegram fluttering to the floor at her feet.

Maxie and Wayne both reached for it at once, but Wayne was the quickest and he glared at Maxie as he picked up the telegram. Without looking at it he spoke to Janelle.

"Do you want us to know what it says, Janelle?" he asked her quietly.

She nodded wordless, and Wayne lifted the telegram and cleared his throat.

"It is addressed to Janelle, of course, and it reads:

"'Puzzled over your wire. Have written you three letters, and sent two wires, none of which were answered. Mr. Lawrence slipped away from hospital more than a week ago, and we have been unable to find any trace of him. Cannot believe news in todays New York papers, yet it could have been Mr. Lawrence, incredible as it seems. Feel this could have been avoided had you come as I asked you to do. It's too late now'."

Wayne looked up at Maxie, and there was accusation, condemnation, in his eyes.

"The wire is signed 'Georgia Judkins'!" he added unnecessarily.

"She—she was—Sherman's special nurse—devoted to him!" stammered Janelle, fighting with all her strength to regain her self-control to grapple with this hideous thing that had so unexpectedly developed. "But —what does she mean by saying that it could all have been avoided had I come when she wired me to? I got no wire from her telling me to come—I've been so worried and so unhappy because I didn't hear from him!"

Wayne looked accusingly at Maxie, who shrugged and said carelessly, yet avoiding Wayne' accusing eyes.

"Maybe the wire was missent—lost—that happens, you know!"

He added briskly, "The things we must do now is to find out just what happened, and decide what is to be done! Who is the woman — did you know her, Janelle?"

Under the spell of the situation that drew them all together, they had dropped the formality of "Mrs. Elliott" and were addressing her as the hurt, frightened child that she seemed, and it made her grateful to them, so that she clung to them a little. They were her friends—they would help her.

"The woman's name was 'Annie Green'—I—did not know her, though I knew of her!" she answered, and then she went on to explain to them the letters she had received, signed "Annie Green" and of the detective's unsuccessful attempt to find the woman, and of the "Personal" that she inserted in the New York paper.

Chapter 61.

A DANGEROUS CONFIDENCE!

THE THREE men, listening to the story of "Annie Green" and the way in which she twisted her life into the pattern of the lives of Sherman and Janelle, looked at each other a little startled.

"Oh, then — this Lawrence DID know a woman named 'Annie Green' — and naturally he would feel bitterly towards her for her part in the kidnapping of your baby! That makes it look—a little bad for him, I'm afraid!" Jim Marvin voiced the thoughts of the other men.

"Oh, but Sherman Lawrence is not the sort of man to—murder a woman he doesn't even know—not even if he had that much reason!" protested Janelle sharply. "Don't you see—he would have talked to her —argued with her—perhaps bargained with her, to find my baby — he would not — have murdered her! Not Sherman—he couldn't do such a thing!"

The three men were unconvinced.

"Well—I don't know! It's—a queer case! There was that liquor, you know — could he have been —

drunk?" wondered Wayne aloud.

Janelle cried out sharply, her nerves near the breaking point.

"I tell you he didn't do it—I KNOW he didn't do it!" she cried. "And besides—I don't believe this woman 'Annie Green' knew anything about the kidnapping—I believe she was just trying to—get in on a little money by pretending to sell information she didn't have!"

Wayne was studying her closely.

"Why do you say that, Janelle? You have some reason for it!" he said quietly.

Calmed by the tone of his voice, a little sobered by the reflection that she had not meant to tell any one at all about the green orchid, she hesitated. But after all these three men were her friends—they had proven that beyond a doubt! They would help her—and it would be good not to have to carry the whole burden of her worries alone any longer. She decided to confide in them fully.

"I—think that I have had a message—from the kidnappers—and—I believe they are right here in California—or near here!" she told them quietly and as calmly as she could.

There was a tiny silence as the three men stared at her in utter amazement.

"What sort of a message?" demanded Wayne swiftly.

"A flower—a green orchid exactly like the one that I found in my baby's bed the night he was stolen!" said Janelle quietly.

The three men exchanged glances, Wayne's eyes were shining with amazement and interest and sheer appreciation of the dramatic, as he leaned towards her, tense and waiting.

"Go on, Janelle—let us have the whole story! What else?" he demanded swiftly.

And so Janelle began at the beginning and told them of the sinister green orchid that Forgio had given her, and of his amusement when he had found that she hated the plant. Of the night her baby had been stolen, when she had found the green orchid on the baby's pillow, and had known it for a silent, but eloquent message from Forgio.

The green orchid had come to be a symbol of the man she had hated and feared — and Forgio had known that only too well.

"So when I came into my room here the first night I was in this house and found the orchid on my pillow, with a note beneath it—I was convinced—as I am now—that the message in the note was from the kidnappers, and that they are watching me constantly!" she finished quietly.

The note was in a small locked compartment of her desk. She brought it to them, and put it into Wayne's hands. The three men read it aloud, puzzled, and wondering.

"This note and the flower came to you here, in this house?" demanded Maxie. "Where was the guard? What am I paying him to be a night-watchman for— if he doesn't night-watch?"

"I don't know where the note came from, nor how it came to be in my room—but I do know that it was there!" said Janelle firmly. "That's why I am sure that this 'Annie Green' was either no member of the kidnappers, or else a very small one!"

There was the faintest possible movement in the hall where the light had been dimmed. Janelle, who sat facing the hall cried out sharply and saw a shadow move swiftly across the light.

"You will tell no living soul one single word of what has happened, or of what is to happen——and you will bring the ransom money in small bills, none larger than a fifty dollar bill! And — you will bring — SIXTY FIVE THOUSAND DOLLARS!"

Janelle caught her breath.

(See Page 580 in No. 19)

"There—in the hall!" she gasped, but Wayne and Jim Marvin had already leaped to the open door. There were sounds of a scuffle in the hall, and then after a crowded interval Jim and Wayne were dragging a man into the room.

A man in the livery of a chauffeur and whose ordinarily yellow face was ashy pale with terror, his dark eyes darting this way and that for some means of escape.

Maxie sprang to his feet, aghast.

"Good God, Satsu—what are you doing snooping there in the hall?" he demanded.

Wayne and Jim released the man, and Wayne, puzzled, looked down at the man.

"Why good Heavens Maxie, it's your chauffeur!"

"Sure—and I'm asking him the meaning of this!" demanded Maxie, irate. "Satsu—what were you doing there? Why didn't you wait in the car?"

To Janelle, looking on, the name "Satsu" rang like a tiny bell far back in her consciousness. At the moment she could not place it. But she knew that she had heard the name before—and suddenly, as the man looked up and met her eyes, half-fearful, half-defiant, she knew him! Alexis Forgio's valet and house-man!

On that never-to-be-forgotten night when she had gone to Alexis Forgio's apartment, frantic with worry for the loss of her baby she had heard Forgio call this man—"Satsu!"

"Please, Mr. Boss—it was very cold in the car —very late—I get sleepy. It look warm and bright in house — I creep in — I go sleep — I no think to scare peoples—I try to creep out, nobody hear—I very sorry!" stammered the chauffeur with every evidence of sincerity.

Janelle stepped in front of him and looked down

at him.

"Satsu—you once worked for a Mr. Alexis Forgio in New York, didn't you? You've seen me there?" she demanded sternly.

The man looked up at her and then swiftly dropped his eyes, with every outward appearance of humility, though Janelle felt that there was derision and defiance in his eyes.

"Please, Missy—no! I not know this man in New York—I never be in New York—me California! All time this country live here!" he pleaded—but Janelle knew in her heart that he was lying.

"Well, get back to the car, Satsu—no, you might as well go on home and to bed. I'll get a taxi when I'm ready to go — run along now — scram!" ordered Maxie, and the chauffeur scuttled out of the room like a scared chicken.

Wayne walked to the window and watched until the lights of the car slipped down the drive and turned into the highway. When he came back to the room, he was frowning, puzzled.

"Now, why the devil do you suppose he was hiding in the hall, eavesdropping?" he wondered aloud.

"He was lying when he said he did not know Forgio—I am positive that he is the man—why, even his name is the same!" said Janelle, and, wide-eyed, she stared at Maxie. "Do you suppose—is it possible—that he is in touch with the people who have my child— acting as a go-between?"

Wayne and Maxie both shrugged, but it was Wayne who answered.

"I hate to say it — but privately, I'm of the opinion that most any darned thing could happen now-adays!"

"But—what the devil would he want to get mixed

up with kidnappers for?" puzzled Maxie.

"Don't be a lame-brain, Maxie—remember that Janelle would probably pay a good deal of money to get her baby back safe!" Wayne pointed out with considerable heat.

"Anything in the world—everything I've got— I'd strip myself of everything I own, and gladly work for him—scrub floors if necessary, to take care of him! There's nothing I wouldn't do to get him back—my poor, little, frightened lost baby!" Janelle broke down, weeping as though her heart would break and Jim put his arms about her tenderly as though she had been his sister, and held her close, comforting her as best he could.

"There, there, dear—you mustn't grieve so—we will get him back for you somehow!" he tried to soothe her.

She made a little swift gesture of heart-break and bewilderment.

"It—it—all seems—so dreadful! First my baby — and then Sherman! Perhaps if I had stayed in Havana—if I had never come here—Sherman would not have left the hospital—I can't help feeling, somehow, that—he was trying to find me—that he was— coming to me——" she stammered before the tears overcame her.

"That's why I think you should wait here—he will come to you here—I feel sure of it!" Maxie told her strongly.

Wayne looked steadily at Maxie, who returned his glance with all innocence.

"For once, I'm afraid you're right, Maxie — though I hate to admit it!" confessed Wayne. "At least, Janelle, wait for the morning papers and see what new developments there are—and then you can decide what is to be done!"

And at last she consented. The pert little maid had been aroused, and it was in her hands that Wayne, Jim and Maxie left the girl when they at last said good-night. Janelle promised them to drink the hot milk and the bromide that Wayne had provided, and to go straight to bed.

The three men left her reluctantly, and her brave, white little smile went with them as they went out into the cool, starry night, and hailed a night-cruising taxi.

Chapter 62.

MAXIE MAKES A PLAN.

HEN HE had dropped the other two at their apartment, M a x i e kept the taxi and had himself driven towards his own place. And Maxie's a g i l e brain w a s working fast. Someway, somehow, he must keep Janelle here in Hollywood and at work on Sound Stage No. 6 until "Legacy of Love" was finished and in the cutting-room. After that he would more or less lose interest in her. What he wanted was the finished picture ready to release to his exhibitors who would pay him "important money" from all over the world, and make it possible for him to realize his ambition of making "The Big Four" become the "Big Five," with XL Productions the fifth unit.

Let us be perfectly fair to Maxie. He saw Janelle Elliott not as a human being with a heart and a brain —not as a woman with a heart that could suffer and be tortured and wrung with sorrow; but as a piece of property that belonged to him, and which he had the opportunity to develope for his own enrichment and the furtherance of his own ambition. In planning ways to hold her here in Hollywood, he had no thought of being cruel or heartless. Just as, when he had held up the three letters and the two telegrams, he had done it just as he would have checked the advance of a competitor in business. Just as he would have had repairs done to a bit of machinery whose faulty adjustment was making business bad for him.

And now, as he thought over the whole plan that was becoming more and more clear to him, the human element did not enter into his thoughts. He would by some means preferably fair but if necessary foul, hold Janelle here until the picture was finished. After that he would do anything in his power to make it possible for her to go wherever she liked—wherever it seemed best for her, in the hope of finding her baby and her lover.

He frowned a little as he remembered that Janelle had money of her own. That he could not hold over her the threat of holding up her salary or the inducement of a bonus at the completion of the picture as a means of keeping her in the studio if she no longer wanted to stay. He was beginning to be afraid that her hope of finding the baby through the completion of the picture was beginning to dwindle. If that hope vanished, he knew that no power in the world would hold her at the studio, now that this mystery of Sherman Lawrence had bobbed up.

As he paid the taxi-driver and let himself into his impressive house, he reached the conclusion that the only way to keep Janelle in Hollywood was by convincing her that her hope of finding the baby was about to be realized.

That, he told himself, was more or less easy. But—how to do it? That was the next thought. He would have to be extremely careful. He must be convincing—whatever he did, he must do boldly and convincingly. Suddenly his eyes brightened and he snapped his fingers in silent exultation.

"Satsu!" he murmured aloud. "Satsu is the very boy for me!"

He went on to his own room and there he gave himself over to working out the final details of his plan. He did not ring for Satsu—he waited until morning, and when his valet came in with his breakfast, Maxie sent for the chauffeur.

Satsu, looking trim and smart and neat, presented himself promptly, a veiled look that was almost fright in his eyes.

"Satsu—you used to work for this Forgio guy Mrs. Elliott was talking about—don't lie to me, you slant-eyed devil—you did, didn't you?" snapped Maxie.

Satsu sucked in his breath with a faintly sibilant sound, and thought swiftly. But he argued the absurdity of trying to deny a thing that could be easily proven if any one cared to go to the trouble, and so he nodded instead.

"Please, Mr. Boss—yess—but so much trouble—so much newspapers—so much talk—make it hard to get job in East—so I come West!" he explained with a pretty pretense of humility.

"And a darned smart idea, too!" commented Maxie. "All right, now, Satsu — what do you know about the kidnapping of Mrs. Elliott's child?"

Satsu's eyes flew wide with fright and a wild declaration of innocence.

"Please, Mr. Boss—I know nothing. Mr. Forgio —him say he do it—I hear him tell Missy Elliott—but me, I know no anything!" he stammered, and Maxie believed him.

"O. K., Satsu—I'll believe you—for the present, anyway!" said Maxie firmly. "Now listen to me—I got work for you to do—and if you do it right, it'll mean a nice little piece of money for you. If you do it wrong, it'll mean you'll have a new job to find! Get me?"

"I get you, Mr. Boss!" Satsu assured him with promptness.

"All right. Do you know what sort of flower this 'green orchid' was?" demanded Maxie.

"Mr. Forgio, he all time crazy about 'em—I see 'em, yes!" answered Satsu.

"Know where you can get one in Los Angeles?" demanded Maxie.

Satsu hesitated and his eyes dropped.

"Maybe so—maybe no. Very expensive—cost a lot of money!" he evaded.

Maxie grunted. "Sure, I expected that! Here's ten dollars—get me a green orchid—exactly like the ones this Forgio used to scatter around! And after that I'll tell you what to do next!" said Maxie, and as Satsu scuttled out of the room, Maxie grinned to himself wickedly.

He would keep Janelle in Hollywood until her picture had been finished, and then he would make amends for everything that had happened by aiding her in any and every way.

The morning papers contained complete accounts of the crime in New York that had been laid at the door of Sherman Lawrence, wealthy and socially prominent young financier. It was discovered that he had been ill for some time in a hospital in Havana, Cuba, but that he had disappeared from there under rather mysterious circumstances in plenty of time to have been in New York on the day of the murder. More, a boat from Havana had docked that morning, although the name of Sherman Lawrence had not appeared on the passenger list.

An autopsy on the body of the dead woman proved that despite the evidences of the half-emptied bottle of whiskey, the stained glasses on the table, the woman had not tasted a drop. Apparently the woman had neither friends nor relatives, for no one claimed the body. Nor had any trace been found of the man accused of the crime of murdering her.

The detectives assigned to the case, aroused to extra vigilance by the fact that the case was making front page newspapers all over the world due to the prominence of the man involved, were puzzled by the complete absence of any clue. Not a finger-print appeared in the room. Only the new collar and neck-tie found in the waste-paper basket, and the suit-case with its monogram of "S. L., Atlanta" and the coat and vest that hung over a chair. The coat and vest bore an embroidered monogram on the inside pocket—and the letters were "S. L.' The coat was part of an expensive suit, but the tailor's name had been carefully cut out. The collar was the sort that can be bought by the dozen in any haberdashery shop, but the neck-tie bore the mark of a smart Havana men's shop. It was new—had evidently only been worn once or twice, for the crease of the knot was quite fresh.

Of course, the old stories were dug up—Sherman's defence of Janelle during her trial for the death of Forgio—Sherman's flight and crash in the jungle—Janelle's and Buck's rescue of him—and Janelle's presence in Hollywood now to make a movie that was designed to help her find her lost baby. Naturally the reporters swarmed the studio and the house where Janelle lived.

Knowing the utter uselessness of denying herself to them, Janelle faced them and told them all she could. And she finished by pointing out to them the utter impossibility of a man in Sherman's condition, wasted by fever and months in the hospital, destroying the woman, "Annie Green," by strangling her. The authorities at the hospital in Havana, interviewed by representatives of the American newspapers, corroborated Janelle's statement. Mr. Lawrence, on the night that he escaped from the hospital, was too weak and ill to walk more than a few feet without assistance. But this fact didn't aid Sherman's defense greatly — for it was only too evident that he HAD walked or had an accomplice on the outside to help him—the hint that he had been "not quite himself, mentally" when he had left the hospital became in the more excited press, the statement that he was "suffering from temporary insanity" and it was brought out that under the stimulus of such a condition, a man may accomplish feats of strength impossible to him under normal conditions.

Daily Janelle devoured the papers in the prayerful hope that some trace of Sherman would be found, and that she could go to him. Maxie and Wayne had convinced her that it would do no good for her to go to New York—absurd to think that Sherman could be hiding there, and the police of that great city unable to lay hands on him. Much better for her to stay here where Sherman could, given the chance, come to her. Much better for her to go on with her work, to occupy her mind—rather than to sit and brood in idleness.

It may be easily imagined that the lovely and spoiled Gladda Romaine did not view this fresh front-page publicity and seeming triumph of her rival with and degree of enthusiasm. Gladda and her affairs, formerly of first importance to her studio, had now become lost in the mass of publicity that without the press-department turning a finger, descended upon Janelle.

Gladda, in the privacy of her dress-room bungalow, faced her personal press-agent and demanded that something be done. Demanded it in such tones that that young man realized he must do something, and do it quickly—or else lose a most profitable client.

"Of course, Glad—there's one thing that can be done and done quickly—one thing that will take her hot-footing out of the studio with the picture still unfinished!" the press-agent pointed out.

"Make it clear—I'm not good at riddles!" snapped Gladda.

"If she were made to believe that her child was in some foreign country—or, say, some very distant state—she'd break her neck getting there without a moment's delay!" suggested the press-agent.

"Of course — but how do I go about it?" demanded Gladda.

"I've been reading up on the case — the early stories about the Forgio case mentioned a peculiar flower—a green orchid—that was used to convey messages of death and destruction — and, no doubt, kidnapping—from the amusing Mr. Forgio to his intended victims! Well—I know a florist here in L. A. who has one of those green orchid plants—the darned thing is a meat-eater, no foolin'—a pretty sense of humor this Forgio must have had. Anyway—this is the plan!"

He leaned closer, and his voice dropped to a whisper, as Gladda, her eyes shining, leaned close to hear.

Chapter 63.

A MIDNIGHT MESSAGE!

TO JANELLE every day was twelve unending hours of suspense and fear. Every night was sleepless with worry and wonder and anxiety. Where was Sherman? What was happening to him? Where was her baby? Was he still alive? Would she ever see him again? She felt as though she were living on the top of a volcano, and heard below her the rumblings of the fire-monster threatening any moment to break forth.

On an evening late in the week she granted her three servants the evening off. The night-watchman was on duty outside the house. She was restless, sleepless, and she sat on alone in her pretty drawing-room, an open book in her lap. But she had not turned a page for an hour or more.

Suddenly the clock on the mantel before her chimed twelve musical, mellow strokes—and as though it had been a signal, the door bell rang—so suddenly that Janelle started violently.

She controlled her nerves and went to answer

the bell, the house brilliantly lighted behind her, sure that a loud call from her would bring the watchman on the run.

She opened the door and saw a man standing there, his cap drawn well down over his face, the collar of his coat turned well up. She could catch only a glimpse of his eyes, shining and dark, between the collar of his coat and the brim of his cap.

Before she could speak, he thrust a small, square box into her hand, and without a word, turned and fled into the darkness. Bewildered, Janelle stared after him through the darkness. And then, with a little rush of fear, she closed and locked the door swiftly, and stood there in the lighted hall, holding the box in her hand.

She stared down at it stupidly. It was a plain square white box, unwrapped, unaddressed, with a string tied about it. She untied the string at last, lifted the cover of the box—and almost dropped the box as she saw lying within it a green orchid!

For a long moment she stared at the orchid, shaken with a creeping sense of fear sweeping over her. The sinister green orchid that was a message from Forgio—and had been a supposed message from the kidnappers!

Beneath the orchid in the box lay a folded note. Touching the flower with shrinking fingers, she drew out the note and unfolded it. Typed on cheap paper, folded twice, the note had neither address nor signature. It read simply:

"If you want to find your baby, ALIVE and well, come tonight to the spot marked on the map on the back of this note. You will drive yourself, and you will come alone—or you will never see your child again. We mean business, so don't delay and don't bother bringing any-body with you. If you do exactly as you are told, no harm will come to you! If you try to give the alarm, or bring the police with you, we will not be responsible for anything that happens. Follow the route marked on the map and don't drive over thirty miles an hour. Somewhere along the route, a man will stop you and tell you what you are to do next."

There was no signature. Merely a little damp spot where the stem of the orchid, freshly cut, had "bled".

Trembling violently, Janelle studied the crudely scrawled map on the back of the note. It marked a route out through the hills along a lonely road to a canyon that was a wild, desolate looking place. A place of unsavory reputation, scene of several gruesome mur-ders and attempted murders. Yet—she must take her car and go there tonight, alone, to find her baby!

The note made it perfectly plain that she would have no opportunity to take any one with her or to give the alarm. She could accomplish her purpose—find her baby—only by risking her life—by obeying the orders contained in this note.

She hesitated only for a moment, then she ran to her room and hastily changed her trailing, soft chif-fon house-gown for a dark, practical suit, a small hat, walking shoes. She ran down-stairs and out to the garage where her car was parked. As she backed out into the drive-way, the night-watchman was nowhere to be seen and she wondered vaguely what had become of him as she drove out to the roadway.

She had fixed the route marked in the map clearly in her mind, but she had brought the note with her as well. Beneath a street-light she stopped and looked at the note again—and as she did so, a big, heavy, powerfully built coupe swung past her, and she saw that two men occupied the seat. Two men who looked at her sharply as they passed, and then speeded on.

Were they members of the kidnap crowd? Were they watching to see that she obeyed instructions to the letter? Had they some news of her baby? Her heart hammered madly in her throat at the very thought as she meshed the gears and drove on.

The streets were practically deserted for it was now close to one o'clock, and Hollywood is a hardworking city that goes to bed early to preserve its "camera-features."

She drove along, keeping the needle of the speedometer down to thirty miles an hour. She saw the coupe speed up ahead of her and turn into a side-street. When a few minutes later she passed the side-street she saw the coupe parked against the curb, the lights out, and she caught the white glimmer of two faces as the men leaned forward to watch her pass.

A little later, looking back, she saw that the coupe was following her and her heart hammered wildly. But she kept on at the steady, even thirty mile an hour pace, leaving the sleeping city behind her and entering the hills.

It was very dark here, and very still. Lonely, deserted. Ahead the moonlight lay a silver path across the road, the silver laced with the black of tree shadows. All about lay the stillness of night in the country, broken only by the sound of her car as it drove slowly along. Behind her she caught the glimmer of the twin headlights of the powerful coupe, and then as she neared the canyon, with its sinister reputation, the lights of the coupe behind her dropped out of sight—

and she seemed utterly, completely, terribly alone here in this dark, evil place.

— ◾ ◾ ▪ ● ▪ ◾ ◾ ▪

Back in New York, a man was being discharged from the hospital. A man who was gaunt and hollow-eyed, whose thick hair had streaks of gray in it, and whose dark eyes wore a puzzled, almost a frightened look.

The doctor who was studying him, shook his head.

"We are so crowded that we can no longer keep a patient who is entirely well save for the fact that he cannot remember his name and address! I suppose, after all, it isn't terribly important, and you are very lucky to have this job of janitor offered to you! It's really only a job as night watchman in a small factory in Jersey — ten dollars a week salary and a place to sleep day-times! In such times as these, a man is mighty lucky in your position, to find work like that!"

"Yes, of course, Doctor—you're very kind, and I'm very grateful! Both for the job and for the new name!" said the discharged patient as a faint smile lit up his gaunt face. "Your friend who offers me the job—I'll try to repay him by—working my best! And maybe—as you say—some day I'll remember what is behind me!"

"Of course you will—quiet, rest, enough occupation to keep you from worrying, and good, plain, substantial food will put you right quicker than we, in this over-crowded, over-worked hospital can do. Good-bye and good luck—John Doe!" said the doctor, and shook hands with the patient who moved with a slow, shuffling step, and the slightly bewildered manner of a soul made timid by the noise and confusion of a big city, out to the curb, where a Ford delivery truck from the factory in New Jersey waited for the "man without a memory" whom the humanitarian owner wished to help.

* * * * * * * * *

Ahead of Janelle in the darkness loomed the wall of the canyon, rising dark and sheer, thickly wooded. Here along the narrow trail that with some difficulty she was following, the moonlight could scarcely penetrate the thick foliage of the trees that lined the road. It was wild and lonely and forbidding, especially locked in the dead silence of the night, broken only by the sound of her car, which seemed alien and unwelcome.

She had almost reached the end of the narrow, twisting, uneven canyon road, and was beginning to wonder if the note and the orchid had been some sort of hoax or if the plan had gone wrong, when suddenly, ahead of her, in the road, a man stepped from the shrubbery and flung up his hand to stop her.

With a shrill of protesting brakes as she brought the car to a too protesting stop, she saw the man, enveloped in a long cape, a slouch-brimmed hat drawn low over his eyes, come towards her.

Continued in Next Number.

"I won't have you sneaking in and out of my house, frightening me to
death!" said Janelle, sharply. The Jap apologized profusely and
bowed himself out. Janelle did not for a moment believe his story about a date with the maid.

(See Page 604)

Chapter 64.

THE RANSOM DEMAND.

S THE MAN stepped from the sheltering shadows of the under-brush along the road, Janelle's heart climb-ed into her throat with terror. She was suddenly appallingly conscious of her lone-liness, her helpless-ness, here on this dark, terror-ridden road. The lights of the coupe behind her had melted into dark-ness. It was very late. The sky was sprinkled with a frost of stars—and she was here, utterly alone with this strange, dark figure ahead of her, who, as she approached, raised his hand as a silent order for her to halt.

As she pressed her foot on the brakes and the car rolled to a halt, the man came towards her, keeping carefully out of the reach of her head-lights. As he came towards her, she saw that she could not guess at his appearance. The long cape huddled his body—she could not tell whether he was tall, or short, light or dark, young or old. The brim of his hat drawn down, the collar of the old-fashioned cape turned up, she caught only the glitter of eyes as the man paused beside the car and looked at her. Eyes that glittered in the faint light from her instrument board, as the man looked her over swiftly.

"You came alone—you told no one—you are very wise!" said the man.

His voice was odd—pitched so low that it was a mere whisper, and unless she heard it again at exactly that pitch, she would not be able to recognize it if she ever heard it again.

"My baby? You have him?" she demanded swiftly, trembling, hanging on his words.

She saw that he shrugged lightly.

"He is alive—he is well—we know where he is! We are prepared to return him to you—on payment of the ransom!" came that odd whispering voice.

Janelle leaned towards him, but as though he suspected her of a desire to search his hidden face with her eyes, he stepped swiftly back from her.

"Stay where you are!" the whisper, had in it the ring of a command. "You will return here tomorrow night over exactly the same route. You will come alone —you will tell no living soul one single word of what has happened, or of what is to happen—and you will bring the ransom money in small bills, none larger than a fifty dollar bill! And—you will bring—SIXTY-FIVE THOUSAND DOLLARS!"

Janelle caught her breath.

"But — sixty-five thousand dollars — it's such a lot of money!" she protested swiftly.

She thought the man shrugged again.

"You have the money—we have the boy! You want the baby—we want the money—of course, if it is too much money——" he spoke indifferently, and he stepped back until the shadows almost claimed him.

"No, no!" Janelle cried out, and flung out a hand

towards him. "It is not too much—I will pay! I will pay—if only you will return him alive and well!"

"That is better!" the man's whisper was more sibilant, and rang with a sort of triumph. "You are wise! Tomorrow evening, at midnight, you will drive along this road until you see our signal—and then you will slow down and throw the money, done up into a bundle, out of the car towards the light that will be your signal. You will drive on two-tenths of a mile—your speedometer will tell you that—and then you will stop and the baby will be put into the car! Now, understand—you must not stop when the child is put into the car. You must instantly speed up and drive on—and not until you have driven five miles, must you stop! Remember — absolute obedience to everything I have said is the only way in which you may be sure of getting the child back. Do you understand?"

"Yes—I understand!" said Janelle, trembling.

"All right—then see that you do exactly as you are told—and that you tell nobody—nobody, do you understand? One single word of to-night to a single living soul—and you will never see your child alive again!" said the man.

Before Janelle had time to do more than agree that she understood, the man had stepped swiftly backward, and the dark shadows of the trees swallowed him up. He had vanished so quickly, so silently, that for a moment she sat blinking a little stupidly.

She looked about her. It seemed to her that the darkness of the night was peopled with strange, dreadful shapes that loomed grotesque and menacing, peering at her through the darkness.

She put her car in motion, and turned back towards town. She drove now as though the fiends of Hell were after her, for a sudden, swirling flood of panic had swept over her, sending her, panting and frightened and upset, back to her pretty house.

As she turned in at the driveway, the night-watchman came hurrying up, and she saw that he was stupid with sleep. He looked startled, and a little sheepish as he recognized her, but he grinned.

"How in the world did you get out, Miss Elliott, without me seeing you?" he demanded as he swung open the car-door for her.

Janelle's smile was faint, and a little mocking.

"Probably while you were asleep, don't you think?" she suggested.

"I haven't been asleep—why, I've been watching the place——" he began, and Janelle interrupted.

"Then you saw the messenger-boy who came here with a telegram about midnight?"

The night-watchman blinked owlishly.

"Messenger-boy? Midnight? Gosh, no—I didn't see anybody!"

"Then you must have been asleep—but it's all right! We won't quarrel about it now—run along and get back to sleep!' Janelle said, and ignored the man's attempts at explanation as she went into the house.

Safe in her own room, she dropped down in a chair and put her shaking hands over her face. She had established contact with the kidnappers. She had actually come face to face with the man who knew where her baby was. A man who assured her that the baby was alive and well and would be returned to her on the payment of a ransom that would practically clean out every penny she had in the bank.

Somehow she did not think for a moment that the man had been deceiving her. There was a sort of deadly seriousness about him. He had meant business so emphatically that she somehow, knew instinctively that he was not deceiving her. That he either had her baby, or knew where it was and that on the payment of the ransom he would bring the child back to her.

Tears were slipping down her cheeks now. Tears that were half of grief, for what her baby had suffered —tears of a tremulous, radiant delight at the thought of the reunion with him. She stood before the picture on the wall—that picture that was her dearest, most precious possession. The picture of an adorable, curly-haired two year old boy, who ecstatically hugged a fat, squirming collie pup and laughed out joyously from the picture. So well she remembered the day that picture had been conceived — the delight of watching it grow beneath the deft fingers of Amelia! The joy when she had learned that the picture had been meant for herself—a birthday present.

This time tomorrow night, she told herself, her heart trembling with joy before the prospect, she would have her baby back in her arms. This time tomorrow night, she and Billy would be together again—never to be separated again!

Another thought crept into her mind. Once she had found Billy, she would be free to take him in her arms, and to begin the search for Sherman. She would find him somewhere—and she would help him to prove that the terrible crime of which he was accused was one of which he was incapable.

The gray light of dawn was creeping across the world by now—and to Janelle the light was symbolical —she was emerging from the darkness of desolation in which she had been robbed of her baby, and of the man she loved. The gradually breaking light showed the discovery of her baby—the rising of the sun would be that glorious, never-to-be-forgotten moment when she would have both her baby and her lover.

Chapter 65.

OUT OF THE NIGHT.

AND WHILE Janelle was taking her life in her hands to answer the summons of a heartless and merciless gang of "baby-snatchers," a new employee of a factory in New Jersey was settling down for his night's work. The work that befitted his convalescence and his clouded mind.

It was a very warm night, and he had brought his chair outside the little "office" and propped it back against the wall of the factory. Before him there was the rolling hill that dipped to the meadows— the factory crowned the slight hill. It was a dark, and moonless night. The sky was sprinkled with the frost-like radiance of millions of tiny stars that are not visible in the rays of the moonlight.

It was very quiet here. Not a sound disturbed the stillness save the cheerful "song" of the frogs at the foot of the hill along the marshy banks of the stream that wound its way along there. There was the fragrance of dew-wet earth, of moist, growing things— the fragrance of a summer night—and as it came to the nostrils of the man who was known only as "John Doe," there came a very faint stirring at the very back of his consciousness. Not clear enough to be a return of memory.

The weeks of quiet, of normal life, of sound sleep and good plain wholesome food, had done a great deal to bring John Doe's body back to its normal condition. Slowly, bit by bit, it had pieced together the shattered fabric of a brain tortured by fever and fear and heart-hunger. And now as he sat here in the quiet, peaceful summer darkness, his mind stirred very faintly, and almost it seemed to him there came a trace of that lost memory.

There was, he knew now, something that he had to do. Something that was tremendously important. Something that he had to do right away. But—WHAT WAS IT? He racked his poor, troubled brain until the perspiration burst forth on his knotted forehead and his hands were twisted together until the knuckles showed white with the strain.

Suddenly there before him, linned against the darkness, he saw a woman. Scarcely more than a girl she was, with a shining, golden head and great, deeply blue eyes. She wore a misty trailing garment of white that swayed and fluttered about her as though blown by a vagrant wind, though the night was still.

While the man who was known as John Doe clutched the arms of his chair and leaned towards that vision, tense, fighting with every instinct within him, to call the name of the woman who stood there, she held out her arms to him, with a pleading gesture—and then—slowly the vision faded.

When at last it was gone, the man arose, crying out a name. A name that he had not known was in his consciousness—the name of the woman who had stood

there before him with her arms extended in that pleading gesture. He knew her now — he knew her now!
Why—her name was Janelle—and he had promised to
do something for her—and he hadn't done it. There
was somebody he had to see—for Janelle. Somebody
who had something that belonged to Janelle, and would
not give it back. What was it? Somebody that Janelle
loved so deeply she could not be happy without it—and
he had pledged himself to get it for her—and he had
failed.

He was on his feet now, trembling a little,
the cold perspiration trickling down his face as he
fought to remember what it was he had promised to
get for Janelle.

Suddenly out of the darkness and the fog that
settled so thickly over his memory, one word stood
out sharp and clear against the darkness—and that
word was—California!

He couldn't be sure just how—but he knew
that the woman, Janelle, and the thing he must do for
her, were somehow, all mixed up with California. He
had to get to California—and there, somehow, it
would be revealed to him what he had to do for
Janelle. Perhaps there, too, he would learn who Janelle was.

He didn't know where California was—but
somebody would tell him. And he had a little money
—all that he had earned here at the factory, for he
had worked all night, and slept all day, and his meals
had been given him in the factory cafeteria, so he
had had nothing to spend his money for. He had
forty dollars—surely, he reasoned, that would be
enough to get him to California, and just as soon as
the engineer, who had been kind and friendly to him,
had come to work in the morning, he would find out

where California was and how he must get there.

The engineer was a little startled at the question, and looked searching at the night-watchman, who was known only as "John."

"But—what do you want to go to California for?" he demanded.

"It's terribly important—something I have to do—I have to go right away!" argued "John." "It isn't very far, is it?"

The engineer waxed sarcastic.

"Oh, gosh, no—practically right across the ferry! Just a step or two!" he sneered good-naturedly.

"Thank you—and good-bye!" said John, and hurried off to change from his overalls into the misfit, but quite clean and tidy suit of clothes that had been given to him when he had been dismissed from the hospital.

The crowds on the train, and, later, on the ferry, worried him. He had spent the past four weeks after leaving the hospital at the factory in Jersey where he seldom saw more than two or three people at a time. To be plunged suddenly and relentlessy into a crowding, struggling, hurrying mass of people who shouted at each other in hideous, jarring accents—who seemed desperately afraid that they would lose a precious moment of irreplacable time, if they dared to offer the faintest courtesy to a neighbor—all sent "Johne Doe" into a trembling spasm of nerves and confusion in which his ordinary manner of talk became a hurried, stammering, dazed thing.

A shabbily dressed man who stood near him in the crowd as the ferry entered the slip on the New York side, grinned at him, and the faint gesture of friendliness drew the bewildered "John Doe" to the shabbily dressed, hard-faced man, whose eyes were furtive and guarded.

"I'm—going to California. I wonder if you could direct me to the nearest route?" asked "John," making a heroic effort to speak clearly and to avoid the stammering that made his speech so confused.

The shabbily dressed man looked a little startled, and then his eyes brightened.

"California, eh? That's a long jaunt, friend —you'll be needing money for a trip like that!" he said genially.

"Oh, I have money!" "John" assured him promptly. "It's just that I don't know the nearest route! They told me it was just a step beyond the ferry, but I don't quite know which way to go!"

The furtive eyed man looked at John closely and noticed the hollow cheeks, the sunken eyes, the twitching hands.

"Been in 'stir', Pal?" he asked, his voice low-pitched with an almost friendly note. "I'm a 'stir-bug' myself—we have to stick together, or get licked again!"

John looked puzzled.

"Stir? I don't—quite—I've been in the hospital—and—I can't seem to remember—it's—damned embarrassing not to be able to remember your own name!" he admitted, humiliated, and the man's expression altered.

"Oh—so you've been in the hospital, eh? And now you want to go to California, but you don't know the nearest route? Well, that's a coincidence —matter of fact, I'm heading for California myself— suppose we go along together!" he suggested brightly.

He had thought this stranger, with his desire

for California, had recently emerged from prison—
"stir." If he had, then he must be protected and
helped—since the shabbily-dressed, furtive eyed man
had himself been out of prison only a short time, "a
stir-bug." And according to the queer code he main-
tained, one "stir-bug" must always take up for, and
help another "stir-bug." Had John been a recently
released prisoner, the shabbily dressed man would
have fought for him and called him "brother." But
since he had not, it was quite all right to take any
advantage of him possible.

John was relieved and grateful that his new-
found friend should accompany him on his journey,
and he went ashore with the shabbily-dressed man.

Instead of taking the Forty-Second Street
cross-town trolley as the majority of the ferry-pass-
engers did, John and his new-found friend walked a
block east, and then turned south along a dirty,
dingy, noisy slum-street.

"Got to stop in here and get my baggage—
come along and have a drink!" urged the new-found
friend as he reached a dingy doorway and led the
way to a door upon which he knocked a strange signal.

The door opened a narrow slit, revealing a
brown, forbidding face which relaxed a little as the
face recognized John's new-found friend.

"Got a pal headin' for California!" explained
the shabbily-dressed man to the owner of the brown,
ugly face. "We stopped in for a drink and my baggage! My roll, you know!"

The door opened a little wider, and the owner
of the face, a swarthy, bearded, heavy-set man allowed
John and the other man to enter. There was a whispered conversation between the two men, but John
was glad to rest in a comfortable chair in the clutter-

ed, smelly, untidy room.

The shabbily-dressed man came over to John, carrying two well-filled glasses.

"Here, pard, down this—it'll make you feel more like travelling!" he insisted genially. John accepted the glass and lifted it to his lips.

He was thirsty and he swallowed a large gulp of the liquor before he discovered the stinging, merciless quality of it. His eyes burned, and watered; his throat was scorched. He gasped for breath—but a moment later a tingling warmth spread along his veins and his head felt light and giddy.

His new-found friend insisted, and John swallowed the last of the fiery liquor in his glass. The room seemed to spin around before him—he saw two men before him instead of one—there was a ringing in his ears, and after that—oblivion.

Dimly he heard a triumphant voice say:

"That shot got him—come on, Andy—let's 'roll' him—he said he had money enough to go to California—I could use it!"

When "John Doe" next became conscious, he was lying flat on his back in a clump of shrubbery beside the highway. His head throbbed dully, his tongue felt swollen and thick, he was tortured with thirst, and with hunger. He managed to sit up, wincing with pain as he did so.

He looked down and saw that the pockets of his clothes had been turned inside out, and that everything he had, including the forty dollars, had been taken. He had been robbed, drugged, and brought to this place and dumped. He managed at last to get on his feet, and to reach the highway. Doggedly, dazedly, he plodded heavily on.

Chapter 66

"SIXTY-FIVE THOUSAND DOLLARS--CASH!"

ANELLE studied her bank balance. Not quite sixty-six thousand dollars. It had seemed a huge amount. She had felt quite safe and rich and secure. She had felt that bulwarked by that much money, she would be able to find her baby and to take excellent care of him. But now she must give up sixty-five thousand of that to guarantee his safe return. It didn't really matter —once she had him back safe in her arms, she could work for him—how joyously, how gladly she would work for him!

She wrote out her check and took it to the teller who had always handled her checks since her arrival in Hollywood.

The paying teller greeted her with a pleasant smile and a cheerful word. He took up the check, glanced at it—and then his eyes widened. He read the amount again, and then looked at Janelle.

"You want—sixty-five thousand dollars—in cash, Mrs. Elliott?" he demanded as though he could not believe his eyes.

"Yes!" said Janelle quietly. "I must have it!"

"But—surely, on a check of this size, you can give us a few days——" began the teller, before he realized that a little line of people, half a dozen or more, standing in line to deposit at the next window, were listening avidly, and then he stopped.

"Just a moment, please!" he told Janelle, cold-ly, and she saw him go out of the cage.

A middle-aged man in the line at the next window, came over to Janelle.

"You'll excuse me, lady—but did I hear the teller say you wanted sixty-five thousand dollars in cash?" he asked so earnestly that Janelle answered him with no thought that he was being impertinent.

"And he don't want to do it?" asked the man.

"He thinks I should have given notice of my intention to withdraw that amount—and I haven't time to wait. It's a matter of life or death! I've simply got to have the money!" explained Janelle.

The middle-aged man was frowning.

"Sure you have—besides, it's your money and in an open checking account—they've got no right to ask you for notice, to give them time to gather up the money. They've got no right to put the money where they have to have time to gather it up!" he mused, and Janelle realized that he was talking as much to himself as to her.

He had a bank-book in his hand, and there was a thick sheaf of bills and checks in it ready for deposit. The deposit slip was fastened on top and Janelle saw the amount at the bottom of the slip—nearly five thousand dollars.

Suddenly the man seemed to reach a decision, and he slipped the bank-book with its money carefully into an inside pocket.

"Thanks, lady, you've given me an idea!" he said swiftly, and Janelle saw him turn to one of the glass desks in the center of the bank, where he drew a blank check towards him, figured for a moment, and then wrote out a check which he took to the paying teller beside the window where Janelle stood.

"Good morning, Mr. Briggs!" said the teller briskly. "Sorry to have kept you waiting!"

"That's all right, young man—just cash this check for me and I'll be on my way!" said Mr. Briggs ominously.

The teller looked startled.

"But I thought you were depositing, not withdrawing, Mr. Briggs!" he protested, and then he read the check, and his eyes widened at the amount of it. "Forty thousand dollars, Mr. Briggs! In cash?"

Mr. Briggs was annoyed.

"How did you think I wanted it—in cigarette coupons? Of course I want it in cash—and now! Get me?" he took no trouble to lower his voice, and others engaged in various businesses in the bank turned to look at him.

It's queer how whispers of panic speed through such groups. Five minutes before they had been depositing sizable amounts, cashing checks, paying loans, renewing notes, opening accounts—all brisk and business-like and matter-of-fact. And then Janelle had laid before the paying teller a check for sixty-five thousand dollars, and his startled comment had reached the ears of Briggs. And now, Briggs, purple in the face, was demanding that his entire balance be returned to him in cash and at once.

And panic stalked, grim and silent and rather terrible, through the bank. A widow whose balance was thirteen hundred dollars thought with terror of the plight of three little children if that was wiped out; a wife whose husband was out of town, remembered their joint account of several thousand dollars and was in a panic; a business man remembered that the entire cash of his firm was in this bank, and that the loss of that capital meant the loss of his firm; a man who had all but starved himself and his family to save enough money to pay a mortgage due next week on his home, felt the palms of his hands grow clammy at the thought of having that money swept away. A retired business man from the east with an invalid wife dependent upon him, felt his heart quiver a little at the thought of what it would mean to himself and that wife, to have this bank fail with everything he had in the world of material wealth in it. A stenographer, here to deposit several thousand for her employers, stuffed the money into her bag and sped to a telephone to spread the alarm.

To see a group of people, sane, every-day, matter-of-fact, swept by the panic of money-fear is a strange and unlovely thing. The fear of the silent thing that creeps closer and closer and that nothing one may do, can fight off, is a thing of horror.

Janelle had innocently tried to withdraw the money that would mean her baby's life and safety. And by so doing she had precipitated a bank run!

The bank manager, sensing the sweep of fear that swayed the group in the bank, as a strong Northwest wind sweeps a field of ripened grain, hurried to the window where Janelle stood and spoke swiftly to the man who faced Mr. Briggs.

"By all means, give Mr. Briggs his money— and when he brings it back tomorrow morning, refuse to accept it!" said the bank manager acridly.

"Don't you worry, buddy—I won't be back here any more!" snarled Briggs, and clutched the money passed out to him.

"And I am sorry, Mrs. Elliott, that you have permitted yourself to listen to any silly rumors about the safety of the bank—your money is quite safe, and we are only too glad to return it to you!" snapped the bank manager to Janelle as he counted the money out to her as rapidly as possible.

Janelle looked at him, puzzled.

"I have no doubt of the safety of the bank! It's merely that I have to have sixty-five thousand dollars in cash by midnight tonight—and this is the only way I can get it. After all, the money is mine! I have a right to it, haven't I?" she demanded.

"Of course you have—and we are delighted to give it to you!" snapped the bank manager.

By now there were lines of people at every paying teller's window, presenting checks for their entire balances. Officers of the bank went about among them, trying to reason, to explain, to argue them into more rational behavior. But the money-panic was upon them, and not until they had their hands upon the money they demanded, were they willing to listen to anything.

The panic spread. As by some mysterious grape-vine telegraph the rumors spread over town, and more and more people poured into the bank. When Janelle with her sixty-five thousand dollars tucked safely in her bag, walked out of the bank, a special cordon of police were trying to keep order, to keep people moving, to prevent their clogging the sidewalks and hindering traffic.

Within an hour the bank officers had to throw up their hands and admitted their defeat. They had lacked sufficient ready cash to meet the incessant demands upon them. To the angry roaring of a frantic mob the doors were closed, the people still in the bank hustled out to join the roaring, fighting, angry mob outside—and those who had not been able to withdraw their money knew themselves as ruined.

The bank was not slow to place the blame where it was due—in their own thoughts, anyway. The evening papers carried a statement from the president of the bank in which he stated quite frankly, that the run had been started by a depositor of the bank who had grown panicy, having no doubt listened to wild rumors, and who had made such a heavy withdrawal that there had been a few minutes delay bringing that amount up from the reserve vaults. This delay had given rise to a silly report that the bank was insolvent, and had resulted in a frantic run, which, assured the bank president, not one bank in a hundred would have been prepared to resist.

"I unhesitatingly lay the blame for the run and the resultant closing of the bank at the door on this woman!" the president finished his statement. "We are having a conference of officials tonight, and it is highly possible that a warrant for the arrest of this woman on a charge of inciting the disastrous run, will be issued!"

Although the statement did not give the woman's name, gossip did and before the day was over, Janelle's name was cursed in the studios of the majority of Hollywood's residents who had been "caught" in the bank's closing.

This gossip reached Maxie's ears, and Maxie sat. for a long moment deep in thought, chewing savagely on a long, thick, black cigar that he hadn't remembered to light. At last he sent for Janelle, and

"I'm not afraid of you," blazed Janelle, making no effort to lower her voice. "I've played fair with you — I've obeyed orders — I've kept quiet when I could have gone to the police and have had their help in capturing you and your whole rotten baby-stealing crowd!"

(See Page 614 in No. 20)

when she came, looking tired and worried, despite her make-up, he asked her to sit down.

"What's all this I hear about you starting a bank-run and closing a bank?" he demanded gruffly. "That kinda publicity won't do you no good, remember!"

Janelle made a little, weary gesture.

"I've been trying to explain to people all afternoon that I didn't doubt the bank—that I never dreamed there would be a run—merely because I had to have sixty-five thousand dollars in cash, today!" she told him wearily. "I didn't dream——"

Maxie was studying her alertly.

"So—you had to have sixty-five thousand dollars in cash—today?" he repeated. "What for?"

"I can't tell you—or anybody else—I'm sorry!" said Janelle.

"And that, of course," said Maxie quietly, "means that you are in touch with the kidnappers of your baby!"

Janelle caught her breath, and all but cried out as she stared at him, wide-eyed, her breath catching in her throat.

"How—how—did you know?" she whispered faintly, one hand at her throat.

"Then I was right!" he said in satisfaction. "I knew that the only thing in the world you'd be likely to need that much money for would be ransom for your baby!"

Janelle was trembling. She leaned toward him, her hands touching the desk, clenched in an attitude almost of prayer.

"You—you won't say anything—about it?" she pleaded. "They warned me that if I said one single word—to any living soul—they would not bring back the baby! You—you won't—betray me?"

Maxie made a little gesture with the thick, pudgy ringed hand that held the cigar.

"Sure—sure—I won't say a word—not a word! it's a little secret between us!" he soothed her graciously. "Besides, you didn't say anything, I just guessed!"

He was staring at her sharply.

"But, see here—how are you going to get this money to the kidnappers? If anybody suspected that you had that much money, your life wouldn't be worth a plugged nickel!" he warned her.

Janelle indicated a package in her lap. A square box, wrapped in the gray paper used by one of Los Angeles' smartest shops. It looked like a package containing a new gown, or some lingerie—a common-place, unexciting looking package.

"I've had it with me all afternoon on the set. My maid holds it in plain sight of me while I am on the set—and I shall continue to carry it with me until I hand it over to—the right person tonight!" she explained.

"O.K.—but you want to be mighty careful! Lugging around that much money is mighty dangerous business , you know!" he warned her, and then, a trifle awkwardly, he offered another warning. "There's something else! It's out around town that you are the woman that Jordan, the bank official meant in his statement this afternoon. There are plenty of folks who were wiped out in the bank crash that might—hate you enough to offer you physical violence—so be mighty careful what you do, and where you go, until all this blows over!"

"You may be sure I shall!" she told him frankly. "The minute I get my baby back, I'm leaving

California to find Sherman!"

She rose, and with another word or two left the office.

Maxie sat for a long moment, the still unlighted cigar clenched between his teeth, while with his nails he drummed a light tattoo on his desk.

Slowly a satisfied grin spread over his florid, round face, and his eyes twinkled a little.

"Maxie, my boy," he told himself, grinning, "you are one smart boy. Yes—you are."

*   *   *   *   *   *   *   *   *

In her dressing-room-bungalow, Gladda Romaine was listening with frank dissatisfaction to the report of a press agent so expensive, and so successful that he disdained the old-fashioned word and insisted on being labelled as "a public relations counsel."

"I know all that!" Gladda cut in, frowning. "But, after all, wrecking a bank to make a movie star disliked by her public, is going a bit strong, don't you think? And what good is it going to do me, that everybody in Los Angeles is on this little up-start's neck? That's not helping me any!"

The "public relations counsel" grinned at her unperturbed.

"But when I promise you that after tonight she will no longer be in this studio—or even in this state—doesn't that make you a little happier?" he demanded.

"Your promise doesn't—but if I come to the studio tomorrow, and a lot of other tomorrows, and she's not here—then I'll even. O.K. that florists' charge of twenty-five dollars for the green orchid plant!" she told him firmly.

*   *   *   *   *   *   *   *   *

Beside a small camp-fire near the railroad, a group of five hobos sat companionably, enjoying the spoils of the day's raid of begging, stealing, and "acquiring." Coffee simmered in a tin can; a chicken roasted delectably over an improvised spit; there were boiled eggs, too, and fruit. There was even a loaf of fresh home-baked bread that one of the vagrants had wheedled from a kind-hearted house-wife. Small wonder that the five were so content as they waited, sniffing the air hungrily, for the chicken to be done.

At a sudden sound from the surrounding shadows, all five men whirled like animals at bay, staring towards the little path that led down from the railroad as two men emerged into the light cast by the camp-fire.

"Hold everything, boys—it's me—the Georgia Cracker!" said the leader of the two new-comers, introducing himself. The five about the fire relaxed at the recognition of one of their own. "And this here is a new pal o'mine I picked up down the road apiece. He's O. K. boys—name's Jersey John! John, meet the boys — Dago Charlie, Broadway Bud, Louisville Lou, Cincy Red and Noisy Pete!"

Jersey John, tall, rather thin, his face burned brown and half-hidden behind a thick scrubble of dark beard, came forward and the men scrutinized him in the darkness as they peered up at him, the scarlet flames of the campfire flickering over the strange scene.

"Just to prove that Jersey an' me ain't hornin'

in on the eats, we got somethin' to share with the gang!" the Georgia Cracker chuckled as he drew out a quart bottle of innocent-looking white liquor. "An' Jersey copped some smokes in the last town!"

The bottle was hailed with delight and passed about from thirsty mouth to thirsty mouth, while the packages of cigarettes were divided equally. By now the chicken was done, and still hot, was torn in pieces and divided among the men.

They ate, drank, laughed, joked—and Jersey John, sitting a little to one side as became a new member of the group still on probation, looked about him, bewildered, trying to think back through the fog of his tired, clouded mind, to retrace the steps by which he had reached this place in company with these men. To a time when he had not been Jersey John, a hobo, a vagrant, bumming his way on freight-trains, now that he was too shabby and too rough-looking to hitch-hike. Stealing food where he could not beg it. Working where he was given the chance to work. Fighting his way as best he could toward a place that was just a name—California. Toward a girl who was a vision of golden hair and blue eyes, and pleading, outstretched hands—a vision in a misty white frock whose name he knew was Janelle. Beyond that his mind would not go. But there was a driving urge, a frantic need of reaching California and that girl—and he did not mind by what means he reached that goal.

So he sat here, a hobo among other hobos, eating chicken torn by not-too-clean fingers, and bread that a kind-hearted woman had baked for her own family's need, and, at last, smoking stolen cigarettes —with the thought of a misty vision always uppermost in his mind.

Chapter 67

"FEARLESS AS A MOTHER'S HEART!"

JANELLE was as tense as a violin string all evening. She dared not by any action betray the fact that she meant to drive out at midnight to a rendezvous with a criminal. She must behave as usual—she could not know where a spy might be lurking in her own household, watching—to relate to the kidnappers some way in which she had failed to obey their orders.

She tried to amuse herself with a book, but the quiet of the big house got on her nerves. And suddenly, as she sat in the living-room, she heard a faint sound in the hall. She knew the servants were at the back of the house. Was this some messenger from the kidnappers?

She got to her feet and slipped soundlessly across the floor. At the door she listened. She felt certain that something, or some one lurked in that hall—and suddenly, she jerked open the door. A man who had been creeping toward the stairs, whirled and straightened as she opened the door. To her amazement she recognized the man—Satsu, Maxie's chauffeur.

"Satsu! What in the world do you mean? What are you doing here?" she demanded, angry and startled.

"Please, Missy—I very sorry—I have—date with maid!" Satsu stammered.

"I don't believe it—and even if you had, how dare you come through the front of the house sneaking like this?" demanded Janelle outraged. "You should go to the service door and ring, and ask for her!"

"Please, Missy—the chauffeur—he no like. The maid, she like—but she afraid of chauffeur—so she say I slip through here—the chauffeur, in the garage —he no see!" stammered Satsu.

"Well, I won't have this sort of thing, Satsu! You go on home now—it's too late for Annie to keep a date tonight—and hereafter, you must make some other arrangements about seeing her. I won't have you sneaking in and out of my house, frightening me to death!" said Janelle sharply.

The Jap apologized profusely and bowed himself out.

Janelle did not for a moment believe his story about a date with the maid. She didn't want to arouse the household at this hour, ten-thirty, to find out, but she determined that in the morning she would have a talk with Annie and lay down the law about such "dates."

Suddenly, as she turned to go back into the living-room, something on the floor at the foot of the stairs caught her attention, and she went over to it. But even as she stooped to pick it up, she recoiled, afraid. For it was one of the sinister green orchids that, in her mind, would always be connected with Alexis Forgio and the kidnapping of her baby!

There could be not doubt that Satsu had dropped the green orchid. And Janelle felt quite sure that Satsu had meant to take that plant, together with a message, to her room. Somehow she felt convinced now that it had been Satsu who had placed that first green orchid on her pillow the first night she had lived in this house. She knew of his association with Forgio—it was thus that he had learned of the green orchid and its message, of course.

But—now the question was—was Satsu still connected with the kidnappers? Had Satsu somehow engineered the first contact that she had had with them? Did tonight's visit, surprised before its purpose could be accomplished, have any bearing on the trip she was about to make, carrying sixty-five thousand dollars in cash?

She could find no answers to these questions. She could only wait and wonder, and at last on the hour of twelve, slip from her house and into her waiting car. Tonight when she came back, she would have her baby with her in the car! That thought was enough to banish any fear that she might feel. Fearless as only a mother's heart can be, she settled herself in the car, the package containing the ransom money on the seat beside her. She released the brakes and let the car slide noiselessly back into the road before she set her foot on the starter and put the motor to work.

As she drove down the pretty pepper-tree shaded street, she watched for the high-powered expensive coupe that had "tailed her" on her journey last night. But she saw no trace of it, and long before she left the highway to drive down that narrow, twisted, rutted road through the lonely dark canyōn, she was convinced that she was not being followed. It added, somehow, to her eery, frightened feeling— the knowledge that she was not being followed.

She seemed utterly desolately alone in this dark shadowy place. There was neither moon nor stars. The sky was thickly overcast with stormy looking clouds, and the wind had freshened. The lights of her car cut like sharp knives through the thick darkness ahead, and she drove slowly, partly to watch for the signal, partly to ease the tortured car over the bumpy, uneven road.

Suddenly ahead of her, a little earlier than she had expected to see it, a light flashed toward her. The round white beam of a spotlight. Behind it she could see the outlines of a man's figure, shadowy and vague. She slowed and the car rolled to a stop, where the man stood holding the spot-light. The round white beam of the spotlight sprayed upon her face, and Janelle flinched a little from the eyes, unseen, that peered at her out of the gloom.

A hand came forward suddenly in the light of the spotlight. A thick, powerful looking hand in a dark glove, the fingers curled upward, greedily.

"The money?" the voice came, a hoarse, imposs-ible-to-indentify croak.

Janelle took up the bundle beside her, and put it into the hand that closed so greedily over it. The flashlight winked out, the man stepped back and she knew that she must go ahead.

She released the brakes and with her eyes on the speedometer she crawled forward, exactly two-tenths of a mile. And then she stopped.

Her nerves so taut-drawn that the dry branch

of a tree, bending low in the night wind, and dragging against the top of her car almost made her scream aloud. She waited—it seemed that hours passed, but it could have been only seconds.

And then a figure loomed up beside her out of the darkness. The figure, she could not tell whether a man or a woman, enveloped in a long, loose cape that completely disguised the figure, a wide-brimmed hat drawn well down over the face, so that only the indistinguishable glitter of eyes could be suggested, rather than seen.

She caught her breath and choked back a little cry as she saw that the muffled figure carried something in its arms—a bundle about the size of a three-year-old child. A bundle that lay quite still, making neither a movement nor a sound.

The door of the car was opened, while Janelle sat rigid at her seat, her hands clenched on the wheel, her white face straining in the darkness toward that bundle that was being laid on the seat behind her. The cloaked figure drew back.

"You are being watched—drive back to the highway before you stop or you'll be sorry!" said the sibilant whisper, and the cloaked, muffled figure was swallowed up in darkness.

Over her shoulder, toward that bundle that lay on the back seat Janelle whispered through her tears, her lips tremulous:

"My baby—oh, my darling baby!"

She turned the car, and drove as fast as she dared. As she came back past the spot where she had given up the ransom money, she saw the lights of a car that were switched out as she came abreast and she knew that she dared not slow up, or stop now to draw into arms that ached with emptiness the beloved little body that lay so strangely still on the back seat.

She drove recklessly, the car rocking from side to side, her teeth sunk deeply into her lower lip. Her eyes straining toward the lights that would show the beginning of the highway. Her heart trembling with impatience and eagerness for the delight of holding in her arms once more that small, precious body.

The car turned at last into the highway. There were lights here, and cars passing occasionally—and now she was safe. She brought the car to a halt at the side of the road, sprang out, and jerked open the back door of the car. She leaned above the bundle, and in the light of a lamp above her that marked a dangerous intersection, she drew back the coverings above that bundle—and at what she saw there her heart seemed to die in her breast, and a great cry tore itself jaggedly from her throat.

Continued in Next Number.

"Mr. Wayne—you said a while ago that Mr. Cason held up mail and telegrams addressed to me—you didn't really mean that, did you?" Janelle created a slight diversion by putting the question. Wayne looked at Maxie, and Maxie cried swiftly: "Of course, he didn't—just a joker, that Wayne!" (See Page 628)

Chapter 68.

A CRUEL HOAX!

IN THE garish yellow light of a street lamp above her, Janelle stood at the open door of the car and gazed wide-eyed, incredulous, at the bundle of rags and paper that had been so carefully wrapped in a baby blanket, and laid in the back of her car under the pretense of the kidnappers returning her child. She had tossed to the kidnappers a bundle containing sixty-five thousand dollars in cash—and they had placed in her car this bundle, which from her place behind the wheel, she had felt so sure was her stolen baby. Obeying the kidnappers' orders that she not stop to see her child until she had driven from the lonely canyon back to the highway. And now, with her heart beating like a trip-hammer, her arms that had ached with emptiness had reached out to cradle the small, beloved body of her stolen baby—and had found— only a grim, ugly huddle of old newspapers and rags, cunningly wrapped so as to carry an amazinly life-like resemblance to the child it imitated.

She had been tricked! It had all been a cruel hoax! She had drawn out of the bank almost every penny she owned in the world—and she had given it to these mysterious, hidden creatures of the darkness —these skulking beasts of prey who were utterly dead to every human instinct—these things of darkness who played with a tremulous, aching heart as carelessly, as coolly, as though it had been a wooden counter in a game of checkers.

The reaction from the sharp delight of thinking that she had recovered her child to the bitterness of the discovery that she had been duped, made her so giddy, so sick that she could scarcely stand. She clung to the side of the car, her head bowed, fighting with every ounce of strength she possessed to down the deadly nausea that swept over her.

And then, suddenly, a seething rage swept over her. An anger so sharp, so savage that it wiped out all fear of the friends who had tricked her They had dared to play with her like this! She had played fair with them. She had allowed herself to be victimized—to be robbed—to be the butt of their cruel and inhuman joke! Well—she wouldn't take it laying down! She'd fight them! She'd show them that a mother, robbed of her child, betrayed, and derided, could fight like a wild thing!

Too hysterical, too excited, too furious to be scarcely conscious of what she was doing, she leaped into her car, whirled it about, narrowly escaping a car that careened to one side to avoid being struck, and headed once more toward the lonely canyon. Of course, it was absurd—it was ridiculous to think that the fiends were still there. That they had waited tamely for her to come back after discovering that she had been duped. They were miles away by this time—common sense told her that. Still, she was too angry, too upset to be able to reason coherently. She was intent on only one thing—the absolute necessity of fighting back at these people who had so cruelly, so maliciously hoaxed her.

This time she did not drive carefully. She drove as rapidly as she dared, the car rocking along, swaying from side to side, jarring against rocks and ruts in the road.

She came to the spot in the road where the man had stepped out with the flashlight and had held out his gloved hand for the money. She paused, and turned the powerful rays of her spotlight on the woods. The spotlight, attached to the side of the car, swung around, its powerful white beams revealing to her in daylight-like clarity the deserted woods. She drove on, watching her speedometer until it had registered two-tenths of a mile, and there, once more, she paused and swung the spotlight about.

The woods stretched away, deserted, not a sound broke their stillness. She switched off the motor of her car and swung open the door. She stood on the running board, drawn to her full heighth, slender and valiant, womanhood defiant at bay.

Now that the motor of her car was silent, the vast, lonely stillness of deserted places fell upon her. Oppressive, still breathless—as though back there, behind the reach of her light, a great evil beast crouched, waiting, watching with evil, lidless eyes. Watching to pounce upon her—and it was to that watching, silent, evil beast that suddenly she flung the defiance of her angry, hysterical speech.

"I can't see you—but I know you are there!" she shrieked the words aloud, defiant, too hysterical and angry and sick with disappointment to be con-

scious of any feeling of fear. "You've tricked me—
you've robbed me again and again—but you shan't do
it any more. I'm not afraid of you—I'll fight you—
I'll hunt you to your to your holes, like the vermin
you are! I'll never stop until every lay-abiding citi-
zen in this whole world joins me in a search to stamp
out all of you and your loathsome breed! I'll avenge
my baby—and all the other babies you and your rotten, filthy crew has touched! I'll never stop until
there won't be a corner in the world where you can
hide! Do you hear me out there in your den, you
beast? From now on it's war between us—a war
that will never stop as long as one single, crawling
member of your tribe lives!"

Her voice was broken with sobs, but there
was so much scorn and anger and outraged mother-
hood in its tones, that it rang like a clarion call
through the dark, lonely, deserted woods. The echo
came back to her hollowly—and suddenly, from the
other side of the car, in the darkness, a voice spoke,
sharply, a whispering, sibilant voice that she had
heard once before.

"Be quiet, you fool!" it said. "Have you lost
your mind?"

She whirled, but before she could spin the
spotlight about to play it upon that unseen speaker,
a hand closed hard over her wrist, and the light
smashed to pieces beneath the butt of a gun. The
darkness swooped like black wings above them, shut-
ting them into a little cell of darkness.

"I'm not afraid of you!" blazed Janelle, making no effort to lower her voice. "I've played fair
with you—I've obeyed orders—I've kept quiet when
I could have gone to the police and have had their
help in capturing you and your whole rotten, baby-

stealing crowd! But because I wanted my baby more than anything else in the world, and because no amount of money that I could lay my hands on was too much to give you, to get him back, I strung along with you! And then you take the ransom money, and trick me! It's war from now on, I tell you—war——"

"Shut up!" snarled the man, and in his excitement, he forgot to be quite so careful about keeping his voice to that sibilant whisper. "What are you saying—you gave the ransom money to somebody?"

"I gave it to you—I followed your instructions to the letter——" began Janelle hotly, but again the man cut in sharply.

"This is the first time tonight that I have approached you, or spoken to you! You've given me nothing. Now, let's have the story. What do you mean by saying you gave me the money?"

In spite of herself, Janelle was forced to believe that the man was quite honest in his amazement. A little feeling of disquiet swept over her. She forced herself to a semblance of calmness.

"I obeyed your orders implicitly!" she told the man. "I drove into the canyon road—a man stepped into the road and signalled me to halt. He asked for the money, and held out a gloved hand. It was what you had told me would happen, so I gave him the money and drove two-tenths of a mile down the road, when another man stepped out of the shadows, with a bundle in his arms that looked like a sleeping baby. He put the bundle into the back of the car and ordered me to drive on. At the intersection of the canyon road and the highway where there is a street lamp, I stopped, and examined the bundle. It was made up of rags and newspapers, done up to look like a sleeping child, all bundled up!"

The man beside her swore savagely.

"That's Far-away Thomas and his crowd—the blankety—blank—blank hi-jackers! They found out about this tonight—and 'muscled'! They stopped you a full mile below where you were supposed to stop—and they got the money and got away! The low-down crooks!" he snarled.

Janelle was staring at him uncertainly, and now that her eyes had become accustomed to the darkness, she caught the glimmer of a white face between the up-turned collar of his coat and the down-turned brim of his hat.

"You are trying to tell me that it wasn't your own crowd who got the ransom money? Is this another trick? It won't do you any good—I'm going straight to the police and tell them everything that has happened and see that you are hunted down! Like the scum that you are!" she cried passionately.

Eyes that glittered in the darkness like the eyes of an animal and he said very softly, a sibilance in his whisper that made her think of the hissing of a deadly reptile coiled to strike:

"I'd—hate to see you do that! He's—a nice little fellow—it would be a shame!"

Janelle caught her breath before the menace in his voice. It laid like a cold hand on the fever of her anger and shock and pain. She stared through the darkness at the pallid oval, lit with glittering eyes, that was all she had ever seen of the face of the man who was her only contact with the kidnappers.

"You—you—mean that—that——" she stammered, and her breath died in her throat.

"I mean that if you go to the police, you sign the death-warrant of your child!" said the man quietly. "Once the police start looking for us—your child is a deadly danger to us! Alive, he is a rope around our necks—dead and—put away, he offers us no danger whatever!"

Janelle uttered a little sharp moan of agony.

"Oh, please—won't you give him back to me? He's so little, so helpless—he's all that I've got left in the world. Give him back to me, and I swear that I'll never appear against you, never make the faintest effort to cause you any trouble. Give him back to me, and you need never have the faintest fear of the police——" she pleaded hopeless yet frantic with the need to make some appeal to this man who had it in his power to give her the thing she wanted most in the world.

"Sorry—that's out of the question!" the man's answer came shortly, as though her plea disturbed him and he were unwilling to be disturbed. "I don't say that I might not listen to you—if it were up to me alone. But—there are others in this with me—people who have taken as many chances as I have—people who feel they are entitled to the money we expected to get. Sixty-five thousand dollars divided among the crowd would have satisfied everybody, and the child would be back in your arms by now. But that blankety—blank Thomas crowd——" he cursed softly, savagely beneath his breath.

Janelle made a little swift gesture of utter hopelessness and weariness.

"But—what am I going to do now? That's all the money I have—I get three hundred a week salary at the studio—but that will be over in two or three more weeks—and I'll have no place else to turn for money! Surely, surely—you don't mean to keep my baby—FOREVER?" she pleaded.

"No!" said the man quietly—so quietly that, for a full moment the ominousness, the dread significance of his words did not penetrate her understanding. "The fellows are getting restless already!"

Janelle's shaking hand went to her throat as though to remove the clutch of an iron band that held her there, threatening her speech.

"You—you—don't mean——" she stammered.

"I mean that—unless we can cash in on the boy pretty soon—it'll be hard to keep the boys in hand!" said the man in the shadows grimly. "You'd better get back to town—I'll get the gang and see what can be done about Far-away and his crowd. I'll —let you hear from me in a day or two!"

And despite her little frantic cry of protest, he turned and melted into the shadows before she could find anything to say that would stop him. She sat there alone in the dark for a little while, feeling utterly exhausted mentally and physically, before at last she set the car once more in motion.

She reached the house without further event, and leaving the car in the drive, she crept wearily up to her own room. It was very late—rather, very early in the morning, too late to think of going to bed, and so she merely sat down on the chaise-longue and hid her face in her hands, completely exhausted, mentally and physically.

She had felt so sure that she would be able to bring back her baby—instead she had come back empty-handed. Robbed of her fortune, and with nothing to show for it but a bundle of newspapers and rags. She wept at the thought—wept with disappointment, wept until she could weep no more, and at last lay asleep, her face hidden against the chintz-covered pillow of the chaise-longue.

Chapter 69.

THE ARM OF THE LAW.

HE SLEPT late and arrived at the studio, late for the first time since she had begun to work there. Wayne, watch in hand, was passing her dressing-room door when she emerged, ready for work and his angry frown faded as he caught the look in her eyes and on her face.

"Is this a nice thing to do to a friend, Janelle? Holding up work while the over-head mounts and Maxie's temperature keeps pace with it?" he demanded, and then, seeing her face he added in concern, "Why, child, what's the matter? You look as though you had seen a ghost!"

"I'm—not sure whether I ought to tell you—something HAS happened, but I'm not supposed to say anything—I'll think about it and maybe tonight I'll tell you and Mr. Cason!" said Janelle wearily, and with that Wayne was forced to be content.

As they walked together toward the set, Wayne was frowning a little. He had no way of knowing what had happened—but he felt pretty sure that whatever it was affected either Janelle's sweetheart or Janelle's baby. And he wondered darkly, if Maxie could have had anything to do with it. He quite frankly didn't trust Maxie, and he didn't care who knew it.

Jim Marvin and the others were waiting on the set, and Jim looked concerned at the look in Janelle's eyes. But there was no time to question her, as Wayne went rapidly to work, anxious to make up for the hour that had been lost through Janelle's tardiness.

Throughout the day as she went through her scenes and spoke her lines, Janelle's thoughts were busy. She had three friends in Hollywood—three men who could help her. Men who would help her if they could. Men of influence like Maxie Cason and Hobart Wayne, her director. Men of youth and imagination like Jim Marvin. Such men would be able to help her a lot—she need only to call on them. She had fought alone for so long—she had obeyed the kidnappers' demands for secrecy—and she had been robbed. Now she lacked the means for paying the ransom even if she were sure that to pay it would bring back her baby. She had stood alone, fought alone—until she was weary unto death. She must have help—friends who would come to her rescue.

And so, in the late afternoon when Maxie stopped to watch a scene, and Wayne, Jim and Janelle were for a moment together, Janelle faced the three men, her hands extended in a little, pleading, eloquent gesture that embraced them all.

"Something has happened!" she told them quietly, her voice restrained through the shadows of tears still lurked in her eyes. "Something that convinces me I can't go on fighting alone. You've all said you would help me if I asked it—and now—I DO ask it!"

Wayne shot a swift glance at Maxie and wondered suspiciously if his startled look was one of guilt. But the three men spoke almost at once.

"Of course, Janelle!"

"Then have dinner with me tonight, and I'll tell you—what has happened!" said Janelle, determined now to finish the job and to have done with carrying her load of secret turmoil. "And—Mr. Cason, will you see to it that your chauffeur, Satsu—is somewhere where some one you trust implicitly can keep an eye on him? I want to be—quite sure that he is nowhere near my house! I'll tell you why tonight!"

Wayne was quite sure now that Maxie looked faintly guilty, but he spoke up with well-simulated surprise.

"Why, what do you mean? Surely Satsu isn't implicated in this mysterious thing that has happened?"

"I'm not sure—but last night, I discovered Satsu creeping through my house. He claimed to be keeping a date with the maid—but—well, I'd like him to be somewhere tonight where we could be sure just what he is doing!" said Janelle frankly.

Wayne spoke promptly.

"You don't trust your house-servants, Janelle?"

Janelle made a little weary gesture, and raised piteous eyes to him.

"I don't trust ANYBODY any more—except you three!" she confessed frankly—and Wayne thought Maxie had the grace to look faintly ashamed.

"Then—why not have dinner at my place?" suggested Wayne. "The walls of my living-room are sound-proof—I'll give my servant the evening off and have dinner sent in from the restaurant in the building, and we'll dismiss the waiter before anything but the weather is discussed. That way we ought to be perfectly sure of being rid of spies!"

And so it was settled. Maxie's car, with Satsu at the wheel, was waiting when the four of them left the studio, but at an expressive glance from Wayne, Maxie dismissed his car and the four of them climbed into Janelle's car, parked in the enclosure reserved for stars and executives of the lot.

Wayne's apartment was on the fourth floor of a handsome white stucco apartment house in Beverly Hills. Janelle parked the car, and with the three men entered the building, and a few minutes later found them in the living-room whose walls, Wayne proudly assured them, were sound-proof.

While Wayne mixed a shaker of cocktails, Janelle told them what had happened the night before, and the three men listened, intent and a little startled at the daring of this slim, young girl who had gone alone two nights in succession to a wild, lonely spot, unarmed, to face emissaries of a dangerous band of criminals.

She told them of the "hi-jacking" last night which had resulted in the loss of every penny she had in the world, with the exception of her weekly salary. She told them of going back, mad with rage and disappointment and hurling her defiance into the woods where she felt sure the kidnappers lurked. Also of the sudden appearance of the man with the whispering voice, who told her that she had been robbed by "hi-jackers" and who had warned her of the danger unless she could pay another ransom.

When she had finished, the three men who had listened to her story stared from one to another in amazement, and back at the slender, pale girl who told this amazing story so calmly.

Wayne suddenly thumped his fist on the table beside him.

"This thing has gone far enough!" he snapped sharply. "We've dilly-dallied along here, and this girl has been tortured and played with by as black-hearted a crew of pirates as ever sailed the Spanish Main! And I claim it's about time we called in the law and had somebody take a hand that knows how to go after these criminals! I'm going to telephone the police!"

Maxie protested swiftly.

"No, no, Wayne—remember, they told her that would mean the baby's death! You must be careful!"

Wayne whirled on him savagely.

"See here, Maxie—have you had anything to do with this?" he demanded. sharply, savagely.

Janelle cried out swiftly, reproachfully:

"Oh, Mr. Wayne—how CAN you even THINK of such an accusation?"

Wayne looked down at her, smiling grimly.

"Because I know Maxie—and because I know there's darned little he'd stop at when it came to a question of 'protecting his investment'—I happen to know that he held up mail addressed to you from the hospital in Cuba, and telegrams, too, urging you to come at once. I know that Maxie would go to great lengths to keep you here until your picture is finished——" said Wayne, but Maxie, purple with rage, was screaming wildly:

"Shut up, you fool—shut up—you're fired!"

"Shut up yourself, you double-fool—I quit!" snapped Wayne.

Jim Marvin suddenly shouted with laughter,

and the unexpectedness was like cold water on the fury of the two quarreling men.

Wayne turned on Jim, scowling.

"You impertinent young pup!" he snapped.

"Keep your shirt on, Old Man!" counselled Jim, grinning. "You were like a very bad imitation of Weber and Fields—you'd have laughed if you had seen yourselves!"

Wayne and Maxie looked at each other, a trifle sheepishly, and then Jim said swiftly.

"Maybe I'm wrong—but it was my impression that we came here to see what we could do to help Janelle—not to quarrel among ourselves!"

Wayne grunted, and Maxie sighed slightly.

"Maybe you're right—anyway, here's dinner, and we'll try to behave like sane people while we eat it!" suggested Wayne, and for the next hour while the waiter was in the room serving the meal they were careful to talk only of surface things.

By the time the meal was over and the waiter had gone, Maxie and Wayne had forgotten their differences, and after sober reflection they were able to discuss the situation quietly and peacefully. It was finally decided that a detective should be called in and the whole story laid down to him.

Wayne had a man in mind, and by rare good luck managed to find the man at home, and willing to take on a case. He promised to come over at once, and while they waited for him, Wayne thought of something.

"Janelle, you said at the studio that Satsu, Maxie's chauffeur was in your house last night—any idea what he was doing there?"

She shook her head.

"He said he had a date with the maid—and

"Of Atlanta, Georgia?" "Of course — Sherman Lawrence, of Atlanta!"
The three men exchanged swift glances, and then the police
chief turned back to Sherman. "Are you prepared to swear to that?" he demanded.

(See Page 644 in No. 21)

that he tried to sneak through the front of the house, so that my chauffeur and yard-man, Robert, would not know of his call!" she explained. "I thought the explanation too glib to be true, so I ordered him out. After he had gone—I found—a green orchid on the floor where he had dropped it!"

Wayne looked startled and a little puzzled.

"A green orchid?" he repeated, puzzled. "What in the world was Satsu doing with a green orchid?"

"What puzzles me is—where did he get it?" said Janelle in answer. "I know that they are quite expensive—the plants, I mean. I once owned one of them—I loathed it! It's like some hideous form of living evil—it must be fed, you know—chopped meat, if it is in a place where it can't catch flies and other insects for itself—Alexis Forgio gave me the plant, and the night my baby was kidnapped, I found a green orchid blossom on my baby's pillow! To me the green orchid has always been—a symbol of evil. The night I moved into this house—I found a green orchid on my pillow with a note supposedly from the kidnappers! The night that I got the first message to meet the kidnapper—the note came enclosed in a square box that held a green orchid. So— you see why I hate the things!"

"And Satsu dropped one in your house last night? Just as you were leaving to keep the appointment with the kidnappers? That's darned funny!" said Wayne, bewildered. "Could it be possible that Satsu is in cahoots with the kidnappers?"

"Ridiculous!" snapped Maxie, who was perspiring a little.

Wayne looked at him shrewdly.

"Well, a plant as rare and expensive as a green orchid shouldn't be easy to buy—no doubt, if we can find out what florist handled one recently, we can find out who bought it and that ought to give us a clue!" said Wayne.

Maxie mopped his forehead with a spotlessly clean handkerchief and avoided Wayne's eyes.

"I don't believe Satsu's having the green orchid meant a thing—except that he was trying to make a hit with his girl friend, the maid!" he said unexpectedly. "You see, I happen to own a green orchid plant—myself!"

There was a little moment of surprise and amazement. The other three stared at him, wide-eyed.

"Since when have you owned a green orchid plant, Maxie?" demanded Wayne suspiciously.

Maxie waved his hand airily.

"Oh—not so long. I got interested in 'em—queer little devils—and when I found out that there was one in town, I bought it—that's all!" he answered carelessly. "I suppose Satsu thought he'd make a hit with his girl friend, so he swiped one of the flowers. I'll deduct it from his salary this week, believe me!"

Wayne grunted. "I DO believe you, Maxie—about 'docking' Satsu, even if not about the reason you bought the green orchid!"

Maxie drew himself up haughtily.

"Are you insinuating——" he began grandly, but Wayne interrupted him baldly.

"I'm saying quite frankly that I suspect you of some kind of a plot to keep Janelle in town until she has finished that dratted 'Legacy of Love'—and whether you'd go far enough to trick her out of her estate, or anything like that, I'm not quite sure just yet!"

"Mr. Wayne—you said a while ago that **Mr.** Cason held up mail and telegrams addressed to me— you didn't really mean that, did you?"Janelle **created** a slight diversion by putting the question.

Wayne looked at Maxie, and Maxie **cried** swiftly:

"Of course, he didn't—just a joker, that Wayne!"

"But Nurse Judkins wired me that she **had** written and telegraphed saying that Sherman **needed** me—and I never got the wires!" puzzled Janelle.

"Janelle, you must know the truth as far **as I** can find it for you—Maxie has held up mail and tele- grams addressed to you. I don't know what else **he** has done——" began Wayne, but Janelle turned **on** Maxie swiftly in outrage.

"That was a despicable trick, Mr. Cason—to try to keep me from the man I love when he needed me. If I had gotten the wire, I'd have gone to Cuba —I might have spared him all this horror—but be- cause you held the wires, I didn't—oh, I hate you for that! I hate you! I'd never work another day for you—never!" she cried swiftly, passionately.

"Am I to blame if out of the thousands of let- ters that reach my studio every day, and the hun- dreds of telegrams, one of them is lost? I ask you!" Maxie protested weakly.

Janelle turned away, unwilling even to listen to him.

There was a ring at the door, and Wayne ush- ered in a stout middle-aged man with the round, cher- ubic face of an innocent child. He was bald-headed, ruddy faced, his eyes blue and guileless. He was dressed in a neat gray suit that his stout body had rendered shapeless, and any one looking less like the average conception of an extremely shrewd detective it would be hard to imagine.

"Janelle, this is Detective Henry O'Hearn—if he can't get to the bottom of this mess for you, then it's hopeless! Hank, this is Mrs. Elliott, who wants you to help her find her lost baby!" Wayne performed the introductions briefly.

Janelle's hand was swallowed up by Hank O'Hearn's pudgy hand, and his blue eyes studied her as he smiled almost bashfully.

"Sure, 'twill be a pleasure to help the likes of this little lady, Hobart, me boy!" said Detective O'Hearn, and acknowledged the introduction to the two men.

"And now, suppose we have the whole story right from the beginning!" suggested Hank O'Hearn, when they were all comfortably seated, and Wayne had poured fresh cups of coffee for everybody.

Chapter 70.

IN THE "JUNGLE."

IT WAS twilight, and beneath the high railroad trestle well out of sight of passing trains, four "knights of the road" clustered about a tiny campfire on which boiled a tin can of coffee. Spread on a clean newspaper near at hand was the food that the four had managed to acquire by begging or stealing during the day. But the four hobos in their "jungle" were intent on something besides food. They were listening to a little, ratty-looking man who occupied a seat in the center of the little group, and who was gesturing busily with not-too-clean hands.

"I tell ye, it's a set-up!" he assured them volubly. "The bank is a one-story building. By having somebody keep an eye on the night-watchman, we can heave a brick through the window and get in without a soul hearing us. Sure—I know what I'm talkin' about. The express goes through at midnight. It blows a signal for the crossing—and it blows loud enough to deaden the noise of breaking the window—specially when there ain't nobody sleeps close to the bank. It's in the 'business block' and one of us can take care o' the night-watchman. And once we're in the bank—the safe is a cheese-box— heck, I can open it on-two-three, just like that! An' there's a cool twenty-five grand in there—ours for the takin'. Not a bit of danger—just walk in, help ourselves, and walk out—and we'll be so far away by the time the hicks find out they been robbed—why, say, they won't even get a glimpse or a smell of us! It's a push-over, I'm tellin' you—a push-over!"

"Sounds good to me!" said one of the men. "Boy, twenty-five grand split four ways ain't hard to take—not a bit!"

"Oke with you, Cracker?" demanded the little ratty-faced man, facing the man who was sort of self-proclaimed leader of the little "mob."

"Sure—it's oke with me, Skeeter!" agreed the Cracker, and turned to Jersey John, who had nothing to say. "How 'bout you, Jersey?"

The man called Jersey John started a little, and faced the three men.

"I'm sorry—I'm afraid I wasn't listening!" he apologized quite honestly.

Skeeter looked startled and a little resentful.

"He wasn't listen'? Say, is this bloke on the level?" he demanded under his breath.

"Sure—he's a pal o' the Cracker's—kind of balmy! Goofy! But he's O. K. Got an awful yen to get to California—some dame out there he's nuts about!" explained the other man while the Cracker talked to Jersey, explaining the plan.

Despite the twisted kink in his brain, that had closed down upon all his past, and that left him blundering along, lost, shrouded in an impenetrable fog, Jersey found himself turning away from the plan that the Cracker proposed. He had stolen before—that had been one of the first things the Cracker had taught him. That the world owed him a living and it was up to him to collect it! By fair means or foul! The whole world, argued Cracker, was against a hobo—a bum—therefore the hobo's hand must be against the whole world. That was only logic. A fellow owned just what he could take—and if he couldn't protect it then it belonged to some one else! That was good, sound common-sense, according to Cracker and his pals.

So now, the Cracker used all his twisted, perverted, fair-sounding arguments to convince Jersey that this plan was one that was fair and legitimate.

When Jersey proved slow to accept the plan, Cracker redoubled his arguments. It was absolutely necessary to have four men on the job—and Jersey was the one to look after the watchman.

"Lookit, Joisey—what about this dame in California that you gotta see? You'll be six months on the way, hoboin'—ridin' the rods ain't what it used to be!" he coaxed. "But with your cut on twenty-five grand—that'll give you six grand, boy—six thousand smackers! Cripes, a fellow could be a gentleman on that much coin! You can go on to Cal, looking like somebody—and most like, the dame'll be a whole lot gladder to give you a tumble if you're all dressed up—and lookit, you'd have a little money—she may need dough, too—sure, all dames need dough! Lookit how glad she'd be to see you if you had a pocketful o' coin—what's the use o' goin' out there broke when all you got to do is push a gat in a guy's ribs an' tell him to keep his trap shut for five minutes? That's more'n a thousand dollars a minute—

sure you're gonna do it—that's the boy!"

The Cracker turned, his face shining.

"Oke, boys—Joisey'll hold the gun against the watchman's gizzard while we get the dough. Come on, let's get goin'—it's quite a hike to the village, an' we gotta be there when the express whistles!" said the Cracker, and the four men hastily finishing their food, doused the tiny campfire and started.

Jersey, striding along beside the Cracker, found himself stirred by the soft beauty of the night. The long weeks of "hitting the road," walking when he had to, begging rides in trucks and wagons, riding the rods, or box-cars with the Cracker and his crowd had restored his body to its full strength, but, unfortunately, his memory was still elusive. The long, sunny days in the open had browned his face and arms, and had lent strength and power to his legs. But the hard, ugly, crude life in which he found himself had kept his brain limp and halting.

He was terribly dissatisfied with his present mode of existence. Hungrily, dazedly, he knew that there was something better somewhere. That he, himself, had known something far better. But—what was it? What had it been? His sense recoiled from the rough, coarse, grimy clothing that he wore—with a wistful shred of memory of a time when he had worn better things, clean—when he had lived decently. But always when he had reached that point in his musings, something of this new life struck him, and the ugliness, the sordidness, the shock of it bludgeoned the faint memory back to earth.

Tonight as he strode along beside the others, through fields that smelled sweetly of dewy earth, and lush, growing things—as he listened to the chirping of crickets, the hoarse croaking of frogs, he was overcome with a violent nostalgia for that old life, that lay just outside of his reach. Perhaps when he reached California and found the girl, whose name would be Janelle—probably then he might be able to make contact with that vanished past.

It was that thought, that hope that sent him now, quite ready to meet tonight's dark work. With more than six thousand dollars, he could have a bath, buy decent clothes, buy a railroad ticket that would take him straight to California and the girl, Janelle, who would be able to help him link up that all-but-forgotten past with the hope of the future.

By the time the four men reached the little village of their destination, the moon was high in the sky and the little town slept peacefully. It was a pretty little town, bordering a wide river. The road climbed the bluff from the bridge, and led the way through the business block and on past to the residential section where pretty, old-fashioned two-storied white houses set neatly back from the road behind trim picket fences.

The bank was on the corner of the street at the top of the bluff. Beside it there was a steep path leading down to the dock.

Above the bank was a doctor's office, and the rest of the two blocks was taken up by the business places—a drug-store, a feed-and-grain store, a department store, a "New York" millinery, and so on.

The bank's plate-glass front faced the river. Below it, where the railroad trestle crossed, there was a junction. When the express came roaring through, the sound of the wheels ringing loudly over the trestle, echoed by the water, the several sharp blasts of the whistle, all created a noise that would easily hide the tinkle of breaking glass.

The four men huddled in an alley back of the bank. Below them was the bluff and the fishing dock. Across the bridge on the other side there was a marsh, covered with shoulder high rank weeds and underbrush, and beyond that, a tiny island also covered with rank river growth.

In the light of the moon, high and serene, the scene was bathed in beauty. The four men who huddled in the darkness, waiting for the watchman, fidgeted a little—but Jersey John felt his soul flooding with quiet and peace and almost happiness.

Suddenly a man came around the corner of the street, tried the door of the bank and then came on toward the alley. Instantly the four men bunched themselves, and as the man reached the alley, they leaped upon him.

He had no chance to cry out. No chance to fight—he went down beneath their vicious onslaught like a man of card-board. He was utterly helpless against them. Jersey John, thrust a little to one side by the ferocity of the others, grew a little sick as he watched the fight—it could scarcely be called that, for it lasted barely a moment—and then the watchman lay still, face down.

The Cracker stood up.

"Come on, fellows—he's out like a lamp! Make it snappy, Jersey—come on, Skeeter. Here, Jersey— if he starts to wake up or moves, let him have it— if you don't, he'll plug you!" he ordered grimly. "When we come out of the bank, Jersey—take it on the lam! We'll scatter and meet at the jungle in time to get the south-bound freight at daylight!"

Jersey could find no words to answer them. His hand closed laxly about the cold, ugly butt of the automatic that the Cracker thrust into it—and then the other three were out of the alley and skulking beneath the shadow of the corrugated iron awning in front of the bank.

Jersey heard the approach of the express. He looked down at the still form that lay in the darkness at his feet. He had had the swiftest glimpse of the man as he had come toward the alley. He had had time to see in the moonlight that the man was old and heavy—his hair was gray and his face was the kind, innocent face of an old man in whose heart beats a love of humanity. This was the man whom he and his companions had attacked—for no reason save that this man was doing his duty.

Suddenly, sharp and loud and clear, he heard the blast of the great locomotive as it rounded the curve and approached the junction. He started— there was the faint sound of tinkling glass, and then the train-whistle again—around the corner from the alley where he stood, all was quiet now—the third blast of the train-whistle—and then the roaring of the train as it crossed the trestle and was gone.

The man at his feet stirred, and moaned.

Jersey John bent swiftly, raised the man's head from the ground and laid his hand on the faintly beating heart. Thank God the man still lived. His shaking hand mopped the perspiration from his own forehead as he made the discovery. The man moaned again, and his eyes opened. The moonlight filtered into the alley enough to give a faint luminosity—the moon was directly over-head and in its rays Jersey John saw the watchman's face, bloodstained—and knew that the watchman saw his.

Suddenly the old man lifted his head with unexpected strength and screamed at the top of his lungs. Jersey John, startled, dropped the injured man and sprang to his feet, his instinct for self-preservation rising above every other thought.

He heard the sound of running feet—the Cracker, Skeeter, Red, came flying down the alley.

"The flatties, Jersey—take it on the lam, boy —croak the old guy and come on!" ordered the Cracker as he passed Jersey, the others in close pursuit.

The injured man screamed again, and Red paused long enough to deal a vicious kick which sent the old man reeling backward, his head striking the stone pavement of the alley—and he was still.

Jersey John was held in a paralysis of horror. The events of the past five minutes seemed to have taken years to elapse. He had stolen—petty raids on unprotected fields and village stores. But this— this deliberate wounding of an old man—the vicious kick—had sickened him to the point of acute nausea.

He stood stupidly looking after the fleeing men —then at the old man who lay so still on the ground. And then, at the mouth of the alley down which the Cracker and his co-horts had vanished, a man appeared. He saw Jersey John standing over the injured night-watchman, and he shouted to someone behind him.

"Look out, boys—here's one of them now! Watch out for him!" he cried, his voice sharp with excitement, and Jersey John heard the bark of a rifle, and a bullet sped past him.

The instinct for self-preservation, that instinct that is the last to be lost, roused him from the stupor of horror that he felt, and he turned, running with all the strength he possessed out of the alley down the street, across to the path above the bluff. At the foot of the bluff lay the marsh with its tall, rank growth, and toward this he headed, scrambling, sliding, slipping down the bank.

Almost instantly, he was in water waist-deep. He ploughed on, conscious that the shoulder-tall grass hid him now as he moved. His heart was pounding like mad in his breast. His lungs felt as though they must burst with the effort of his breathing—and he was cold and clammy with a sick memory of that old man, lying so still and helpless back there in that dark alley.

Behind him he heard the shouts of men. Guns fired into the air. A bell ringing—obviously to arouse the little village to news of the dastardly crime that had been committed here.

Beyond the marsh was the small island. He knew that he could swim that distance. There must be dry land on the island—tiny as it was. There perhaps, he could hide for awhile. Maybe even plan some way of escape.

But as he struggled to reach water deep enough for him to swim toward that island, a sudden fearful glare leaped up behind him—and, with his heart climbing into his throat, he saw that the pursuers had fired the tall, dry marsh grasses and that in a few moments he would be surrounded by flames—roasted alive!

The marsh grasses, their tall tops dry to the edge of the water, rustling dryly in the faint night-breeze, offered a tinder-like surface to the torch. With a shout of triumph, the pursuers saw that they had trapped the criminal whom they sought.

There was no choice for Jersey John. Trapped there in the roaring flames—the wall of fire between him and the open water that would permit him to reach the island, behind him the fury-maddened

men with their guns and their dogs—to linger meant
a dreadful death—to turn and go back meant a death
almost as certain by means of a bullet—but at least
a death more swift, more merciful.

With his breath catching in his throat, his
flesh scorched by the flames, he turned and staggered out of the marsh. As he plunged out to face the
circle of men who waited tensely, his arms were
above his head in surrender—but as he plunged out
and into the open, a man flung up his gun.

"Give him a chance, Bud—he's surrendering!"
he heard a voice say in that split second, and answering voice, harsh and trembling with fury:

"Chance, hell! What chance did he give my
Dad—damn him?"

The words ended with the bark of a gun, the
spat of a bullet—and an agonizing pain tore through
Jersey John's shoulder, flinging him forward on his
face. He was plunging into a bottomless well of oblivion—the black waters lapped up and over his face
—and as he went down, there was a wild roaring in
his ears.

*   *   *   *   *   *   *   *   *

In the severely white-walled ward of a small
town hospital, a man who had lingered for several
days at the very gates of death, opened his eyes and
looked weakly about him. The place was utterly
strange to him. Though it was a hospital ward, and
there were half a dozen beds in it, his bed was the
only one occupied.

He saw that there were bars at the windows,
and only one door. High up in that door there was

a grating, across which were more stout looking bars. The place was severely clean—cheerless, ugly, and faintly odorous of a vigorous antiseptic.

He was very weak and tired—but his head was quite clear, though he had the hardest time trying to remember where he was or how he came to be here. It was really too much trouble to try to think, though, so he finally drifted off to sleep, and awoke only when the clanking of a key turning heavily in a lock foretold the opening of the door.

He watched anxiously and saw a burly looking man wearing a white linen jacket, coming into the room, carrying a tray on which was an evening meal.

The man on the bed watched him with interest, and the man in the white jacket discovered with almost equal interest that the patient was awake.

"Oh—so you've waked up, eh?" he grunted. "Ready to talk? There's plenty o' folks anxious to listen!"

The patient looked puzzled.

"Ready to talk? About what?" he demanded.

"Who you are—who your pals are—and where they are!" answered the patient promptly.

"I'll gladly tell you who I am—but I'm afraid I haven't any pals. I'm Sherman Lawrence of Atlanta—does that help any?" laughed the patient good-naturedly—and saw the attendant's eyes widen, -his mouth drop open with astonishment—and the next moment he turned and sped from the room, leaving the patient staring after him, bewildered.

"Odd sort of fellow—wonder where Nurse Judkins is! And if there was a letter this afternoon from Janelle—bless her!"mused Sherman, and turned with a healthy appetite to the meal on the tray beside him.

Continued in Next Number.

"Who are you?" she demanded swiftly. "Keep your voice down!" ordered
the man sharply. "And don't ask questions! I've got a
message for you — about — green orchids!"
(See Page 669)

Jan., No. 21

Chapter 71.

WANTED FOR MURDER!

HERMAN discovered that his arm and shoulder were painful when he tried to move them, and that he was very weak. Otherwise, he felt fine. He gave strict attention to the plain yet wholesome food on the tray beside him, and was just finishing the last of the baked apple when the door opened and the white-coated attendant accompanied by the doctor and a man in the uniform of a police chief, hurried into the room.

The faces of the three men registered their excitement. The doctor, with a little gesture to the police chief, went forward first and examined the patient's temperature. Satisfying himself that the man was in a condition to be questioned, he stood aside and the police chief, bristling with importance and excitement, stepped forward.

"Did you tell Guy here that your name was Sherman Lawrence?" he demanded.

"I did—it is!" answered Sherman, succinctly, puzzled.

"Of Atlanta, Georgia?"

"Of course—Sherman Lawrence, of Atlanta!"

The three men exchanged swift glances, and then the police chief turned back to Sherman.

"Are you prepared to swear to that?" he demanded.

"Certainly, if it's necessary!" returned Sherman promptly. "And in return, suppose you tell me why I am in a ward instead of my own room, and where Nurse Judkins is—and any other little facts like that! My mind's not very clear on how I happened to get here!"

The three men exchanged swift, sharp glances, and the police chief's face darkened a little.

"Oh—so that's gonna be your alibi, is it?" he demanded with sarcasm rife in his tones.

Sherman looked up at him, puzzled. He looked from one to the other of the three unfriendly, suspicious faces about him, and in spite of himself, a tiny tinge of fear touched him.

"Alibi? I don't get you! Why should I need an alibi?" he wanted to know reasonably enough.

"I suppose murdering a man in cold blood doesn't call for a stiff alibi?" the chief was elaborately sarcastic.

Sherman gasped as though ice-water had been flung into his face, and cried out sharply:

"Murder? What the devil do you mean? What are you talking about?"

"I mean that you are under arrest for murder —the murder of Lance Hayden, as fine a man as ever walked in shoe-leather! I'm talking about you shooting him down in cold blood so your partners could rob the bank! That's what I'm talking about!" thundered the chief, who had been an old friend of Lance

Hayden and who grieved sincerely for his death.

Sherman listened to him in blank amazement.

"Wanted for murder!" Why—it was ridiculous—absurd—impossible. He, Sherman Lawrence, a murderer? An assistant to bank crooks? Why, the man was crazy!

"I never heard of anything so idiotic in my life!" he cried when he had at last regained breath sufficient to answer. "I can prove by my nurse that I haven't been out of the hospital in three months!"

"Hey—lay off that!" snapped the attendant roughly. "You can't prove nothin' by me—except that you come into the hospital yesterday mornin' when the sheriff managed to get you away from the mob that was gonna lynch you!"

Sherman raised himself a little on his pillows, wincing as the movement disturbed his injured arm and shoulder. He glared at the attendant savagely.

"I don't know who the devil you are! But you certainly are not my nurse! I was referring to Nurse Judkins—and if you will call Doctor Rodrigguez, I am sure he will vouch for the length of time I've been here!" he snapped.

"That's not necessary—we all know how long you've been here!" cut in the police chief. "You've been here since early yesterday morning, when a mob, led by Lance Hayden's boy, smoked you out of a marsh along the river bank, and would have lynched you if the sheriff and his posse hadn't risked their lives to get you here!"

There was something deadly in the assurance of his tone. Something that for the first time convinced Sherman that they were not indulging in some grisly joke. It was only too plain now that some ghastly mistake had been made. They thought

that he was a criminal—it was a case of mistaken
identity. He began to feel cold at the pit of his
stomach, and his mouth went dry.

The police chief, assured by the expression on
Sherman's face that his words had gone home, leaned
a little closer over the bed.

"There's just one faint hope for you buddy—if
you'll tell us who your pals were—and where they
went—you may get off with a life sentence in prison!
But—if you don't—it's the electric chair for you sure
as shootin'!" he said grimly.

Sherman made a little distressed, weary
gesture.

"This is all such infernal nonsense! I've told
you that I've been here in the hospital for months—
I've got the haziest possible notion of slipping out of
bed at the hospital, while Nurse Judkins was out of
the room and of trying to go somewhere—I think it
was to catch a boat for the States—but the next
thing I knew, I was back here! So you see it wouldn't
be physically possible for me to have killed a man,
and to have gotten back to the hospital in one night!
And I'm paying a pretty stiff price for a room with
a special nurse—I don't care a whole lot about being
thrown into a smelly ward like this! You might tell
Doctor Rodriguez that when you see him!" he protested wearily.

The three men looked from one to another,
and then the police chief, puzzled in spite of himself,
asked a question.

"Who is this Doctor Rodriguez bird that you
keep talking about?"

Sherman looked his surprise.

"Surely this doctor and attendant know the
senior physician of the American Hospital, don't

they? If not. how does it happen that they are here working in the hospital?" he demanded.

The police chief pushed his cap back on his head, and scratched his head in token of bewilderment.

"Listen, buddy—you are in the prison hospital in a block of the jail in Yamacraw, Mississippi! And there ain't no Doctor Rodriguez, nor no American hospital in a good many miles!" he said wearily.

Wide-eyed, astonished, Sherman stared at him.

"You mean—I'm not in the American Hospital, in Havana, Cuba?" he gasped.

"Not by several thousand miles!" said the police chief.

"You mean—I'm back in the United States?" gasped Sherman. "But—how did I get here?"

The police chief grinned wearily and without mirth.

"We're waitin' for you to tell us!" he admitted, and it was plain that he did not believe Sherman's amazement.

Sherman put a shaking hand to his forehead dazedly.

"But—I can't remember—a thing beyond that walk—at night—through the oleanders and the jasmine—trying to catch the boat to the States! It's —all a blank!" he puzzled. "What—what day of the month is it?"

"July 5th! And the year is 1932!" said the police chief with a humor that did not reach Sherman.

"July 5th! And—the last I remember was— the first of May!" gasped Sherman, and his eyes were wild. "Oh, my God—what's happened? I've— lost two months out of life.

"Plenty's happened—and that old 'lost mem-

ory' alibi ain't gonna do you no good! There were
plenty of people saw you with their own eyes—you
killed Hayden—you're as guilty as hell—you better
think fast, buddy and decide to play ball with us!"
said the chief grimly.

Behind him the door burst open, and a man
in uniform dashed in.

"Good grief, Chief—you know who this bird
is?" he demanded, and thrust into the police chief's
hand a square of paper containing a photograph, and
across the top the words:

"Wanted for Murder!"

The chief looked at the picture, then at the
man on the bed. Hurriedly he read the lines beneath the picture, and then he whistled and pushed
back the cap from his forehead.

"Listen to this, boys!" he spoke to the three
grouped about him, ignoring the man on the bed who
listened, wide-eyed, incredulous with horror. " 'Want-
for Murder: Sherman Lawrence, financier and prominent socially, of Atlanta, Ga., accused of the murder
on the 14th of May in New York City, of a woman
known as Annie Greene. Lawrence is approximately
six feet tall, and weighs about one hundred and
eighty-five pounds. Dark hair and eyes. Considered
very good looking. Well-educated and accustomed to
travelling in the best of circles. A reward of $1,000
will be paid for information leading to the arrest of
this man!' "

The police chief looked down at the white-
faced, horror-stricken man in the bed.

"So you're Sherman Lawrence, are you? And
you're prepared to swear to it, are you? And you're
well-educated and accustomed to travelling in the
best of circles, eh? Reckon you kinda stepped out of

your circle lately, ain't you? Murder and robbery? You must be one of them 'Trill Slayers' the big city papers write about! Well, boys, reckon we're gonna have a nice little thousand dollar melon to cut pretty soon!" he chuckled gleefully, and rubbed his hands together happily.

But Sherman, despite his frantic efforts to keep his brain clear, was overwhelmed with the shock and the weight of this horror—and once more the black waters of oblivion rolled over him, and he lost consciousness.

Chapter 72.

A COWARDLY ATTACK!

TO JANELLE, the next few days were a horror. She was pointed out on the street, ordered to the district attorney's office for an investigation.

"You say you drew this money to pay the ransom for the recovery of your child? But of course, that was foolish of you—you had no assurance that the child would be returned after the money had been paid. You were tricked—the chances are that the people who 'contacted' you knew nothing really of the baby—it was merely a chance to rob you and you let them do it!" the district attorney was annoyed, and resentful. "Mrs. Elliott, if the public would co-operate with the police and guardians of the law, this country wouldn't be riddled by gangsters and crooks! If you had come straight to my office when you were contacted for this ransom, we could have put men on the case —we could at least have captured the ransom-seekers!"

"Which would have resulted in the death of

my baby—they warned me of that!" Janelle pointed out quietly.

The district attorney made a little annoyed gesture.

"I doubt it. Alive, the child means a fortune to them—dead, all their time and effort has been wasted. That's the very last thing they would do!" he assured her so convincingly that she almost believed him. "The reason these kidnapping operations have spread so alarmingly is that so many mothers and fathers become hysterical and pay any amount the kidnappers seek, rather than to turn the case over to the law and let the police handle it!"

"Perhaps you are right—anyway, it's too late to do anything about it now!" said Janelle wearily. "I've paid out everything I have—I couldn't pay another ransom—so they won't ask for another. But— I had no intention of wrecking the bank by withdrawing the money.

For the first time the district attorney smiled.

"I'm quite sure you didn't! And we'll try to do what we can—what you will let us—to help you! You may be surprised to find that we can do rather a lot, too!" he assured her as he shook hands with her and saw her to the door.

Outside in the bright hot sunshine, she decided to walk instead of hailing a taxi.

Before she had gone three blocks, she knew that she was being followed. A rough looking man in a cheap gray suit and a battered hat, was loitering behind her, taking pains not to come too close, yet careful not to lose sight of her.

Her heart suddenly hammered in her throat. What did he want? Was he from the kidnappers? Did he want to give her a message? Or did he mean her bodily harm?

Suddenly she realized that she was passing a department store. She did not believe that the man knew she had discovered his presence. Moving carelessly as though she had just remembered a purchase she meant to make, she went into the shop. Once inside she all but ran across it to another entrance below the one through which she had come. She stepped out on the side-walk—and, sure enough, there was the shabby man, standing at one of the windows, staring idly in at a display of children's toys.

Boldly because there were people on the street and she knew this man could not harm her, Janelle walked up to him.

"Are you following me?" she demanded sharply.

Startled, the man turned swiftly about and stared at her, a vast pretense of innocence in his eyes. Eyes that grew bolder as they swept over her taking in every line of her lovely figure and her charming face.

"Well, no, I wasn't!" he admitted reluctantly. "But I'd be easy to persuade—you wouldn't be hard to follow, you know!"

The insolence, the calculated significance in his tone, brought the hot blood to her cheek, and she stood back as though he had struck her. He grinned as though her fright and her anger amused him. And then without another word, he turned and was swallowed up in the crowd.

Janelle stood stock-still, staring after him, wide-eyed, her color high. The impudence of him! The insolence! Behaving as though she wanted him to follow her—apologizing because he wasn't following her!

She knew that he was lying. He HAD been following her ever since she left the district attorney's office. But what his purpose might be—whom his employer might be—that she had no way of knowing. She went on at last, home, still puzzled and bewildered.

The next day when she reached the studio, it was with the comforting assurance that one more week would finish "The Legacy of Love," barring any unexpected delays. She was anxious to get away from the studio—away from the glowering, sullen, catty Gladda Romaine, who never overlooked an opportunity to humiliate and embarass the new star whose "rushes" and whose newspaper publicity seemed destined to make her a real studio "bet."

Also, Janelle told herself, she would be happy to have the picture out, telling her story graphically, showing photographs of her baby, enlisting the sympathies and the aid of the whole world in tracking down the kidnappers.

Her studio was waiting for her with the day's costume spread out, with all its accessories. Janelle had learned to apply her own make-up now, and she seated herself at her dressing-table, slipped off her dress, and bound a towel about her head to protect her hair from the make-up.

"Dis hyer sho' is a pretty dress, Miss Janelle!" said Mattie, the maid, as she shook out the folds of a yellow tulle frock ready for Janelle's wearing.

"It IS pretty, isn't it?" agreed Janelle as she dipped her fingers into her cold cream jar.

She turned her head to look at the dress and, carelessly, her thumb and forefinger worked the cream together—and Janelle cried out with pain. Startled, she looked at her hand—and saw blood oozing through the milk-white of the cream!

"Lawsy, Miss Janelle, whut you done, honey?" gasped Mattie, dropping the dress and catching up a towel to wipe away the cream.

Janelle's fingers were cut in a dozen tiny places! She picked up the cold-cream jar, and held it in the morning sunlight. It showed rough and lumpy, rather than smooth and creamy as it should have been—and a cautious investigation proved that it was full of powdered glass!

Wide-eyed, utterly amazed, she stared at the tiny particles of glass that her paper-knife lifted from the cold-cream and spread on her dressing-shelf. She looked up at Mattie, shaken and frightened.

"Why, Mattie—how—who——" she gasped.

Mattie was ashy with horror.

"Lawsy, Miss Janelle, effen you'd jest a rubbed dat cold cream on yo' face like you allus does—you'd a be'n ruint' fo' life! It would 'a' cut yo' pretty face to pieces!" she whispered as though she could not speak the words above a whisper.

"Who could have done it, Mattie? How did that jar of cream get there?" demanded Janelle, a little sick and shaking with horror.

"Lawsy, Miss Janelle, I don' know, honey! I ain't teched de dressin-table dis mawnin'. I be'n busy gittin' dis dress and de odder things ready fo' you!" said Mattie, and Janelle was sure of the girl's loyalty.

Then there was a knock at the door.

"Ready on the set, Miss Elliott!" called the assistant director's voice, cheerful and matter-of-fact.

Janelle flung open the door.

"Ask Mr. Wayne to come here just a moment,

Bill, please—it's terribly important!" she asked, and because she was pale and trembling, her eyes wide and frightened, the director's assistant asked no questions, he merely obeyed.

Five minutes later Wayne was in the doorway, frowning a little, displeased when he saw that she was not dressed and made up. Quickly she explained and showed him the jar of cold cream. Wide-eyed, amazed, Wayne listened, and when she had finished he stood for a moment in silent and deep thought.

"Who could it be who would want to do a thing like that to me?" demanded Janelle, anger and outrage trembling in her tones. "I've injured nobody on this lot—I never willingly injured anybody in my life—why should any one try to do a dreadful thing like this to me?"

"There are a lot of people who might have done it, child—a star jealous of your success—some body who had money in the bank, and is sore at you because they think you wrecked the bank—some crank who resents the fact that you have a certain amount of money while he has a very uncertain amount—a movie fan in love with Marvin and jealous of you. About the only person I can safely say is entirely innocent would be Maxie—he's too anxious for you to finish the picture!" said Wayne, and he was trying to make his voice sound light and gay and amusing, for he saw that the girl was badly frightened and that her nerves were unsteady. "However, forget it now, and get a make-up on and come along. If we work very hard for the next five or six days, we ought to be through—and you'll be free—unless Maxie can coax you into another contract!"

Janelle pulled herself together with an effort, and managed a pale smile.

"O. K. boss—I'll be right along!" she assured him, far more gaily than she really felt, and Wayne hurried away.

Mattie brought out a fresh jar of cold cream, still sealed, and opened it. Assured that it was innocent of any harmful ingredients, Janelle donned her make-up, put on the yellow tulle frock, the golden slippers, and hurried out to the set where she began the day's work.

Meanwhile, Gladda Romaine, in her dressing-room bungalow, was expressing herself in no uncertain tones to her "public relations counsel."

"You probably have completely forgotten that our original idea was to rid the studio of this woman before 'Legacy of Love' is finished!" she reminded him with elaborate sarcasm. "AFTER the picture is finished, it will be too late! I'm sick of seeing her around here—I'm sick of seeing her picture plastered over every newspaper and every magazine in the country—I'm sick of hearing the publicity department sing her praises—and once the picture is finished—well, if she stays here until it IS finished, you can look for another job!"

The "public relations counsel," a dapper, well-dressed young man, looked at the beautiful Gladda with distinct distaste in his dark, long-lashed eyes. He hated her cordially—nothing would give him more pleasure than the privilege of telling her to take the job and go to blazes with it. But if he did that, he would have to go out and hunt another job—he might have to actually work! And he didn't like to work.

"I'm not bothering about hunting for another job—your enemy will be out of the studio before another twenty-four hours, and her picture junked!

Rest assured of that!" he said far more convincingly than he should have said it. "Afraid it'll cost you another hundred or so, though!"

Gladda gave him an ugly look.

"Another blonde to be taken to dinner, I suppose!" she sneered. "Get rid of this woman—and you can take them all to the Brown Derby—and I'll pay the bill!"

"It's a date!" the "public relations counsel" assured her with a light laugh, as he rose to go, her check in his hand, his light stick swinging gracefully in his gloved hands.

Chapter 73.

THE GREEN ORCHID MURDERS!

HAT evening Detective Hank O'Hearn had asked for a conference at Wayne's apartment, and there Janelle, Jim Marvin, Maxie and Wayne dined and waited for O'Hearn who arrived about nine o'clock. It was obvious from his expression that he had some news to relate, and they waited, tense and interested.

"I'll relieve your suspense at once, Mrs. Elliott, by telling you that I don't know any more about where your baby is than I did when I first talked to you about him!" he said swiftly. "However, something that has just been reported to the police an hour ago, has some connection, I feel sure, with your case!"

"Tell me!" Janelle begged swiftly.

"I'll have to begin at the beginning! To make it all clear!" said Hank quickly. "A couple of years ago when the rum-running industry was in its most flourishing stage around here, there were two rival crews that were always getting in each other's way. One crowd was headed by a man known as Curly Duke.

The other by a fellow named Thomas. They were constantly cutting in on each other's territory—and Thomas wasn't above hi-jacking an occasional load of Curly's liquor if he thought he could get away with it. Now and then, Thomas ran afoul of the law —and always escaped by offering an air-tight alibi that proved he was 'far away from the scene of the crime'—until at last, he became known as—Far-away-Thomas!"

Janelle cried out sharply.

"Why—the man I contacted about the ransom said it had been a man named Far-away Thomas who had hi-jacked the ransom!" she remembered.

"Sure—that's what I caught when you were telling the story!" said O'Hearn. "I may be all wrong—I often am—but I had a hunch that if Far-away was mixed up in this, Curly Duke might be, too! They're ancient enemies—Far-away would rather hi-jack fifty dollars worth of Curly's liquor than five thousand dollars worth of somebody else's! And if Far-away could cut in on sixty-five thousand dollars in cold cash of money that was headed Curly's way—well, that would be, in Far-away's imagination, a perfect crime!"

"Then you think these rum-runners have the baby?" demanded Wayne swiftly.

"Hold on, hold on—I didn't say that! I only said that the discovery that the supposed kidnapper who talked to Mrs. Elliott and who made arrangements for the ransom, mentioned Far-away Thomas the moment he found the ransom had been hi-jacked, made me suspicious!" protested O'Hearn. "You see, rum-running hasn't been so good these last few months—the people that used to buy cases of liquor at a time, are buying quarts now—or hitting the wagon. And rum-runners and their crews have to eat—and a ransom of sixty-five thousand dollars is important money!"

"You said something was reported to the police an hour ago! What was it?" Wayne remembered suddenly.

"I'm coming to that!" answered O'Hearn, who liked to be allowed to tell his own story in his own way. "A man was found murdered on a lonely road outside the city—a road leading to a beach where it has been rumored that rum-runners unload most of their cargos. The man has been identified as a man suspected of belonging to Far-away's crowd—a fellow named Virge Estes! Well, pinned to the man's coat was a small white card on which there were fourteen straight marks—little up and down figures —and one of the figures had been marked out. A line drawn across it, slanting. There are fourteen men in Far-away's gang—or there were fourteen until tonight!"

Hank O'Hearn looked across at Janelle, then at Wayne, and Jim and Maxie.

"That's not all!" he told them quietly. "The little card was pinned to the man's coat—but— in the man's button-hole was—a green orchid!"

There was a little moment of stunned silence— and then Janelle shivered and covered her face with her hands. The very mention of the sinister green thing with its fang-like purple blossoms and the bloated head with its purple spatters made her ill.

"Then you think that Curly Duke has the child —that Far-away hi-jacked the ransom—and that for revenge, Curly and his men intend to wipe out the Far-away crowd?" demanded Wayne sharply.

"That's what I THINK—but, mind you, I can't prove it!" protested O'Hearn conscientiously. "Thinking a thing, and proving it's so, are two entirely different things, you know!"

"It's the darndest thing the way this green orchid is always bobbing up in this case! I thought green orchids were rare and expensive—but, by golly, I'm beginning to believe they are as common and as easy to get as dandelions in spring!" complained Jim Marvin quite frankly.

"That's where you're wrong, son! I've been checking up on the dratted things. Only one florist in town—and he's a wholesaler—had 'em. He's sold out. He had five of them a week ago—and every one of them has been sold!" said O'Hearn, and drew out a little red notebook. "I got a list of all the buyers—the first one sold here was sold to Mr. Maxie Cason!"

Wayne looked accusingly at Maxie, who squirmed a little and would not meet Wayne's eyes.

"The second one was sold to—Miss Gladda Romaine, of your company, Mr. Cason!" said O'Hearn quietly.

Even Maxie looked startled.

"Gladda? Now what the devil does SHE want with a thing like this?" Wayne pondered aloud.

"Maybe for that new white and jade-green living-room she's had William Haines design for her!" suggested Jim. "The fact that the darned thing is rare and expensive, no matter how ugly it is, would make Gladda want it—Gladda's like that! Maybe she intends to bring it to the studio in the hope of worrying Janelle—Gladda, you may have discovered, is jealous of Janie in a great big way!"

"The third green orchid," O'Hearn read aloud

from his notebook, "was sold to a Japanese who would not give his name—and who insisted on taking the plant away with him. The description of the man, I might add, tallied to a gnat's whisker with your chauffeur, Mr. Cason!"

Maxie looked startled and a little apprehensive. Wayne looked more accusing than ever. Jim looked a little bore, and Janelle completely mystified and distinctly uneasy.

"The fourth plant went to a society matron in Bel Air, who had a newspaper writer up to do a story about the plant with pictures of herself feeding it. Polite and gentle publicity is all she's after, I'm convinced, for she is a woman whose social position and all that are unquestioned! The fifth and last plant was bought by a man who came into the shop at closing time. Who wore a broad-brimmed hat drawn well down over his face, his coat-collar turned up, and who did not question the price of the plant. He seemed disappointed when he found that there was only one left, and counted the blossoms before he bought it. He seemed relieved when the florist pointed out that there was half a dozen buds that would be open within two or three weeks. There were eight blooms, the florist remembered—and seven buds!"

O'Hearn waited, and the others looked startled.

"There are fourteen men in Far-away's outfit— there WERE fourteen until tonight—and fifteen blossoms, counting the buds!" said O'Hearn quietly.

There was a tiny silence in which the shrill clamor of the telephone bell made them all start. Wayne answered the phone and turned a moment later to O'Hearn.

"For you!" he said and held out the receiver.

O'Hearn clamped the receiver to his ear, spoke a moment or two, and turned back to them, his face grave, a shade pale.

"And now—there are only twelve men in Far-away's gang!" he said quietly.

The others stared at him, wide-eyed, startled.

"You mean—you mean—another murder?" stammered Janelle, her throat dry, her hands, clench-ed together, clammy with horror.

"Found beside the highway in a deserted part of the city!" answered O'Hearn. "With a card pinned to his coat, with fourteen straight lines, two of them crossed out—and with a green orchid in his button-hole!"

There was a little shiver in the thought of the grisly humor—a man murdered, his murderer paus-ing to fasten a flower in his lapel, a flower that was a symbol of death.

Janelle caught her breath and gave herself a little shake, as though the physical action might clear her mental faculties.

"Mr. O'Hearn, I want to ask you a question, and I want you to promise me on your word of honor to tell me the whole truth—don't try to 'spare me'—tell me the truth, brutally, if need be! Will you promise me that?" she demanded.

"I sure will—word of honor!" agreed the de-tective promptly.

"Then—do you honestly believe that my baby is—still alive?" asked Janelle steadily.

So promptly, so sincerely that she could not doubt the honesty of his words, O'Hearn answered:

"I am convinced of it, Mrs. Elliott!"

Janelle drew a long, uneven, shaken breath.

"What makes you so sure, O'Hearn?" demanded Wayne.

"I'm not only convinced the child is alive—I'm convinced that Curly Duke and his crowd have the child! Otherwise, there'd be no point to these murders of Far-away's men! He and Curly have bickered and fought and raided each other, and once in a while somebody first on one side and then another. has been killed. But—these two deaths tonight were cold-blooded, deliberate murders. And the green orchids were not put there just for a fancy touch! The orchids were put there as a sign, a symbol of reason for the death of the men! All right—but why that particular sign and symbol? Why go to so much bother for just that special sign? Because, throughout the kidnapping of the child, the whole business, a green orchid has been the symbol used. Therefore, I am convinced that Curly and his men are after Far-away and his men, and that the reason is that they hi-jacked sixty-five thousand—hence the use of the orchid!"

O'Hearn spoke so firmly, so positively, that his very words carried conviction. But when he had finished, he looked around the little group as though almost startled at the intensity of their attention.

" Now, mind you—I'm just saying that's what 1 THINK—but I can't PROVE it—yet!" he explained.

"But you DO believe my baby is alive?" insisted Janelle, tremulously.

"I do—with all my heart, Mrs. Elliott. And —I'm going to help you get him back, if there's the faintest chance in the world!" he assured her solemnly.

And Janelle thanked him, with tears in her eyes.

Chapter 74.

OUT OF THE PAST.

THE following morning when Maxie came down to breakfast, he sent for his chauffeur. Satsu came promptly looking neat and trim in his well-cut uniform, his sleek dark hair well-brushed. There was a trace of a harried, hunted look in his eyes as he waited to learn what his master wanted with him.

"So you got yourself a green orchid, too, eh Satsu?" demanded Maxie unexpectedly.

Satsu blinked, looked bewildered, **and then** guilty.

"Please, sir—I steal one single flower—it very old flower—nearly ready to wilt. I want give it my girl-friend! She like very much!" he apologized humbly.

Maxie made a little swift gesture with his hand.

"I don't mean that you've taken a blossom from my plant—I mean you've bought a plant for yourself!" he explained, and eyed his servant steadily.

Satsu looked honestly bewildered.

"I buy plant that cost two, three months salary? No, sir—I save my money—some day I go back—and see cherry blossoms in Japan!" he protested, and Maxie felt the boy was telling the truth.

He dismissed the chauffeur, and later, at the studio, he sent for the lovely and glamorous Miss Rómaine. On her way across the lot, to the executive building, she saw Janelle arriving for the day's work, looking cool and sweet and lovely—and Gladda's famous pearl-like teeth ground together with rage as she went on to Maxie's office.

"All right, Maxie—what's up? You want to cancel my contract so that you can concentrate all your activities on Janelle Elliott, I suppose!" she snapped as she entered the office. "Well, you can't cancel it—but I'll sell it to you for a hundred thousand dollars—I'm sick of the XL lot, anyway—and sick of amateurs!"

"How's your green orchid plant getting along, Gladda?" asked Maxie gently.

Gladda looked startled and dropped her eyes.

"What do you care?" she demanded angrily.

"I should think picking so many blooms off it at once would be bad for it!" mused Maxie. "Mine seems to resent being picked!"

"No blossoms have been picked from my green orchid plant—I dare any one to touch it!" snapped Gladda. "For Pete's sake, Maxie, you didn't send for me at nine in the morning to discuss orchid culture, did you? I've got work to do!"

"O. K.—run along—it wasn't important anyway!" agreed Maxie, and Gladda, in a rage flounced out of the office.

The door had scarcely closed behind Gladda before it flung open again, this time to admit Janelle, with her eyes shining like stars, her cheeks scarlet with excitement.

She carried the morning paper in her hands and dropped it on Maxie's desk as she spoke.

"Look—look, Mr. Cason, they've found Sherman—Mr. Lawrence, my fiance! I didn't have time to read the morning paper before I left home this morning—but Mattie, my maid, had this one here at the studio for me and I've just seen it! Look—isn't it glorious?" she stammered wildly.

Maxie read the headlines and the first paragraph of the story before he looked up, bewildered.

"Glorious? You call it glorious that you find this man, your sweetheart, in a Mississippi prison, charged with two murders? Glorious, you call it? My child, have you gone crazy?" he demanded in quite honest bewilderment.

Janelle made a little expressive gesture with her hands.

"Oh—that doesn't amount to anything—it's all some absurd mistake—we shall be able to prove that easily! The glorious thing is that he's been found and that I shall be able to go straight to him just as fast as I can get a plane!" she cried, and turned toward the door.

"Wait, wait—Janelle, you're not going to walk out on the picture now, when it's almost finished?" pleaded Maxie, and Janelle paused, uncertainly.

"But, Mr. Cason, you don't understand. This is the man I love with all my heart—he's in trouble, he needs me. I've got to go to him—he's ill, injured —when I was in trouble he threw everything aside to help me! Even if I didn't love him, it would be my duty to go to him!" she pointed out.

"Yes, yes, of course—but after all, just three

days, Janelle—only three more little days and the picture will be 'in the can'—and then you can go to your lover and know that the picture is going on its way to help you find your baby—that it will be shown in hundreds of cities, in thousands of theaters before millions of people—it's a big thing, Janelle— a tremendous thing to think of the power of the motion picture——" pleaded Maxie persuasively.

"But it's a big thing, too, Mr. Cason, to be in love and to know that the man you love needs you— and to be able to go to him! I've—I've got to go! It's been so long—I've been so lonely—oh, I can't stay, I CAN'T!" she all but sobbed.

"Look, child—I do this for you! I tell Wayne, and we'll all work day and night—we'll finish the picture in thirty-six hours—and then you can go— just thirty-six hours—remember old Maxie, and how he has helped you and worked for you—you wouldn't let him down now, would you? Think of all the money I've spent on the picture—it'll all be wasted if the picture isn't finished! Be a good little sport, Janelle—send him a wire—we'll put through a long distance telephone call—you can talk to him—explain, he'll tell you to stay and finish the picture before you come!" pleaded Maxie.

But it took an hour or more of pleading from Maxie and Wayne and Jim before, reluctantly, she consented. A long distance telephone call went through to the little Mississippi town, and Janelle talked to the chief of police. Cautiously he assured her that "the prisoner" was in no danger, but that he was unable to come to the telephone. He assured her that he would see that "the prisoner" had every possible comfort and that he would be given Janelle's message.

There was chill comfort in this unsatisfactory conversation, but it was all she could hope for. She went back to the set, determined to finish the picture as quickly as possible so that she might be free to go.

Only Jim, the character actress, and a pretty little ingenue were in these scenes with her, and their sympathies caught by Janelle's predicament and her eagerness to reach her lover, they unhesitatingly agreed to work straight through until the final scenes had been shot.

It was quite late that night as Janelle waited off-stage for her entrance. She stood behind a door that would open into a handsomely furnished set. Where she stood behind the scene it was quite dark, and there was a great clutter of scenery and cables and properties. She was very tired, and while she waited for the lights to be fixed and for her signal, a voice spoke out of the darkness behind her.

"I've got a message for you!" the voice said very low, and though she whirled, the speaker stood in the shadow of a piece of scenery so that she could not see his face—she could only see the bulk of his body.

"Who are you?" she demanded swiftly.

"Keep your voice down!" ordered the man sharply. "And don't ask questions! I've got a message for you—about—green orchids!"

Janelle caught her breath sharply, and tried to peer into the darkness to discern the features of the man who stood there, but she was powerless against the darkness.

"Green orchids!" she whispered, and knew that she was trembling violently.

"The man with the green orchids—who has

something that you want very much—is prepared to
return that—something—to you if you will obey orders implicitly!" came the whisper from the darkness.
"There must be no risk to the man or his friends.
The—piece of property you want to regain is—too
'hot' for him to handle, but he wants to return it to
you—ALIVE AND WELL—with no danger whatever
to his own friends. Do you agree to that?"

"Of course—I don't want anything but my
baby!" said Janelle swiftly.

"And you will make no effort to punish the—
people who have—your property? You are willing
for them to go free?" insisted the whisper.

"Oh, yes—yes—I only want my baby!" pleaded
Janelle swiftly.

Apparently satisfied, the man moved a little.

"When this scene is finished, walk across to
the door, as though to get a breath of air. I'll be
waiting for you there, and I'll take you to where
—your property is—and bring you back within an
hour! Is that agreed?" he demanded.

"All right, Janelle—come on!" she heard
Wayne's voice sharply.

She made a swift gesture of assent to the man
in the shadows, and bracing herself, she opened the
door and walked out into the set in the glare and
brilliance of the full flood of lights.

She went through her scene as smoothly as
she could, though her pulses were hammering, and
her heart was beating thickly. Her eyes were like
stars. She was trembling with excitement. The
man had said he would take her to where her baby
was—and he would bring her back—within an hour.
That meant that the baby would be returned to her
and she would be back here in the studio within an

hour!

And within a few more hours she and her baby would be on their way to Sherman, and please God, the three of them need never be parted again. So much of loneliness, so much of heart-hunger, so much of fear and doubt and despair had swept over them—when all they asked was to be together in peace and happiness.

"Cut!" called Wayne, and as the cameras stopped grinding, he walked over to Janelle. "Good work, my child! Why—what's up? You're trembling like a leaf!"

Jim, who had not been in this scene, came up, his eyes startled, and a little afraid.

"I just saw Mr. Cason!" he said so low that his voice reached not farther than the ears of Wayne and Janelle. "O'Hearn telephoned!"

Wayne and Janelle looked swiftly, questioningly at him.

He nodded and swallowed.

"Another of Far-away's men has had an orchid pinned in his coat-lapel, and a card on his chest with three figures marked out!" he answered the unspoken question in their eyes and shivered. "This stuff gets on a guy's nerves!"

Janelle looked up swiftly, and across the sound stage. The door had opened and a man had let himself out into the darkness of the lot. She had had only a glimpse of him—he had looked rather bulky and powerful—she shivered a little, for she had no doubt that he was the man who had whispered to her from behind the piece of scenery.

He had said he could bring back her child if she went with him. She had no moment of fear for herself. She excused herself to Wayne and Jim who were discussing the next scene while the technicians fussed with lights and camera-angles.

She walked across the stage and opened the door. She stepped out into the darkness. Ahead of her, in a faint patch of moonlight, was a parked car —a coupe of a heavy, powerful, expensive make. It stood where moonlight filtered through the branches of a eucalyptus tree. As she stood hesitant on the steps, a hand came out of the darkness of the car and beckoned to her.

And Janelle, brave because she was going to find her baby, went forward to the car, and as the door swung open, got into it. In the darkness she could not see the driver. The door slammed shut, the powerful motor purred, and the car drove away, bearing Janelle and her unknown, unseen driver— where?

Continued in Next Number.

The man's hard brown fist clenched on the white table-cloth and his jaw set hard. "I said—get back to your own quarters!" he snarled savagely. Janelle looked at him in amazement. (See Page 687)

Chapter 75.

TRAPPED!

A S JANELLE got into the coupe beside the unseen driver who was merely a bulky figure in the darkness, she felt a little qualm of fear. But the thought that this man had promised to take her to her baby was enough to down the fear. After all, she had risked so much for her child—why should she hold back now?

As the man drove swiftly through darkened streets, Janelle's thoughts were busy. He had said that his crowd considered the baby "hot property"— that meant, she knew, that they were afraid of being captured with the baby in their possession. They had therefore decided to give the baby back to her— to take the loss of the ransom money—or perhaps they had managed to find some way of settling the ransom-trouble with the hi-jackers.

No doubt they knew that detectives, the police, men from the district attorney's office were now at work on the case and realized that every hour that they kept the baby in their possession meant an added danger. She could readily understand their eagerness to rid themselves of that danger by returning the child to her. By gaining her promise that she would not appear against them in court—would make no attempt to prosecute them. They could be reasonably sure, that way, of making a clean get-away. Of escaping the heavy penalty the law required for kidnapping.

She was a little uneasy because the driver took so long.

"I must be back at the studio within an hour!" she reminded the man at the wheel.

"O. K.!" he grunted, and the car speeded up.

Ahead of them there was a dark, lonely curve in the road. Not even the moonlight could penetrate this spot, and as they approached it, the car slowed a little and slid to a stop in the deepest shadow.

"The gang is to meet us here—get out!" ordered the man at the wheel, and pushed the door open beside Janelle.

A little frightened, hesitant, Janelle stepped out into the road. She was conscious of several darker shadows who crept closer to her and she heard a voice answering a swift question, the voice of her driver answering it—and then something black and soft and stifling was flung over her head and shoulders, and strong arms closed about her in an overpowering grip.

She fought savagely, terrified, kicking, fighting, trying to scream aloud. But the stifling folds of the smothering cloth strangled the cry in her throat, and the arms that held her were like iron bands against which she was powerless. She was lifted, still kicking and fighting, and flung heavily into the back of a car. Probably a truck, she thought hazily, as she felt the rough boards of it.

A heavy covering, perhaps a tarpaulin was flung over her and a moment later she heard the heavy roar of a powerful truck engine. The cumbersome vehicle began to move, gaining speed. She was shaken and bruised and battered as the truck raced onward.

It seemed to her that hours passed while she lay, cramped and half-smothered by the thick black cloth and the heavy tarpaulin that covered her. Once as the truck sped on its way, she heard dimly the two men on the front seat exchange swift, startled words and knew that someone ahead in the road had signalled them to stop.

"The road patrol! What'll we do, Walt?" she heard one man say dimly.

"Do? We'll stop, you fool—what else can we do? Stop and trust to luck!" she heard the other man answer, and then she felt the slowing of the truck.

She was powerless—gagged by the black cloth which was wound about her in such a way that she could not move. The smothering weight of the tarpaulin added to her discomfort and her powerlessness. Only faintly could she hear what was being said as the truck slid to a halt.

"Who are you and where are you going?" the hail came from the road-side.

"Couple o' truckers, headin' for the coast! Got a job haulin' some fish!" the man on the front seat answered. "Truck's empty now—take a look!"

"O. K.!" Janelle heard the word from the highway, and with all her strength she fought to move, to tear the smothering black folds from her mouth, to scream to high heaven. But—she was powerless.

Rescue, help, revenge, was here at hand. Within reach of her, and she was powerless to take advantage of it. The thought maddened her. She heard foot-steps coming along the paved road, and knew that somebody lifted the corner of the tarpaulin. But she lay at the very front of the truck almost beneath the driver's seat—and the inspection was so casual that the inspector did not raise his eyes to her body as it lay, like a fold in the tarpaulin, at the other end of the truck.

She felt her heart sink to her very boots when the man walked away from the truck, and she heard the roar once more, and felt the painful jar as the truck began its course once more.

She wept forlornly, miserably, as she lay there, bounced and battered and bruised by the speed of the truck, her helplessness to spare herself from the jarring against the rough boards.

It seemed to her that long hours passed before, at last, the truck came to a halt, and she heard footsteps coming around to the back of the truck once more. This time, strong, carelessly brutal hands yanked her forward, dragged her out of the truck.

They stood her up on the soft, yielding sands of the beach and whipped the black cloth from her head and shoulders. She swayed, dazed and dizzy, as she stood before them and pushed back the tangled, dishevelled golden hair from her forehead and looked about her.

She stood with two men on the beach. A lonely, deserted strip of beach without a sign of human habitation as far as she could see. Overhead, the moon was beginning to wane. The stars were cold and far away. The night-wind from the ocean swept in, chill and dispiritingly damp.

Cold terror laid like an icy wind against the girl's heart.

"What—what are you—going to do with me?" she stammered after a moment, as she looked at the men.

In the moonlight she saw them—roughly dressed in sweaters and trousers, unshaven, powerfully built—terrifying looking.

One of the men hitched up his trousers and an ugly grin touched his ill-favoured face.

"We're gonna let you be queen of the rum-runners for a while!" he told her grinning. "Won't that be nice?"

"Mr. Cason—the people at the studio—they'll never let you get away with this!" she told them swiftly. "They'll find you and you'll go to prison for life for this!"

The man grinned wickedly, and widened his eyes in mock surprise.

"No! You don't mean to tell me!" he gasped in mock amazement. "Gee whiz, Stubby—ain't you scared?"

"Purt' nigh to death!" agreed the other one sarcastically.

Suddenly his voice quickened and he pointed.

"Look, Walt—there's the light—they're comin'!" he said excited, and for a moment neither one was watching the girl.

Instantly Janelle took advantage of this. She turned swiftly to the road where the truck stood, and ran as fast as she could. Hampered by the frail yellow tulle frock in which she had been working before the camera, and with her feet in frivolous, high-heeled, golden satin slippers, she hadn't a chance, for before she had gone twenty feet the two men were after her.

As they caught her she fought them savagely with small, doubled fists, and with manicured nails that raked Walt's ugly face, leaving a row of scratches that bled a little.

"You damned little wildcat!" snapped Walt, and his doubled fist caught her at the point of the jaw and knocked her unconscious.

When she next regained consciousness, she lay flat on her back on the deck of a ship, and beneath her, she could feel the steady, even throbbing of the powerful engine. Over her head, the sky was the deep, unrelieved blue that marks the darkest hour before dawn.

For a little while she had difficulty in remembering where she was. Her jaw ached dully. She was stiff and bruised and chilled through, 'for she wore only the frail yellow tulle gown that left arms and shoulders bare.

Memory returned to her in a swift flood of horror, and she managed to sit up, and to look about her. The ship was a good-sized one, masquerading as a fishing boat.

She managed to get shakily to her feet and to move to the rail—and as she did so, a man came toward her across the dimly lighted deck.

"Oh, so you're feeling better? That's good! Sorry I had to be so neglectful of the comfort of a fair guest, but the truth is, you were a bit troublesome at first, and we had to get the ship under way as rapidly as possible! But if you'll come below deck, I'll try to make amends for being such a poor host!" he greeted her cordially, courteously and in a pleasant, good humored tone.

Janelle shrank from him. She could see only that he was dressed in a dark suit, across which there was a dull gleam, probably of brass buttons, and that on his head he wore a yachting cap. For the rest, his face was scarcely more than a blur.

"I—I—don't want to go below deck—all I want is for you to give me back my baby and take me ashore!" she cried unsteadily.

The man uttered a little low laugh.

"Now isn't it just too bad that a gentleman who is so anxious to please should have to refuse both of the first requests of his guest? It happens that I haven't your baby—believe me, that is the truth! And it also happens, unfortunately, that I can't take you ashore.

"The boys and I have a little date with the 'mother-ship' well outside the twelve mile limit, and the boys insist that you go along with us!" he assured her, and she saw that he was enjoying the situation immensely. "You might as well be sensible and come along — I have some coffee waiting down below deck, and I assure you, I could do with a cup — and I'm sure you could, too!"

Janelle hesitated, and when the man spoke again his voice was sharp, devoid of the easy, amused courtesy of his first words.

"Snap out of it—I'm ordering you below deck —or shall I have Walt THROW you there?" he snapped, and she could not doubt that he would do exactly that.

He took a step toward her, and Janelle, already battered and bruised and sore at the hands of his gang, shrank with fear.

"I'll—I'll—go!" she stammered, and followed

him to the stairs and down the companion-way to a
door which he flung open and stood back once more
polite and courteous for her to enter ahead of him

It was a luxuriously appointed lounge. Small,
but fitted up in perfect taste and comfort. The port-
holes were shaded by cretonne curtains. The furniture was designed for comfort as well as beauty. On
the table in the center of the small room a lace
cloth had been spread, and on this, a handsome silver
coffee-percolator, bubbled with a delicious savory fragrance. There was a platter of thin, dainty, appetizing sandwiches. A bowl of salad. A silver platter of
French pastry.

Janelle stared at it in amazement. No charming Beverly Hills drawing-room could have offered a
daintier or more attractive picture.

The man, watching her and reading her
thoughts, laughed.

"One might as well be comfortable, even if
most of one's life IS spent on the high seas! With
occasional flights from the government's earnest
young men!" he laughed as he drew out a chair
for her.

She accepted the chair that he drew out for
her behind the coffee percolator, and watched him
as he sat down across from her. She saw that he
was an extraordinarily handsome man of between
thirty and thirty-five. Sun-bronzed to the color of
old copper. His hair a thick, dark red. His eyes
blue and dancing.

His clothes were as expertly tailored as any
she had ever seen on the movie sets or the Beverly
Hills drawing-room. Blue flannel, double-breasted
coat with a double row of buttons, a scarf twisted
carelessly about his throat, his visored cap set at a

jaunty angle over one eye.

As though her eyes on his cap had suddenly made him conscious of his bad manners, he laughed, and tossed the cap lightly to a near-by chair.

"Forgive me—I'm afraid a man doesn't gain a drawing-room polish out here on the high seas! It takes the appearance of a pretty woman to keep a man on his toes about such things!" he apologized. "Now, may I have a cup of coffee, please? It will taste much better if poured by a pretty hand, I'm sure."

Dazedly Janelle poured the coffee into fragile, exquisite Wedgewood cups, one for him, one for herself. There was thick, sweet cream in a silver jug, lumps of sugar in a matching bowl. The man held the plate of sandwiches toward her, and Janelle realized that she had eaten nothing since dinner, and was hungry.

"The salad is very good—it's my own recipe and it took me a year to teach Sing Lee to make it —but he's an artist,now!" he assured her as he served a plate of the salad for her.

She was staring at him, wide-eyed, as he served himself and her, and began to eat. Suddenly the words burst from her, almost without her consciousness that she had been about to say them.

"I think you're the most extraordinary man I ever met!" she blurted.

The good-looking, sun-bronzed young man laughed and bowed gaily.

"And permit me to say that I had no idea you were so pretty until now—really, your pictures don't half do you justice!" he assured her gravely. "I'm delighted at the prospect of getting to know you— better!"

"Why did you bring me here? What does it all mean?" she demanded straightly.

A little cruel look slipped swiftly over the man's face and he seemed suddenly to lose interest in the really delicious salad.

"That is something you will learn later!" he told her harshly. "My original purpose in bringing you here was—revenge! But—now that I have seen you—well, my plans have taken a slight turn! I'm —not quite sure just now!"

Janelle tried again. She leaned toward him across the table.

"Tell me just one thing: is my baby here—on the boat?"

"No!" said the man so quickly, so firmly that she believed him.

"It was not you who kidnapped him?" she demanded, a little startled at her own boldness.

"It most certainly was not, dear lady!" the man assured her as promptly. "Whatever my faults may be—and I grant you they are many!—they do not descend to the kidnapping of helpless infants! When I kidnap a baby—I see to it that she is—over eighteen and pretty! Those are the only babies in whom I am interested!"

He was laughing a little as he said it, and his dark blue twinkling eyes slipped over the girl who sat before him with an almost caressing glance. It made her sharply conscious of her bare neck and shoulders, her white arms bare from the shoulders down.

"Too bad Walt and Joe mussed your pretty frock—such clumsy louts, both of them!" he apologized as he took in the crumpled, stained, torn gown. "But never mind, I'm sure we can find something aboard that will make an effective substitute. The Molly E. often entertains feminine visitors though she has never been quite so honored as tonight!"

He bowed to her again, but the look in his eyes frightened Janelle and she shuddered. He was tremendously good-looking—but he made her feel as though she were looking at a very handsome and deadly reptile.

He was daring, and resourceful — he was entirely without fear — but some feminine instinct told her that he was equally without mercy. That he could be as ruthless as he was daring if necessary.

Chapter 76.

WOMAN AGAINST MAN.

UT, COME—you're not eating! The salad —you don't like it? Then another of the pate de foie gras sandwiches — or a chicken — perhaps — another cup of coffee? Or a bit of pastry?" he was the perfect host once more.

"Thanks — no, I'm not hungry!" stammered Janelle.

Behind the man the door had opened very softly, and Janelle looked up to see a woman coming almost soundlessly into the room. She was a tall, voluptuous looking woman, with thick very black hair closely waved to her proudly held head. She wore a trailing tea-gown sort of negligee of pale rose colored chiffon velvet, that had long, wide sleeves of frail, creamy lace. Her feet, as she moved, showed the tips of silver slippers, and there were jewels about her throat and on her wrists and her fingers.

In the look that was in her eyes as she saw the man, Janelle knew that this woman idolized the man. But when the woman's eyes slipped to Janelle, the girl saw in them a green flame of jealousy and hatred.

"Oh, so here you are, Steve—I was wondering what had happened to you!" said the woman smoothly. The man turned swiftly, startled and resentful of her presence. "I've been waiting for you for more than an hour!"

The man whose manners toward Janelle had been so perfect, did not even trouble to rise when the other woman entered the room. He merely turned his head, looked at her with anger and disgust in their blue depths that were no longer twinkling.

"Well, go back to your own room and wait some more!" he snapped insolently.

The woman's face flushed as though he had struck her. Her head went up and she strolled around the table, one hand on her hip, the other touching her beautifully waved hair.

"Oh, I don't think I shall! I'll just sit here and—meet your little friend!" she drawled coolly, and dropped into a seat across from the man.

Janelle was startled at the look that swept over the man's face. Darkening it with rage, lightning flashing from his eyes. He was utterly furious.

"Get back to your own quarters—do you hear?" he snarled at her savagely.

The woman flung up her head and caught her breath. She was suddenly pallid beneath the expertly applied rouge on her cheeks, and her eyes were blazing.

"Who the hell do you think you're talking to? I'm not a dog, or a discharged servant!" she cried hotly.

The man's hard brown fist clenched on the white table-cloth and his jaw set hard.

"I said—get back to your own quarters!" he

snarled savagely.

Janelle looked at him in amazement. All semblance to the airy, amusing grace and charm of the man was gone. He was revealed now as a bully and a brute—she shivered in repulsion.

The woman wilted a little beneath the words, and the glare in the man's eyes. And then she sat back down doggedly.

"And I said—I would not!" she answered, though her voice trembled a very little betraying the fact that she did not feel as bold as she tried to sound.

The man pushed back his chair and stood up. The woman got to her feet, afraid, yet valiantly fighting.

"Steve—you've no right to treat me like this! After all that I've been to you for all these months —after all that I gave up for you—a home, a decent place in respectable society——" she cried sharply, but the man cut in savagely:

"You were nothing to me you didn't want to be! You gave up nothing for me that you didn't want to give up. I've paid you well for all that you've been, and all that you've lost! And now—I'm sick of the sight of you! Get out!"

The woman cowered away from him.

"I won't—I won't, I tell you. I won't be thrown over for this silly little idiot! Just because she's —younger than I am—a little fresher—a little prettier—you want to throw me into the discard—for her! But you shan't do it—you shan't!" she wailed, shaken, frightened, yet still fighting.

The man's little laugh was like a stinging whiplash.

"And who's going to stop me?" he asked as

though he enjoyed the woman's stark terror and abject pleading.

"I am! I'll kill her before I'll let her take you from me!" cried the woman wildly.

Insane with jealousy and wounded love and anger, the woman caught up the silver coffee pot, half-filled with boiling coffee, and flung it with all her strength straight at Janelle.

With a cry of horror and fright, Janelle sprang backward and away. The silver pot struck the wall, its boiling liquid contents spattering over the wall and furniture. A stinging handful of drops spattered Janelle, but she had escaped the worst of the unexpected onslaught.

The woman was huddled in a corner, weeping now, looking fearfully at the damage she had created. The man called Steve assured himself swiftly that Janelle was not seriously hurt, and then he turned to the woman.

"And now," he said grimly, his voice thick with menace, "I'm going to beat you to death for that!"

The woman cried out, whimpering, as the man caught her and dragged her out of the corner. With the first blow that he struck the cowering woman, Janelle was out of the cabin and flying up to the deck, seeking help.

Two sailors lounged on a hatch, talking in low tones, and Janelle flung herself upon them.

"Quick—quick—he's going to kill her! He told her so—he's beating her!" she cried sharply.

The two men sat erect, startled.

"Mama Louise and Far-away? Come on, Lafe—O. K., miss!" said one of them, and sped down the companion-way stairs to the cabin.

Janelle stood still for a moment, stunned by the two names. "Mama Louise"? The man had called the woman "Louise" and the woman had called him "Steve." But this man called him—"Far-away!" The man who was supposed to have engineered the hi-jacking of the ransom money! Far-away, who was known to be the leader of a well-organized gang of rum-runners! And the man had told her, earlier in the evening, that he and "the boys" had a date with a "mother-ship"—that was what rum-runners called the ship that brought in the contraband liquor to the twelve mile limit——

She turned and hurried back to the cabin, fearful of what she would see, yet drawn by a fasinated horror. She paused in the door of the cabin and looked fearfully inside.

The woman lay huddled in a little heap, her face hidden against her arm, her little broken sobs pathetic. Her rose-colored chiffon gown was torn to ribbons through it her back gleamed with great red welts laced across it. Her hair that had been waved so beautifully was dishevelled about her face. She was a picture of abject woe.

The man stood at the table breathing hard, a short, thick, wicked looking dog-whip still in one hand. His hair was tumbled, and his face was damp with perspiration. He dropped the whip as he saw Janelle, and brushed his hands over his hair, pouring himself a drink of water—settling the scarf about his throat.

"Mama Louise has had her weekly 'petting,' boys—you'd better take her to her own quarters now—I imagine she will go now!" said the man grimly.

The two sailors were resentful.

"I know, Far-away—giving a dame a clout on the conk now and then keeps 'em in their place, and they love it. But to take a dog-whip to a woman—that's going too far!" one of them protested.

The man whirled upon him, his anger newly roused.

"Don't give me your back-talk! I don't require any instructions in behaviour from you! Get that woman out of here and make it snappy!" he snarled.

The two men looked at each other, and then at the man. One of them shrugged, and walked over to the woman who still lay huddled, weeping brokenly.

He stooped and lifted her carefully in his arms, and when she moaned, Janelle heard him say:

"Take it easy, Mama Louise—old Lafe ain't gonna hurt you none!"

As the two sailors passed Janelle in the doorway, one of them gave her an ugly, menacing look from which Janelle shrank.

When the two men had gone, carrying the woman so gently, Janelle paused a moment. The man inside the cabin turned to her with an effort donning again, like a discarded garment, his easy, graceful manner.

"A rotten shame that you should have been subjected to such a scene your first night aboard the Mollie E!" he apologized. "I shall have Louise sent ashore as soon as possible, so you need have no fear of a recurrence of such a thing!"

He came toward her, smiling, easy, graceful, but Janelle shrank from him, her eyes blazing.

"You—vile beast!" she cried into his face. "Don't you dare even touch me! I— loathe you! I—

despise you!"

The man paused, and for a moment his eyes snapped. But then he controlled his swift spurt of of anger and shrugged.

"Oh, you'll get over that!" he told her confidently. "You rather liked me tonight when you first came aboard—I could see it in your eyes. And you will like me again—other women have!"

"Are you Far-away Thomas?" demanded Janelle.

The man's expression altered a little. Plainly he was rather pleased with the title.

"A few of my friends and all of my enemies call me that!" he assured her. "But—to my friends —especially my feminine friends—I am—Steve!"

"Then—it was you who—hi-jacked the ransom that I was trying to pay the kidnappers of my baby!" accused Janelle hotly.

The man smiled and drew out a handsome platinum cigarette case, offered it to Janelle, and raised an eye-brow when she refused. He selected a cigarette, lighted it, and returned the case to his pocket.

"So you don't smoke! Good! That will be a novelty! I adore feminine women with none of the masculine vices! We must see that you acquire a few feminine vices, however—it would never do to have a little saint aboard the Mollie E.—she would be far too lonely!" he laughed.

"Then you did steal the sixty-five thousand dollars?" asked Janelle again. It was a statement of a fact rather than a question.

The man looked annoyed.

"I don't like that word 'steal'—it was an illegitimate business transaction, if you like—it was a

case of Curly Duke getting it or my boys—and Curly
has no finesse about spending money. He would
have blown it in vulgarly—so my boys and I decided
to take the money ourselves! I might as well tell
you frankly, though, that the net result to you
would have been the same, had Curly gotten the
money!" he assured her.

Janelle looked puzzled. "What do you mean?"
she demanded unceremoniously.

"I mean that Curly Duke hasn't even got your
baby—what's more, I don't believe he knows who
has it or where it is!" said the man frankly.

"He was tricking me—just as you were?" demanded the girl.

"Nothing else but!" agreed Steve. "But—I'll
tell you something: I can find your baby and bring
it back to you—if I choose to do so!"

Janelle's eyes widened and she took a little
eager step toward him.

"You know where he is? He's all right?" she
demanded swiftly.

The man's eyes lighted with appreciation of
her young beauty.

"So that wakes you up, does it? Now I know
how to go about arousing you to a pleasant emotion!" he laughed. "I don't know where the child is
now—but I am willing to bet you anything you care
to risk that I can find him within thirty-six hours!
And bring him back to you in very little more time
than that!"

Janelle's cheeks were scarlet, and her eyes
were shining like stars.

"Oh," she cried, "if you only would!"

The man came closer to her, so close that
Janelle, in a momentary panic, stepped back and

away from him.

"And—what would you give me, if I did?" demanded the man, his tone dropping a little to a tone that meant to be seductive and alluring.

"I'm afraid I couldn't give you very much!" she stammered, a little afraid of him. "Practically every penny I had in the world was in that sixty-five thousand dollar ransom that you've already had!"

The man made a little impatient gesture with his hand.

"I don't want money—I know where I can lay hands on all the money I want! What I want from you is—something besides money!" he told her very low.

He put out his arms and caught her in them. She fought him savagely, but he only threw back his handsome head and laughed aloud at the futility of her struggles, until Janelle ceased to struggle, and stood like a woman carved of stone, rigid, unresponsive, white-faced, her teeth set in her lower lip—a prisoner in the circle of his arms.

The man looked down at her. Brutally, he forced her head back and kissed her. A kiss that was brutal and hard and that bruised her mouth. She made no effort to resist him, knowing the uselessness of such an effort, and too proud to amuse him by her struggles. But she was as unresponsive as though he kissed a stone image, and after a moment, angry and unsatisfied, he let her go and stood looking down at her, frowning a little.

"No," he said at last, "not like that! I want you—but not against your will. But—don't think you can escape me! You are here on my ship—a prisoner. You haven't a chance in the world of escaping—so you may make the best of it!"

She offered no answer—and suddenly the man said swiftly, eagerly:

"I'll make a bargain with you: your caresses, your response, your love freely given, if I return your child to you! That's the only ransom I shall ask! Is it a bargain?"

Janelle hesitated. The picture of Sherman, lover-like, devoted. Sherman, holding her close in his arms, and taking her kisses almost as though to him they were sacred. The picture of the lovely little family group—herself, her baby, Sherman—

She shivered a little.

"Remember, I haven't the child—but I have —connections—that can locate him for me in thirty-six hours—and there are ways to bring him back to you, safe and sound, within a very short time after that! And I'll do that—if you promise to—belong to me, afterward!" insisted the man.

In Janelle's mind there was the beginning of a plan. She must fight craft with craft. She must use every weapon at her command as mercilessly, as ruthlessly as this man and his associates used theirs. So she looked up at the man who waited eagerly for her decision.

"It's a bargain! I will—belong to you, AFTER you have brought my baby back, alive and well!" she said firmly. "And now, if you don't mind—I'd like to be alone for a while. I'm—rather tired!"

"Of course, you are—you lovely thing, you! Come along, I'll show you to your room!" and at the sudden look of fear on her face he grinned. "Don't be afraid, it has only one door and the key is on the inside! You're quite safe!"

Chapter 77.

WITH THE RUM-FLEET.

OWN THE CORRI-DOR they went to a door which Steve pushed open, and where he felt for a light switch. The room was flooded with light, and he stepped back for Janelle to enter ahead of him. The room was small, but immaculate, and prettily furnished. There was a narrow wooden bed, a gaily decorated chintz wing chair, a dressing-table with black and silver toilet articles upon it. There was a small closet, a chest, and a shelf of books.

Steve opened the chest and Janelle saw a pile of apple-blossom tinted silk and crepe and lace.

"Use anything you find here—it's all yours!" he assured her. "And you'll find some things in the closet—I'm a very hospitable person, you'll find!"

He laughed and for a moment she thought he was going to kiss her again. But instead he turned back to the door, and said a casual, almost a hurried good-night as though he were afraid to trust himself any longer in her presence,

The moment the door had closed behind him, she sped across and turned the key in the lock. An open door at the other side led to a small, but exquisitely comfortable and immaculate bath-room. She assured herself that there was only one entrance to this, and that was through the bedroom.

Then she proceeded to make herself familiar with her surroundings. From the chest filled with delicate lingerie, she selected pajamas of heavy silk, and a negligee from the open closet. There were backless bed-room slippers adaptable to almost any sized foot, and armed with these, she went into the bath-room and ran a tub of hot water.

There was a huge jar of bath-salts on the bath-room shelf, and she poured liberal handfuls into the hot water, delighting in the fragrance. She bathed luxuriously, getting rid of the aches and the stiffness of her body before she donned the silk pajamas and the negligee. She found a package of toothbrushes, still sealed in their cellophane wrappers. There were small boxes of powder of several shades, rouges to match, half a dozen lip-sticks, dozens of small powder-puffs. The brush and comb to the toilet set on the dressing-table was quite new and unused. There were several tall crystal bottles of perfume on the shelf—apparently, the man whom his enemies called Far-away, and his friends called Steve, was a host who over-looked nothing that would provide for the comfort and daintiness of his feminine guests.

Daylight was creeping over the water when Janelle crept into bed, worn and tired from the eventful night, but with her brain still spinning with the things that had happened and the things that threatened to happen.

Chapter 78.

THE ALARM IS GIVEN.

AYNE ran his fingers through his hair, sighed wearily, and sat erect in his chair.

"All right, Griffin —tell Miss Elliott we are ready for her!" he spoke to his assistant director over his shoulder. "Come on, fellows, let's get this scene over with and go home!"

The tired technicians straightened, and with the thought of the extra pay-check that tonight's over-work would bring, they went back to work. Cameras were adjusted. Sounds were tested out. Lights were wheeled into place.

The pretty golden haired girl whose luck it had been to be exactly Janelle's height, weight and coloring, and so had landed the job of being Janelle's "stand-in girl," moved to the position Wayne had checked so that the camera-man could figure out the best angle at which to shoot. Mary Gray, the "stand-in," thought wistfully of the fun it must be to be a star and have someone else do the tiresome things like standing in for lights, camera-angles, and to fit gowns—and wondered if some day, she herself might be a star with a "stand-in girl" to take all her present hard work.

The assistant director came hurrying to Wayne, wide-eyed.

"Afraid Miss Elliott has done a Garbo on us, Boss—'ay tank she go home'!" he explained.

Wayne looked puzzled. "What the devil do you mean?"

"Well, she's gone—she's not in her dressing-room, and nobody has seen her for an hour or so!" explained the assistant.

"I call that a pretty rotten trick to play on the rest of us when we are working like dogs just so that the picture can be finished in time for her to get away!" protested the character man who had just overheard the news.

"And so do I! I passed up the party at the Mayfair tonight, just to accomodate her—and now she checks out on us! The best party of the season, too—and I had a new frock for it!" cried the pretty little ingenue resentfully.

"Wait a minute, folks—Janelle Elliott never checked out on anybody in her life—there's something wrong about all this somewhere!" cut in Wayne sharply.

He looked at Jim Marvin.

"Call Hank O'Hearn, Jim—better call Maxie Cason, too!" he ordered quickly.

Jim hesitated.

"Heck, Wayne—it's after midnight— maybe she fell asleep some where!" protested Jim.

"Probably at her own home, in her own bed!" sneered the ingenue, mourning the lost Mayfair party and the pretty frock.

"All right—we'll look! Everybody! Lights on all over the place! And everybody is a member of a searching party—let's go!" called Wayne, and almost instantly lights sputtered on, people began to spread about the place.

But an hour's search proved that Janelle was nowhere about. The night watchman at the gate had seen her come out of the studio door as though for a breath of air. The next minute she had crossed to a waiting car parked in the shadows, and had driven off.

Wayne heard this news with mixed feelings. He still felt quite sure that Janelle would not slip away from the studio for more than a few minutes without telling him. She had an hour or more before her next scene, when she had finished the last one. She would not have gone away for longer than that without saying something about it.

Hank O'Hearn was called, and Maxie Cason was called. The police, at last, were notified, and a search began. In Maxie's office that morning Maxie and Wayne held a conference.

"Only half a dozen scenes left to be done before the picture is ready!" mused Maxie. "Scenes at the beginning of the picture—not too much close-ups, not too much acting—but scenes that we need. All right, Wayne—we put Mary Gray into Janelle's costumes, and make-up, and we finish the picture and get it on the screens!"

Wayne stared at him, not too much surprised.

"I suppose it could be done. She's a smart youngster, this Gray child, and she's exactly Janelle's height and weight. Make-up ought to take care of the rest! Sure—we'll do it. But—Maxie, what the heck do you suppose has happened to Janelle?"

Maxie shrugged, though he looked trouble.

"Maybe she ran away to find her sweetheart —she wanted to go, you know——"

"Don't be an idiot, Maxie—she promised us she would stay—and she meant it. Janelle doesn't break her word!" Wayne protested.

Maxie stared at Wayne shrewdly.

"Seems to me you fight pretty hard for her, Wayne—she's just another little star you know! And you're a great director!" he suggested mildly.

Wayne's face suddenly looked drawn and old and tired.

"I'm a very great sap, one of the world's most complete fools!" he said quietly. "I'm—in love with her, Maxie. Don't bother to look surprised— you've known it all along!"

"She owes you a great deal, Wayne!" said Maxie quietly.

Wayne smashed his fist hard on Maxie's rosewood desk.

"She owes me nothing! I knew all along that she—just about worshipped this fellow Lawrence— and that she could never see me as anything but just—a rather tiresome old man of forty—forty DOES seem old to a girl like Janelle, you know——" he stood up suddenly. "What the blazes? I'm behaving like a snivvling nine-year-old—forget it, Maxie!"

"It's forgotten, already!" Maxie assured him, and the two men who worked together and bickered and quarrelled and fought but who remained friends underneath it all, gripped hands for a moment before Wayne went back to the difficult task of fitting

Mary Gray into the first half dozen scenes of Janelle's picture.

*   *   *   *   *   *   *   *   *

In her dressing-room, Gladda Romaine faced her "public relations counsel" and she was so gay and radiant and smiling that the "public relations counsel" looked a trifle wary and startled. As he had entered the room he had been prepared to offer some glib alibi or apology—but the moment that he saw smiles, instead of thunder-clouds on the lovely face of the pampered star, his voice died in his throat, and cautiously he waited for her to speak first.

"Good boy, Donny—you put it over! I don't know how you did it—I don't want to know how—I only know that you did! Here's your check—and if you can KEEP her away, now that you've GOT her away, I can probably scare up another little check later on!" she bubbled happily.

The man accepted the check with becoming modesty and took himself off. Outside the dressing-room he stared down at the check perplexed.

"So she's gone, is she? And Glad thinks I had something to do with the vanishing act? Well —we'll let Glad think so—but—what the heck do you suppose DID happen to the Elliott blonde?" he mused to himself.

However, after a moment he came to the conclusion that this was none of his affair, and that about the wisest thing he could do was to pocket the check, and keep his mouth shut. Which he promptly proceeded to do.

*   *   *   *   *   *   *   *   *

Throughout that day and the next, Wayne and his unit worked on the final scenes of "Legacy of Love" and by midnight they were finished, and the film ready for the developing, printing and cutting rooms. Wayne said good-bye to the assembled company, and assured the excited Mary Gray that he would have something for her in his next production.

Wearily he entered his car and drove to his apartment where his man was waiting to let him in.

"A gentleman to see you, Mr. Wayne! He's been waiting quite some time. A Mr. O'Hearn, he said his name was!" said the servant. With his heart beating swiftly, Wayne hurried into the living room where O'Hearn was waiting patiently.

"Hello, Hank—any news?" he demanded eagerly.

"Well—I'm not sure that it affects Mrs. Elliott —but—I've got news of a sort! You remember that her fiance, Sherman Lawrence, was in jail in a little town in Mississippi, accused of murdering a woman in New York, and of at least complicity in a bank-robbery and a murder in Mississippi?" asked O'Hearn gravely.

"Yes, yes, of course I remember!" Wayne snapped pettishly, for it hurt to be reminded that Janelle could never be anything more to him than just a lovely dream.

"Well—Lawrence escaped tonight!" said O'Hearn quietly.

"Escaped?" gasped Wayne incredulously.

O'Hearn nodded.

"Some friends of his came to the jail about midnight—there's two hours difference in the time between here and there, you know—and they sawed through the bars and got him out. Got him away as slick as a whistle!" said O'Hearn.

Wayne stared at O'Hearn wildly.

"Surely, O'Hearn, you're not suggesting that —Janelle could have had a hand in that? Why—she wouldn't have had time to get there—she's only been gone from here since night before last!" cried Wayne.

"A plane left the local air-port an hour and a half after she was seen leaving the studio and geting into a Cadillac coupe. There was a woman on board. The plane made a stop early the next day at a town fifty miles from Yamacaw!" explained O'Hearn, and then, "I'm—kinda afraid she might have lost her head, Wayne—women in love do funny things! At any rate—the law thinks she helped and —they're hunting her, and him, too!"

Continued in Next Number.

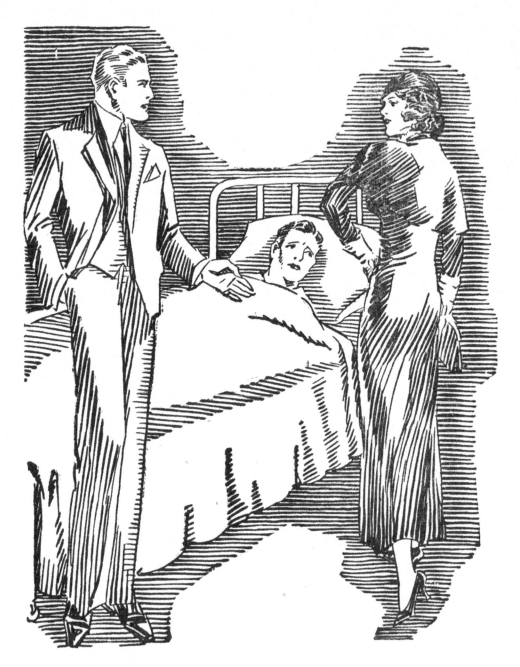

"Er — I'm his lawyer — just what HAVE you been to each other?" he
asked, politely, guardedly. The girl lifted her head proudly. "We
were married the 22nd of May! He is my husband!"
she said, firmly. Sherman could only stare at
her, speechless. (See Page 736)

Jan., No. 23

Chapter 79.

THE PRISON BREAK.

HERMAN was conscious, even in his sleep, of some faint noise that disturbed his slumbers. Not enough to arouse him fully—just enough to annoy him a little, and make him restless. But suddenly, a voice spoke near him, and he sat erect, wide awake.

The window at the foot of his bed across which there had been bars, was now open to the midnight sky.

The bars had been sawed through, pulled back, until a man could slip through. In fact, a man had.

He stood at the foot of Sherman's bed, listening, tense, and rigid.

"What do you want?" demanded Sherman, but the man at the foot of the bed swiftly cautioned silence.

"Pipe down, Joisey—it's your old pal, the Georgia Cracker!" cautioned the man coming around to the bed, and bending low above the man who lay there. "I've come to get you out o' here!"

"But I don't want to get out of here!" Sherman told him, vigorously. "At least, not until after the trial—I'm innocent——"

"Aw, shut up—what's the use o' that stuff to me? Ain't I the Cracker? Ain't I your pal? Wasn't I with you when the old guy was croaked? Think the Cracker's gonna leave a pal to rot in a dump like this? Come on, Joisey—the boys are out-side!" the Cracker was rough and hasty.

He flung back the covers, started to lift Sherman out of the bed, his powerful arms making light of Sherman's wasted strength.

"You fool——I tell you, I won't run away!" began Sherman, but the Cracker clapped a hand swiftly over his mouth, and looked about him.

A towel hung over a chair beside the bed, and the Cracker caught it up and swiftly knotted it into an effective gag, with which he silenced Sherman's further protests.

As he lifed the injured man, Sherman tried to fight him—and the injured shoulder sent a wave of excruciating pain over him.

He felt himself lifted, shoved through the window, and the pain and the roughness of the handling to which he was being subjected, robbed him of consciousness......

When he next knew what was happening about him, he found himself in a van, that was fitted up like a tiny bungalow. He lay on a bunk that was fastened to the wall, and that could be pushed up, out of the way, when not in use.

There was a tiny oil stove, beneath a cupboard on which there were dishes, cook-things swung below it, and there were canned victuals of all kinds.

A vast assortment of bright, shining new tinware took up most of the space in the van, and altogether, it was the weirdest contraption in which

Sherman Lawrence had ever travelled.

Through the window beside him, he could see that they were passing through the country—pretty, lush fields and green woods, and now and then the wheels of the van rumbled heavily across a bridge below which he caught the glimmer of a stream.

He could not see the driver, but he knew that the van was drawn by horses—he could hear the clop-clop-clop of their feet on the dusty, unpaved road.

He yelled loudly, and heard the driver speak to the horses.

The van turned from the road, and jounced and jarred along a few feet until it came to rest at last beneath a giant tree.

Somebody came around to the back of the van, and opened the door.

A big man, approaching middle-age, grizzled and battered by life. A man whose broad, good-humored face was laced by lines etched that by wind and weather —yes, and perhaps by hard living as well.

He wore clean, but faded overalls, and a violently checked shirt. On the back of his head, perched an utterly disreputable hat.

"Well, pal—glad to see you got your senses back! Thought last night you'd clean took leave of 'em!" the man greeted Sherman, cheerfully, almost affectionately.

Sherman raised himself a little and stared at the man, bewildered.

"And who the devil might you be?" he demanded, sharply.

The man who lounged in the doorway grinned, and bit off a sizable wad of chewing tobacco, as he considered his answer.

"We-e-ell, I might be the Prince o' Wales—or Andy Mellon—or President of the United States!" he answered, cheerfully. "Matter o' fact, I'm best known as the Georgia Cracker—a fact you ought to know right well by now—Joisey John!"

Sherman frowned, puzzled and a little angry.

"Why do you call me—Jersey John?" he demanded, irritably. "My name is Sherman Lawrence!"

"O. K. by me, Pal—only it's a damn' fool trick to pick a name for yourself that the cops all over the country's trying to hang on a murderer!" agreed the Cracker, sensibly. "But have it your own way!"

Sherman made an angry gesture with his unhurt hand.

"Darn it, I didn't pick the name—it was given to me at birth! I'm trying to tell you that that is actually, my name! And I don't know what you mean by trying to say that I am — this ridiculous — Jersey John!" he exploded.

The Cracker drew up a little stool and seated himself beside the bunk.

"Now, son, you listen to me a spell—I'm talkin' sense, even if you don't realize it now! You will, some day—believe you me!" he said, very seriously.

"I met up with you couple, maybe three weeks ago. You was all of a whip-stitch to git to California, account of a lady named Janelle! That was all you knowed. You didn't have a dime in your pocket—you was half-starved, and more'n half batty.

"I was sorry for you—and I took up with you. Me 'n' you bummed our way clear from New Jersey out here—we was pals—we strung along together— what was mine was yours and vicey-versy. Do you remember all that?"

Sherman's anger had melted, and he laid his uninjured hand on the man's knee for a moment.

"No—I don't remember—but I'm grateful—truly

I am!" he said. sincerely.

"That don't make no difference!" said the Cracker as though the words of gratitude embarrassed him. "Well—I got you into this bank stick-up—it was Skeeter that croaked the old guy—but Skeeter and Dopey and me got away—with the swag—and left you there, holding the bag.

"Skeeter and Dopey thought it was all right to let you take the rap for all of us—but I couldn't see it that way. I still had the swag—it hadn't been divided —so I was in what you might call a position to argue with 'em. I told 'em that not one cent would they lay fingers on as long as you was in clink.

"So they agreed to help me get you away—and then I give 'em their split, and they beat it. I got yours and mine. Now do you see why you want to forget about this Sherman Lawrence gag?"

"But I tell you it isn't a gag! It's my real name!" protested Sherman, half-laughing, half annoyed.

The Cracker made a little gesture.

"All right, it's your name—so what?" he pointed out, grimly. "What about the dame you are supposed to have croaked in New York? What about an alibi for that, eh?"

"I didn't do it, of course, any more than I killed the night-watchman!" protested Sherman, vigorously.

"All right, maybe you didn't. That's your story —but how are you gonna make anybody believe it?" demanded the Cracker, unimpressed.

"By proving I'm innocent! The courts can't convict an innocent man!" said Sherman, swiftly.

The Cracker's little contemptuous laugh was half a grunt.

"Don't make me laugh!" he derided. "The reason I made Skeeter and Dopey help me get you out of that hoose-gow was because I know just how easy it is for a feller to get convicted, innocent or guilty. And the only way to prove that you didn't kill the watchman, is to find the man who did—and Skeeter's plenty far away by now, and still travelling.

"The minute you go on the stand to tell your story, then it's me, and Skeeter and Dopey at the wrong end of a man-hunt — and since you ain't got sense enough to see that the only way to keep your own neck unstretched is to lay low for awhile, and then leave the country, it's up to me to see that you don't get a chance to squawk.

"I bought this tin-peddler's outfit for a hundred and fifty dollars cash—it's as good a disguise as I could find. And you can stay right there in your little beddie-bye until you're strong enough to get out on your own —and until you can, I'm the boss o' this layout!"

"But, you idiot, don't you know that the fact that I escaped, and ran away, will be considered proof positive that I'm guilty?" demanded Sherman, angrily.

"Well, what if it does? Guilty or not guilty, they can't hang you if they can't find you, can they?" demanded the Cracker, reasonably enough.

He turned to the shelf of canned goods above the stove, with a gesture that said plainly he had said all that he intended to say on the subject. That his mind was made up and it was a sheer waste of time to argue with him.

"And now—how'll you have your corned beef and baked beans—hot or cold?" he wanted to know, cheerfully, and set about the preparations for dinner.

Sherman lay still, lost in troubled thoughts.

The case against him had been black enough—his lack of memory, the fact that, after all, he COULD have been guilty of the horrible things of which they accused him—all this had been bad enough. His only hope had been to face the trial, and prove his innocence.

But now, his absurd "prison-break," this ridiculous "escape" had sealed the case against him. Even his friends would have some trouble believing him innocent, he realized, with a sinking heart.

He realized that the Cracker's motives in freeing him by practically kidnapping him, had not been entirely unselfish. The Cracker had feared to see Sherman on the witness-stand in his own defense—he had feared Sherman's memory of the exploits of himself and his companions.

Of course, the Cracker knew and admitted that Sherman was innocent of the murder of the old night-watchman. Of the murder of the woman, "Annie Greene," the Cracker of course knew nothing.

Frankly, Sherman admitted to himself that he knew very little himself. He lay there, lost in thought while the Cracker went about the task of preparing a plain, yet wholesome and appetizing meal, now and then flinging a curious glance at the man who lay in the narrow bunk.

Sherman was trying with all his might, to fling his mind back along those eight or ten weeks that he had, somehow, lost out of his life.

It was a terrifying thought, really, that for eight or ten weeks, he had been—and done—and seen—things that now he could not remember. That the eight or ten weeks were as they had never been.

Yet — things had happened — rather terrible things, he was afraid. Things for which now he was to be called to account, even though the man who had done those things was a man a thousand miles apart from Sherman Lawrence.

With an effort that made his head ache dully, he

cast back in his mind to the night he had left the hospital in Havana. That he could remember perfectly.

Nurse Judkins, leaving the room to get his nourishment due in a few moments. Himself, climbing out of bed, his legs wobbly, clinging to the posts of the bed for support as he managed, with trembling hands, to drag his clothes on.

Out of the hospital—yes, he remembered that. And the velvety darkness that enfolded him as he hurried away, his foot-steps wavering but his purpose rigid as life itself.

Even now, he could close his eyes and recall the fragrance of that velvety, tropical darkness—the scent of blossoms—the glimmering, ghostly white of great pompoms of oleander blossoms that spattered their white petals upon him as he walked along beneath them.

He frowned, set his teeth, and his fists clenched as the man he saw in his memory—that plodding, staggering, wavering creature—seemed to melt into a fog —a mist settled down upon him—Sherman could see him no more.

What happened to him after he vanished into that fog? He all but groaned aloud as he tried to pierce the fog, and, at last, knew himself beaten.

His next conscious memory was of awakening in the hospital, with the beetle-browed, burly attendant in the white coat standing beside him, the Chief of Police reading the notice of a reward for the capture of Sherman Lawrence.

He was wanted for the murder of "Annie Green." The name awakened a new thread of memory—he saw himself on the verandah of the hospital in Havana, with Janelle beside him. Janelle was reading a letter—and the letter was from Annie Greene. She claimed to have information about Janelle's lost baby. He had hired detectives to investigate the case — they had learned nothing.

There had been other letters from "Annie Greene"—and now he could remember that the reason he had slipped away from the hospital that night had been a final letter from Annie Greene—he had been trying to reach New York to see the woman—to have a talk with her—to find out once for all what, if anything, she really did know!

And now, a cold and clammy horror swept over him. HAD HE SUCCEEDED IN REACHING NEW YORK AND A CONFERENCE WITH THE WOMAN?

Had they, perhaps, quarrelled—had she refused to give up the information she had claimed to have—and had he—oh, was it possible that—after all—he WAS guilty of this terrible crime? Had he, under the spell of a temporary insanity, strangled this woman who had tortured Janelle by withholding vital information?

He was writhing a little, white-faced, his teeth set, his hands twisted into the covers of the bed, his brow beaded with cold perspiration when the Cracker came over to him, and touched his shoulder. In his other hand, the Cracker held a plate of steaming, savoury food.

"Here you are, partner—what's matter? Been having a nightmare? Well, snap out of it, and fill your tummy with some good hot grub! That'll put you straight!" said the Cracker, matter of factly.

Sherman was conscious of an almost passionate gratitude towards the vagrant. As grateful for being aroused from his bitter, terrifying dreams, as for the food, for which he found himself surprisingly hungry.

Chapter 80.

THE THING THAT HAD TO BE.

HEN JANELLE arose at noon, after a sound sleep of utter exhaustion, she found that the day was perfect, and the ship was ploughing along steadily, as though with a very definite goal in view.

Janelle bathed, and when she was ready to dress, looked about her, The yellow tulle frock that she had worn last night was completely ruined. The chest of drawers revealed nothing suitable for day-time wear, though there were frail and costly garments—lingerie, negligees, night-gowns, satin pajamas, slips, piles of stockings rolled into little balls and looking like delicately tinted blossoms.

All were quite new and there were several sizes among them. She was able to find a pair her own size, and strapped sandals in another drawer that fitted well enough.

The door of the closet as she swung it open, revealed dresses, gowns, things suitable for wear aboard a ship.

She found a white linen frock, sleeveless, belted, jaunty-looking, an amusing feminine variation of a sailor suit, that she donned, and then, conscious that she looked very trim and neat and attractive, she stepped out on deck.

The sky was a cloudless blue. The water reflected the blue, broken with great, rolling breakers and dancing white-caps and there was an exhilarating breeze. If only she might have relaxed and let herself go—if only she were free to enjoy all this!

But she gave it scarcely a glance as she heard foot-steps behind her and turned, to see a Chinese cabin boy, who greeted her with a beaming smile, and twinkling shoe button eyes.

"Ah Sing bling blekfus fo' missy on deck!" he assured her, and indicated a cushioned wicker chair, beside which a small wicker table had been drawn.

The cabin boy pattered away and Janelle sat down in the comfortable chair. A few minutes later, the boy was back with a tray on which there was a slender silver pot of coffee, a tray of golden brown toast, a pat of butter, a little bowl of marmalade, and a melon, its pink flesh gleaming rosily from its nest of ice.

It was as dainty and delicious a breakfast as would have been served to her on one of the finest ocean liners, and as she ate, with the healthy appetite of youth, she puzzled a little about this man, Far-away Thomas, who lived in such princely luxury aboard this ship—and earned the luxury by smuggling liquor into a country where, ostensibly, prohibition flourished.

She was half-way through with her meal, when Far-away came along the deck, immaculately groomed in the double-breasted, blue flannel brass-buttoned coat, and spotless white flannel trousers.

"Good morning!" he greeted her, and his eyes

lighted with appreciation of the picture she made. "The acid test of a pretty woman is—how does she look in the brilliant noon-day light! Needless to say, you pass the test with flying colors! What a charming break-fast companion!"

"Twelve hours of the thirty-six have passed!" Janelle reminded him, minus any other greeting.

The man frowned, in annoyance, and accepted the interruption of the cabin boy who brought him a tray identical with the one that he had brought to Janelle.

Another small wicker table drawn to another comfortable, cushioned wicker chair, and the man began his breakfast.

"I might say," he answered her, surlily, "that your manners scarcely keep pace with your looks!"

"I'm afraid I'm not thoroughly posted on the etiquette of being kidnapped! Being held a prisoner against my will, I didn't know I was expected to be—entertaining!"

Far-away looked up at her, from his melon, and there was a shadow of menace in his eyes.

"You'll find it to your advantage to—keep a civil tongue in your head!" he warned her, grimly, and there was the click of a whip-lash in his voice.

Last night, he had been gracious, charming, a little drunk. This morning, he was entirely sober, with a slight headache—and he was in no mood to be trifled with.

Yet Janelle dared a little farther, despite the brutality she had seen him display to the woman, "Mama Louise" last night.

"Then—your promise about—finding my baby and bringing him back to me—was not true? You did not intend to do it, at all?" she asked, quietly, her heart sinking a little. Somehow, she had felt that he COULD do this thing if he would! And—she had believed that he would.

He lifted the empty melon-hull and flung it carelessly over-board, wiping his fingers delicately on the embroidered linen napkin.

"I may—I haven't quite decided yet! First of all, I shall want to know who has the child——and then I'll decide whether it would be worth-while to—take it, or not!" he told her, carelessly.

Janelle rose, swiftly, without a word to him, and turned. Without looking back, she walked away from him down the deck.

At the far end of the deck, out of sight of the man, she paused, and leaned against the rail, looking out over the blue waters, with their dancing white caps and long breakers.

A sound behind her caused her to turn, startled, and she saw the woman, "Mama Louise," huddled in a steamer chair, her breakfast tray untouched beside her.

"Mama Louise" was weeping, trying a little to stifle her sobs, and she was quite unconscious of Janelle's presence, until Janelle stood beside her and spoke.

"Why are you crying?" asked Janelle, quietly.

Startled, the woman lifted a face swollen with weeping, a great ugly bruise on one cheek bone, a cut against her temple.

She wore pajamas, with voluminous trouser legs and a tight little brassiere top, with straps laced across her back. Her back, bare save for these narrow straps, showed swollen bluish stripes where the dog-whip had taken its toll of her last night.

As she saw Janelle, and recognized her, her distorted face became ugly with hatred, and her eyes flashed fire.

"Why am I crying? Because there was sugar instead of salt on my melon this morning—because it didn't rain today—because gulls don't sing—why do you suppose I'm crying? You've an infernal gall to ask that!" she sneered, savagely.

"If—you're jealous of—me—perhaps it would please you to know that I have nothing but loathing and disgust for—Far-away!" said Janelle, steadily.

A little of the hostility went out of "Mama Louise's" manner, but she lifted one shoulder in a little shrug.

"A lot of good that will do you!" she answered, lifelessly. "He's crazy about you, for the time being—and out here, he is the law—he rules! Whatever he says, you'll do—or wish to God you'd never been born!"

"If he is such a beast—oh, I know he is—but—how can you possibly — care for him?" demanded Janelle, puzzled.

The woman shrugged again, and a little faint smile touched her red mouth.

"I—adore him—I worship him—I'm mad about him—yet—he is a brute and a beast, and, lately, he has treated me like a dog! Yet—like a beaten dog—I crawl back to him and lick his hand! Because—in spite of everything—I love him—and—I can't stop loving him!" she answered, and her voice sounded dreary and dead.

She looked up, suddenly, at Janelle, and a queer little smile twisted her lips. A bitter, derisive little smile—and Janelle knew, somehow, that the bitterness and derision was directed at the woman herself, and not at Janelle.

"Mama Louise" spoke suddenly.

"You dispise me for that, don't you?" she said, quietly. "I don't blame you—I despise myself! But

—I can't help myself! I was well brought up—my mother and father were well-to-do people—I had advantages—education—I went to college—I was ambitious—I had hopes of making a name for myself.

"And then—I went to a dance one night—at a public dance-place—it was a sort of joke—a lark! And —I met Steve! It was love at first sight—I went mad about him. I—let him take me home with him that night—the next day we came aboard the Mollie E.

"I haven't seen my parents since—they loved me —were very proud of me—I suppose I—broke their hearts.

"But—it was a thing that—had to be! A thing so much stronger than I—that—I couldn't even fight it! I didn't try—it was something—as big as life, as strong as death, and as inevitable!"

She was silent for a moment, her face turned towards the sea, and Janelle studied her curiously.

A beautiful profile, slightly thickened by approaching obesity due no doubt to the liquor that she drank so carelessly and to the indolent life she led aboard ship. A woman who had been a great beauty — who was still beautiful — and Janelle's heart was touched with pity for her—a deep, almost an aching sympathy.

"Mama Louise" looked up, suddenly.

"I suppose you can't understand a love like that! Few women would be capable of it—thank God, few women are tortured by it!" she said, evenly "But— for the first year—Far-away was true to me—and—I lived in Heaven. Our love was—glorious--superb. A flame that lifted us both to the heights! It is—the memory of that year that keeps me chained here—I'll never leave him—I—couldn't, even if I tried!"

Janelle looked down at her, and saw that there

were tears on the woman's lashes, though a tremulous
smile touched her lips.

"And—some day—he'll come back to me—and
love me again—as he did that first year! That's—
worth waiting for—worth—enduring anything for!"
she said, quietly.

And Janelle, feeling that she intruded by merely
looking at this woman's face, touched as it was by an
almost rapt look, turned and slipped away............

   *   *   *   *   *   *   *   *   *

The afternoon passed quietly. Far-away seemed
busy with some purpose of his own, and when he passed
Janelle, he scarcely looked at her.

She lay in a steamer chair, in a shady spot,
watching everything that went on about her, saying
nothing, apparently lost in thought.

But in reality, very little escaped her. She knew
that Far-away was intent on some serious purpose.

He and the entire crew, which seemed much too
large to be needed by this rather small ship, were busy
all afternoon, and she discovered, to her alarm and
amazement, that, mounted fore and aft were small,
but very practical looking guns of the most modern
sort.

Far-away spent a good deal of time on the bridge,
discussing the course with the navigator, and as darkness fell, the feeling of tenseness increased.

At dinner, which she ate in the cabin with Far-
away, Janelle found him abstracted, excited, and almost
unconscious of her presence, for which she was heartily
glad.

There was no sign of "Mama Louise" at dinner, but afterward, when Far-away stepped on deck, and paused, for a moment, in the light that fell from the companionway, Janelle saw "Mama Louise" come up to him.

She was beautifully dressed in an amber satin evening gown, her hair beautifully waved, the ugly bruise on her cheek almost hidden beneath artfully applied make-up.

Far-away gave her a glance, and turned indifferently away.

Janelle unnoticed behind them in the companionway, felt her heart ache for the woman who had tried so humbly and so painstakingly to make herself beautiful for this man who gave her scarcely the most indifferent glance.

"Steve," said "Mama Louise," swiftly. "What is this thing you are planning for tonight?"

Far-away turned, swiftly, almost angrily.

"What do you know about it?" he demanded, sharply.

"Nothing," answered the woman, very quickly. "Nothing except that I've seen the men working over the guns today—and I know that whatever it is, it's dangerous! Please don't!"

"Don't talk like a fool!" snapped Far-away, roughly. "Curly Duke's ship is bringing in a fifty thousand dollar cargo tonight. We are going to get to him thirty minutes before his own boats—and we're going to land it ourselves—that's all!"

"Mama Louise" cried out, sharply.

"Oh, no, no—Steve, you mustn't! I tell you, you mustn't!" she cried, wildly, and put both shaking hands on his arm, in a pleading gesture, clinging to him as he tried to shake her off. "It's dangerous, I tell you

—Steve, you mustn't!"

The man flung her off, and glared at her, his own nerves taut, resentful of her excitement that could not but agitate him a little.

"Have you lost your mind? Since when have I stopped a job like this just because it's dangerous? Are you losing your nerve, Mama Louise? If you are, it's about time I was getting a new 'mama'!" he sneered, roughly.

"But this is different—Steve, I tell you, something awful will happen tonight if you try to carry this plan through! Steve, you've GOT to listen to me!" cried the woman, and her agitation, her excitement were so intense that, in spite of himself, the man now paused.

"I cut the cards today, Steve—a dozen times—a hundred times—I cut them, and almost every time the death card came up. Trouble—and death! You've got to give up this crazy scheme!"

For a moment, in spite of himself, the man was shaken. And then he thrust the woman away from him, savagely—the more angry since, for a moment, he had been inclined to listen to her—to be swayed by her.

"Don't be a fool!" he snarled, savagely. "You and your damned fortune-telling cards! I've hi-jacked many a boat-load of Curly Dukes' stuff, but nothing that ever gave me more pleasure than this! Think I'm going to stop just because you've had a crazy brain-storm? Get back to your room, and cut the cards some more—and find out whose death it is—so you can be prepared—if necessary!"

There was an ugly, ominous threat in the last words, and he shoved the woman out of his way so viciously that she would have fallen to the deck had she not managed to catch the railing, and support herself, for a moment.

Janelle, still standing in the doorway where she had heard and seen everything that had taken place, found herself clinging to the frame of the door, shaken and terrified by what she had heard.

Far-away was planning another of his hi-jacking operations! Guns were to be employed—it would be a dangerous business—death and destruction, in the wake of the rum-runners! She shivered, and grew cold with fear and horror.

Chapter 81.

ON THE MERCY OF THE COURT!

ALL THROUGH the night, Sherman lay wakeful and bewildered.

He was wise enough in the ways of the law to know that he could follow no more dangerous course than to run away from the accusations and terrible charges on which he had been arrested.

His only hope of ultimate freedom was to throw himself on the mercy of the court, and, somehow, someway, prove his innocence.

Now, he was a hunted man—a fugitive from the law. He did not doubt but that at this moment, there was a price on his head — a liberal reward for his capture.

He MUST go back and give himself up. He MUST hire a lawyer, detectives, if need be, and prove himself innocent of the charges against him. Or—and here his heart sank, plummet-wise, to his boots—or, if he were guilty, he must take his punishment!

He shuddered at the bare thought of being proven guilty. And yet, if he HAD, under the spell of a temporary insanity, during those eight or ten weeks that he had lost out of his life, committed this crime, it would be better to know it—to have it proven against him, and to take his punishment, than to skulk, cowardly, a fugitive from the law, a fugitive from justice, not knowing whether he was guilty or not.

The next thing, having made up his mind that he must give himself up to the law, was how to go about doing it.

He was unable to walk—he was unable to slip out of the wagon, while the Cracker was asleep, and to make his way, how many miles he had no way of knowing, to the nearest officer of the law, to whom he could surrender. And the Cracker had made it only too plain that he would not allow Sherman to give himself up.

There was only one way out — and that way meant that not only he, himself, but the Cracker, must face imprisonment. He solaced his conscience with the thought that he could use power, money, influence, all to help the Cracker as well as himself. They must both throw themselves on the mercy of the court—and take whatever punishment was meted out to them, when their guilt or their innocence had been finally established.

He busied himself with a well-laid plan, and when morning came, he assured the Cracker that he was suffering terribly. That the wound in his shoulder had broken open and that he must have medical attention at once.

The Cracker was troubled. Unwilling to run the risk of going to a doctor, yet unwilling to see his pal suffer.

At last, reluctantly, he hitched up the two horses, and the big van, with its rattling load of tinware clink-ing merrily, lumbered into the road.

Sherman had not had to pretend very much about his injured shoulder. It WAS paining him terribly—and he was running a temperature.

He set his teeth, as the clumsy old van jogged along, shaking him, jarring the injured shoulder, but, at last, in a tiny village off the main highway, the van came to a halt in front of a neat white cottage, that wore its doctor's shingle swinging proudly above its front gate.

The Cracker climbed down from his perch in front, and, with obvious reluctance, went up the walk to the house. Through the window, Sherman saw the man talking to a neatly dressed, gray-haired woman, and then, a moment later, the Cracker came down the walk, beside a middle-aged, kind-looking man, bare-headed, who carried a medical bag in his hand.

Sherman was breathing a little harder when the doctor and the Cracker stepped into the van, and the doctor looked about him, curiously, even before he sat down to examine his patient.

"Cozy little place you have here — I envy you, getting about, seeing new faces, new scenery, every day!" he commented, as he unbottoned Sherman's shirt, and leaned above him, to examine the wound.

The Cracker lounged in the doorway, looking on, restless, worried. Sherman found the doctor's ear close to his lips, and whispered, almost soundlessly,

"Send him away! Send him away!"

The doctor hid a startled movement, and his eyes flashed to Sherman's, and then he turned to his bag, fumbled for something, and said to the Cracker,

"I wonder if you'd mind running up to the house and asking my wife to send me a roll of half-inch bandage. I don't seem to have any here!"

The Cracker hesitated—looked at Sherman, who lay with closed eyes, as though unconscious, and then at the doctor. He could scarcely refuse such an innocent request, however, and, after a moment, he stepped down to the ground, and hurried, his ragged coat flopping about him, up the walk to the house.

The instant he saw him go, Sherman caught the doctor's sleeve, and drew the man towards him.

"Listen, Doctor—I've only a minute—I've got to talk fast. I'm an escaped prisoner—Sherman Lawrence, wanted for a murder I did not commit, and also for a jail-break that was not my fault. I want to give myself up to the law, and stand trial—but the Cracker is implicated, too, and he won't let me give myself up because it will mean his arrest, too. Report to the Sheriff that we are here—have us arrested before we get out of town—there's a stiff reward out, and it's yours if you'll do this!"

The doctor was pallid with amazement.

"You want to give yourself up?" he stammered.

"Of course—I want to stand trial and be acquitted, or convicted, one—I don't want to be a fugitive, hiding out all the time—quick, he's coming. Say you'll report to the sheriff!" urged Sherman.

"Of course—at once!" said the doctor, swiftly, and when the Cracker came back into the wagon, the doctor was putting a finishing touch on a very neat job of dressing the shoulder-wound.

"Oh, you didn't need the half-inch bandage, after all!" said the Cracker, and there was suspicion in his eyes and his manner.

"Er—no, I decided that the inch and a half would make a neater job. Sorry to have troubled you—but I think you'll find that quite all right now!" said the doctor and tumbled his instruments and medicines carelessly into the shabby little bag, obviously eager to be gone.

"How much, Doc?" demanded the Cracker, fishing into his capacious pocket.

"Oh—a dollar will be enough!" said the doctor, and pocketed the money, as he hurriedly took his departure.

The Cracker looked after him a moment, suspiciously, and then down at Sherman, who lay quite still, with closed eyes.

"Now I wonder what's eatin' that bird?" mused the Cracker. "Guess you'n me'd better be travellin' along!"

He climbed into the front seat, spoke to the horses, and the van began to move again, lumbering down the village street and on into the open country again.

Sherman lay tense, watching the road behind them, that was visible through the open door. He saw the little village drop behind as the horses took up a brisk pace.

He all but held his breath, watching for some sign of the approaching sheriff down that long, dusty road—and, at last, he saw a battered, but still defiant little flivver come rocketing along, in a cloud of dust.

Eagerly, he watched it—raising himself a little on his pillows, as it came closer and closer.

The Cracker did not discover the car until it essayed to pass him, and then, startled, he pulled the wagon to one side, and the flivver passed, went a few paces up the road, and then turned, sharply, blocking the road.

Four men, all armed with shot-guns, hopped out of the flivver, and came running back towards the van.

"You're under arrest — the both of you! For murder, robbery and jail-breaking!" thundered the leader of the men, a wiry, grizzled little man who wore a shiny badge that half-hid his meagre chest.

And the Cracker, looking back at the man who lay in the bunk in the wagon-van, cursed him until he had no more breath to curse with ....

*   *   *   *   *   *   *   *   *

Out on the broad bosom of the Pacific, a ship rode lazily, its lights out, several men tensely on the look-out. In the ship's hold, fastened in sacks so that each bundle could be swiftly dropped over the side, was a fifty thousand dollar cargo of fine liquors.

Well outside the twelve mile limit, so that there was no danger of any difficulty with Uncle Sam's upholders of the prohibition law, and flying the flag of another nation, the ship and its men were quiet and at ease—unafraid.

And hidden now in the darkness, another ship crept closer to the one that flew a foreign flag. A ship whose empty hold yawned for the fifty thousand dollar cargo—and whose owner's pockets yawned hungrily for money that he had no right to take.

Suddenly, those aboard the Mollie E. saw the faint glimmer of a signal light—winking for a moment, and then lost in the darkness. Instantly, Far-away returned the signal.

A length of stove-pipe held steady upon the railing of the ship, one end in the direction from which that swift light had come—the other end against Far-away's stomach. He moved back, inserted an ordinary flashlight in the stove-pipe, and pressed its light on. A signal light, visible a tremendous distance across the water, yet giving no sign visible anywhere around the ship. An accepted signal of the rum-running fleet.

Far-away flashed the light on, off, on, off—on a bare second—off two seconds—on three seconds—off two seconds. A moment delay, and then the answering signal from the ship that loomed away in the larkness.

"That's her, all right—she returned the signal. Up and at 'em boys—and remember, no trouble unless it can't be avoided. The liquor to be transferred as quickly as possible—and if we can, we'll get away without them knowing that we're not Curly Dukes gang!

"But—if we can't do that—then let 'em have it!" ordered Far-away, and in his low, exultant voice, there was a throb of delight, of excitement. It was obvious that the man thoroughly enjoyed the consciousness of danger—that he relished it.

Outside the range of the group of men who clustered about the signal light, Janelle and "Mama Louise," two women whose grievances and enmities were forgotten in their common peril, huddled together, watching terror clutched at their throats, a trembling excitement crisping their nerves.

Slowly, but surely, the two boats came alongside. The liquor-carrier stayed very carefully well outside the legal limit, and the Mollie E had to step over that imaginary boundary to come alongside the rum-ship.

But finally, the boats were side by side, and the exchange of signals had satisfied the rum-ship that the Mollie E was her customer.

"They're half an hour early, boss—we didn't look for 'em until around one o'clock—it's just a little after twelve!" a man on the rum-ship reminded his skipper.

"Oh, well, that's their look-out, not mine! Go ahead and transfer the cargo, and let's get going!" ordered the skipper.

It was a moonless night, though the sky was sprinkled with a frost-like glimmering of stars. Against that faintly illuminated starry expanse, Janelle saw a great crane-like contrivance dip into the hold of the rum-ship and come up, carrying in its great maw, a lumpy looking bundle.

A turn and the crane-like thing was depositing its bundle soundlessly below decks on the Mollie E. Again and again the crane made its trip. Tireless. Faithful. Soundless with well oiled machinery.

At last, the rum-ship rode high, while the Mollie E. wallowed a bit, her hold stuffed with fifty thousand dollars worth of contraband. The signal came from the rum-ship—she was empty. The Mollie E. flashed her signal back.

The engines of the Mollie E. began to thump again—steadily, tirelessly. The ship began to move— Janelle held her breath. Had it, after all, been accomplished without danger? Had they escaped the terror that she and Mama Louise feared—so easily?

She held her breath—and suddenly, back in the direction from which they had come, she caught the flicker of a light. On a second—off two seconds—on three seconds................

She heard the men cry out, softly.

"There's Curly's crowd now!"

Far-away gave a great, triumphant shout of laughter, heard aboard the rum-ship.

"Thanks for the load, old man—tell Curly Dukes he's been 'frazzed' again—and by Far-away Thomas!" he yelled, his caution overcome by his eagerness to "crow" over the man he had robbed once again.

There came a yell of rage from the rum-ship— Far-away's own men hushed him sternly — and the skipper signalled "full-speed ahead."

The two women, clinging together there in the darkness, shuddered, and Janelle prayed, inarticulately—perhaps "Mama Louise" did, too, in her own way, for the man whom, in spite of everything, she loved with a blind, dog-like devotion. Then, suddenly, crashing across the water with a hideous, tearing sound — came the whine of a bullet! It crossed the bow—an eloquent messenger of what was to come............

* * * * * * * * *

To Sherman, in the hospital at Yamacraw, again, came Bert Hastings, from Atlanta. A member of the law-firm in which Sherman had, as he expressed it, cut his political teeth. One of the cleverest, shrewdest, most capable lawyers in the business.

The two men gripped hands, wordless because their delight in meeting again was too deep for words.

"And now what I want to know, Sherm, old son, is how in the name of the seven fiends of Hades, you ever got yourself into such a hell of a mess?" demanded Bert, frankly.

"I'm not quite sure myself—it's a long story!" said Sherman, and proceeded to tell Bert the high-lights of it.

It WAS a long story, and the telling of it took considerable time. Bert listened, in utter amazement, and when he had finished, Bert stared down at his old friend, wide-eyed and a little aghast.

"Son, you don't need a lawyer—boy, you need a magician!" he admitted, frankly. "Ye gods, to think of YOU, in such a mess as this—it's enough to make a fellow's hair curl!"

"The thing that ought to make your hair curl, old

man, is that I expect you to get me out of this mess!" Sherman assured him, firmly. "Tell me, have you heard anything from Janelle? I mean, has she wired, or anything?"

"There was a wire the day you stepped out for your airing, with your friend, the Cracker. There was also a long distance telephone call—said she'd be here in three days! But—I'm afraid something happened to upset her plans!" admitted Bert, reluctantly.

Sherman stared at him in bewilderment.

"What do you mean? Tell me!" he ordered, swiftly.

"I suppose I might as well—you'll have to know sooner or later!" admitted Bert. "I don't know, of course—it may be studio publicity—but the newspapers say that Janelle Elliott, who had just finished the final scenes in a picture she was making at some dinky studio in Hollywood, has vanished—and they fear foul play!"

"What?" Sherman was pallid.

"Now, take it easy, old man—the whole thing may be just a publicity stunt, and she may, right this minute, be on her way here. That may be the movie studio's gentle way of horning in on some publicity, while Janelle beats it here——" Bert was interrupted by the opening of the door, and the arrival of the white-coated attendant, whose manner had undergone a complete change since it had been proven that the prisoner really WAS several times a millionaire.

"A lady wants to see you, Mr. Lawrence—the warden says its O. K. if you want to see her!" he said, and grinned a little. "I'd see her if I was you—is she a peach?"

Sherman cried out, swiftly,

"It's Janelle!" and to the attendant, "bring her in, of course!"

The grinning attendant vanished, and, a moment later, a girl stood in the doorway. Sherman was conscious first only of a bitter disappointment at the discovery that the girl was not Janelle. She was young and almost startlingly beautiful. Dark of hair and eyes, and beautifully dressed in a trim dark suit, smart little hat, with a tiny veil.

Wonderingly, he stared at her, as she stood in the doorway, and then he said, politely,

"You wished to see me?"

The girl caught her breath on a little sob, and stumbled towards the bed on which he lay.

"Oh, my darling, my darling—what have they done to you?" she sobbed and collapsed beside the bed, weeping hysterically. "To find you in this AWFUL place!"

Sherman stared, wild-eyed, at Bert and then at the girl.

"Who is she?" demanded Sherman.

Bert grinned, wisely. "Oh, no—YOU tell ME!" he insisted.

"I never saw her before in my life!" protested Sherman.

The girl lifted her head, her lovely eyes flooded with tears, and cried out, reproachfully.

"Oh, how can you say that? After all we've been to each other!"

Bert started, and his eyes widened.

"Er—I'm his lawyer—just what HAVE you been to each other?" he asked, politely, guardedly.

The girl lifted her head, proudly.

"We were married the 22nd of May! He is my husband!" she said, firmly.

Sherman could only stare at her, speechless.

Continued in Next Number.

"Just when did you first meet this man you say is your husband, Miss——?"
asked Bert very carefully and deliberately. The girl lifted
her head haughtily. "I am Mrs. Sherman Lawrence——not
MISS anything!" she protested haughtily.
(See Page 761)

Chapter 82.

PIRACY ON THE HIGH SEAS!

S THE SHOT went across the bow, a little spasm of excitement sped over the men on board. Quickly the guns on the forward deck were uncovered, ready for action. A light flashed a signal closer at hand, and those on deck whirled the gun, aimed it directly at the light — and waited.

"The fools!" Janelle heard Far-away growl savagely, and he cursed luridly. "Do they want to bring the whole darn United States Navy down on our necks?"

Again the light flashed, this time to the left of its previous position, and again the gun was swung about.

Far-away swore and raved.

"Don't you see what they are doing, you blasted idiots? Those signals aren't coming from the mother-ship—they're coming from the mosquito fleet—it's done deliberately to deceive us!" he cried.

Janelle and Mama Louise, huddled in a corner in the darkness, cried out suddenly, sharply, as a dark figure lifted itself above the railing, from the very sea itself, it seemed. But even as they cried out, the dark figure stood upright, and in its hands was the barrel of a hand machine-gun.

"Up with 'em, Far-away—way up!" ordered the voice of the shadow grimly, and Far-away whirled on his heels with a savage oath of dismay.

By now others were swarming over the railing and Janelle knew that there must be boats below there —boats that, while the crew and Far-away had been absorbed in watching those decoy signals, had quietly slipped close enough for their crew to climb aboard unseen.

The deck now was a seething mass of men— working quietly, so quietly that there was something eery about their movements.

Far-away and his men were at the mercy of these men, and they knew it—accepted the fact with what little grace they could muster.

In the dim light that swung above his head, Far-away lifted his hands well above his head and said grimly,

"O. K., Curly—you win!"

"Win?" said the man facing him, and his voice was grim and ugly. "Of course I win, you dirty, thieving, hi-jacking rat!"

Janelle caught her breath and almost cried out. For the voice hardly lifted above a whisper was the one she had heard before on a lonely, deserted canyon road—the voice of the "contact man" who had told her of the ransom demand.

She started forward, but Mama Louise caught her swiftly and pulled her back, a hand over her mouth, warning her to silence.

"There have been times when you didn't win,

Curly!" Far-away reminded Curly grimly.

"Maybe—but this isn't one of them!" said Curly with equal grimness.

He spoke to one of his men.

"All right, Jay? You've got the hoist ready? Then tell the skeeters to get going!" he ordered crisply though in an undertone.

And Janelle, huddled there in the darkness, saw one of the amazing sights of one of the best organized illicit industries in the country—the loading of a rum-cargo to the fleet of speedy, powerful little speed-boats that takes it in and lands it on the beach.

The small boats, built to be the expensive toys and playthings of sons and daughters of the idle rich, capable of maintaining a terrific speed, began to circle the Mollie E.

Their motors muffled until the sound was like a continuous hum, they sped past, paused a moment while the hoist lowered into the small boat one of the bulky bundles encased in sacking.

Instantly, the little boat darted away like a water-bug and another took its place. Efficiency was the watch-word. More rapidly than one can talk about it—the transaction was finished.

While Curly stood with the hand machine-gun slung in the crook of his arm, one hand carelessly but purposefully on the trigger, his eyes never leaving Far-away, the little boats sped up, were loaded, sped away, swallowed up in darkness, until the hold of the Mollie E. was as empty as it had been when the ship had sailed from port.

"And now, Far-away, I hope you've learned your little lesson!" said Curly coolly as he turned towards the railing. "Meddle in my business just once more—and it'll be the last time. You get me, I hope. I'm about fed up with you and your hi-jacking, anyway, you yellow rat!"

This was too much for Mama Louise. Thrusting Janelle roughly aside, Mama Louise stepped from her hiding place and confronted the two men.

"That's a little too much, Steve—even from Curly Dukes with a gun in his hand! Are you going to take it?" she demanded.

Curly stepped back as the woman revealed herself.

"Oh—so it's Mama Louise! The same spitfire she's always been! I wonder, Far-away, that a woman with the spirit of Mama Louise could ever take up with the likes of you!" he sneered, his tone expressing hatred and contempt.

"Keep your hands off Mama Louise—and your tongue, too — you blowhard!" snarled Far-away savagely, his up-lifted hands twitching a little as though they ached to twist themselves about the throat of this ancient enemy.

"Oh, that gets a rise out of you, does it?" sneered Curly viciously.

Suddenly, a diversion was created. Across the water came a cry:

"Ahoy there! Who are you?"

"A Government boat—been trailing me all evening!" whispered Curly tensely, and now the scene shifted.

Curly and Far-away, and their men were no longer ancient enemies. Now—suddenly—they had a common cause—fear of this guardian of the law that was approaching, a slim, gray avenger of the laws they so callously broke.

"Answer them, you fool!" Far-away hissed to one of the crew, and turned swiftly to Curly, Mama Louise, and Janelle. "Into the cabin—quick. The salon, there ahead !"

"The Yacht Mollie E, out of Frisco, headin' for the South Seas!" the sailor yelled back to the approaching gun-boat.

"We're coming aboard!" the answer floated back, and Curly, Mama Louise, Janelle and Far-away were in the salon, where Janelle had first dined with Far-away.

To her amazement she saw Mama Louise, Far-away and Curly seating themselves about the table. Cards appeared as if by magic — hands were dealt— cigarettes lighted—there were even glasses on the table, and ash-trays.

"AND a grand slam!" laughed Mama Louise gaily, as she flung down her cards.

"And that leaves us in the hole again, partner!" said Curly with a rueful laugh, smiling at Janelle. "Oh, well, we had poor cards — and luck was with them!"

The door was pushed open, and a young officer in an immaculate white uniform, the brass buttons glinting cheerily in the light, his cap at a jaunty angle above his good-looking, sun-tanned young face, was staring from one to the other of the four people who sat about the bridge-table.

Janelle opened her mouth to cry out—and in that instant, felt something jabbed against her side. She dropped her eyes—and saw the round blue barrel of an automatic pressed hard against her side—and held in the quite steady, very capable looking hand of Far-away who sat opposite Mama Louise. There was no mistaking the meaning.

Far-away did not even look at Janelle—yet the silent threat of the gun was enough. She knew that if she opened her mouth to speak, the gun would silence her forever. Far-away and Mama Louise would manage an explanation—they would risk a great deal to keep her from telling her story to this young man. She wisely held her tongue.

"Well, officer—to what are we indebted for this honor?" demanded Far-away, making it plain that he resented this intrusion.

The young officer saluted.

"Sorry, sir—we've been trailing a rum-runner all afternoon, and have orders to search all suspicious looking craft in this neighborhood!" he answered quietly, his eyes, steady and honest and blue, went slowly from one to the other of this party, apparently interrupted at their game.

He saw two men, obviously successful business men, dressed in yachting clothes; he saw one very beautiful young woman in an attractive evening gown, and a slightly older but no less attractive woman, also in evening attire.

He was covered with confusion. Obviously this was exactly what it claimed to be — a pleasure cruise of well-to-do people. He saw with shame, that the very pretty younger woman seemed strangely agitated —no doubt he had frightened her by his unceremonious entrance, and he was sorry.

"And you think ours a suspicious looking craft? By George, Henry, the boys at the office will certainly give us a good razzing for that one!" laughed Far-away bluffly.

"You said it! We'll have to keep still about it —and trust to luck they'll never find out!" returned Curly, and lighted a fresh cigar from the humidor beside the table.

"I told you, Bill, that you should have had this

boat overhauled and painted before we started out in it!" accused Mama Louise fretfully.

"I'm sorry, sir—my apologies!" the young officer, a little flushed, started to withdraw.

Far-away stood up, bluff, genial, good-natured, apparently what he pretended to be—a successful business man on a holiday.

"Not at all—not at all! Such mistakes are bound to happen!" he assured the young officer. "Have a look at the ship's papers if you like—the captain will be glad to permit it under the circumstances—have a cigar—since I don't dare offer you any liquid refreshment!" he laughed.

As Far-away stood up, Janelle thought herself free of the gun—she half-rose in her chair, but Mama Louis was also on her feet, and she pushed Janelle back into her chair with a friendly hand on her shoulder, and laughing, flirting with the young officer, she bent low to whisper loud enough for the young officer to hear.

"Hasn't he the most GORGEOUS eyes?" then, in a whisper that reached only to Janelle's ears she said savagely, "One peep out of you, and you're finished—you fool!"

The young officer took himself off. Far-away went with him to the deck, and Curly stood watchfully waiting. his back to the wall.

When Far-away came back, he spoke to Curly contemptuously.

"Put that gun away! You've got the liquor—that deal is over—why hold a grudge?" he sneered ill-naturedly.

Curly pocketed the gun and turned toward the door.

"Well, if the 'arm of the law' has withdrawn, I'll

dash along, too! Thanks for a delightful evening!" he said cynically.

Janelle could no longer be restrained. She thrust herself forward, facing Curly, and lifted her white face to his.

"Mr. Dukes — don't you remember me? I'm Janelle Elliott—you told me you could bring back my baby for a ransom of sixty-five thousand dollars!" she cried swiftly.

Curly stared at her, startled. Obviously in all the tenseness and excitement of the last few moments, he had not had time to observe her closely. But now his eyes widened, and he caught his breath in amazement.

"Well, I'll be damned!" he gasped, "What in blazes are you doing here?"

"She came at my invitation!" said Far-away quietly. "And—I have promised to get the kid back for her!"

Curly laughed aloud and raised his eyebrows a little, in an expression of mock surprise.

"So? Well, considering the fact that you hijacked the ransom money, you really are the person who should restore the missing child to its grieving parent!" he laughed derisively. "And, boy, I'd like to see you do it!"

The two men eyed each other like strange bulldogs.

"Meaning that you've got the kid, of course!" said Far-away.

"Meaning that you've got the money!" said Curly.

Far-away grinned wickedly.

"But—you can't spend a three year old kid— and you CAN spend—sixty-five thousand dollars!" he pointed out calmly.

Curly studied Far-away for a moment as though he had never seen him before in his life. And then he smiled. A faintly wolfish smile that sat oddly on his ruddy, rather round face, and that did not reach to his wary dark eyes.

"You always were a piker, Far-away!" he drawled coolly. "I suppose, to you, sixty-five thousand dollars is—important money!"

"It's not exactly—cigarette coupons!" Far-away protested.

"True—but it's not half a million, either. And the kid is worth just half a million to us!" said Curly quite simply.

Janelle cried out sharply.

"I could never pay that—I haven't any more money — the sixty-five thousand wiped me out............" she stammered.

"I'm not expecting it from you, lady," Curly assured her gravely. "But—it wouldn't be the first time a millionaire paid plenty to make the woman he loves happy!"

Janelle stared at him uncertainly.

"A—a millionaire?" she repeated, puzzled.

Curly made a little inclusive gesture with his hand.

"Scarcely a day passes but that some man, worth millions, squanders a couple of hundred thousand on a bauble of some kind to make his lady-friend happy. I know of a man who gave a woman five million dollars worth of emeralds—that, of course, was before the stock market crash — but half a million dollars would seem like small change to some men, if it were spent to make the woman he loved happy!" he pointed out to her, smiling.

Janelle caught her breath.

"You — you mean — Sherman Lawrence?" she gasped.

Curly nodded. "I mean exactly that. We've checked him up. He's worth five or six millions at a conservative estimate. He'd fork over half a million dollars as quickly as the average man would buy his sweetie a box of candy, once he is assured that your child will be returned safely to you!" he returned in a careless tone.

Far-away and Mama Louise were listening breathlessly, staring from Curly to Janelle. It was Janelle who spoke.

"You know so much—I suppose you know, too, that Sherman is in a prison hospital in a little town in Mississippi, charged with murder?" she demanded resentfully.

Curly laughed.

"I know even more than that—I know that he was not guilty of either murder—and I also know that —he is no longer in prison!" he answered promptly.

Wide-eyed, breathless, Janelle cried,

"You mean—they've acquitted him?"

"I mean he escaped! Darn fool thing to do—it may slow us up in making contact with him and getting the half million—but we'll get it eventually!" answered Curly carelessly.

He glanced at Mama Louise and Far-away, still laughing lightly.

"And now I'll be going — good-night — pikers! You've always been small-timers, both of you—and I suppose you'll never make the big leagues! Too bad! But thanks for a pleasant evening, anyway!"

Janelle put herself before him.

"Just one thing—please tell me—just one thing!

My baby—is he—is he—well? Is he alright? Does he —cry for me?" she stammered eagerly, and there were great crystal tears in her eyes and slipping down her lovely cheeks.

Curly looked down at her—restively, as though something in her eyes, her helplessness, her innocence before the brutality to which she had been subjected made him ashamed.

"The baby is alive—quite well—and receiving the best of care. You needn't worry about that! And —no, he doesn't cry for you! He is—quite happy!" he said with an unaccustomed gentleness.

Behind him there was a knock at the door and a man's voice.

"All clear, Curly—let's get goin'!"

Curly spoke over his shoulder and still facing the three in the room as though he did not trust them sufficiently to turn his back to them, he fumbled behind him for the door knob, turned it, opened the door and stepped through it. He quickly closed it behind him, and immediately afterward they heard swiftly running foot-steps along the companionway, and overheard a subdued confusion.

Far-away stood where he had, when he faced Curly. There was a look of wolfish greed on his face, anger and puzzlement, and a wild sort of planning. The look that he turned on Janelle was one in which there was nothing of admiration, or lust or desire. Only a cold, calculating, merciless look that poured over the girl like iced water.

"So the kid is worth a cool half-million to Lawrence, eh?" he said at last just above his breath. "Well, then—I've got a double reason for finding him now— you, and the half-million!"

Janelle caught her breath and shuddered. These

two men who controlled her fate and that of her child talked as though neither she nor the child were human —alive.

She grew sick at the thought of her baby, so little and helpless and innocent at the mercy of these human wolves, used like a bit of inanimate clay—a counter in their insane game of easy wealth—her poor little lost baby!

She turned blindly and felt her way out of the salon, and to the room that had been assigned to her. And here, for the first time tonight, she gave way to the storm of terror and bewilderment and pain that plucked at her heart.

Chapter 83.

A HOLLYWOOD PRE-VIEW.

THE LAST SHOT of the film flickered out, with Janelle and Jim Marvin clasped close in each other's arms, and the word, "Finis" danced before the spectators eyes.

For a moment there was silence—and then a brisk spatter of applause that was music in the ears of the three who sat well down front hunched in their chairs, listening tensely to that sound of applause and the words of commendation about them.

"It's a hit, Maxie!" Wayne told his employer.

"It's not bad!" agreed Maxie happily.

"Not bad, you old hypocrite! It's swell, and you darned well know it!" snapped Wayne and punched his employer in the ribs.

"I can't help wondering where Janelle is!" said Jim Marvin. "Gee, she screens great, doesn't she?"

"I think I know where she is!" Wayne said quietly.

The other two turned upon him swiftly.

"You mean you've heard from her?" they cried

in unison.

"Not directly—but Hank O'Hearn went down to that little town in Mississippi when it was reported that her boy-friend—that Lawrence bird—had given himself up after that crazy prison-break of his! And late this afternoon I had a wire from Hank—Lawrence's wife has bobbed up to help him, and the fact that she refuses to see Hank, convinces him that it's really Janelle and that she has some wild idea of helping Lawrence!" answered Wayne heavily.

"You think she dashed down there and married Lawrence——" began Jim, but Wayne shook his head.

"No—she hasn't had a chance to do that without the whole world knowing that it has just happened. I believe—and Hank does, too—that she is going to pretend that they have been married all along—and that she is going to try to prove some alibi for him at the time of the crime. It's a crazy idea, of course, and she can never in a thousand years get away with it. But —it would be rather like Janelle to try something like that!"

The house-lights were on now, and the theatre was all but empty. The picture had been screened for a pre-view in a little theatre in Glendale. Later it would be brought into Los Angeles with a great fanfare of publicity trumpets, and if Maxie could manage it, a premiere at Grauman's Chinese or Egyptian Theatres.

In the lobby a newspaper reporter spied the three men and came over.

"Congratulations, Mr. Cason — you've got a darned good picture!" said the reporter. "But what's the low-down on all this 'true story' business? You're not trying to make us believe that this star — Miss Elliott — really had a baby kidnapped and that the picture was made in the hopes that it would arouse people to help her find it, and too, to help stamp out the crime of kidnapping?"

"It's the truth I'm telling you!" said Maxie solemnly.

The reporter grinned, unbelieving.

"Oh, come now—of course, it's a grand gag and the dear public will fall for it, hook, line and sinker, and love it -- and the picture will probably gross a million and all that—but on the level now—come clean with a fellow—I won't squawk, I promise you! That idea of beginning the picture with a trailer of the star begging the public to help her find her baby and all that—it's swell stuff—it's too darned swell to be on the level!" he protested.

Maxie sighed heavily.

"You newspaper guys are so smart you're a little dumb!" he said frankly. "The facts of this story are a matter of public record—go to the 'morgue' in your own office and trace this case back to the trial of Miss Elliott for murder—and her acquittal when the real murderer confessed—and follow it right down to the present day, and you will see that the whole story is true—every word of it!"

The reporter, convinced in spite of himself, looked from one of the men to the other, and could not doubt the seriousness of their faces, the utter lack of levity in their eyes.

"Then—what's the connection between this and the rumor that Miss Elliott was kidnapped a few minutes after the picture was finished? Is that on the level, too?" he demanded, his eyes eager now.

"I wish to God I could say it was a gag—but it's only too true. My boy, I'll give a five thousand dollar reward in cash to any man, woman, or child, who can tell me where Miss Elliott is, so that we can find her! That's on the level, too — you — you — doubting Thomason!" snapped Maxie rashly.

"Boy, oh, boy—what a story! And picked up on my night off! I'll ring the bell with this, Mr. Cason— and I'll put the reward in big letters, too, and mention the name of the picture at least a couple of times!" promised the reporter, and was off, yelling "Taxi, taxi!" at the top of his very sound lungs.

An hour later an extra was on the street, shouting the name of Janelle Elliott and rehashing the story of her crowded, tumultous young life that had been climaxed now by this kidnapping hard on the heels of the finish of her first starring picture, in which, agreed the reporter, she was surprisingly good for a newcomer.

The morning papers, of course, carried a more complete story, and the mention in substantial letters of the reward that Maxie Cason would pay for information that would lead to the recovery of Janelle and her return to the studio.

Those papers were read with interest throughout the city. But in several places they received more than interest.

One of these places was an almost oppressively luxurious apartment in a discreet apartment-house on the fringe of Beverly Hills. A plump, rather florid woman in an elaborate rose satin and lace negligee, read the paper as she insulted her healthy appetite with a tiny cup of black coffee and a postage-stamp sized square of very hard toast, while she looked with envy and hunger at the large cup of coffee, creamed and sugared, the delicate brown buttered toast, and marmalade that lay on the plate of her breakfast companion.

"See here. Curly—there's a five thousand dollar reward out for the Elliot woman!" she said swiftly. "I could use that five thousand—but more than that, I'd like to see you take the dame away from that blankety-blank Far-away!"

"Give us a look, Honey!" said Curly, and took the paper.

He studied the photograph of Janelle—one of her studio-stills.

"Yep, that's her, all right!" he said at last. "The five thou' would wrap you up that ermine coat you've been hankerin' for, wouldn't it? And the look on Far-away's face when I copped the lady would be worth more than he has cost me this last year! Yes—I think you can telephone the shop that you'll **have the coat** delivered!"

He reached for the telephone.

*   *   *   *   *   *   *   *   *

In Maxie's office he interviewed his chauffeur. The little Jap stood quiet, waiting—but his almond eyes were wary.

"Seen the morning papers, Satsu?" Maxie demanded.

"Yes. boss!"

"Read the reward that I am offering for information about Miss Elliott?" asked Maxie carelessly.

The Jap's eyes narrowed a very little, but his answer came promptly.

"Yes, boss!"

Silence—then—"Five thousand dollars in American money is a lot, you know. Satsu! It would go a long way—if one wanted to change it into Jananese money and go home and watch the cherry-blossoms bloom!" said Maxie quietly.

The Jap looked startled, and more cautious than ever.

"Yes, boss!" he agreed politely.

Maxie leaned towards him across the table.

"See here, Satsu—let's get right down to brass tacks. If you know anything about what happened to Miss Elliott—it's worth five thousand dollars if you tell it. If you don't—you're liable to sweat plenty in jail here! Now if you know anything—spit it out!" he snapped.

Satsu was agitated, frightened.

"Please, boss—I know nothing! A man who know my boss in New York, he say to me, 'Satsu-- twenty-five dollar you take message and flower to Missy Elliott'—and I take. That's all!" he stammered.

"Who was this man?" demanded Maxie swiftly.

Instantly Satsu's eyes were veiled again and wary.

"Please, boss—I know not. In New York he bootlegger—out here—I no know what. But he have much money — much fine clothes!" he explained graphically.

"Where did you meet him?" demanded Maxie, quite sure now that he was about to learn something of importance.

"He come to me when I am wait for you in car —at the studio one time—in front your house one time —in front Missy Elliott's one time! I no know where he live!" explained Satsu.

Whether he was lying or not, Maxie could not tell. But somehow he felt that there was at least a grain of truth in the man's story. He let the chauffeur go after awhile, and did not see the man's expression of acute relief as he left the room.

Maxie had learned, he felt, a few things that might help. He knew now who it was who placed the orchids with the messages on Janelle's pillow; he did not know who had bribed his chauffeur to do this, but he did know that it was a man whom Alexis Forgio had known in New York — no doubt Alexis Forgio's bootlegger. No doubt out here the man was in the same business—at least, Maxie felt with some satisfaction, he had a hazy idea that might possibly develop into a clue.

And the lovely and glamorous Gladda Romaine had also read the story in the morning papers. With her lovely, airy thin brows drawn together in a little ugly frown, she promptly telephoned the dapper young man who was her "public relations counsel."

That young man, awakened from a sound sleep at ten A. M., arrived at Gladda's home cross and irritable, and without having set eyes on the morning paper.

So when Gladda tossed it to him and he read, his eyes widened and the sleepiness quite vanished from their depths.

"I just wanted to tell you, Tommy, that if she ISN'T found for the next couple of months, I'll double Maxie's reward!" said Gladda suavely.

The man looked up, swiftly.

"You mean——" he stammered.

"I mean that if you are entertaining any little idea of restoring the lost star to her frenzied producer—and telling the true story of how she came to disappear—I wouldn't if I were you! You can get me into some trouble by claiming that I put up the money and that I planned the whole thing—but it will be my word against yours, and after all, you actually did the dirty work of the kidnapping—and that carries an ugly sentence out here!" she warned him smoothly.

The thing had gone too far to suit the young man, so hastily and quite frankly, he told the truth.

"Sorry, Glad—but the truth of the matter is that I had nothing whatever to do with the lady's disappearance. I didn't plan anything like this—frankly, I'd never have the nerve to try to carry through such a thing. I'll do your little dirty jobs, but when it comes to kidnapping—that's out!" he confessed quite frankly.

Gladda sat erect and flung aside her half-smoked after-breakfast cigarette. Her eyes were snapping, and her face was drawn in an ugly grimace.

"You had nothing to do with all this?" she demanded.

"I did not!" answered Tommy frankly.

"But you let me pay you, thinking you had?" she snapped, her tone ugly.

"I let you pay me, yes, for publicity services—but not for kidnapping!" answered the man.

"You're fired!" snapped Gladda sharply.

"Your mistake — I've resigned. And am beginning work in the morning, doing a column on activities of the movie folks for the Record!" said Tommy, smiling contentedly.

Gladda's face whitened back of the carefully applied make-up.

"You're — you're going to — write a movie column?" she gasped.

"A la Walter Winchell!" the man returned happily. "The Record reasons that with my understanding of the—er—shall we say inside workings—of the movie colony, I ought to be able to get just the intimate, inside stuff that the fans go for!"

He met Gladda's frightened eyes for a long moment, and Gladda moistened her lips carefully before she stammered with a little artificial laugh,

"But, of course, you won't be too busy to continue to—er—handle advantageous publicity for me—at your old salary?"

The man laughed.

"Of course not, Glad—delighted!"

"It's—blackmail!" snapped Gladda roughly.

"You set the trap, baited it yourself — then walked into it!" Tommy pointed out grimly. "It's—merely legitimate business!"

And he walked out of the patio, leaving Gladda to writhe in helpless fury, knowing that she dared not offend this young man whom she had trusted with enough secrets to ruin her if he cared to betray her. And she knew all too well how little affection or liking he had towards her to counsel mercy. So she sat and chewed her fingernails, and plotted.

Chapter 84.

THE STRANGER-WIFE.

OR A LONG MOMENT, there was tense silence there in the dingy hospital cell, when the very attractive young woman had claimed the dumbfounded Sherman for her husband.

She was weeping, managing somehow to remain beautiful even in the midst of her tears, and the lawyer stared from her to Sherman, and back again to the woman.

She was beautiful, young, well-dressed, a girl of evident culture and refinement.

"It's all a—a lie!" gasped Sherman, when he had in a measure recovered his breath, and without an apology for his lack of chivalry. "Why, I never saw this girl before in my life! She's a rank stranger to me!"

"Sherman!" gasped the girl, as though heart-broken beyond words. "Oh, Sherman, my darling— how CAN you say that? How CAN you?"

"Because it's true! I don't know what kind of a game this is—but it's not on the level. Bert, for the love of Heaven, tell her she's crazy. Why, I never saw the woman before in my life!" protested Sherman wildly.

"Just when did you first meet this man you say is your husband, Miss——?" asked Bert very carefully and deliberately.

The girl lifted her head haughtily.

"I am Mrs. Sherman Lawrence—not MISS anything!" she protested haughtily. "I first met him the 15th of May when he came into the little tea-shop that I kept on the outskirts of a little town in Ohio. I thought he was a motor-tourist—my shop was on the highway and a great many people stopped there to eat. He came back a number of times. He was—terribly nice—I—guess it was—love at first sight with me! And—with him, too, I thought!"

Once more her lovely eyes were drowned with tears, and she raised her dainty handkerchief to her face, to all appearances completely overcome by her emotions.

Sherman was lying perfectly still, staring at her wide-eyed, filled with a sinking sense of horror. After all he had lost eight weeks out of his life—almost ten. His last memory was of the first of May—this girl mentioned the 15th, as the day when she had met him first. Could it be possible that—he put the thought away from him savagely, and waited for the girl to go on.

When she had controlled her emotion a little, she went on with her story.

"I had no close relatives—no one to be interested in what I did, and so, when Sherman made love to me, and begged me to marry him, I consented. I loved him dearly — I believed he loved me — I was lonely, and starved for love—and so—we were married!" she controlled a choking sob. "He suggested that I sell out my little tea-shop and go back to Atlanta with him. So I did——"

Bert gave a little half-humorous grunt.

"Don't tell me you gave him the money!"

The girl's dark eyes flew wide and the tears dried on her lashes.

"But—that's just exactly what I DID do—how did you guess?" she gasped.

Bert gave a little groan and turned to Sherman, quizzically. He tried to make his remark sound as though he considered it all a joke, but his manner was none too successful.

"You didn't happen to do a little plain and fancy arson and some horsestealing along the way here, did you, Sherm? That seems about the only thing you overlooked!" he complained. And then turning back to the girl again, he inquired simply, "And what happened then?"

"Why, we went on a honeymoon! It was glorious—I was never so happy in my life—and then, one morning, when I woke up, Sherman was gone!" she wept again at the memory. "He left a note and a hundred dollar bill, and told me that he had been called away suddenly by some very urgent business, that he had paid the hotel bill and the hundred dollars would be enough to get me back to Ohio—and that I would hear from him later! But—I didn't until I read in the paper about him being arrested here, charged with this terrible murder and robbery!"

She wept again at the thought.

"So, of course, you came out to add your charges of desertion and what not to the rest of the charges against him! I understand!" said Bert a trifle heavily and wearily.

The girl's head went up proudly and her eyes flashed the fire of resentment. Her hand, wearing its plain platinum band beneath a modest solitaire, went out swiftly and covered Sherman's uninjured hand, holding it close.

"I did nothing of the sort!" she cried hotly. "I came because I love Sherman and because I am his wife. The place of a wife is beside her husband when he is in trouble!"

Startled, Bert stared at her, and Sherman's own eyes widened.

"You mean that in spite of everything he has done to you—you still love him? You still want to help him?" cried Bert.

"Of course—it's my duty—and even if it were not — I can't stop loving him just because he is in trouble." said the girl dramatically.

To Bert's keen, shrewd ear, it was a little too dramatic to ring true. He stared at the girl hard—but whatever was in his mind, he kept it to himself for the time being.

"The fact that you discovered through the newspapers that he is worth a considerable fortune, had nothing to do with bringing you here?" he accused so suddenly that the girl drew back as from a physical blow and whitened a little.

"How dare you?" she breathed at last in a tone of complete outrage, and then to Sherman, "Surely you aren't going to allow me to be deliberately insulted—after all that has happened?"

"Sorry — I meant no insult!" apologized Bert. "After all, I am a lawyer, and you will have to be prepared to face a good many ugly questions when you go on the stand to defend your husband!"

Suddenly Sherman's stunned brain began to

function once more. He raised himself a little on his pillows, and stared at the girl so wildly that she recoiled a little from him, puzzled and startled.

"What day was it that you said I came into your tea-shop?" he demanded sharply.

"The 15th of May!" answered the girl.

"You are sure of that?" he urged.

"I could scarcely forget such a day!" she told him swiftly. "I wrote an entry in my diary about it! Besides, it was my birthday!"

Sherman turned swiftly to Bert.

"Don't you understand? The woman in New York that I am accused of murdering was killed on the 15th of May! I couldn't possibly have been in two places at once!" he cried eagerly—and a tiny, enigmatic smile played for a moment about the girl's lips. She lowered her eyes lest a gleam within their dark depths should arouse these two men to a suspicion she could ill-afford just now.

Bert made a swift exclamation and banged his fist on the edge of the little night-table that stood beside the bed.

"Darn it, that's right! Buddy, there's your alibi! You couldn't possibly have killed one woman in New York, and met another one in Ohio on the same day! There's our case!" he gasped.

He turned swiftly to the woman.

"You've got a certificate to prove you were married on the 22nd, as well as the diary to prove you met on the 15th? No doubt other people can be found to swear that Sherm was in the town in Ohio on the 15th —now let's see the marriage certificate!" he ordered briskly.

"Of course!" said the girl, promptly and opened her smart dark leather bag and drew out a stiff, folded paper.

Bert took it, unfolded it, and read its contents swiftly. He started to fold up the paper, then apparently read it a second time. Finally he looked up at Sherman, wide-eyed, puzzled.

"What was the name of the woman you're supposed to have killed?" he asked quietly.

"Annie Greene!" said Sherman, who never spoke the name without a little involuntay shudder. "Why do you ask?"

Bert handed Sherman the marriage certificate, and Sherman read, astounded.

"Why," he cried to the girl, "your name is— Annie Green?"

"Yes!" said the girl—quietly and simply.

*   *   *   *   *   *   *   *   *

To Janelle, the night and the day that followed the attempted hi-jacking were nerve-wracking in the extreme. For one thing she was entirely grateful. The discovery that Curly Dukes believed her baby worth a ransom of half a million dollars seemed to have completely destroyed Far-away's half-laughing, wholly amorous desire for herself. He paid her little attention indeed, for he and Mama Louise spent considerable time in close conference.

Janelle saw that Mama Louise revelled in this undivided attention from the man whose slave she was —and Janelle was glad for the woman whom she sincerely pitied.

The Mollie E. plunged its way southward, and the weather became warmer. Late in the afternoon of that day, the ship cast anchor, and off to the left Janelle could see a low-lying dark smudge that she knew must be land. Whether the mainland of California or some island, she couldn't tell.

Where was Sherman? Curly had said that Sherman had escaped from prison, and while she knew that Sherman stood charged with a double crime for which the state would demand his life, she bewailed the fact of his escape. She knew that it would be taken as a silent confession of his guilt—and she knew in her heart that Sherman was not guilty. She couldn't, she wouldn't believe that!

To think of him in a prison cell had been horror enough. But to think of him now, a fugitive from justice, fleeing from the law, skulking, hiding, afraid to show his face—she felt that that was a horror almost more than she could bear.

Her poor baby — the man she loved! To be separated from both of them—to be held here a prisoner, unable to help either of them—oh, it was cruel, it was terribly hard and unfair! She bowed her head on her hands and wept.

A voice spoke behind her — Far-away's voice, grim and almost surly.

"What are you mooning here for? No use your trying to escape—the water between here and the coast is infested with sharks—you wouldn't last five minutes! Look!" he told her, and into the fading light of day, he flung something out into the water.

Shuddering, Janelle saw a gray shadow lift to the water—saw the sharp line that marked the great sea-beast—and saw it sink again. She shuddered and hid her face in her hands.

"So, even if you think you could swim that distance—you see what little chance you'd have! And as for a boat—well, that's as silly as trying to swim. There isn't a life-boat aboard that can be handled by less than half a dozen men! So I'm afraid you'll be here until I am ready for you to go ashore!" he told her.

From behind him a woman's voice spoke—a woman's voice that had an edge of jealousy and sharpness to it.

"Far-away!" it said.

Mama Louise was a few feet behind Far-away, and as she spoke his name, Janelle saw the look of annoyance touch Far-away's face. But he obeyed the summons as though for the moment he thought it to his interest to keep the woman quiet. He turned and walked to her, and together they walked along the deck.

The three of them dined together in an almost sultry silence, and Janelle was glad to escape to her own cabin after dinner. She crept into bed, mentally and physically exhausted, and after a short interval, she cried herself to sleep.

The Mollie E. rode lazily at anchor. The slim young new moon slipped out of sight. The stars came out like a sprinkling of hoar frost, and the sea was beautifully calm and still.

Aboard the Mollie E, all save the two sailors on watch went to bed. Quiet and peace and utter stillness settled over the ship, and the night rode on.

Around midnight a boat crept close to the side of the Mollie E. Crept so cautiously, with muffled oars, that neither of the members of the watch heard the faintest sound.

While two men in the boat held it against the gang-plank of the Mollie E. four men swarmed soundlessly up the side and over on the deck. Two of the invaders crept up and overpowered the guard without a sound.

With a little signal two of the men crept swiftly, soundlessly down the deck and to the door of the cabin behind which Janelle slept.

Her door was locked, but it was the work of a few moments for one of the men to expertly force the lock.

The door slid open. Janelle slept soundly. One of the men caught up a blanket from the foot of her bed and wound it swiftly about her. A handkerchief soaked in chloroform was over her face. He raised the blanketed form and hurried out of the cabin, while the other man, looking swiftly about him, grinned a little and laid on the pillow where Janelle's head had made a little dent—a green orchid.

And then he, too, slipped quietly out of Janelle's little room and closed the door very carefully behind him.

Continued in Next Number.

Frowning, she picked up the top picture and held it to the light. And then came quick recognition and then a gasp, a cry was torn from her lips. For smiling up at her from the snapshot was her baby son! Her little lost baby!

(See Page 800)

Chapter 85.

HUMAN CHATTEL!

ANELLE awoke to consciousness in a pretty, if slightly gaudy room. There were cream-colored, ruffled net curtains at the windows, fussily pinned back with tiebacks in the shape of pastel-colored flowers. There was jade-green enamelled furniture painted with sprays and baskets of flowers about the room, and the walls, of cream-color, were decorated with brightly colored French prints. The carpet was thick and soft and blue.

Janelle lay still for a long moment after awakening, looking about her, dazedly. She had gone to sleep aboard the Mollie E. She had cried herself to sleep with the swish of the ocean in her ears, her body settling to slumber to the accompaniment of the gentle rising and falling of the ship on the water. Yet she had awakened in this dainty, if slightly over-adorned room, surrounded by an almost oppressive luxury.

Save for a slight headache and a heavy feeling that sometimes comes from an unrefreshing slumber, she felt quite all right. She was about to get out of bed to try to find out where she was, when the door opened cautiously, and a bright blonde head was thrust into the room.

"Oh—hello!" and the bright blond head, attached to a plump body clad in a blue chiffon and silver lace negligee, came into the room.

She smiled cheerfully and genially at the dazed Janelle.

"How do you feel? Hope the boys didn't hurt you last night or frighten you—they had their orders, and they know they have to obey them!" said the woman breezily.

"I'm all right!" answered Janelle dazedly. "But —where am I?"

The woman smiled triumphantly.

"Oh, this is Curly Dukes' place—Curly and I felt you had been a guest of that—hi-jacker long enough. We didn't want you to think the whole—er—organization was like Far-away Thomas and Mama Louise—so Curly insisted that you come over and visit us awhile!" she answered with a little laugh. "I'm Bertha—Curly's 'mama'!"

Janelle looked bewildered.

"But—why should you—or—Curly want to bring me here? What possible interest could any of you have in me? I've nothing to do with you—all that I ask is that you give me back my baby—and let me go!" she stammered. "It won't do you any good to hold me —you see, I haven't any money—I can't pay you any ransom—every cent that I had in the world was the sixty-five thousand that Far-away hi-jacked!"

Bertha laughed.

"My dear—don't be absurd! You are our guest —we wouldn't think of mentioning money to you!" she answered, though her eyes were gleaming a little.

"You'll find that Curly is not a piker and a small-timer like Far-away—we have plenty of income—we don't go around — stealing from widows and orphans as the Thomas crowd does. We have—er—legitimate sources of income!"

She walked to the closet, opened it, and flung some garments across the foot of the bed.

"There! Slip into those and come on out to breakfast—Curly's anxious to meet you!" she said, her manner suddenly brisk.

She turned and went out of the room. Janelle slid out of bed and found a small, but well appointed bathroom opening from her own room. Here she had a brisk shower that all but did away with the dull little headache.

The garments that Bertha had thrown across the bed were dainty lingerie and a black silk Japanese kimona across the back of which stalked a gorgeous crane, beautifully embroidered.

When Janelle emerged from her room, she stepped into a sunny, wind-swept living-room out of which opened a sunny dining-room already laid for breakfast.

Bertha was waiting, and with her the man who had come aboard the Mollie E. — Curly Dukes. Two other men lounged at the back of the room, and Bertha and Curly took no more notice of them than if they had been pieces of furniture.

Curly greeted Janelle with cordial friendliness and laughed a little.

"I'd give a lot to see Far-away's eyes this morning!" He's probably the maddest hombre on the broad Pacific!" he laughed.

"Did you bring me here just to amuse yourself—to get even with Far-away—or for any real purpose?"

demanded Janelle swiftly.

Curly sobered instantly.

"I brought you here, my dear girl, so that you could be returned to the movie studio that is grieving so sincerely for you—so that you could go to the rescue of your fiance—and, eventually, so that we could return your child to you! Isn't that reason enough?" he told her almost sternly.

"You see," Bertha laughed, "Curly and I are your friends—aren't we, Curly?"

"Of course!" said Curly, and he and Bertha exchanged a swift, significant glance. Janelle thought the two men at the back of the room grinned.

The dining-room door was filled suddenly with the form of a negro maid, dressed in an ill-fitting black dress and a slightly soiled white cap and apron.

"Miss Bertha, I cain't keep dis hyeh coffee hot much longer—'lessen yo-all wants me to mek fresh coffee, yo-all hed better come an' eat!" she ordered sullenly.

"We're coming, Mazie — come on, Janelle — you don't mind if I call you Janelle, do you?" suggested Bertha chummily, and the three moved to the dining-room.

The table looked dainty with its Basque cloth of cool green, striped in narrow, brilliant stripes, and set with yellow china and black-footed crystal glasses. There was a bowl of marigolds in the center of the table, and Bertha indicated the gay, sunny, cheerful table as they sat down.

"Cute, isn't it?" she laughed. "I get fat if I even look at a decent bit of food, and Curly will stop loving me if I get really fat—so I have to get my fun at meal-times out of making the table look pretty!"

Janelle sat in silence while the meal was served.

She looked about the place with considerable interest. The room, as had the others, bore all the evidences of wealth—of luxury—there was little indication of good taste, and certainly no trace of a sense of the artistic in the interior decoration and furnishings, but obviously a great deal of money had been spent lavishly in getting this place together.

She thought of her experiences these last few days. Had they been related to her by another she would have found difficulty in believing them. But they had happened to her, Janelle, and while the sudden transformation from her regular existence and the wild transplanting into scenes of melodramatic action seemed nothing short of a dream she had to admit that it was all true — too true. The involuntary guest of one of the most notorious and deeply hated "hi-jackers" on the west coast; and now the guest of the acknowledged head of the rum-running industry along that same coast. She, Janelle Elliott, here in the apartment of a bootlegger and his mistress. A bootlegger who had not hesitated to become a kidnapper as well. First he had become tangled in some way, she could not yet know how, with the kidnapping of her baby. And now at his orders, she had been kidnapped and was a prisoner here in this place. That she should be sitting peaceably at his breakfast table in a scene and surroundings so perfectly placid and home-like in their atmosphere might have appealed to her sense of the ludicrous to the point of uproarious laughter if she had not been so alive to the dangerous possibilities of her situation.

And in the meanwhile she wondered—what about Sherman? She had been gone almost a week—she had had no direct news from Sherman. She had not seen a newspaper. What had happened to him?

Curly, with a word of careless apology to whose answer he did not even listen, unfolded the newspaper that lay at his place and glanced incuriously through it for all the world like any ordinary business-man at his breakfast table, surrounded by his family. Suddenly he gave a little exclamation and handed the paper to Janelle.

"By George—there's something that will interest you!" he said, and indicated a two-column headline.

Janelle saw Sherman's name and caught the paper in both tense hands.

"STARTLING DEVELOPMENTS INCREASE INTEREST IN LAWRENCE CASE.

"Yamacraw, Miss.—This little town along the Mississippi River is in the throes of a wild excitement today with the latest development in the case of Sherman Lawrence, well-known capitalist of Atlanta, Ga., who is held in jail here awaiting trial for the murder of a man and a woman.

"Lawrence, who broke jail several days ago and then seemed to think better of it and surrendered himself and his companion, known only as 'The Georgia Cracker,' for re-arrest, is still in the prison hospital, and was joined yesterday by a woman who claims to be his bride.

"The young woman, who is about twenty-two or three years old, and extremely pretty, claims that Lawrence came into her tea-shop on the 15th of May, and that following a whirlwind courtship of seven days they were married in the village of Canal Winchester in Ohio.

"A fact that makes her information of extreme interest to the police is that it was on

May 15th that Lawrence is accused of murdering a woman named 'Annie Greene' in a hotel of shady repute in New York—a fact which, if proven, will establish an air-tight alibi for Lawrence and clear him of this grave charge of murder.

"Another fact that the police learned with interest is that the pretty young brunette who claims to have married Lawrence in the Ohio village on May 22nd, was before that alleged marriage a Miss Annie Greene! Whether this is merely a strange coincidence, or whether there is some connection between the two women who had the same name and such violently contrasting fates, is yet to be learned.

"An interesting side-light on the case which is as full of side-lights as any thriller of the Sherlock Holmes school, is that Lawrence has been for several months the fiance of Janelle Elliott, who was acquitted more than a year ago of a murder-charge and who is at present engaged in the making of a motion picture that will depict some of the interesting high-lights of a career that has been extremely eventful, to say the least of it. Miss Elliott was acquitted of a charge of murdering a man whom she accused of kidnapping her baby, and her search for that lost baby has taken her over most of the United States, and even in the jungles of South America!"

As Janelle, startled and puzzled dropped the paper, staring wide-eyed at Curly and Bertha, she caught a significant, almost an amused glance that sped between them.

"Oh, but that can't be true. It's all some horrid mistake. Why, Sherman could not possibly have married another girl when he was in love with me!" she cried wildly.

Curly shrugged lightly.

"You must remember—it's been a long time since you've seen him—men change, you know!" he returned carelessly.

"Men like Sherman don't! Why—he's been in love with me for years——" Janelle picked up the paper, seeing that there was more to the story under a Los Angeles date line:

"At the XL Art Productions Studio where Janelle Elliott has been employed for some weeks in the production of a movie based on her own life, it was stated that Miss Elliott vanished from the lot under very mysterious circumstances, and that a reward of five thousand dollars has been offered by Maxie Cason, president of XL Art for information that will lead to her return. Whether this was a bona fide disappearance or merely a gag in preparation for the opening of the Elliott feature at a down-town theatre could not be definitely ascertained."

Janelle looked up swiftly.

"I understand, of course, why I became your guest, instead of Far-away's!" she said coolly. "It's for the five thousand, of course!"

"Oh, but not entirely I assure you! You must give us credit for appreciating good company—Mama Bertha has been lonely!" he assured her quietly, smiling courteously.

Janelle stood up suddenly, unwilling to remain

any longer in the presence of these people who seemed so alien in every thought and instinct. To them she was no more than a human chattel—something they could use for barter. They could take her from Far-away Thomas just as they took away from him a cargo of liquor — and for the same reason. She was utterly helpless—at their mercy.

In her own room — the gaudy, pretty room in which she had awakened, she huddled in a chair and put her face in her hands. She was here, a prisoner; somewhere her poor baby was equally at the mercy of these people or others like them. And there in Mississippi, Sherman was in prison, and a strange woman claimed that he had married her!

It was all such a hideous mess! Janelle was sick and shaken with despair at the thought of it all. She knew that it would be worse than useless for her to try to escape from this apartment. She looked out of the window and saw the street far below. The fire-escape would, of course, be out of her reach. Her captors had seen to that before they put her in this room.

She was bitterly puzzled about the woman who claimed to be Sherman's bride. Not for a moment did she doubt Sherman. There was some horrible mistake —just as there had been some horrible mistake about the murder of the woman named "Annie Greene" in New York. The thought that this strange woman who claimed to be Sherman's bride claimed also the maiden name of "Annie Greene" seemed strange and almost, somehow, sinister.

Janelle remembered the letters she had received in Cuba, signed with that name. Could either of these women have written those letters? Badly spelled, badly phrased, almost illegible—obviously the writer had been

an almost illiterate person. But which had it been—
that poor soul who had been done to death in New York
— or the woman who was in the little Mississippi
village?

If only, she thought dully, she could get free
from this place and go to Sherman! If only some way,
somehow, she could get to him and talk to him and find
out the truth!

Suddenly she became conscious of voices in conversation on the other side of the bath-room door. She
crept quietly across the bath-room and put her ear to
the crack of the door. Bertha and Curly were in there,
and for the moment apparently forgetful that Janelle
was so near.

"But, good grief, Curly, if the man has already
fallen for some other woman—and gone so far as to
marry her—how do you expect to be able to get anything out of him for this woman's baby? Frankly,
Old Boy, I think you are stuck for one kid — that
greaser's going to want your hide if you don't come
through pretty soon!" she heard Bertha say. Janelle
felt her heart beating so loudly that she was afraid they
would hear it, and laid her hand above it as though to
still it.

"Don't you worry your thick head about that.
mama—you leave such big thoughts to the men of the
family!" she heard Curly say lightly. "In the first
place, there's something that smells fishy to me about
that bride business! It doesn't ring true to me! I'd be
willing to lay a bet that the Forgio crowd is back of
that!"

Janelle put a swift, shaking hand over her mouth
to choke back the little scream at the mention of Forgio,
and listened with her breath held, praying that they
would say more.

"I wouldn't be much surprised—that gang will never get over the way you lifted the kid right out from under their noses when they tried to 'frazz' you on that wine deal—and you beat 'em to it!" answered Bertha carelessly.

They were silent for a moment, and Janelle knew by the faint sounds that they were dressing for the day—perhaps to go out.

"Well, anyway, daddy — what's the lay-out? How do I get the Janelle girl back to her producer and get my five grand? My coat is being delivered to-morrow!" said Bertha lazily.

"I'll pay for the coat—I'm not anxious to let the dame go! I'd like to hold her here awhile and worry Far-away—besides that, I want to see what develops out of this 'bride' business with Lawrence!" answered Curly grimly. "The minute you let the Elliott woman loose, she'll hot-foot it to Mississippi—and then it'll be too late for any under-cover work! We'll just keep an eye on her for a spell and see what comes up!"

Janelle heard a sound that made her believe Bertha or Curly was coming towards the bath-room. Holding her breath and moving without a sound, she sped back to her own room, closed the door very, very carefully and turned the key in the lock.

She was trembling with excitement. She knew now that Curly had taken her baby, her little Billy-boy from Forgio's gang in reprisal for something the Forgio gang had done to him. Her baby had been simply a human chattel.

What did Bertha mean by saying that "the greaser would be sore if Curly didn't" do something about the child? Did that mean that the baby was in Mexico in the hands of a "greaser" or Mexican family? Or did it mean, perhaps, that he was here in Los Angeles in the Mexican quarter?

And—he had said that he did not believe the girl in Mississippi was really Sherman's bride! Something about that smelled fishy! In spite of her fear and her dislike of Curly, Janelle felt a tiny thrill of gratitude to him for that.

Sherman, too, felt that there was something wrong about that — but she had not dreamed that it might reach back to the Forgio crowd! And — who were the Forgio crowd? She had known Alexis Forgio as a very wealthy man who amused himself with sculpture, and whose work was considered so good by those who knew of such things, that he had frequently given "one man shows" in the austere and high-brow art galleries of Madison Avenue and Fifth Avenue.

Now to find that he had been allied with a gang that had dealings, as a matter of course, with Curly Dukes, acknowledged leader of the west coast illicit liquor industry, was a bit startling.

Chapter 86.

THE TANGLED WEB.

HE TWO MEN who sat in the prison hospital ward stared at the very pretty girl with marks of tears on her face, and both men looked wide eyed and utterly astounded.

"Your n a m e is — Annie Greene?" demanded Sherman again as though he could scarcely believe it.

The girl bridled indignantly.

"I don't see anything funny about that—naturally, its a rather common name, and I suppose people get tired of it——" she began, but Sherman interrupted her almost roughly,

"Did you ever write any letters to Mrs. Elliott, in Havana?"

The girl looked surprised, a little startled.

"No, of course not — I don't know any Mrs. Elliott!" she returned pettishly.

"You know that the woman I am supposed to have—murdered—was named Annie Greene?" asked Sherman.

The girl made a little fluttering gesture with

slender, dainty hands on one of which twinkled a modest diamond solitaire above a shiny new platinum band.

"Yes, of course—I read about it in the paper!" said the girl, a little too readily. "But that's only a coincidence—it—it doesn't mean anything!"

Sherman was staring at the girl, his eyes narrowed a little, frank suspicion in their depths.

"Did you ever know a man named Alexis Forgio?" he asked, and he could have sworn that the girl gave a tiny start before she controlled herself and masked the start with a movement to pick up her bag that had slipped to the floor.

"No—I never did! I'm sure I'd have remembered—the name is—sort of odd!" she said without the trace of a stammer in her cool, pleasant voice.

Bert decided to terminate the scene.

"We'd better be toddling along, Sherm, old boy! You've had enough excitement for one day! I'll be back in the morning!" he said pleasantly. "And if you will permit me, Mrs.—er—Mrs. Lawrence, I'll see you to your hotel!"

Sherman offered an objection.

"You know, of course, that it will be September before I come to trial? I'm afraid it's going to be tiresome for you hanging around a little town like this waiting——" he said, but the girl interrupted him dramatically.

"Nothing could be tiresome, darling, that would give me a chance to help you! And I know that I CAN help you by proving that you were with me in Ohio on the day you were supposed to have done—that dreadful thing."

And then to Sherman's amazement and, it must be confessed, slight embarrassment, she bent her head and set her mouth on his in a loving kiss. When she stood up her eyes were swimming with tears.

"How on earth can ANYBODY think for even one moment that YOU could do anything so—awful?" she stammered, and with her handkerchief pressed to her lips, she almost ran from the room.

Bert, grinning a little, bent over Sherman.

"You lucky dog!" he grinned. And then, "I'll be back!" he hissed and followed the weeping "bride" from the room.

Sherman lay still for a long time there in the room where the ghost of an exquisite, if slightly heavy perfume still lingered as though to keep him reminded of the girl who had just left the room.

He knew that during those eight or ten weeks in which he had lost his memory, he might have been capable of a great many things—but it seemed so utterly incredible that he could have married some one else when the vision of Janelle had been so strong in his heart. Murder he might have committed — theft — yes —but surely not marriage!

Yet—this woman had a marriage certificate duly filled out and witnessed, dated, and quite authentic. It would be easy enough to prove the truth or the falsity of her statement.

His heart sank at the thought of Janelle. If it was proven beyond all question of a doubt that he HAD, while temporarily insane, married this girl, and she had come so unselfishly to his side when he was in trouble, then he knew he was bound to her with bonds that he could not break.

If he was really married to her — if there had really been a week's honeymoon — if he had really deserted her on that honeymoon, as she claimed, and vanished overnight with the money she had obtained from the sale of her tea--room — and if, after these offenses against her, she had still remained loyal enough and devoted enough to come to his side, to offer this alibi that would save him from at least one of the most serious charges against him — then he owed her the loyalty of sticking to his marriage vows no matter how repugnant to him the alliance was even though he had assumed them when technically he was not mentally responsible.

Lord! What a tangled web he was in! Like a fly caught in the devilishly tricky web of an enormous spider — buzzing and fretting and fighting to escape, and only tangling himself the more deeply with every struggle!

If this woman really WAS his wife—then Janelle could never be! If this woman had married him—and was still loyal to him in the face of his many offenses against her—then he could not set her cold-bloodedly aside the moment he won his freedom—in order to marry another woman.

Janelle seemed to stand before him, slender and radiant and lovely. Janelle, with her valiant small hands and her indomitable courage, and the great, loving heart of her! Janelle whom he had loved since she had been little more than a child, racing off to a football game, red-cheeked, starry eyed, a brown beret clinging to the side of her gay young head—a game in which she was to see her young, adored secret husband go to his death.

Sherman saw her again as she had sat beside him at the beginning of the game — her arms laden with chrysanthemums that marked her sponsor of the game — her eyes eager and ardent and glowing, following the tall, splendid young captain of the team —not until a long time afterward, was Sherman to learn that that young captain had been for three months, Janelle's secret husband.

He wrenched his thoughts away from that as the cell-door opened and Bert came back into the room. He looked startled—and he carried a folded newspaper in his hand.

"I've got news, Sherman, of Janelle—but you've got to keep a stiff upper lip, boy—and take it on the chin!" said Bert with kind, merciful brutality. "She's —gone! Disappeared!"

Sherman lay still against his dingy pillow as though Bert's words had been a physical blow lashing him in the face. The color ebbed away from his face until he was utterly pallid, and his jaw was hard and set. And then his hands clenched into hard fists, he said very quietly,

"How—did it happen?"

"The people at the studio don't know!" answered Bert. "She was anxious to get to you—they had a hard time persuading her to stay on a couple of days and finish the picture she was working on. But she finally agreed and the studio speeded things up by working nights. They were hard at work one night— Tuesday—when she stepped outside the studio for a breath of air—and that was the last any one saw of her.

"The studio gate-keeper says a coupe was parked outside the gate, beneath a eucalpytus tree, but it was so dark that he couldn't see any one in it. He saw Janelle cross the lot and get into the car and it drove away — and that's the last that's been heard from her!"

"That was Tuesday night?" asked Sherman swiftly.

Bert nodded.

"And this is Saturday! My Lord, ANYTHING could have happened to her since then! What are they doing? What kind of a search are they making?" demanded Sherman frantically.

"They're combing the city, the hills, and the bay. They've wired a description all over the country—they are doing everything possible, Sherm—keep your shirt on, old boy—they'll find her!" argued Bert, but Sherman had turned his face to the wall and would not answer.

Meanwhile in the best room that the little village hotel afforded, the former Annie Greene who must now be hailed as Mrs. Sherman Lawrence was writing a letter.

"Things are going even better than I dared to hope. He and the lawyer are both convinced —not a trace of suspicion. Will wait here for the trial—trust you to see that everything in Ohio is handled right. Miss you like the dickens, but guess a trip to Europe and living on the fat of the land from now on, is worth a few weeks or a couple of months in a stick-in-the-mud place like this. Some dump, believe you me! But— Paris and the Riviera will be just twice as heavenly after I get away from here. Will keep you posted."

The letter was unsigned. It was sealed in an envelope, addressed to a gentleman in a room in one of New York's swankiest hotels. This envelope, in turn, was sealed inside of another and the second one in turn was addressed to a public stenographer's attention in St. Louis.

This having been attended to, Mrs. Lawrence got

out of her smart dark gown, hat, and slippers, and into a pair of the most exotic lounging pajamas that the eyes of Yamacraw had ever beheld—not, of course, that Yamacraw was to behold these!—and, with her feet cocked on another chair, a flask from her suitcase close at hand, a box of cigarettes beside her, she proceeded to bury herself in a book whose lurid passages had caused it to be banned throughout the United States, so that the copy she read had been smuggled in at great expense.

Like a good workman who has done his job well and rests content, Mrs. Sherman Lawrence devoted her amused, engrossed attention to the book.

Chapter 87.

CATS AND THE MOUSE.

THE NEXT DAY or two passed so slowly that Janelle felt as though she must go insane with the inaction. She grew nervous and jumpy from lack of exercise and fresh air. As the hours passed and she was watched by the two men and by Curly and Bertha, she began to feel like a mouse in the power of four cats who, knowing that the mouse can't possibly escape, watch with cruel amusement the scampering attempts at escape.

The second evening when dinner was over and they were in the living-room, the telephone rang and the man whose duty it seemed to be to answer that insistent instrument, caught up the receiver and spoke into the transmitter. A moment or two — he spoke cautiously, in monosyllables, and when he turned back he looked startled.

"The blue serges have nabbed Jumpy Joe for dipping a poke!" he snapped.

"WHAT?" snarled Curly savagely, as though he couldn't believe his ears.

"Blake just telephoned! Said Jumpy Joe was shy of the dust and jumpy as the dickens. Blake wouldn't let him have any dough—your orders, Curly—and so Jumpy Joe lost his head—and now the blue serges have got him!" answered the man.

"The damned, dirty little so-and-so!" grated Curly through his clenched teeth, his fists doubled. "If I had my hands on him I'd wring his neck! The blankety blank so-and-so!"

His curses were so savage and so lurid that they seemed to Janelle to turn the air blue about him. Bertha and the two men seemed almost as upset as Curly.

"He's off the dust—then that means his nerves are shot—and he'll squeal like a trapped rat!" said Curly after a moment, forcing himself to the semblance of a calmness he was far from feeling. "What does he know, Eddie?"

"Nothing much, Chief—he knows there's a kid, but he doesn't know where! And he knows about that stuff you took from Far-away—and a few things like that. Nothing that can do a lot of harm!" said Eddie soothingly.

"Then we'll bluff it out!" snapped Curly. "If the dicks show up here, we'll bluff it out! And the next time Far-away Thomas feels like sprinkling any bullets and green orchids about—let's hope Jumpy Joe is the first elected."

A voice spoke from the dining-room door.

"I'll see to that, Curly—always glad to oblige!" said Far-away Thomas' voice, and the four looked up in amazement to find Far-away standing in the door-way, behind him three watchful, furtive-eyed, lynx-faced young men, each with a business-like automatic at "attention" trained on one of the people in the room. "And now, if you don't mind, I'll take my guest back. She's been here long enough! Too long, in fact! Come on, Janelle!"

Janelle sprang to her feet so swiftly that her chair overturned behind her.

"I won't!" she cried vehemently, passionately. "I won't be handed back and forth between you two as though I were a piece of—of—furniture that neither of you wanted very badly. I am not a human chattel to be thrown first this way and that — and bartered for!"

"Stow the chatter and come on—or, so help me, I'll plug you!" snapped Far-away. "Even Curly might have a little difficulty explaining the discovery of a murdered woman in his joint—so you either come with me, or I swear I'll plug you where you stand!"

"Better run along—that's about Far-away's speed —plugging helpless women! He'd rather shoot babies, of course, but women are almost as good game!" said Curly, and the tone of his voice made the words a burning insult.

Far-away's gun moved a little and the round tiny hole of it covered Curly's heart.

"For two cents, I'd let you have it right through the gizzard, you——" he hurled an unprintable name at Curly, and Janelle saw Curly's muscle quiver a little, though he controlled the fury that shook him as he held his hands above his head.

"Oh, no, you won't, Far-away—you haven't got the guts!" sneered Curly. "You're too yellow to shoot anybody but helpless women and babies—you're a hi-jacker—a rotten, dirty, yellow hi-jacker. You haven't got the courage to go out and take things on your own —you wait until some MAN takes the risk and then you help yourself to what he has taken!"

Far-away was reeling a little with rage, and suddenly he flung the gun away and hurled himself towards Curly. The two men grappled—Curly's two men moved as though to help their leader, but Far-away's gun-men motioned them back, a slightly harried, not quite frightened but distinctly uneasy look in their eyes. Plainly they were on the verge of bolting — but as Curly and Far-away crashed and fought and struggled, Far-away's gun-men hesitated.

So absorbed were the whole roomful of people that they were not conscious of a faint sound of disturbance at the back of the house, and it was not until the room was surrounded that a voice spoke from the doorway.

"Hands up, everybody—the law! Snap out of it, Curly—let him go, Far-away—part 'em, boys!" said a cool, calm voice, and with a gasp Curly and Far-away separated to stare startled at the stout, burly-looking man in the doorway with his automatic and with the half-dozen or more stern-eyed, armed men behind him.

"Blue serge!" gasped Far-away's men, and turned to flee through the dining-room.

Far-away, with a single glance at the men in the doorway, leaped after them, disregarding the detective's cry of "Stop—halt!" As Far-away reached the doorway, the detective's gun spoke, Far-away slumped, and fell face down.

"Get back there, Curly—you, too, Eddie and Bill —easy Bertha—I'd hate to shoot a woman!" ordered McCarthy, the detective, and the men behind him surged into the room.

Janelle stumbled towards the detective, weeping, laughing, hysterical.

The detective stared at her, puzzled.

"Say, sister, you're a new one to me—where'd Curly pick you up? 'S a wonder Big Bertha ain't

scratched your eyes out or carved her initials on you
—I can't understand you not being all scarred up!" he
commented grinning.

"I'm Janelle Elliott!" she told him swiftly. "Far-
away Thomas and his crowd had me kidnapped—Curly
Dukes and his men brought me here!"

McCarthy whistled and swept off his hat, his
eyes wide with amazement.

"Janelle Elliott, the picture star? Why say,
there's a whale of a reward out for your discovery!"
he gasped.

"I know it—and I know something else!" said
Janelle swiftly. "This man here knows where my kidnapped baby is—make him tell! He admitted to me
that he had the child——"

"Well, if he has, he'll give it up—he'll talk and
then some, believe you me, sister!" snapped McCarthy
decisively.

He turned to Curly.

"Come on, Curly—step on it! We got a little
pal of yours down at the station-house — boy named
Jumpy Joe! He was a little short of cocaine dust—and
when we gave him a little, he told us plenty! We'll
offer you the hospitality of the city for quite a spell!"
he said happily.

Curly sneered, though his eyes looked a little
startled.

"Don't be a fool, McCarthy—I'll be 'sprung' before I have been at the station thirty minutes!" he
snapped.

McCarthy grinned undisturbed.

"Oh—I ain't so sure of that this time. There
wasn't no kidnapping charge against you when we had
you down there before! This time you're gonna find
things a little different! Let's get going!" he ans-

wered.

The four of them were herded downstairs while one of McCarthy's men waited with the still and silent Far-away who was lying sprawled on the dining-room floor. Another mercifully released the terrified negro cook who had been gagged and bound to her chair in the kitchen.

At the police station, Janelle answered the questions addressed to her and then was permitted to go home. A taxi took her to the door where the night watchman greeted her with almost tearful joy. She had scarcely reached her room before the telephone was ringing frantically, and Maxie, who had heard the news of her rescue from McCarthy, assured her that he was on his way over.

Janelle had just enough time to change from Bertha's dress that she had, perforce, had to wear for the past two days into one of her own before she heard the sound of Maxie's car in the drive-way and as she hurried downstairs, Maxie and Wayne were entering the house.

Maxie greeted her with a great, bear-like hug, and a sound kiss. Wayne, his eyes shining with happiness, caught both her hands in his, and suddenly, as though this were not enough he bent his head and kissed her.

"You know what tonight is?" Maxie demanded, his eyes shining, so excited that he was stammering a little. "Tonight is the premiere of 'Legacy of Love' and at Grauman's Chinese it's playing! And tonight, Janelle, my child, you are going down to the theatre with Wayne and me and hear them applaud you and laugh and cry with you. The picture, it's a big hit—I'm telling you, Janelle, you're great!"

"Tonight, Mr. Cason? Oh—must I go tonight?

I'm so tired!" pleaded Janelle.

"Don't be a brute, Maxie—can't you see the girl is utterly exhausted? Have a heart!" snapped Wayne roughly.

Maxie's face fell so hard that Janelle was sorry for him. She looked swiftly at the clock—it was almost nine o'clock. Strange, it had seemed to her that it should be midnight at the very least.

"All right, Mr. Cason—I'll go! But tomorrow morning, the very first plane that flies east is going to take me with it to Yamacraw, Mississippi!" she decided swiftly.

"O. K.—I'll have a plane ready for you—I'll charter it myself—a special plane! But tonight—tonight is the premiere of your picture—you are a star —you must be there!" said Maxie happily.

"I'll go and dress!" Janelle hurried out of the room.

She had gone through so much in the last few days that she felt numbed, unable to think or to feel very keenly. Almost automatically she got out of her house-gown and into her newest and smartest evening gown. When she came back downstairs, Maxie and Wayne were waiting for her. Outside, Satsu, at the wheel of the Rolls-Royce sat with his expressionless face turned straight ahead. Not by the flicker of an eyelash did he give the appearance of seeing Janelle, of being surprised at sight of her. He was like a mechanical doll there on the front seat small and yellow, and capable in his smart bottle-green, silver-buttoned uniform.

The Rolls-Royce drove smartly until it came within the circle of the traffic drawn by the premiere. It was not the picture, an ambitious production from Poverty Row, that drew this vast assemblage of fine cars and beautifully dressed women and excellently tailored men, of struggling fighting "fans" so numerous and so noisy and so anxious each to see his own favorite of the screen that it required fifty policemen to hold them in check.

It was not the picture that drew the superbly gowned feminine stars—it was the desire to see and be seen. The thing that drew the masculine stars was, partly, their women-folk, partly the necessity of being seen at such places in the hope that a producer might decide one was "just the type" for a certain part.

The small-part people, featured players, and so on came to see and be seen—and the fans came not because of the picture—probably half of them didn't even know the name of the picture—but they came to see in person those glamorous people whose pictured lives they followed with so much zest.

Janelle who had witnessed other premieres was not too excited by the fact that she was the star in the production about to be screened. She knew too well of how little real importance she was to these other stars —and to the fans she was an unknown name that had leaped at them again and again from the front pages of their newspapers.

So when the Rolls-Royce at last reached the curb, and Wayne helped her out of the car and with Maxie on her other side, crossed the lobby, she was not tremulous with excitement. It was all a part of the show.

About the microphone that recorded the arrival of the famous folk were grouped the announcer, and a star who was making the usual stereotyped little speech. Only this star happened to be Gladda Romaine, and at her side, Tommie, who had formerly been her "public relations counsel," but who now had become a full-fledged columnist.

Gladda, reaching the end of her little "wish-you-were-here" speech, saw Janelle and Wayne, with Maxie trotting beside them. Tommy heard Gladda catch her breath suddenly and saw her square her shoulders. But she was sharply conscious of Tommie beside her, and so she quickly recovered herself and cleverly masking her feeling, cried gaily over the microphone.

"And now I'm going to take the announcer's place and have the pleasure of introducing a new star—Hollywood's very newest—whom I'm sure everybody who sees her picture is going to love as we here in Hollywood love her! Janelle Elliott, everybody — Janelle, meet your public, honey!" laughed Gladda charmingly, and with one arm about Janelle, drew her to the microphone.

"I'm very happy to be here!" said Janelle quite clearly. "And of the public—I ask only that when they have seen this picture, they will help me to do two things—first, to find my little lost baby, and second, to stamp out in our country and the whole world the crime of kidnapping!"

She turned away from the microphone, and Gladda with a sweet smile said silkily, half under her breath,

"You never step out of character for a moment, do you, darling?"

Janelle and Wayne, still with Maxie trotting along beside them, crossed to the entrance, but there an earnest-eyed, excited young man rushed up to Janelle.

"Won't you give me your autograph, Miss Elliott?" he begged, and presented an autograph book and a fountain pen.

Janelle, smiling, took the book, wrote her name,

and handed the book back to the boy. As he turned away, her evening bag, caught on the edge of the autograph book, flew out of her hand. The boy, confused and bashful, stammering a little, leaped to recover it and hand it back to her. She thanked him and he melted into the crowd, as though confused and embarrassed by his awkwardness.

Janelle and Wayne smiled a little at the boy's bashfulness, and went on into the theatre.

The experience of seeing herself on the screen was an odd one. Janelle felt awkward and bewildered a little—she felt quite sure that given the opportunity, she could do much better the next time—but when the picture had flickered off the screen there was polite applause and congratulations.

She excused herself from the party that Maxie had planned, and Wayne took her home. He stood in front of her for a moment, there in the hall, saying good-night to her.

"I've — worried a lot about you, child — it's— mighty good to have you back again!" he told her quietly, and then to her surprise he lifted her head, turned it palm upward, and set his lips against the cool pink flesh with a little almost convulsive movement —and then he was gone.

Janelle stood there in the hall for a long moment, a little disturbed by something she had seen in his eyes. It couldn't be possible, she told herself, after a shaken moment, that Wayne was in love with her— why—that was absurd. He was a great man, famous, one if the greatest directors in the business. She was just a little nobody.

But she went upstairs at last to her own room, shaken and weary and on the verge of a collapse. In her own room she dropped her evening bag that was made of tiny seed pearls on the dressing table. The catch was loose and as she dropped it, the catch opened and half the contents slid out on the dressing-table top.

Her silver compact. her lip-stick — and a picture. Two small kodak pictures! Puzzled, she stared at them without touching them. She hadn't put them in her purse. How had they come there?

Frowning, she picked up the top picture and held it to the light. And then came quick recognition and then a gasp, a cry was torn from her lips. For smiling up at her from the snapshot was her baby son! Her little lost baby!

Continued in Next Number.

"I want to marry you!" he said. Janelle gave a little soft cry of distress, turned her head to one side, and would have drawn away from him, but he held her two hands firmly and would not let her go. (See Page 830)

Jan., No. 26

Chapter 88.

LOVES CLEAR CALL!

J A N E L L E stood amazed and bewildered, staring down at the snap-shot in her hand. It showed a baby of about three years old, standing against a light-colored stucco wall. Above him spilled the dark glory of some blossoming vine that half-hid the wall. The sun was in the child's eyes, and he was smiling, shyly, happily— a smile that clutched at Janelle's heart.

To her there could be no doubt but that it was her baby. Older than when she had lost him, taller, yet the same. Her beloved little Billy-boy who had been so cruelly snatched from her arms a year ago— a tear dropped on the kodak print. Carefully she wiped it away.

How had the picture gotten into her bag? She had taken the bag, completely empty, from the drawer of her dressing-table when she dressed for the premiere. She had slipped into it her flat silver compact, her handkerchief, her lip stick and a small amount of money for an emergency. All these things were still in the bag just as she had put them there—but the picture had been put there, somehow.

Suddenly she remembered the awkward, eager, bashful boy who had asked for her autograph and who had knocked her purse from her hand, and restored it with such confused blushes and stammering apologies. He had had an opportunity if he worked fast, to slip the picture into the bag, then—had he done so? She tried to remember what the boy looked like.

He had been young — not over twenty — and he had been flushed and eager-eyed and — well, she couldn't see him very clearly in her memory.

She had not paid especial attention to him—but wracking her brain now, she came to the conclusion that this boy was the only one who had had a chance to put the picture into her bag — and she remembered how he had melted into the crowd, as though covered by embarrassment at knocking the purse from her hand.

What was the purpose of that little picture? Was it merely to prove to her that her baby was alive and well? Or—was it meant for a clue that would show her where her baby was? If so, no matter how hard she studied the picture, she could not grasp that clue.

The stucco wall was like any one of thousands of stucco walls, half hidden behind smothering masses of blossoming vines.

Suddenly she picked up the telephone beside her, and called Hank O'Hearn. His voice, quiet, matter of fact, composed, greeted her as casually as though it had been half-past two in the afternoon instead of half-past two in the morning. Casually he assured her he would come over at once.

He seemed to think it nothing unusual or out of the way, that he should receive a telephone call at two-thirty in the morning, demanding his presence at a given place. Almost before she had time to realize what she had done, she heard the sound of his taxi stopping at the gate. She knew by the sound of murmured voices that the alert night-watchman was demanding Hank's credentials before allowing him to enter the gate.

Janelle opened the door as Hank came along the little flagged walk.

"It's shameful to get you out at this hour of the morning!" Janelle attempted to apologize.

"It's a pleasure!" Hank assured her quite sincerely. "And besides, my think-tank works much better between midnight and dawn than in the day-time —perhaps one of my ancestors might have been a night-owl!"

Janelle switched on the living-room lights and handed him the picture, explaining swiftly and concisely where she had obtained it, she described as well as she could the young man who had given it to her—or rather, the man she suspected of having put it in her bag.

"Do you suppose its meant merely to reassure me that the baby is alive and safe?" she asked Hank as he studied the picture very closely. "Or—is it meant as some sort of clue?"

"I believe its meant as a clue—skunks who steal babies don't bother themselves with efforts to reassure the mothers!" said Hank grimly.

He took from his pocket a small, but very powerful magnifying glass. Holding the picture under a very bright light, he went over it inch by inch while Janelle watched him, closely, scarcely breathing, in her intense concentration and the deep hope that he would be able to discover something.

Suddenly he gave a little gasp and drew her towards the picture. Holding the glass, indicating with his thumb where she should look, he asked very swiftly,

"There! What does it look like to you?"

Janelle studied the spot indicated, magnified enormously by the powerful glass and suddendly she cried,

"Why—it looks like—a word—no, two words. Calle—Sol—I can't see the last letters! What is it?"

Hank's eyes were shining and his round, full moon face was ruddy with delight.

"It's a street sign!" he told her jubilantly. "Calle Soldat—I can't be sure of the last letters, but I am convinced that's what it is. Street of the Soldiers! Somewhere below the border, for Calle is a word meaning 'street' to the greasers! Now, if we can find a wall like that, on the Street of the Soldiers——"

"But—what town? What part of Mexico?" demanded Janelle eagerly.

Hank looked startled and then his face fell.

"Gee—that's so! There's a gang of towns and villages down there—it COULD be most any of them, couldn't it?" he agreed. "And I thought it was all over but the shouting!"

Janelle's heart fell, too.

"You mean—then there's not much chance after all of the clue being any good?" she asked desolately.

Hank looked at her sharply.

"No, ma'am, I don't mean that at all—it's a darned good clue, and I'm going to make it work! It'll take a little time—but if you'll leave everything to me, I know we can get somewhere!" he told her promptly.

Remembering. she told him then of her experience at the hands of Far-away Thomas and Curly Dukes. And of the conversation between Curly and Bertha that she had over-heard.

Hank listened in mounting excitement. When she had finished he pounded one big, ham-like hand on his knee, and said roundly,

"By gollys, this gives us something to work on —the first definite lead we've had since I came on the case! It's a cinch Curly and Bertha will be 'sprung'— released on bail. They've got the slickest and the crookedest attorney this side of Hades, and a bond's a cinch to arrange for them! And from then on I'll have somebody trailing them every step they take—I'll make THEM lead us to the baby! Meanwhile I'll find out where the Street of the Soldiers is! Just you leave things to me for a few days, Mrs. Elliott!"

Sharp and clear above the tumult in Janelle's heart came a call that was clarion-like — the call of love.

Freed for the time being of the responsibility for the search for her baby, she was free now to listen to the call of love. With Hank O'Hearn on the case, it would be safe for her to go away for a few days to see Sherman—and her heart leaped with delight at the thought.

"You won't need me for a few days?" she asked Hank, to be doubly sure. "If you don't—I'm going to see—my fiance!"

Hank looked up quickly.

"You mean—Mr. Lawrence? I was down a few days ago—fine young man!" he told her quietly.

"You saw him?" cried Janelle eagerly.

"Yes," said Hank. "I think it would be great for you to run down and see him—he's plenty worried about you!"

"Then—I will. I'll go in the morning—no, THIS morning!" said Janelle eagerly. "And — if anything happens and you should need me—you can wire me there!"

"O. K." said Hank, and a few moments later said good-night and took himself off.

Janelle, who had already made investigations, knew that there was a passenger plane leaving the nearest air-port at nine that morning, that would get her to the air-port nearest Yamacraw at four in the afternoon. From there it would be necessary to hire an automobile.

She went to bed at last, so exhausted that she was asleep almost before her head touched the pillow.

Chapter 89.

AN ANGEL OF THE DEFENSE!

T WAS six o'clock on the evening when Janelle reached the little town of Yamacraw, and she knew that she could not go to the prison to see S h e r m a n this late. She would have to get in touch with Sherman's lawyer, Bert Hastings, and get him to pull a few wires and make a few arrangements.

"Ain't but one hotel in town, lady, and that's it!" the driver of her hired automobile assured her, as he jerked a thumb towards a ram-shackle two storied white frame building that had a long, sagging "gallery" that ran across its front, with rocking chairs painted a billious, time-stained green.

The driver placed her two bags on the hotel steps, where an aged porter with a reproachful look at Janelle, took them and carried them into the house. Janelle followed him and found a dried up little old man behind the dilapidated desk. He whirled an ancient register at her, an Janelle wrote her name, and followed it with "Los Angeles, Cal."

"A room with a bath, please!" she mentioned carelessly.

"Ain't got it!" the old man assured her importantly as he blotted her signature, and squinted at it near-sightedly. "Ain't but two rooms in the house what's got private baths — and they're both took. I kin give you one right alongside the other bath!"

And Janelle had to be content with this. It was a bare, cheerless room furnished quite simply with a white-painted iron bed-stead, a dresser and an old fashioned wash-stand that held a bowl and pitcher with two towels folded aggressivly across the mouth of the pitcher. Limp curtains at the two long windows, and a hand-made rag rug on the floor completed the room's decoration.

Janelle sighed, smiled, and opened her bag, selecting fresh clothing.

She was dressed, almost ready to go down to dinner and in search of Bert Hastings, when there came a knock at the door. When she called permission to enter, the door swung open and a very pretty girl, dressed in a frock of black-and-white printed silk, a broad-brimmed black hat in her hand, dusty black patent leather slippers on her feet, came into the room and closed the door.

"Forgive me for intruding!" she said pleasantly, though there was a wary look in her beautiful eyes. "But you're the first human looking person I've seen in this town since I came here, and I simply had to come and talk to you!"

Janelle smiled cordially.

"I'm so glad you did! Yamacraw DOESN'T look so exciting!" she laughed.

"It's simply—deadly!" said the other girl, and gave a little despairing sigh. "If it were not for my husband being here, I wouldn't stay another moment!"

"Your husband is in business here?" asked Janelle politely.

The other girl lifted her head a little, almost defiantly, and said frankly,

"My husband is—in prison here!"

Janelle caught her breath and her eyes widened. The color seeped from her face, and she stared at the other girl as though she had suddenly become some strange and deadly thing.

"In—prison?" she repeated, and tried to fight away the thing that somehow she knew this girl was going to say.

Even before the girl spoke, she felt in her heart the words that she was about to hear.

"Yes—he's Sherman Lawrence—but—he's not guilty, I tell you! He's not guilty! I am his wife— and I KNOW that he is not guilty!" cried the girl dramatically.

Janelle said very quietly, her eyes steadily on the other girl's face, unwavering,

"Yes, I know that he is innocent—I am—Janelle Elliott!"

"I'm Mrs. Annie Lawrence!" said the other girl, for a moment as though unconscious of what Janelle had said. And then as though the name penetrated her consciousness for the first time, she caught her breath and her eyes widened. "Janelle Elliott! Then—you are the girl—who is in love with—my husband!"

Janelle clenched her hands and drew a long breath.

"We have been—engaged for—a year!" she said, levelly.

The other girl's face sharpened—lost its beauty, and her eyes flashed wickedly. She threw up her head and with one hand on her hip, she laughed insolently.

"Oh, well—I don't mind his being engaged to you—as long as it was ME that he married!" she sneered.

The hot color flooded Janelle's face, but she set her teeth and controlled her resentment before she answered.

"You and I have nothing to gain by insulting each other! Nothing to gain by being enemies. I want only one thing out of this—and that is Sherman's happiness. If you can make him happy — then I have nothing to say! Except — congratulations! He's — rather a fine person, you know!"

The other girl laughed.

"Oh, sure—and, of course, the fact that he is worth six or eight million dollars doesn't detract from his fine points!" she answered coolly.

Janelle studied her gravely.

"Meaning, of course, that—you married him for his money!" she accused.

Annie laughed.

"I thought we were not going to insult each other!" she reminded Janelle contemptuously.

Janelle made a little confused gesture and turned away.

"I'm sorry!" she stammered. "I—didn't mean to say that!"

There was a knock at the door, and the aged porter stuck his head in at the door.

"Gent down stairs is a-askin' fer the lady that jest arrove!" he delivered his message, "Says his name is Hastings!"

Janelle saw the other woman start, and thought she grew a bit pale. She flung her lighted cigarette into an ash-tray as she turned to the door.

"He's my husband's lawyer!" she said swiftly. "Danny must have made a mistake—I'm sure that it is me he wishes to see!"

She thrust the porter out of the way and hurried out of the room. The porter looked after her, shrugged, and took himself off.

Janelle stood alone at the window, looking out into the darkness. The majestic river, justly called the Father of Waters, rolled on his way, a hundred yards or so away from the main street of the little village, seeming to say that the affairs of these puny humans were of so little importance.

Janelle had known, of course, that the woman who claimed to be Sherman's wife was here in this little town. That she had arrayed herself beside her husband and had manifested her determination to help him in the coming fight for his life. But—to read of the woman in the paper, and to come face-to-face with her in real life seemed so different. The woman of whom she had read had not seemed quite real. But there could be no doubt about this flesh-and-blood girl who had faced her so arrogantly—and who had taunted her with being in love with Sherman.

She shivered a little and hid her face in her hands. Was she to have to make this sacrifice now? Was she to have to give up the man she loved to this other woman? How had it happened that Sherman had married this woman? How could a man like Sherman get himself tangled in such a hideous mess? To be accused of murder, complicity in a robbery out of which had grown another murder, and then on top of it all, to be revealed as a man who had married a girl he had known less than a week, while he was still engaged to a girl whom he had known for years——

Behind her Janelle heard the turning of the doorknob, and she whirled about to face Bert Hastings.

"I knocked and I thought I heard you say come in!" he greeted her, smiling. "I'm Bert Hastings, Sherman Lawrence's lawyer! And you, of course, are Janelle Elliott the movie star!"

Janelle tried to smile an acknowledgement of his pleasantry, but she felt far from smiling.

"Won't you come in and sit down, Mr. Hastings?" she invited politely. "And—how is Sherman?"

Bert smiled as he accepted the comfortless chair which was all the room afforded.

"I left him rejoicing in delight over the news that you had been present, alive and unharmed, at the premiere of your picture, and that you had escaped the hands of bandits!" he answered.

"May I see him — tonight?" begged Janelle humbly. "Will you arrange it?"

Bert's expression altered a little, and he looked away from her out of the window towards the river, a dark, moving, powerful body that could be sensed, rather than heard through the thickening darkness.

"That's what I've come to see you about, Miss Elliott!" he said gravely. "After I lay the case before you—after I give you the angle of the defense—it will be for you to decide—whether you see him or whether you go straight back to Hollywood — without seeing him!"

Janelle stared at him, wide-eyed, bewildered.

"But—I don't know what one earth you're talking about!" she cried sharply. "Of course I intend to see him—you can't mean that he doesn't WANT to see me?"

Bert was still looking away from her out of the window, as though he hated having to say the things that he must say, but knew the inevitability of them.

"No, no—he wants to see you. If he knew you were in town, I doubt if the prison bars or his weakness would have any effect on him—he'd probably walk right through the bars, and into this room—he's that anxious to see you!" he answered quietly. "The choice — the decision—must be up to you!"

Janelle drew a long hard breath and squared her shoulders. She faced him with her head erect.

"You must have a very good reason for saying things like that—as though there could be a choice after I have come out here to see him. I'm waiting to know what you could possibly have to say that would make me willing to go away without seeing him. After all—I love him, you know!" her voice broke a little on the last words, and there was the glimmer of tears in her eyes, but she still faced him straightly.

"I know you do—and that's why I believe that when I have finished, you will decide of your own free will to — go away without seeing him!" said Bert, quietly.

"I'm waiting!" said Janelle as quietly.

There was a tiny breathless pause. They were like two fighters who silently take each other's measure, before the first blow is struck—each sensing the other's weakness before beginning the attack.

"Miss Elliott. Sherm is—in a mighty tight spot! Our defense plea on the first charge hinges on only one thing — the time. If we can prove beyond the shadow of a doubt that he was in Ohio on the 15th of May it will prove his innocence of a charge of murder! You, of course, understand that!" said Bert at last carefully.

"Of course!" said Janelle.

"Public opinion is a funny thing!" Bert went on after a moment. "The fact that Sherm's 'girl-bride' arrived so promptly and testified to his presence in Ohio on May 15th has helped establish a doubt of his guilt. Her loyalty and devotion to him here, despite the seriousness of the charge against him, has created a favorable impression. We have decided to concentrate on that one angle—that, in view of the fact that he was with Annie Greene in Ohio on May 15th, he couldn't possibly have murdered another Annie Greene in New York on the same day. We are anxious to concentrate public opinion on that one point — and the fact that a well-known movie star, who claims to have been engaged to Sherm at the same time that we contend he was wooing and winning Annie Greene in Ohio—has flown here to visit him in prison is going to disturb the picture we are trying to impress on the public mind—the picture of a loyal and devoted bridegroom, hero of a whirlwind courtship—do you begin to see what I mean, Miss Elliott?"

"Yes, of course — but — it seems unnecessarily cruel that I should not be allowed to see him now—after I've made such an effort—I love him so!" it was a little heart-broken cry from the girl's heart.

Bert, knowing shrewdly the wisdom of the angle of defense he was planning, hardened his heart against the distress in her voice and the misery in her white face.

"But—had you stopped to realize, Miss Elliott, that after all, this girl who has endured so much at Sherman's hands, is entitled to some consideration?" he asked brutally. "After all, you know, she IS his wife, and she has come to his support—her testimony will clear him of this charge. She could have been forgiven, I honestly believe, for refusing to have anything whatever to do with him after she found out what a mess he was in!"

Janelle looked startled.

"Do you realize, Miss Elliott, that she married him after only a week's courtship? That she sold the little shop that was her only means of livelihood, and gave him the money? And that, a week later, he deserted her on their honeymoon, leaving her only a hundred dollars of HER OWN MONEY, and a callous little note saying he was through?" he demanded almost sharply.

"I don't believe it!" cried Janelle sharply. "Sherman could never do a thing like that—he's not capable of it!"

"Nevertheless the facts prove that he did, just exactly that!" said Bert sternly. "And after that, this girl has sacrificed her pride to come here, and to help him—and I don't mind telling you that it is going to be practically her testimony alone that is going to clear him! I repeat — she is entitled to every consideration!"

Janelle was listening, wide-eyed, white-faced.

"You mean — that for me to visit him — would make him seem—disloyal to her?" she whispered.

"Not only seem, but actually be disloyal!" said Bert quietly. "After all, they ARE married—I have proofs of that! She is his wife—she has done nothing to merit a divorce—the marriage could not be annulled, since it has been consummated by a week's honeymoon. He cannot cast her aside, once her usefulness to him is past—no matter under what circumstances they were married, after she has proven her loyalty and her devotion as she has!"

Janelle's heart sank like a plummet. She could see the truth of what Bert said. This other girl was Sherman's wife — she, Janelle, could no longer have even the smallest place in his life. She must go away

—she must not even see Sherman.

"The town is full of newspaper reporters—correspondents of the large city newspapers all over the country. I don't want them to know that you are here! I bribed Seth, down-stairs not to let them know that you are here—and I've got a car waiting to take you back to the air-port tonight!" said Bert and then as he caught the expression on her face, he said swiftly, "Try not to hate me, Miss Elliott—I am doing only what I see as best for both of you. You are as eager as I am to see Sherman free of this awful mess—and once he IS free of it, you and he may take whatever course seems best to you. I only ask that, for the duration of the trial, you allow me to use my judgment!"

Janelle stood straight, her face paper-white, and reached for her hat.

"I—do understand—perhaps you are right—you are wiser than I—I will do whatever you say!" she told him, and there was a deathless agony in her voice that she was too proud to put into words.

Bert had no words with which to answer her. He merely picked up her two bags and walked downstairs with her, and put her into the waiting car. And then, as she held out her hand to him, smiling a little despite the tears in her eyes, she said, her voice choked and uneven,

"Please—take good care of him—and—tell him that—I love him!"

"Of course!" said Bert, and unexpectedly to himself as much as to her, this hard-headed, shrewd, matter-of-fact attorney lifted her hand and kissed it. "You're — a game little sport!" he said, and stood back as the car sped away into the darkness.

Janelle put her face in her hands as the car

gathered speed, and wept as though her heart would break.

As the car drove away, two newspaper reporters who had been having dinner in the hotel, came out and spoke to Bert.

"Hey, Mr. Hastings, who was the lady that just left? You're not holding out on us, are you? You promised us all the story as fast as it broke!" one of them reminded him.

"That was my maiden aunt from Sedalia—funny thing, the old soul always visits me on my birthday and leaves a swell box of cigars — try one, boys!" said Bert with a perfectly straight face, and offered fat, tempting perfectos.

The reporters looked hard at him, but Bert beamed back at them so innocently that they were convinced in spite of themselves, and thought no more of Bert's mysterious visitor.

But from an upper window, a pair of dark, vindictive eyes watched Janelle's departure with triumph riding high in those eyes.

"And that," said Annie Green Lawrence happily, "is that!"

She turned back into the room, established herself as comfortably as the room would permit, and resumed her book.

Chapter 90.

AN ATTEMPTED REBELLION.

HE FOLLOWING MORNING when Bert arrived at the jail for his usual morning visit with his client, he found Sherman in gay and jubilant spirits, the morning paper spread before him.

"Hi, Bert — I'd be willing to lay you a bet that before dark tonight you'll have a chance to meet the prettiest girl you ever set an eye on!" he greeted his lawyer.

"Says you?" Bert was polite but unimpressed.

"Says me!" he answered happily. "Janelle will be here before night—or I'm a one-eyed mule-driver.

Bert hesitated, but decided he might as well get it over.

"Janelle was here — yesterday, Sherm!" he said gently.

It took a full moment for that to penetrate Sherm's consciousness. But when it did he lay quite still, staring at Bert as though quite sure that he had made some mistake—that he had not really heard what he thought he had heard.

"You—you said——" he stammered at last, and Bert finished the sentence for him.

"I said that Janelle arrived late yesterday afternoon!"

Sherman's face lit up with a wild delight.

"Then—where is she? She's outside—go get her, Bert!" cried Sherman eagerly.

"She's — gone, Sherm!" said Bert.

Sherman stared at him, wildly frowning.

"Gone?" he repeated, unbelieving.

Bert nodded.

"Yes, Sherm—I sent her away! I thought—I knew—it was best!" he returned, and braced himself for Sherman's cry of anger and bewilderment.

"You sent her away? Who the devil gave you such authority? How dared you do that? For two cents, I'd climb out of bed and give you the thrashing you deserve. YOU sent her away! Without even letting me see her! After all she's been through — to be bundled off as though I didn't want to see her—Bert, why, why, WHY?" At first he raged and swore, but at the last his voice broke on a confused, bewildered, heart-sick note that made Bert sick with pity.

Bert tried to explain to Sherman as he had done to Janelle. But where Janelle had listened and reasoned and agreed at the cost of heart-break and a disappointment almost too sharp to be borne, Sherman refused to listen or to be convinced.

"Suppose I AM married to this woman — she's nothing to me—I don't even remember her—I've loved Janelle Elliott for years, and the minute I'm out of this, she's going to be my wife!" snarled Sherman savagely.

"Of course," said Bert quietly. "The minute you are out of this—you are going to disown the woman whose loyalty and self-sacrifice made it possible for you to get out of this — so that you can marry some one else! Naturally, Sherman, I know that YOU would do exactly that!"

There was a delicate edge of sarcasm in his voice, a tone that made Sherman look at him sharply, closely. For a moment the two men exchanged glances. It was Sherman's eyes that fell first.

"I—I see what you mean, Bert," he said at last quietly. "I — couldn't do that after all, could I? No —I'm hooked! There's—no way out!"

"None that a man of your sort, Sherm, could follow!" said Bert. "She's your wife—she married you in good faith and she has been loyal—I see no way you can be free—and still keep your self-respect!"

There was a little silence, and then Sherman asked heavily.

"I suppose—there isn't any doubt but that—we ARE married?"

"None at all as far as I can see!" answered Bert. "I wired the Justice of the Peace who signed the marriage certificate, and he sent back an affidavit, attesting to the fact that he performed the marriage himself, on May 22nd in his office at Canal Winchester! He offered to come and testify if he was needed. Of course I subpoenaed him."

There was a little silence. And then Sherman asked with a trace of hope.

"You talked more to her—to—I CAN'T call her my wife, but you know who I mean — do you think there could be a chance of—her asking for a divorce— and—er—a settlement?"

"Afraid not, Sherm. She doesn't seem to want money—she seems to be genuinely in love with you. She is busy making plans for going home with you to

Atlanta when all this is over — your friends will accept her readily. Sherm—she seems—a nice enough young-ster! And darned pretty!" Bert tried to sound en-couraging.

Sherman's grin was faint and without humor.

"But—she's not Janelle!" he pointed out quietly, and turned his face to the wall as a sign that he did not wish to talk about it any more.

Bert hesitated, then he got up and left the room. Sherman's heart was a whirlpool of bitterness. For long months he had dreamed of Janelle, longed for the sound of her voice, yearned for a sight of her—trembled before the glory of the thought of her kiss. And last night she had been almost within the sound of his voice — and he had not seen her. She had traveled all this way, eager for a sight of him as he was for her—and they had been kept apart.

And now, said Bert, they must be this way—always. His duty was to the woman who had endured much at his hands, and who was staunchly supporting him now—his clenched fists beat sharply at the pillows as though his helplessness must find some physical outlet.

*   *   *   *   *   *   *   *   *

Bert went from the jail down to the postoffice, where he collected his own and Sherman's mail. A rather amazing amount of it, since the world is full of so many queerly developed people who invariably write letters to those more or less fortunate whose names are front-page newspaper copy.

Bert went back to the hotel and selected a chair in a shady spot on the wide veranda. It was cool here, with a fresh little breeze that rippled the broad expanse of the river below him, and here he would read his mail.

He had hardly seated himself before Annie Greene Lawrence — he always thought of her by all three names — came along the porch, looking fresh and dainty and cool in a becoming frock of yellow eyelet embroidery that revealed her bare arms and round throat enchantingly. She, too, had a little sheaf of mail, and with a pretty smile she sat down beside him.

"We'll read our mail and then we'll talk—shall we?" she suggested with a bright, warm little smile.

"Of course!" said Bert, and as he swung a chair about for her, he dropped some of his letters.

Annie bent and picked up three of them as Bert gathered others and as she held out the three, her eyes caught on one of the envelopes. She caught her breath on a little gasp, and grew pale, her wide eyes on the envelope.

"Why — what is the matter? Is the writing familiar?" demanded Bert quickly.

The girl recovered herself and smiled, though she was still pale and her eyes were wide and a little frightened.

"Of—of course not! It's—it's—just that—bending over so swiftly—made me—a bit dizzy—it's so—warm! I—I think I'll go to my room—and—and—lie down awhile!" she stammered, and before Bert could recover his wits sufficiently to try to hold her, she was gone, skimming along the porch like a frightened swallow and into the house.

Bert looked down at the envelope that had so excited her. A cheap envelope of the sort that can be bought by the package in any ten cent store. The address was in a scrawling, almost illegible hand, and the postmark was City Hall station, New York City. It was addressed to Bert. After a moment he tore it open and drew out the single sheet of cheap, rough ruled paper that it held and unfolded it.

> "If you wantta find out something that'll be interesting to Sherman Lawrence, send me railroad fare to come to you. It'll be worth it to you both. Send it to me at this hotel.
> "Al Fesson."

Bert sat for a long time staring at the note, and when at last he folded and put it back into his pocket, his face was a study. He knew that Annie had recognized the writing, and that it had alarmed her. She had some reason for fearing this man—but what it was, he of course, had no way of knowing. But—he was not the lawyer he thought he was, he told himself firmly, if he didn't find out before the trial!

Chapter 91.

TANGLED CLUES.

HEN JANELLE returned to Hollywood several days earlier than she had been expected, she found that Maxie and Wayne had not been idle. They came and took her to dinner the second evening that she was at home.

They took her to dinner at the famous and popular Brown Derby, where it seemed that all the movie notables who had thought it a bore to dress formally for the more elaborate Cocoanut Grove dinner, had gone to dine.

Once before she had dined here, and had been awed at the sight of Bebe Daniels and Ben Lyons, happy, devoted, handsome, dining at an adjoining table; the lovely, fragile-looking Constance Bennett and her titled husband in a party that included "the littlest Bennett," Joan, with her own new husband; the beautiful, aloof Marlene Dietrich and her handsome, blond young husband, with Josef von Sternberg, the eccentric and gifted young director who claimed the discovery of the exotic Marlene; Tallulah Bankhead, vivid, charming, stimulating, making one of her infrequent public appearances.

The close and intimate proximity of all these and many another famed figure of the silver screen—the fact that she was actually sitting in the same room with them—could reach out and touch them if she had had the temerity to do so — had thrilled her beyond words.

But much had happened since then.

Then Janelle had been an outsider, awed and thrilled and delighted with her glimpses of the great and the near great.

But tonight, after weeks of working beneath the lights and before the cameras of movieland, after having attended a premiere of her own picture and being congratulated by some of the greatest of the stars, she had a warm, cozy little feeling of being completely at home in these surroundings.

Maxie and Wayne watched her when the waitress had gone with their order. It would have been apparent to Janelle—had she not been so pre-occupied with her observations of the assemblage of prominent men, handsome men and beautiful women — that these two had some thought in common which they hitherto had not disclosed to her. And Maxie smiled at Wayne knowingly.

"We signed a new writer today, Janelle — his first job will be your new picture!" said Maxie rather casually.

Janelle looked up, startled.

"My new picture?" she repeated.

"Of course—I forgot to tell you, we're taking up your option—it's a shiny new contract for three years—the first year at $750 a week, the second year $1,000 a week, the third year $1,250—and no options!" said

Maxie firmly.

Janelle hesitated, and Wayne said, clearing his throat a little,

"Of course—unless you are going to be married right away!"

Janelle's face tightened. To an interested observer the change in her expression from one of alert pleasure to one of dark despair was startling.

It seemed to Wayne, who loved her and wanted her happiness more than he had ever wanted anything in all his life, that he had never seen any one who looked quite so miserable.

"No," she said very quietly. "I—am not going to be married! Ever!"

Wayne's eyes lighted a little, and he looked at her squarely.

"You see—that's why I came away so soon!" she explained, for she felt that these two people who had been so truly and so sincerely her friends deserved to know all about her present situation. "His—wife is with him—and—I no longer have any right to—even be with him!"

Maxie looked startled and perturbed by her expression. Wayne said suddenly,

"Let's dance, dear!"

Janelle welcomed the chance to get away from this moment by the action of dancing, and rose instantly.

Wayne's arms closed gently about her, holding her lightly yet securely, as though he would never let her go.

And by the time they had finished the dance and were once more at the table, Maxie was so excited about his plans for Janelle and the new picture, that there was no more mention of Sherman or the unhappy finish of the hurried trip she had made to Mississippi.

When they left the Brown Derby, and Maxie indicated the Rolls-Royce, Wayne shook his head, drew Janelle's hand through his own arm and said firmly to Maxie,

"No! I'm taking her home tonight—in an open roadster so she can feel the wind on her face, and smell the orange blossoms and see the moonlight! Goodnight, Maxie—we'll be seein' you!"

Maxie looked swiftly from Wayne to Janelle, and unexpectedly his face softened.

"Good-night, Janelle—and—good luck, Wayne, my boy!" he said quietly.

Wayne flashed him a swift, almost boyish smile, his manner eager and suddenly young. He drew Janelle to his roadster parked near at hand, and helped her into it.

"Now just relax and don't try to talk or be amusing or anything — and let me drive you a bit!" he begged.

He drove out through the hills, along roads that were silver ribbons unwinding beneath his speeding wheels. Along roads from which the sleeping city lay twinkling among its leafy darknesses. Chains of lights that made a fair necklace of beauty—when at last the roadster came to a halt in front of Janelle's house, Wayne turned to her with that almost boyish eagerness.

"Let me come in for a moment, Janelle — I've got to talk to you. I thought I could wait until tomorrow—but now—well, I can't, after all! Let me come in with you for a little!" he begged insistantly.

Janelle smiling, led the way and in the livingroom, with lights blooming like soft flowers against the dusk, he looked down at her and took both her hands.

"Janelle, I thought the time would never come when I could tell you this—but now to know that you — are not going to marry Lawrence — well, to know that you are free gives me the right to say that — I love you very much, my dearest — and that more than anything in the world, I want to marry you!" he said.

Janelle gave a little soft cry of distress, turned her head to one side, and would have drawn away from him, but he held her two hands firmly and would not let her go.

"I know what you are going to say, dearest — that you don't love me! Sweetheart, I don't ask you to love me—I don't expect it, now! But afterwards, some day, there will be a time when you will come to me and say 'I love you' and that moment will be worth waiting for! All that I ask now is — that you marry me! I do not ask you to be my wife in any-thing save the name—until you have learned to love me. But—Heart's Dearest, I'm so lonely—I've always been lonely — and now that I have — a great deal of money — I've found that that only makes one that much lonelier——"

She was listening, looking up at him fascinated, held in spite of herself.

"I want a home, Janelle — not just an apart-ment. I want a home high in the hills — and some one to live there with me to make that house a home! I can do a great deal for you, Janelle — as my wife, you'd have any career that you wanted—luxury——"

"But — you would give me so much — and I could give you so little! You — wouldn't really want to marry me — knowing that — I loved some one else!" she stammered wildly.

"If your love is completely hopeless — and I know that it is since this man is married — then I'm perfectly willing to take a chance, for — if I were very good to you and very patient and very kind — you would some day learn to love me — a love like mine cannot help winning a response!" he pleaded eagerly.

And in the end, because he promised her a relief from loneliness, a friendship that wrapped her about as a shining garment — because she liked and admired and respected him — more, because she trusted him implicitly, she said yes. She would marry him on his own terms. She was to be merely a guest in his house until that time when she had learned to love him, and when she could come to him of her own free will and lay her hand in his and ask him to take her as his wife.

He left at last in the seventh heaven of delight. Just when he had despaired of ever winning her, she had melted into his arms, and had let him kiss her. A cool, chaste little kiss that made her heart cry out, hungry and lonely and frightened for a man whom she must forget for that other man was already married!

She sat on alone in the living-room for a long time after Wayne, jubilant and joyous, had gone. It seemed strange to think that she was engaged to Wayne —one of the four greatest movie directors the industry had known. A man whose income was many thousands of dollars weekly — a man who was already wealthy by his own efforts, and whose name on a production was accepted by the public as a guarantee of the worth of that production.

She rose at last to go up-stairs, but as she went

along the hall towards the stairs the telephone rang, and she paused to answer it, puzzled that it should ring this late at night.

A voice sharp with excitement rang in her ears.

"Miss Elliott? Hank O'Hearn told me to call you—he's found your baby! You must come at once!" cried the voice and gave an address swiftly before it rang off.

Janelle stood quite still, the dead telephone in her hand, her heart hammering madly, her eyes wide in a sightless stare. Her baby was found! Her little lost baby was found!

She forgot everything but that. Her baby had been found! With a little soft, sobbing cry, she turned and ran fleetly down the corridor and out into the darkness.

She murmured the street address over and over as she went, trembling in her eagerness to fill her arms once more with the precious, warm sweet weight of her little boy.

Continued in Next Number.

GLOSSARY

acceded – agree to a contract.

arrayed – page 813, no. 26. placed herself next to him with a sort of martial-like pride.

ashy – pallor, or pale skin.

austere – severe or strict in manner, attitude, or appearance - *encyclopedia.com*

basque cloth – a woven textile used in furnishings. infoor and outdoor use originating from France.

bewailed – expressed great regret.

billious – greenish-yellow bile color.

blithe – joyous, happy.

bromide – sedative.

bulwarked – wall of defense, safety.

chaise-lounge – an elongated bedroom chair that supports the legs.

chattel – property.

chintz – a printed, multicolored cotton fabric with a glazed finish.

clarion – a war trumpet.

copped – nab, steal, get a hold of.

coquettish – flirtatious.

cretonne – a heavy cotton fabric used for upholstery, often with floral patterns.

decolletage – a woman's low neckline dress or top.

derisively – expressing contempt or ridicule.

deuce – raise hell.

dewily – cool dewy grass.

dissipation – self-indulgence, debauchery.

enmities – a feeling of being actively hostile to someone.

flivver – a cheap car in bad condition.

forties – indicating the streets in New York numbering in the forties. for example "42nd Street."

furtiveness – shiftiness, sly.

garrotted – strangled.

garroting – strangulation.

haberdashery – men's clothing and accessories.

henna – orange, red hair dye.

hoar frost – dew-drops which have frozen into ice crystals to form a white deposit on an exposed surface.

ingenue – a young woman stock character who is endearingly innocent.

incessant – something unpleasant that continues without pause or interruption.
incredulous – unable to believe something.
indolent – inactive, lazy.
livery – clothes indicating a chauffeur driver.
paper-knife – utensil used in makeup application.
odious – extremely unpleasant. repulsive.
organdie – a stiffened, translucent silk or cotton fabric.
ostensibly – evident, apparent, or conspicuous.
pallid – pale, feeble.
pate-de-foie-gras – a rich, smooth paste made from goose or duck liver.
perfectos – a cigar that is thick in the center and tapered at each end.
perforce – inevitability or necessity.
piker – one who speculates with small amounts of money.
posted – informed.
reproachful – expressing disappointment or disapproval.
sibilant – hissing sound.
skulking – a move stealthily, sly.
succinctly – clearly expressed manner.
sultry silence – hot and humid, uncomfortable.
tarpaulin – waterproofed canvas.
temerity – excessive boldness, audacity.
tulle frock – a fine mesh net fabric outer garment.
tumult – confusion or disorder.
veranda – a roofed platform along the outside of a house, level with the ground floor. - *oxford languages*
wheedled – flattery used persuade someone to give one something.
Yamacraw – small town.

PHRASES

"also ran" – page 541, no. 17. slang originating from horse racing. someone that participated but never won. just someone else who "also ran" in the race.

RANSOM! The Story of a Lost Child; Intimate Chapters of a Film Star's Life – Volume 2

was crowdfunded at Kickstarter thanks to these contributors.

Chelle Anna
Michael Aus
Kurt Beyerl
Matthew Bieniek
Brian R. Boisvert
Michael R. Brown
Nellie Cole
Jeff Connor
Jangus C. Cooper
Eric O. Costello
Rachel Daugherty
Christopher Davis
Patricia Erdely
Kerrington Fier
Zack Fissel
Nanette Galinski
John M. Gamble
David Greenberg
Gavin Greene
David Guiot
Wesley Hoffman
Dave Holets
John Howie Jr.
Heather and Jenn

Rick (RJDiogenes) Hutchins
Fidel Jiron Jr.
Chris Larson
Peyton Light
Will Lorenzo
Keith and Cheri Martin
Ami Morrison
Mike Pasqua
Francis Peters
Old Pops
Robert Price
The Reimans
Robert Slaven
Ron Spayde
Jared Stearns
K.L. Stokes
Rebecca Strickland
Steph Tasker
Tim Tucker
Tina M. Van Dusen
Ian Viemeister
Brian Weisberg
Kimberly Wilkerson
Stephen M. Wolterstorff
Gerry Zaninovich